We Burn Daylight

We Burn Daylight

a novel

Bret Anthony Johnston

RANDOM HOUSE
NEW YORK

We Burn Daylight is a work of fiction. Apart from the well-known actual people, events, and locales that figure in the narrative, all names, characters, places, and incidents are the products of the author's imagination or are used fictitiously. Any resemblance to current events or locales, or to living persons, is entirely coincidental.

Published in the United States by Random House, an imprint and division of Penguin Random House LLC, New York.

RANDOM HOUSE and the HOUSE colophon are registered trademarks of Penguin Random House LLC.

LIBRARY OF CONGRESS CATALOGING-IN-PUBLICATION DATA
Names: Johnston, Bret Anthony, author.
Title: We burn daylight : a novel / Bret Anthony Johnston.
Description: First edition. | New York : Random House, 2024.
Identifiers: LCCN 2023046862 (print) | LCCN 2023046863 (ebook) |
ISBN 9780399590122 (hardcover) | ISBN 9780399590139 (ebook)
Subjects: LCSH: Cults—Fiction. | LCGFT: Novels.
Classification: LCC PS3610.O384 W4 2024 (print) | LCC PS3610.O384 (ebook) |
DDC 813/.6—dc23/eng/20231013
LC record available at https://lccn.loc.gov/2023046862
LC ebook record available at https://lccn.loc.gov/2023046863

Printed in the United States of America on acid-free paper

randomhousebooks.com

1 2 3 4 5 6 7 8 9

First Edition

Book design by Ralph Fowler
Title page image © WocLeeds - stock.adobe.com

For Bill—
worth slightly more* than a gold-plated Susan B. Anthony dollar

We think the fire eats the wood.
We are wrong. The wood reaches out
to the flame.

—Jack Gilbert, "Harm and Boon in the Meetings"

We burn daylight . . .

—*Romeo and Juliet*

Hidy there, everybody. Good afternoon. Or evening. Sorry to be tardy, but we've had ourselves a dustup at the ranch. As you've heard by now, people have taken to calling me the Lamb, which is sure nicer than other names I've been called. Anyway we've had these pork choppers flying at us. I don't mean to tease. I appreciate y'all tuning in, I do. Well so, okay, it's the eighteenth day of February 1993, the year of our Lord, and I'm talking at you, through your radios, in your homes and cars and places of commerce, about the revelation of Jesus Christ. That's the big to-do. All y'all listening know the standard of God's righteousness is law. It's a system of cause and effect that's always been. When a man broke the law of God, he had to shed an innocent lamb's blood. There were other sacrifices—turtle doves, goats, oxen, red heifers, and so forth. Not a good day at the office, I'll tell you what. But such sacrifices could keep a man from sinning, couldn't they? Elsewise he'd lose all his livestock mighty fast, and then what? Lights out. Well that's about where we are now: The suffering's here, the wait is gone. We recognize it. We've been preparing, checking our timepieces. How will it all end? you ask. Who's going to donate his most precious blood? Well, let's see. Let's just get that sorted out once and for all, okay?

Part One

The White Horse

January 1993

Roy

In those raw first weeks of 1993, before my family broke apart and before the March fires, before the world turned its lurid attention our way and before her and before everything else that changed me, I was fourteen years old and learning to pick locks. I could open car doors with wire hangers, school lockers with a pocketknife, and almost anything else with tools my brother had sent me. Mason had been an infantry corporal in the marines, but he'd stayed in Iraq after the war to work as a contractor. He'd just turned twenty-one. We hadn't seen him in years, and although he was supposed to return home in the fall, I couldn't stop myself from imagining a future without him. Occasionally, when I struggled with a difficult lock, I'd pretend Mason was trapped on the other side of the door and his safety depended on my opening it in time. Sometimes I saved him, sometimes not.

My parents didn't know about Mason's tools or the pillowcase full of locks under my bed or the hours I spent picking when I should have been sleeping or studying. My mother was a hospice nurse then and my father was the high sheriff of McLennan County. Their minds were on graver subjects. At supper, one of us would say grace and then we'd tell a little bit about our days, hers tending to the infirm and his at the sheriff's office and mine at school. We weren't a family of bean-spillers or bucket-mouths. We curated our lives, gave each other wide berths. They knew Rosie had dumped me over Christmas vacation, but not that I'd stopped catching the bus from school to avoid seeing her on Isaac Garza's lap the whole ride. And I knew my parents, who claimed not to smoke, shared cigarettes in the backyard when something rattled them at their jobs or with Mason. But none of this came up at the table. We just listened to the sounds of our forks and knives, our glasses being lifted and put down. We asked each other to pass the fried okra or the jar of tartar sauce. We said how good it would be when Mason came home, speculated on what he'd want to eat and do first. We made plans for the happier times ahead. This was how innocent we were, how gullible. This was Waco.

ON THE LAMB

PODCAST EPISODE 12
GUEST: Sheriff Elias "Eli" Moreland (retired)
RECORDED: July 2024
                    Waco–McLennan County Central Library
                    Waco, Texas

Thank you for coming on. Ever since starting the podcast, I've wanted my listeners to hear your perspective. You were sheriff of McLennan County until 1993. Sammy Gregson was your deputy. Your son was—
Sammy had a bead on what was coming before I did. I'll give him that. I'll keep the rest of my opinions to myself.

Understood.
I've been away some thirty years. Down in Camp Verde now. Most days it's still too close.

I don't think you're allowed to smoke in the library.
If you want to hear what all I have to say, I'm going to smoke. I'm just as pleased to get back on the road and miss the traffic. Your call.

I'll see if I can scare you up an ashtray.
See if you can scare up a couple.

Roy

We lived on the western edge of town where the Blackland Prairie gave way to wetlands. Acres of scrub brush and bluestem grass stretched between us and our neighbors. Our house was a two-bedroom ranch with a sagging fence. Root-buckled driveway, wood paneling, an avocado-green kitchen counter and matching phone mounted to the wall. My room was in the back corner of the house, north-facing, with matted brown carpet. Mason and I had shared it, but after he enlisted, I just used his bed as a place for my folded clothes because my dresser drawers were stuck shut. I had two windows and a television my parents bought cheap from the Olde Towne Motel when it went under. On my walls were posters of the Houston Oilers and *The Terminator* and a monster truck doing a backflip; Mason's wall was covered by a huge Semper Fi banner. I'd been planning to change my side up over Christmas vacation, to hang manlier posters and rearrange my furniture, but after Rosie broke things off, it didn't seem worth the bother.

Mason called on holidays and, if he could, every third Sunday; he used a satellite phone that made him sound even farther away than he was, like his words were echoing toward us from the past. He rarely sent photographs and letters, but when a new one arrived, my mother pinned it to the fridge with fruit-shaped magnets. More than once I'd come into the kitchen to find her rereading what he'd written. She seemed to be searching for a hidden meaning, some clue she'd overlooked. That Mason stayed in-country after his deployment had wounded her. She saw it as tempting fate, but also an affront: He'd had the opportunity to return to us, and he'd declined. I viewed it that way, too, and despite the tacit silences in our house, I worried one of us would cop to our bitterness. Or one of us would say something we'd regret if he didn't come home. If she hadn't heard me behind her in the kitchen, I'd ease out of the doorway and close myself in my room; I'd pull a random lock from the pillowcase and make myself crack it before venturing back into the kitchen. If she did hear me, we'd pretend she was upset about one of her patients.

"Mr. Raybourn might be glory bound soon," she said one evening in early January. I'd come into the kitchen for some milk and found her wiping her eyes. She opened the fridge and squatted behind the door to gather herself.

"He has the wiener dog," I said.

"That's him."

"We've never had one of those."

Our pets always came from my mother's patients. Sometimes their owners wrote her into their wills, sometimes the surviving family guilted her into taking the animal. We'd had as many as four dogs and three cats at one time. We'd had a blue macaw and a pair of box turtles. When she wasn't working, my mother was finding homes for left-behind creatures. Forever homes, she called them. She placed ads in the paper, contacted veterinarians and ranchers, cajoled friends. She'd given goats to the 4-H club at my school, an aquarium of impossibly bright fish to the museum downtown, and an elderly hound to my friend Coop's mother, though it didn't last long. If she couldn't find homes for the animals, we carted them out to my grandparents. They had land near San Saba and took in what others wouldn't. That January, we were down to a black-and-white cat named Panda. She disappeared for days on end, and though we hadn't had her long, her absence made the house feel lifeless.

"Mason likes wiener dogs," I said, not because it was true but because hearing my brother's name could buoy my mother's spirits.

"Does he?" She took a beer from the fridge and started hunting for the bottle opener in the drawer. The clock on the wall ticked, ticked, ticked. My mother had gotten it as a grocery store promotion a while back; it had songbirds in place of numbers. She said, "Then he'll be tickled come September. Yes, sir, he'll be happy as a puppy with two tails."

ON THE LAMB

PODCAST EPISODE 12
GUEST: Sheriff Elias "Eli" Moreland (retired)
RECORDED: July 2024

Waco–McLennan County Central Library

Waco, Texas

They don't have any ashtrays.
I'll make do.

If someone from the library—
I was good to those people, even-handed. If there was word of some trouble, I'd call Perry and tell him to come in and we'd get it sorted. Civil-like. Aboveboard. I sent CPS out there, too. Clean reports. Those folks had their beliefs, but laws weren't broken.

We thought of them as a different country, a territory with its own customs. They kept to themselves mostly. When they ventured into town, they were courteous and quiet. Never panhandled or pestered you with leaflets or spoke in tongues. They were friendly. I was trying to stop the raid right up until it happened.

Roy

My father had been sheriff since before Mason was born. Grandpa Huey had worn the badge before that. The clear plan was for Mason to come home, be deputized, and run for the office when my father retired. Part of why he'd enlisted in the marines was because Huey had fought in Korea. War heroes won elections. Not that anyone would run against him. Voters in McLennan County equated the name Moreland with the sheriff's office. My father had gone unopposed in his last two bids. He wore a pager on his belt, along with his sidearm, which was a Colt Python. People liked him, considered him fair, courted his approval. He rarely paid for meals at restaurants or to have his uniforms pressed. The office occupied the drab basement of the old limestone courthouse, but every Christmas it turned bright and crowded with wrapped gifts from strangers.

Sometimes he took me with him to serve warrants. They were mostly quiet affairs, but I'd seen him get sliced at with steak knives and tackled down a knoll that dropped into Cypress Creek. He wanted me to see how people we knew—grocery store cashiers, parishioners from church—could turn unrecognizable if things went sideways in their lives. Men who were mean as water moccasins fell to their knees weeping. Women who served on the PTA cursed and punched walls. "The difference between a night at home and a night in jail is usually a bad day," my father said every time we drove to someone's house. I listened to criminals plead, invent alibis, hurl threats like bricks. He always kept calm, his voice low and tight. Even when he got into scrapes, he stayed composed. "You're all right," he'd say to whoever was coming at him. "Get all that out now. You're okay there."

With each warrant, I tried to see myself handcuffing a man in front of his family or reading Miranda rights to a kid my age while his parents stood by without hope or power. Even in my mind, I caved. The man rushed me before I snapped the cuffs; the teenager pleaded, and like a fool, I let him off with a warning. By the time we arrived back at the office, I'd tallied a hundred ways I would disappoint my father. I didn't know what I wanted to be, had no idea where I wanted to work or live, but I knew my father's life—and my brother's and grandfather's—wouldn't be mine. I didn't pray as often as I should, but when I did, I asked to be less afraid.

So on the second Friday in January when I was walking home from school and my father's Bronco pulled to the curb, I steeled myself. The afternoon was slate gray, the drizzle soaking through my jacket and staying there. He said, "Need a lift, detective?"

His cream Stetson was pulled low on his head, the band dark with years of sweat; he kept a picture of each of us—my brother, my mother, and me—tucked into the lining. His thermos was knocking around my floorboard. The heater chugged.

"Was the bus full up today?"

"I just felt like walking," I said. I rubbed my hands together between my knees.

"In freezing rain."

"I don't know," I said.

We passed the boarded-up Live Oak Mall. It had been bustling when I was young—a two-level building with a glass elevator and mosaic fountains. My mother used to take Mason and me there for school clothes, and my father had liked the Salisbury steak at Woolworths. But once the outlet shops opened on the interstate, the mall went belly-up. After it shuttered, my father was called out because a group of bums had started a campfire inside. Another time someone broke in and graffitied the walls. Now a hurricane fence surrounded the property.

A turkey vulture was perched atop a telephone pole, black feathers plumed thick against the wind and its ugly red head turreting the fields. If my mother had been with us, she'd have said, "He's looking for supper." Every time I saw a hawk or vulture, whether she was with me or not, I heard her say it. Probably my father did, too. The sun had an hour left, maybe less. We were heading east, away from home.

"There's a gun show this weekend," my father said. "Tonight's the early bird bit. I figured we'd have a look-see."

"We can get Mason something. Mom's putting together another care package."

"The snack bar should be open," he said. "They make those Frito Pies."

"I had a big lunch," I said. Really, I'd spent lunch period roaming the halls. I'd picked into a few lockers only to find predictable stashes of candy and cigarettes.

"Your mother thinks you've lost weight since you and Rosie called it," he said. The Brazos River was high and frothy from days of rain. The junipers and ash on its banks had thinned, bare branches like hatch marks against the sky. Everything wet and dripping and rinsed of color. "A hunger strike won't bring her back."

"I know," I said. To our left spread the small airfield and its single runway. A few Cessnas were parked by the hangar. My parents used to take Mason and me out there to watch pilots practice their touch-and-go landings.

"Sammy called a little bit ago," he said. "Sounds like there was some static."

"With the Lamb?"

"I reckon," he said.

Sammy Gregson was a righteous, short-tempered man. He was a Catholic who went to Mass three times a week and crossed himself often and worked as a part-time deputy. Winters were busy for the sheriff's department—people had more or less money than usual, found themselves in close quarters with family they avoided the rest of the year, drank too much—so Sammy'd been getting extra shifts.

The drizzle had almost completely obscured our windshield, but my father waited to flip on the wipers. He always held off as long as possible. Maybe it felt like giving in to him. He was a man who valued willfulness— "He's got the patience of a buzzard circling a sick calf," my mother liked to say—and he often seemed to be testing himself, exercising the muscles of his resolve.

"Did you hear me, detective?" my father said.

I turned to him. The windshield was water-streaked and blurry. "Do what?"

"I said it won't hurt forever. You'll survive this."

"Okay," I said.

"Trust me," he said, flipping on the wipers, "before too long, this will all be a long time ago."

ON THE LAMB

PODCAST EPISODE 7
GUEST: Sammy Gregson
RECORDED: January 2024
Keller-Williams Specialty Realtor
San Antonio, Texas

You served as Sheriff Moreland's deputy.
Eli's a good man. Even when we disagreed, I saw that. You could argue I got what I deserved, but not him.

You're no longer in law enforcement.
That chapter of my life ended in May of '93.

Are you surprised some of the survivors still maintain their beliefs?
They're brainwashed, son. They're always going to paint him with the angel brush. Perry could scramble people, twist their ups and downs.

Roy

I aim to get right what no one else has: Perry Cullen was not a charismatic man. He was not articulate or intelligent. He bragged about leaving school before finishing eighth grade. In his youth, kids took to calling him Perry the Fairy and beating him so often that his mother kept him home. She'd been a prostitute, which he also flaunted. "I'm the son of a whore, spawned from the seed of a double-dealing husband," he'd say. He was not handsome. He wore bottle-thick glasses and still had to squint to read Scripture.

But people put their faith in him. They listened to his claims of decoding the Bible, and it lit a glassy, faraway glow in their eyes. They signed over their savings and pensions. Sold their homes and property, shed careers and uprooted their families to live in squalor twenty miles outside town. They marked their days with Bible studies, one at dawn and another at dusk. If Perry was hearing the message clearly, he'd hold forth for hours. He'd eat spinach from the can at the pulpit. He'd drink the juice. A year or so before the fires, they started calling him "the Lamb."

When they weren't worshipping, they scavenged lumber and tools to build up their property—a couple hundred acres, mostly scrub and chaparral, bequeathed to Perry by an elderly woman many believed had been his lover. His followers raised the chapel first, then the barracks and kitchen, then a gymnasium and mess hall. The structures went up piecemeal, a halting and haphazard progress determined by which materials were cheapest. They had electricity and a phone line, but the only running water was in the kitchen. They fenced a pasture for livestock and built horse stables at the peak of their hill. There was a small pond where people swam and bathed, where women washed the congregation's laundry.

And there was a shooting range, which was part of how Perry kept his books in the black. Come the weeks before hunting season, he could hardly stock enough paper targets. He liked shooting with his customers, showing off his guns and talking Second Amendment rights. My father took me out there once or twice. A hand-painted sign read: KIDS UNDER TWELVE SHOOT FREE.

The group also rented booths at weekend gun shows. They dealt in guns, ammo, and apparel—T-shirts and baseball caps. What sold best were Bullet Bibles. Unopened, the Bibles appeared normal from every angle, but the inside was hollowed out to fit revolvers and semi-automatic pistols. Once, my father bought one as a gag for my grandfather. Everybody laughed when Grandpa Huey unwrapped it that Christmas. A year later we sent one to Mason in Iraq.

On early bird night in January, Sammy Gregson had pushed his way into the booth in search of contraband—steel pins used to convert semi-automatic rifles to full-auto or live grenades or armor-piercing bullets which were nicknamed Cop Killers. He dumped out boxes of T-shirts and hats. He knocked down a pyramid display of Bullet Bibles. Moping away, he said the Lamb and his whole lot would burn in hell.

The Lamb relayed everything to my father in the coliseum's parking lot. He'd been waiting for us in the wet dusk, leaning against an old pickup and smoking a cigarette. My father had planned to chat with Sammy first, but the Lamb intercepted us.

I was looking at my boots, trying to keep my face out of the wind. The asphalt was puddling.

"Any reason he wanted to toss the booth?" my father asked.

Smoke dribbled from the Lamb's nostrils. He said, "You know your man likes griping at us."

My father thumbed up his Stetson and surveyed the area. The Lamb's cigarette was down to its filter. He dragged on it then flicked the butt into a puddle where it sizzled out. My father said, "I'll check with Sammy and see how his story squares against yours."

"Every dealer on that aisle will vouch for us," the Lamb said. "He came in with a mind to knock shit down."

If I squinted, I could see Sammy beside the coliseum doors. His job was checking that any weapons brought into the show were unloaded. I knew he itched to tell his version, knew he resented the Lamb had gotten to us first. I didn't care. I was wondering if Rosie was with Isaac. They might've been at a Young Life meeting, sitting in a circle with Bibles and highlighters, sharing their Jesus love. She'd asked me to join, but whenever I went with her, I felt out of place and underdressed. Young Life kids were drill team girls and football players, kids who'd spent months of their lives in the orthodontist's chair. When Rosie broke up with me, she said she needed to be with someone who shared her beliefs. Isaac's father was a pastor. They had a swimming pool and a hunting lease.

"Rodeo?" the Lamb said. He'd called me that for years. After one of my mother's patients died and left behind two horses, my father and I had brought them out to the Lamb's pasture. The plan had been to eventually take them to my grandparents in San Saba, but the Lamb's kids had cottoned to them. Depending on who you asked, he might have as many as ten children. One boy was named Kanaan.

"Rodeo," he said again, "your daddy's talking at you."

My father was fishing his billfold from his pocket. He peeled off ten dollars.

"Go see if you can scare up something for Mason," my father said.

"How's he faring over there?" the Lamb asked. "I'll add him to our prayer list."

"Nothing wrong with more prayers," my father said.

A stiff wind came across the prairie and sliced through the parking lot. Drizzle pelted our faces, and we turned away in unison. Once it passed, I looked at my father and said, "Don't you want to come in?"

"You scoot. I'll talk to Sammy, then come grab you."

"The rain'll be heavy soon," I said.

"'Open up, O heavens, and pour out your righteousness,'" the Lamb said. "Isaiah 45:8."

"We'll be all right," my father said.

"I'll be quick," I said.

"Don't you worry on us, Rodeo," the Lamb said. "Ain't nobody here made of no sugar, okay? Ain't neither of us fixin' to melt."

Jaye

My mother was not religious. She was not a seeker or spiritual or even especially curious. She was a cleaning lady married to a man who threw a morning paper route for a living; when she came home at night, he was just waking up. In the summer of 1992, when I was about to enter high school, her boss paid her a hundred dollars to spend a weekend prepping a rental property for a new tenant coming from Texas. The house was just outside Highland, California, in the foothills of the San Bernardino Mountains. One wall was a giant mirror marbled with gold veins. The shower was glass bricks. The house had a sunken living room, too much carpet, and too little light. Hard soapy nests of hair in the drains. The living room ceiling fan hung a foot below its housing by two wires. My mother offered me twenty dollars to scrub tile and polish windows.

The tenant pulled in just before lunchtime on Sunday afternoon, a day ahead of schedule. Perry Cullen was reedy and talked with a twang. He wore a sweat-soaked tank top and amber-tinted glasses. He had two grease-blotted sacks of burgers, like he'd planned to bring us food all along. He asked if we'd mind if he prayed before eating, which seemed weird but polite, then the three of us ate on cool grass, small-talking and listening to tales of Perry's travels. To anyone driving by, we were a family picnicking in the yard of our new house. After lunch, Perry helped us clean, and we loaded the garbage into the bed of his old truck. Then he strummed songs on his acoustic guitar. In the beginning, he was a man who arrived early and could carry a tune. A man who brought food and picked up after himself and paid attention. My mother never stood a chance.

Roy

Even on early bird night, the gun show was so packed I slipped past Sammy without notice. Just beyond the doorway, Shawn and Shane Buford were in their Boy Scout uniforms selling candied pecans. Men were arranging their booths and sizing up the competition. They wore camo and coveralls, welder caps and Stetsons. They had beards and paunches and arms smudged with faded tattoos. Some of the women looked like they'd driven straight from a hunting lease while others wore heels and sprayed-up hair. They sold goat's milk soap, turquoise jewelry, and cross-stitch samplers with sayings like, *Want a Stable Relationship? Get a Horse.*

Every few minutes a stun gun crackled somewhere in the building. A couple of men sauntered around with rifles on their backs and FOR SALE flags extending up from the barrels. Bobbing above the aisles, the flags put me in mind of buoys on a lake. Along the room's back wall was all the war memorabilia—helmets and bayonets and patches. A booth sold nothing but antique Bibles and had a lighted display for one a soldier had carried in the Civil War. It cost a thousand dollars.

The Lamb's booth was still in disarray. Bullet Bibles were strewn like they'd been dropped from the ceiling. A man and woman were hustling to tidy their displays. They had shirts and hats printed with a logo that read, *God, Guts, Guns*.

"Excuse our mess," the man said. He was in his thirties with a thick Cajun accent and a thicker shock of black hair.

"Virgil," the woman whispered, "that's the sheriff's boy."

Virgil peered at me. He had a dimpled chin, milky blue eyes.

"How much are those hats?" I asked, just being nice.

Virgil took a hat from the floor and slapped it against his thigh to knock off dust. Then, with a flourish of his wrist, he placed it on my head.

"How much?" I said.

"From our house to yours."

"I have cash," I said. "I can pay."

"Nothing wrong with walking-around money for the weekend."

I thanked him. Then, because it seemed like what my father would do, I shook his hand.

"Sammy's Catholic," I said.

"Then he ought to know better."

"My father's talking to him. He'll set him straight," I said.

"If yours don't, ours will," Virgil said. Then he winked.

ON THE LAMB

PODCAST EPISODE 10
GUEST: Virgil Bernthal
RECORDED: April 2024
                    The Chapel of Light
                    Waco, Texas

A complete aberration is what I'd call it. On American soil, no less. Men, women, children. If you ask me, it was an aberration of justice. A *debacle*. That's the word I'd use. I'd call it a miscarriage or debacle or—

And how old are you, Virgil?
Sixty-seven.

And you're from?
Lafayette. I thought this was about the Lamb.

It is.
We were his students. *Disciples* would work just as well.

And how long were you a disciple?
Thirty-nine years and counting.

So, despite everything, you still believe in the Lamb's teachings?
No.

You said "and counting."
You asked if I still believed despite everything that's happened. I don't believe despite what happened. I believe because of what happened.

Of course. I'm sorry.
You should be.

Jaye

We returned to the Highland house the next morning to find the front door open. Perry, barefoot and bare chested, was tiptoeing on a wooden chair in the middle of the empty living room. The chair wobbled, teetered. My mother must have thought he was hanging himself because she threw her purse into my arms and was bolting across the room when he casually said, "Hidy there, friends."

He'd just finished remounting the ceiling fan. His chest was concave and pale under curls of dark hair. He wore a belt with an ichthus buckle, but his pants sagged enough to expose the frayed band of plaid boxer shorts.

"We came back to finish up," she said. She was shamefaced, flustered by her overreaction or his nakedness. She was also lying, and not for the first time that morning. When my father had returned from throwing his route, she said we were leaving to collect her paycheck and buy groceries. Now she said, "We were going to dust and vacuum. We wanted to make sure you were settling in."

"I surely am," he said. Stepping off the chair, he balanced himself with a hand on my mother's shoulder. In his back pockets were pliers and screwdrivers. He had trouble slipping into his ratty shirt; one of the sleeves was inside out, so my mother helped him. He said, "I like fixing things as much as I like company."

They did laundry most of the morning; Perry seemed to have a closetful of unwashed clothes. When I tried to help, he shooed me away. He said girls my age should spend weekends listening to rock and roll that made parents frightful for the future. Then he snapped his fingers—eureka!—

and jogged out to his truck. He was still shoeless. He brought in a boom box and three leather briefcases full of cassettes; he carried them like a stack of pizza boxes. He positioned the radio on the wobbly chair then spent ten minutes considering what to play; he reviewed track listings and liner notes before deeming each unworthy. When he finally chose ZZ Top, he slid the tape into the deck with unruly, boyish delight. He cranked the volume. He wailed on an air guitar. He squinted as his fingers worked imaginary frets, grimaced as he soloed, and arched his back against my mother's. She covered her face, giggling. His tinted glasses flew off as he headbanged.

When he insisted on treating us to lunch, we expected more burgers. Instead, Perry returned with three rib-eye steaks wrapped in butcher paper. He doused the beef in Dr Pepper and grilled it over charcoal in the backyard. This time he didn't ask before saying grace. He suggested we dip each bite in yellow mustard, which we did, and it was outrageously delicious. He said he'd come to start a landscaping service with some California hippies because people didn't value lawns in Texas. He boasted about friends on every continent—clergymen, outlaws, mathematicians, bricklayers, and mystics. He said he'd made mistakes in his life—"nothing too illegal, but getting close"—but he believed in redemption and had been blessed to meet others who did, too. He said his father had been a cruel man, and his mother had passed on. He'd inherited a spread of land in Texas, and for years he'd been working with like-minded folks to build a community for people who needed help. He was involved in business ventures there, too—small engine repair, a shooting range, an outfit that sold products to weekend warriors. "You know," he said, "these white-collar types who memorize all them *Rambo* movies." He liked manual labor and cowboy churches and Dr Pepper, which had been invented in Waco, Texas, his hometown. He'd never tried sushi or been drunk or played golf.

After lunch, he rinsed our plates then brought out his acoustic guitar and played a funny song about a lonely Texas snowman. The next one followed an angel attempting to pawn a dented halo. When no one wanted it, she yanked it down and wore it like a necklace. My mother and I clapped. Perry turned bashful and said he'd worked up a powerful craving for ice cream. He raced to his truck so fast he had to come back for his keys. He'd also forgotten to ask what flavors we liked, so when he returned, he had ten different quarts, a tower of five balancing in each upturned palm. He'd almost made it to the kitchen before they tumbled onto him.

A clown, I thought. A clown in want of a circus.

ON THE LAMB

PODCAST EPISODE 2
GUEST: Constance Cullen
RECORDED: August 2023
              Phone Interview

I had him young. His daddy liked to beat on us a little. If not for me, none of this would've come to pass.

Because you were his mother.
Because I wasn't meant for mothering. I place too much trust in men. Always have. His daddy forced Perry to memorize the Bible. Made him recite pages before he was allowed to eat. If that boy missed one word, a single solitary word, he went hungry. It stunted his growth is my belief. The next night, he'd have to try again with additional pages required. If he botched it, then he got the belt. Clarence said his way taught discipline. He said it ensured a devout life. When he caught me sneaking food to Perry, I'd feel the rod. A couple of times he brought one of his friends over and Clarence watched him take a turn on me. If he made Perry watch, I've blocked it out.

You mean he would—
Perry never really stood a chance is all. After Clarence, there were plenty of other men coming through the house. If I was out of work, they were customers. If I had a job, I hoped we'd marry.

And you think the Lamb—
He's just Perry to me. My baby boy. He got picked on in school, called horrible names. Why wouldn't he turn to God? When he ran off—in junior high, mind you—I hoped he'd find his way into the army or clergy. God forgive me, I didn't think it'd be so bad if he met an early end. A car crash maybe, but quick. Put him out of his misery. Listen to the words coming out of my mouth, Christ almighty.

After he ran away, did you have contact with him?
Not so much. By the time he was eighteen, he was vagabonding around the world, doing his teachings. I wasn't part of that. Apparently he told folks I'd died. Wishful thinking, I'm sure.

Jaye

My mother started dieting, growing her hair out, visiting the Highland house between cleaning jobs. When she passed me in the hall or kitchen, the air blossomed with new sugary perfume. I felt sorry for her, the way I felt sorry for myself at school, but there were also times when I enjoyed seeing her fight to contain her eagerness. She seemed younger than me in those first months of his courting, and I expected her to ask my advice on what to wear or say or do. Like I had any experience at all. Like the same desperate blood wasn't surging in my veins. Like I wouldn't have done anything at all with any boy at any time had any of them just asked. Like mother, like daughter.

Sometimes she took me with her. With each visit, the Highland house grew more crowded. The sunken living room filled with pawn shop instruments—electric guitars, amplifiers, a sprawling piecemeal drum kit—and frizzy-haired men working out shambling tunes. Some people were living on the property while others were transient. They came from California and Texas, from England and Brazil. I gathered most were strangers to each other, buoyant and strained and deferential, as if the house were a bus station and they were waylaid travelers. While men cobbled together songs, women baked and cleaned and sat on tasseled pillows in the living room, brushing out each other's hair.

Perry celebrated our every arrival. He clapped and hooted. He danced. People watched him greet us, tracked how he offered us plates of food or, even when the music wasn't blaring, put his ear close to my mother's mouth when she spoke. Once, sitting beside her in the backyard, he peeled off his glasses and blotted tears from his eyes with his wrist. She could've been confessing some wanton jealousy or guilt, or maybe talking about my father. He was a decent and aimless oaf, perpetually vexed by anyone who exerted more than minimum effort. When we first started visiting the Highland house, I assumed she included me to allay his suspicions. It seemed illicit but harmless enough. Eventually I understood I was there to save her from herself. To keep her, if not honest, then in check. Without me, she might step out on my father or, maybe worse in her mind, proposition Perry and learn how she'd misinterpreted the nature of their connection. At the end of our visits, he gave her vigorous shoulder massages— a trainer sending his boxer into the ring. He changed the oil in her car, replaced her brake pads. For her birthday, he presented her with a used tape recorder he boasted about haggling down at a swap meet.

He seemed unable to sit still. He was constantly flitting between rooms and engaged in multiple conversations at once. Someone was always knocking on the front door—acquaintances he'd made at a junkyard, someone's sister who'd been evicted after being a day late on rent, a fiddle player or drummer, an investor interested in staking one of Perry's entrepreneurial endeavors. Once, a delivery man showed up with cases of Bibles on a dolly. After Perry signed for them, the people in the house swarmed the boxes like starving refugees. One woman got knocked to the floor and started crying. Perry helped her up and pressed his forehead to hers. Immediately her tears stopped, and she smirked like he'd implanted a dirty joke in her mind. The Bibles were the orange of traffic cones.

"I ordered them like that! The color makes you pay attention," Perry said. "That color says, 'Shit's about to get real.'"

I assumed he planned to sell them and put the profits toward sitars and tambourines, maybe a harp. Despite Perry praying before meals, no one in the house seemed holy to me, least of all him, so the Bibles might as well have been Avon.

And then he'd disappear for days, weeks. He drove back to Texas at least once, returning with a long flatbed trailer stacked with small engines. Then he went to Mexico. Then Hawaii. Then Israel.

When he traveled, my mother's mood curdled. The air around her stopped smelling of perfume. She went back to eating French fries and drinking wine coolers. Perry had never sent her anything—he didn't even know our address—but I could tell she marked her days by checking mail. Maybe he'd promised a postcard. Maybe he'd written our address in the notebook where he scrawled his Jesus lyrics. Probably it was nothing more than the doomed hopefulness of a lonely woman. One night when I opened my mother's purse—occasionally, out of boredom, I'd swipe a few dollars—I found one of those orange Bibles. Another time, after Perry'd been in Israel for almost a month, I passed my parents' closed bedroom door and heard what I thought was the sound of weeping. I pressed my ear to the door and understood my mistake. She wasn't upset. She was singing into her tape recorder and playing it back, adjusting her pitch and adding little runs, making her voice beautiful for him.

Roy

I spotted the dueling pistols at an antique weapons booth. Their cherrywood case had a glass lid and plush wine-colored lining and a label stating the pistols were from 1860. They cost three thousand dollars. I didn't care about the guns, but the lock on the case was a brass Bramah. I'd only seen one in library books but immediately recognized it. Mason's tools would've been too big; picking it would require extra thin needles, and even with those, I might not be able to push in without catching the pins. The dealer asked if I needed help and hovered suspiciously after I said no.

Then a voice: "Sweet hat."

Beside me, standing close enough that her arm rubbed against mine, a girl wearing a gas mask. Her dark red hair was tamed into a thick braid that dropped forward when she leaned over to inspect the pistols. When she faced me again, my reflection showed in the mask's lenses. I appeared small and scared, wearing a cheap hat that sat too high on my head.

"I said I like your cap," she said, her voice made distant and watery by her mask. "The polite thing to do would be to offer a compliment of your own."

"I like your mask," I said.

"It's lacking the filter. If someone launches a chemical agent in here, we'll keel over at the same time."

"We're probably safe," I said.

"So, you're an optimist. If you're so sure of the future, why're you pricing pistols?"

"I'm not. I pick locks. I was seeing if I could open that case. The guy who invented that lock made them so secure no one figured out how to pick them for seventy years. I did a book report."

"We could just grab the box and make a run for it, smash it open later."

"That would work, too," I said. "I'm not really interested in the pis—"

"Do you go to the high school?" She cut me off. "Do you have a sweetheart?"

"You ask a lot of questions," I said.

"I'm trying to save time in case there's an attack."

"Do you know something I don't?"

"I know a lot you don't."

My ears were turning red. It happened when I got nervous. I hoped she couldn't see clearly through the lenses. I tried to straighten my posture without her noticing. Behind us, a stun gun went off.

"I'm a freshman," I said. "My girlfriend broke up with me over Christmas break."

"That tramp. I never liked her for you."

A few aisles over, a man said, "Shit, Yvonne!" Maybe because of whatever was happening with the stun gun. I couldn't figure what to do with my hands; they'd turned cumbersome and foreign, like I'd put on oven mitts.

"My mom and I are from California," the girl said. "I'll eventually start at the high school. I have a gentleman caller. He's older. He has a family but wants to make an honest woman out of me."

The dealer was hovering again. I realized he probably assumed the girl and I were a team. It was exhilarating, flattering. If we grabbed the case and ran, I could just pick the lock later. I said, "Do you *want* to get married?"

"Easy, pilgrim. You're moving a little fast."

"I meant to the gentleman caller," I said.

She adjusted her gas mask. I glimpsed dry lips and ruddy cheeks.

"How many locks have you picked today?" she asked.

"I don't know. A few."

"Well, that's a few too many for Johnny Law."

"Do what?"

With the chin of her mask, she motioned behind me: my father striding up the aisle. He wore a strange expression, somewhere between stern and baleful. What I thought of were those times when we served warrants and people we'd known for years turned into pitiful or dangerous strangers. The dealer with the dueling pistols said, "Son, can I help you with anything here?" I didn't answer. My mouth might as well have been packed with dry leaves. My father was closing in, nodding kindly to people but fixing me with his eyes every few paces, as though he expected me to flee. I wanted to. I wanted to grab the girl's hand and break through the doors and vanish into the dark rain, but even without turning, I knew she was long gone.

Jaye

Perry returned from Israel in September of 1992. His clan threw a party like he was getting out of prison or wanted one last hurrah before beginning a life sentence. The yard and living room were strung with Christmas lights. The landscaping equipment disappeared to make room for picnic tables. Someone rigged a stereo to the amplifiers, and everyone brought food—fried chicken, macaroni salad, heaping plates of rolls, and pimento cheese sandwiches cut into little triangles and staked with toothpicks. My mother made a green bean casserole and bought him a cowboy shirt with silver piping. I thought it was too much until another woman gave him a motorbike. I worried my outshined mother might try to distinguish herself by serenading him.

And she might have if he hadn't been so undone by whatever he'd experienced in the Holy Land. Perry dropped his duffel by the door then collapsed onto the couch. Again he reminded me of a convict, a gaunt shell of a man who'd been paroled and returned to a world that wearied him. He pantomimed appreciation for the party, though it only conveyed that such frivolity was beneath him and whoever had organized it should've known better. Someone shut off the music. He asked that the plate of fried chicken be taken out of the house.

"I'm off meat," he said.

Without his bidding, my mother fetched him a glass of water. Perry awarded her a serene nod. I was proud and ashamed of her. The house was so quiet I wanted to stomp my feet. We listened to each other's breathing. We listened to him swallow—a noise that seemed indecent in such fraught silence. We watched him hand the glass to my mother and lid his eyes, at once anointing and dismissing her. The Christmas lights dappled him in gold. He looked beatific, stricken. His fatigue, which seemed so pure it edged toward divine, was an indictment. Who were they to expect him to regale them with stories? Who wouldn't be sacked after such a pilgrimage? My mother and I slipped out the door with a Hawaiian family, but most everyone lingered. They unplugged the lights and watched his reposed reflection in the mirror. He slept for two days.

When he woke, he was frenetic. He paced and told tales that ran together for hours. He couldn't speak fast enough. He ate standing up and talked with his mouth full. Food dropped from his lips. He mashed it into the carpet with his bare feet and never noticed. The sunken living room had become his theater and seats filled up fast. The unlucky crowded the kitchen or sat on backyard picnic tables, straining to hear through the sliding glass doors. Everyone was rapt. They leaned forward, twitchy with reverence. Here was the reason they'd left their homes to sleep on his floor. Perry was making good on a tacit promise, delivering the manna for which they'd been starving. After the first day, my mother started taping as much as she could with her recorder.

"Okay, see, up on Mount Zion, over in Israel," he said, "I met with seven angels. They set me straight on certain notions confounding my head and I was given wings. And a chore. I was called upon. I talked with old Enoch, too. Enoch who had been translated! He described the Merkabah, which is kind of like God's flying saucer."

Okay, I thought. Okay. I expected my mother to lead us out of the house again and drive off while the whole loony flock jeered, to make me promise to run screaming in the opposite direction if Perry ever approached me on the street. She couldn't get enough, though. No one could. They relaxed and wept and scribbled notes. A man kept taking noisy Polaroids. The longer he talked, the less I understood.

In one version, Perry's chore was to spread word that the staging ground had moved from Israel to Texas. His shirt was open; it flared and lifted as he paced. His toenails hadn't been cut in months, and I kept waiting for one to snag the carpet.

"In olden days," he said, "when somebody said 'you've gone to Texas,' they meant you'd gone bananas, but now folks'll head there because they're seeing straight. Our constitution says every citizen in America has the right to rebuttal the government. See, Texas understands what the rest of the country is missing. Guns? Sure, we'll have them. Sure, we'll use toilet paper. You're all welcome to join in. You're either in or you're out. Maybe we are a little crazy."

In another version, he needed to raise the New Light, which seemed to be children who would inherit the earth after the Wave Sheaf scrubbed it of sin. "This is real Jews and Babylon stuff," he said. "There's a lot on my shoulders here, see?" Or he needed to convince the world the Holy Ghost was female. "Right? It adds up, don't it? The father is the daddy and the son is the son, so she has to be mama. Plain biology. Simple as sin." The only consistency through the versions was how his efforts would be met with powerful resistance. Nonbelievers would challenge the means and the message. Assyrians would outnumber his people. They would distort the truth. They would win unless Perry figured it all out. Either way, he was going to die.

"And I guess I need y'all to start calling me the Lamb," he said, pacing the living room and eating a tomato like an apple. "I've got visions behind my eyes and they ain't good. Rivers of blood. Mountains of bone. I'm seeing sacrifice, okay? I'm seeing lakes on fire and some mighty fucking scorched earth."

Roy

Coop and I had been friends since elementary school. As a kid, he'd eat or drink whatever you put in front of him for a dollar—a spoonful of mayonnaise and sardines, whole habanero peppers, a jar of pickle juice mixed with cocoa powder. His father had bailed years before, just strolled out the door and never returned. Coop lived with his mother and grandmother a few miles away. His house smelled of dryer lint and wet coffee grounds, scents I would forever associate with grief.

On weekends he stayed up watching Cinemax. The goal was to record movies with nudity, graphic violence, or, dream of dreams, both. After my parents went to sleep on Friday, I called and told him about the gas-mask girl and asked him to come to the gun show on Saturday morning. "Can't help you," he said. *The Erotic Island* was airing later, so he wanted to stay up and then sleep in. Coop could be petulant, stubborn. But I knew he loved gun shows and was just resisting because I might have a chance with a girl. I said I'd pay his entry fee and buy him a Frito Pie. Then I promised that if we found her, I'd ask about friends of hers who might be interested in him.

"You have to say I'll probably be on the football team next year."

"You say that every year and never try out," I said.

"And say I'm thinking about starting a band, probably called Love Puddle."

"You don't play any instruments," I said.

"The logo will be a heart-shaped puddle, but it'll be running into the gutter. We'll be hardcore. Or at least punk."

On Saturday, the line circled the building. Men breathed smoke and spat tobacco juice into Styrofoam cups. An NRA lady with a clipboard milled about collecting signatures. Sammy was inspecting people's firearms, and Shawn and Shane were back hawking Boy Scout pecans. Shawn was a year older than Shane but had flunked ninth grade. They started a lot of fights and lied about bagging deer on Isaac's father's hunting lease. Coop swiped a bag of pecans without paying.

We had to sidestep through the packed aisles. I saw people from church and people my father had arrested. The dueling pistols weren't out yet. Coop talked to a vendor about night-vision goggles and then to another with prosthetic legs about nunchucks. The first few times we passed the Lamb's booth, he clapped and pointed at me: "Now there's a man with magnificent taste in headwear!" I was wearing my *God, Guts, Guns* hat. It itched and still sat too high on my head but felt lucky. An hour later, the Lamb said, "You boys lost?" An hour after that: "Walking in circles always leads to the same place, Rodeo."

"He wants to recruit you," Coop said. He was wearing his favorite camouflaged cargo pants, the ones he knew I'd always envied. "At least you'd see the tunnels."

Rumors of the Lamb's secret tunnels were as common as cows. The tunnels were said to start in the barracks or gymnasium, out by the shooting range or under the chapel's stage. They ran for miles under the Blackland Prairie. They boasted a track for a miniature train that could reach Dallas faster than a Lamborghini. The Lamb had getaway cars parked by exit points. Or the tunnels led to safe houses in our own neighborhoods. When I asked my father about them, he said, "Tunnels or toilets, detective? Which would you install first?" But Coop put stock in them. He also believed in chupacabras and UFOs.

"Let's go back to the front," I said. "I can ask if Sammy's seen her."

"Why don't we just print up posters? Wanted: Nameless, Faceless Girl, Engaged to Older Married Man."

"She's not engaged."

"You ever wonder why she wore a gas mask? Acne is no joke. This could be a real Leatherface situation."

"She has to have ties to a dealer to get in on early bird night," I said. "Maybe her dad has a booth."

"Do you know how many times I've snuck into early bird night? The only reason I didn't yesterday is because it was sack-freezing cold," he said. "*Erotic Island* was good by the way. Super good. On this island, all the ladies—"

"I want to do another loop," I said.

"It might be time to cut bait, hoss."

"One more," I said. "Then we'll eat."

"Suit yourself. I'm going back for those nunchucks."

I went through the aisles on my own. I tried planning what to say if I found her, but nothing sprang to mind, which made finding her seem inevitable. Sammy caught sight of me, but I pretended to read a pamphlet about game-processing services. Coop swiped another bag of pecans, then another. The coliseum grew more crowded by the hour. I used the last of my money to buy Mason a gas mask.

When the show closed for the day, my mother pulled into the parking lot behind a line of trucks. Brake lights and blinkers flared through billowing exhaust, smearing the world in red and yellow. We had to wait a long while to exit; our headlights reflected bright off the chrome bumper ahead of us, and a soft rain sifted through the beams. My mother told Coop not to knock himself out with his nunchucks. When I showed her the gas mask, she said, "That's real thoughtful, sweet potato." She'd started calling me that recently, and though I didn't normally care, now it made me wish Coop hadn't come with me today. I knew he thought I'd invented the girl and now he'd call me sweet potato at some embarrassing point in the future. I clicked on the radio to discourage any more conversation. *Hank Williams's pain songs, Jerry Jeff's train songs, and Blue Eyes Crying in the Rain.*

ON THE LAMB

PODCAST EPISODE 6
GUEST: Jim Grant
RECORDED: December 2023
Grant Firearms
Waco, Texas

My wife, Hassie, and I own Grant Firearms. We're on I-35 North, same exit as the mammoths. We started out in the Live Oak Mall, but they hiked the rent and all the retailers moved out; now they're kaput and we're still going. There's a lesson there. We've been in business for over thirty-five years.

When we met Perry, he knew diddly-squat about firearms. He was a Bible thumper who wanted to be a guitar god. When all was said and done, he probably knew more than me and Hassie put together. We're the ones that turned him on to the gun shows, showed him the money to be had. We're culpable in that way. We're on that hook.

Jaye

On the Saturday before Perry left for Texas, my mother and I helped clean out what remained in the Highland house. Most of the furniture had been sold. The refrigerator and washing machine, too, though we'd later learn they'd belonged to the landlord. The cupboards were empty save a few cans of vegetable broth and a box of instant rice. The living room smelled like an overfull vacuum cleaner bag.

I was sweeping the garage when Perry leaned against the door and said, "I've got a buyer in Temecula for the riding mower. I need me a navigator."

My mother was inside, scrubbing the countertops. I looked for her through the sliding doors and in the marbled mirror but couldn't find her. If she went with Perry to Temecula, I'd be stranded here for hours. Dinner would be vegetable broth poured over rice.

"Your mother thought you might enjoy a little behind-the-wheel time," Perry said. His hands and clothes were patched with oil. "I told her I'd bring back some paper towels."

"Me?" I said, incredulous. The garage floor was clean, but I kept sweeping. "I don't know how to drive."

"Give me an hour and we'll remedy that problem," he said. He was suddenly mobilizing, harried, maybe realizing he was already late. He lowered his truck's tailgate and positioned two wooden planks as ramps to get the mower into the bed. With anyone else, I would have rushed to help.

"Why doesn't she want to go?" I asked.

"Who said she don't?" He shifted the mower into neutral. He had to angle and stretch himself to get enough leverage to push, then he steered with one hand. He said, "But there's only room for one other person in the cab and she thought we might appreciate getting to know each other. Your mother and I are thick as thieves, but me and you haven't hardly shook hands, let alone hallelujahed the county."

"I'm not Christian," I said.

"Neither was Jesus. You're in fine company."

"Did you hit your head in Israel?" I asked. Then, because I recognized a suspicion that had been gnawing at me, I added, "Or wherever you went."

"I hit my head on the Word, and believe me, truth is harder than iron," he said. "And it'll squeegee your eyes real good, too. I can see the writing on the wall now."

"What wall? What writing?"

"You hear about what happened up in Idaho?" he said. "How the government took out that Green Beret's wife and son because his way of living offended them? If they'll do that to one of their own, what'll they do to me and you?"

"I don't know what you're talking about. You've changed. Either you were wearing a costume before, or you are now."

"It ain't in the cards for people to change," he said. He stopped pushing the mower and set his eyes on mine. "Not for me, not for your mama or papa or little old you. Wherever we go there we are, just as God intended."

"I don't believe in God." I didn't know if this was true, but I liked how definitive it sounded, how provocative. I wanted him to know I wasn't as gullible as the others.

"That's sorry news for your soul, but all I asked was if you wanted a driving lesson," he said. "Last I checked, everlasting salvation wasn't required for getting a license."

Roy

Middle of January, glaucoma gray and cold. Temperatures fell and stayed down, defeated. Panda disappeared. I put on heavy clothes and tromped through frost-crusted fields, calling her name. Then one morning she appeared on our porch, cleaning her face with her paw. When I opened the door, she trotted inside with an air of annoyance.

My father had been working late. Our phone rang often and at odd hours. Always for him. If I answered, he had me hold the line until he picked up the extension in the garage. He'd spliced it in after Mason deployed so we could all be on the line together. Some of my father's calls lasted a couple of minutes, others stretched beyond an hour. If one ran long, my mother brought him coffee and his Eisenhower jacket. After hanging up, he'd come in looking wrung out, the edges of his voice frayed. He seemed to be receding. Those hours on the phone were waves batting him farther away from our shore.

Despite the mean-feeling cold, my parents smoked in our backyard just about every night. I cracked my window to listen, but they stood by our far fence, their voices borne away on night winds. What words I could hear made no sense. One night my mother said, "What does Idaho have to do with Texas? Did you ask that? I bet they'd have some clever answer that doesn't mean shit." Another night my father said, "What they're calling a stockpile is just *stock*. He's a licensed dealer, and goddamn it, I ought to know." When they came in, my mother soaked in a hot bath, and my father set himself up in the living room. He found a western or space movie on television and worked with brushes and cloths in his recliner, rubbing saddle soap into all our boots. It was one of the few things that relaxed him.

Before the gun show, he'd been wearing his duty jacket and jeans to work; now he emerged from the bathroom each morning in full uniform—khaki shirt, dark green trousers, shined holster, and polished nickel badge. He slapped on aftershave and slicked his hair back with Brylcreem. He scrambled eggs and fried sausage and toasted rye bread and brewed coffee, then ate at the kitchen table by the narrow light above the stove. The kitchen smelled of skillet grease and the Tabasco sauce he spooned onto his eggs. Sunrise was at least an hour off. If I'd ventured out of my room, he'd kiss my head and say I should get back to sleep. He didn't mind me being up, not really, and soon enough he'd make me some toast. After the *Tribune-Herald* hit our porch, he'd flip through the headlines and drink another cup of coffee standing at the counter. He'd clip his pager on his belt and kiss my head again. Then he'd leave and lock the door behind him. He never turned on his truck's headlights until he was down the road.

"I guess Dad's having trouble sleeping," I said to my mother on Friday morning. We were about to leave for school.

"With everything happening, he can't quiet his mind. If this goes on much longer, he'll polish our boots into sandals."

"I don't know what all's happening," I said.

My mother regarded me. She was leaning against the sink. In the window behind her hung our dingy lace curtains. She'd tried to "antique" them by soaking the cloth in tea, a project to pass an afternoon shortly after Mason deployed. They just looked sad and soiled, though I'd complimented them more than once.

She said, "I'm too tired not to tell you."

"Not to tell me what?"

"Sammy's after his job, sweet potato."

"Sammy's only part-time," I said, like it mattered.

"But his bellyaching is a full-time position."

"Nobody'll vote for him."

"They might if he runs Perry out of town," she said. "He's gotten the government in a lather. Last night, the FBI called. The night before was some other alphabet agency. They want to know what's the what."

"I bet it'll be okay," I said, hoping to sound resolute, hoping to sound like my father.

"I'm glad someone thinks so," she said. I was trying to think of what to say, maybe something about Mason or a hopeful future, when she asked, "Did you have any dreams last night?"

This was one of her favorite questions. I rarely remembered my dreams, but over the years, I'd come to understand that dreamless nights disappointed my mother, so I usually made something up. I said, "I had one where we lived in an underwater world and swam from place to place. Everyone wore flippers."

"That's a good one," she said. She straightened my jacket, raised my collar. She assessed me and patted my arms. "I bet you're feeling like you need to get out from under something. I bet you're overwhelmed."

"I don't know," I said.

"I don't either," she said, glancing up at the bird clock. "I'm probably just telling on myself."

Jaye

This was a period of life when I was waiting for disruption—an illness, a car accident, an earthquake that closed school. My classes were tedious and dispiriting. I ate lunch alone, watching other girls snicker and flip their hair and throw away most of their food. I watched the boys watch the girls. I picked out the queen in each group and tried to emulate her swagger, strutting into a room like I'd just conquered a country. My efforts inevitably hit left of the mark. I wore the right boots years too late. I learned to dance to the wrong album. I wasn't despised or ridiculed or a source of gossip. I was a wraith. If they remember anything, it would be my hair. They'd say, "Oh, the girl with the long red hair? What ever happened to her?"

I'd grown my hair out so I could hide behind it.

But I thought some misfit would eventually take a shine to me. A boy would come along, and we'd link up and emerge bigger than we were by ourselves. Or one of the girl groups would adopt me like a stray. Or I'd get sick or one of my parents would and it would alter the way I navigated the world. It could happen. Darla Boeck's brother had been killed in a car accident; Bobby Gonzales had been stabbed in a street fight; Polly Farnsworth had gotten pregnant. It was easy to believe I was in line for transformation—not because I was special, but because I wasn't. I never spent the money I slipped from my mother's purse. In my mind, I was socking it away for a prom dress or an abortion.

So, on a Tuesday night in September, when my mother crept into my room, I knew the wait was over. My father was already bagging morning papers in the Ralphs parking lot. My mother sat on my bed, and I said, "Let me guess: You're leaving."

"I used to think of Texans as oil barons or cowboys. It seemed a place outside time. I imagined it in black and white, I think."

"And now?"

"Now it's a lush green. It's people building something, working together. Now it's the future."

"I think of bandanas and tumbleweeds."

"Your father and I lead separate lives," she said. "Maybe that's not a news flash."

"I have eyes," I said.

"I do, too, but they've been closed. Perry opened them," she said. "The Lamb, I mean."

I suppressed the urge to baaaaa like a sheep.

"He misses you, you know," she said. "He wants to put your name in one of his ballads. He calls me sometimes."

"I hate my name," I said.

"So change it," she said, not unkindly. "You can choose a different road than the one you're traveling. 'Then I saw a new heaven and a new earth, for the first heaven and the first earth had passed away, and the sea was no more.'"

She'd never said anything like that before. It repulsed me so completely I wished I'd made the sheep noise. I felt distance open between us, a sense that I could trust her less than when I'd gotten into bed.

"They have a phone line out there, but I guess it costs too much for long distance, so he calls collect," she said. "We never talk long. He just wants to check on me, and on you. He wants to know our daily goings-on."

"And he wants you to come to Texas," I said.

"It'll just be a visit," she said. The bed shifted when she wiped her eyes. She said, "I want to see what they're making. I've never been to Texas. He thinks I'd like it."

"What do *you* think?"

"I think it's rare to find a connection with someone, especially when you get older. I think I'd like to see myself the way he does."

"I didn't know you even believed in God. Have we ever been to church?"

"Life seems bathed in possibility now," she said. "I feel lucky, like I could contribute value to the world."

"Perry makes you feel that way? Perry who skipped out on rent because he met with seven angels on a flying saucer?"

"When he and I are talking, it's like everyone's been overlooking me my whole life, like he recognizes what only I can offer. He makes me feel . . . I don't know—"

"Special? Alive? Chosen?"

"I was going to say, 'Not invisible.'"

A sudden lump in my throat, a tiny death of a cruel feeling in my chest. I said, "Does Dad know?"

"Well, apparently, collect calls, no matter how short, appear on phone bills," she said. Mischief in her voice, the sound of a hesitant smile. "I'm sure I knew that at one point. I'm sure I was in denial."

"Maybe you wanted to get caught," I said.

"Maybe I wanted to get caught." She took a breath, then said, "So yes, he knows. And he knows I'm heading down there. He just doesn't know when."

"Meaning he doesn't know you're leaving tonight," I said.

"I'll only be gone a week. Ten days tops. No more than two or three weeks at most," she said. "I keep expecting to move beyond it, beyond him, but there's this loving gravity. I'm sorry I'm not stronger or a better mother. Part of me hopes I get out there and hate it and start driving back without ever leaving the car. That would make everybody's life easier."

"How long's the drive?"

"A couple of days? I don't really know," she said. "I've got a thermos of coffee, and I've got my tapes. I packed peanut butter and bread. I'll pull over if I get tired."

None of this shocked me—not the collect calls or her plan to drive through the night or even Perry making her feel visible. This was why I'd been squirreling away her money.

"You really don't care if I change my name?" I said.

"I want you to be happy. I want the world to call you what you want to be called. You'll have to make harder choices than that."

"Are there horses on his ranch?"

"He's mentioned a couple, yes," she said.

"Give me fifteen minutes," I said.

"For what?"

"To pack," I said.

Roy

My brother called that Sunday, and each of us picked up different receivers: my mother in the kitchen, my father in the garage, and me in my room. Mason said he'd just gotten back from a bazaar where he traded a jeep battery for a case of flea collars. The sand fleas were getting worse but wearing the collars around your ankles helped. His plan was to keep half for himself and sell the rest to other contractors. Even without seeing her, I knew my mother was writing down *flea collars* so she'd remember to send some in his next care package. That night, Mason sounded cheerful, and his tone lifted us, too, but shortly into the call our reception crapped out. This happened so often with satellite calls we were more disappointed than concerned. We blurted goodbyes just before the call dropped, then, as was our habit, convened in the kitchen to debrief. My mother said how clever it was to use flea collars that way. I said it was smart to swap a car battery, and my father recalled how frugal Mason had been as a child: Instead of buying baseball cards, he'd drawn his own and sold them to friends. Then the phone rang. Of course we assumed it was Mason, but when my mother answered, it was for my father. He went wordlessly to the garage.

After school on Monday, I took the long route home by myself. Coop had gotten detention for bringing his nunchucks to campus. I cut across a soggy stubble field and watched a pickup pull onto the distant shoulder of Goat Trail Road. It was a faded red beater, though when I was halfway across the field, I tricked myself into thinking it was Shawn and Shane, then Isaac and Rosie. The fan belt squealed when the truck pulled away. At the property line, I hopped the split-rail fence and headed west across another field. My cheeks and ears and knuckles were numb in the cold. It was, I guessed, around midnight for Mason. Did he wear flea collars around his ankles when he slept? I had the lonely feeling that comes after those startling moments when you hear your own voice, plain and trifling, in your head.

When the pickup appeared again, I knew it was Sammy Gregson. Fear dive-bombed me from unforeseen angles. Tragedy had befallen my mother or father or Mason, maybe even Coop, and the deputy had been dispatched to escort me to the hospital. *This is when it happens, in this field, on a stupid Monday afternoon.*

The truck moved slowly forward like it was stuck in neutral. Despite the cold, the windows were down. I didn't know if I should run toward the truck or away from it. When I was close enough, I saw it wasn't Sammy behind the wheel. The driver looked nervy, young, and for a moment, I had the thought that she wasn't tall enough to reach the brake pedal.

"You preferred the gas mask?" she asked.

A rushing through my body, a tilting in my head. I said, "Hi! I didn't know you were you."

"Trippy."

"I didn't think you were old enough to drive," I said. Her age now seemed a new obstacle, another way the deck was stacked against me.

"I'm not. I'm illegally running errands for my mother's dipshit lover."

"My father's the sheriff," I said and immediately wished I hadn't. The truck started picking up speed. I was almost jogging.

"I'm aware. I'm trusting you not to rat me out."

"I won't," I said.

She stomped the brake and almost hit her throat on the steering wheel when the truck stopped abruptly. "Then hop in."

The vinyl seat was split, exposing sickly orange foam. Hairline cracks webbed out from a windshield ding. The radio was gone, the ashtray full. I hoped she didn't smoke. I started preparing answers in case she asked if I did. I tried to remember doing anything weird in the field, singing or picking my nose.

She drove timidly at times, boldly at others. She took corners without signaling or slowing down. I wondered how long she'd been driving. I wanted to buckle my seatbelt, but she wasn't wearing hers, so I hung my arm out the window to clutch the door. I locked it with my armpit.

Her face was smooth and open and plain—no makeup, no earrings. She wore an oversized sweatshirt that read WORLD'S GREATEST FATHER.

I must have been staring. She said, "Really, I can go grab the gas mask if it'll help."

"I just didn't recognize you," I said.

She brought her left knee up to the seat, sat on her foot while she steered. We passed a kolache shop and a barber and a store for beekeeping supplies.

"Waco's weird," she said. "Does anyone ever call it Whacko?"

"Everyone does," I said.

"Last night, the dinner conversation was all about something called the Crash at Crush. Have you heard of this? In the 1800s? They sold tickets so people could watch two trains collide."

"We read about it in Texas History class," I said. "I think some spectators got killed."

"Because there were *forty thousand* of them!" she said. "Forty thousand people *paid* to watch two locomotives barrel into each other."

Her nails were unpainted and chewed down. Her lips a little chapped. I kept sneaking looks when she was concentrating on the road.

"It's weird you have Texas History," she said. "In California, and probably everywhere else, that class is just called History."

"I like your shirt," I said.

"I stole it," she said. "Don't tell your father that either."

We were out by the truck stop with the backroom slots parlor. After that, there were only oil fields. She gave the engine some gas. It seemed important not to ask where we were going. I wanted to appear ready for adventure, as though a random girl chauffeuring me around was old hat. Really, I worried my mother would arrive home to an empty house and be angry or scared or both. I worried my father was already out looking for me. I worried he'd use the siren. The sun was fading.

"My brother's in Iraq," I said.

"I know that, too," she said, distractedly biting her cheek. She hooked a U-turn behind the truck stop. Scattering gravel pinged the fenders. The back tires slid like we'd hit ice; I bounced off the seat as the pickup straightened out.

We started toward the old feed mill. After a mile, I said, "You know a lot about me. I don't even know your name."

"Who cares about names? Would you not have gotten in the truck if my name were Baby Snot?"

"Nice to meet you, Ms. Snot."

"Charmed, I'm sure," she said in a tone that sounded like I'd passed a test. "Tell me about big brother in Iraq."

"He's supposed to come home in September, but I keep thinking he'll die before then," I said. I was speaking in a way I never had, forthright and casual, like someone she might be interested to know. And I was telling the unvarnished truth, something I only realized once the words were out. "I keep imagining what that would do to my parents."

"Then I was wrong at the gun show. You're a realist, not an optimist," she said. "I don't like a man with his head in the clouds."

"I'm pretty grounded," I said. "Pretty laid-back."

We pulled into the feed mill's caliche lot. She steered beside the abandoned loading dock, shifted into park, and situated herself to face me. Her gaze was hard and unblinking, and I averted my eyes.

"This isn't my first time stalking you. I've driven by your house," she said. "I've seen your mother on the porch petting a black cat. She's very pretty."

"Her name's Panda. Her owner died last year."

"I meant your mother, pilgrim," she said. "Your turn. Tell me a secret."

"I bought a gas mask because it reminded me of you."

"Safety first," she said. She leaned across the cab—her chest pressed against my knee, her hair on my jeans—and rummaged in the glove box until she found an old blue marker. She sat up faster than I would have liked. She raised her sleeve and scooted closer. She laid her arm on my lap, palm up, like she was giving blood. She handed me the marker.

"Let's get this out of the way," she said. "Use your best penmanship."

"For what?" I asked.

"The number to call when I'm in distress."

I wrote the numbers large and slow and careful. It reminded me of *Sesame Street* segments where a puppet painted a perfectly proportioned number on a trash-can lid or a man's bald head. That didn't seem like a thing to mention. Her skin was feather-soft.

When I finished, she pulled her knees to her chest and leaned back against her door. She blew on her arm to dry the ink. Her eyes were green or blue. I said, "Can you read it?"

"I could read it from Jupiter."

"I guess I wrote it kind of big," I said. "I want to know your name."

"Trust me, you don't. It makes me sound like I'm from another century."

"My real name is Royal," I said. "My brother calls me Champion even though the only thing I've ever won is a dictionary for getting second place in a spelling bee. There's a nutjob outside town who calls himself the Lamb and calls me Rodeo."

"Rodeo," she said. "It suits you."

"Your turn," I said.

I could feel her relaxing. She rested her cheek on her knees, stared at me sleepily. Maybe her eyes were dove gray, or the color of ice in slow-moving dreams. She smiled a private smile.

"Call me Jaye," she said.

"Jaye," I said. "It's perfect."

"It's just a name, Rodeo. Just a bunch of letters that don't mean anything at all."

"I think it means something," I said.

The late sun was gilding the clouds that unspooled on the horizon. In the failing light, the land appeared lush and peaceful. I could smell damp soil and the coolness coming on with evening, but also the truck's overfull ashtray, and I suppressed the urge to empty it out the window. The first stars were firing, crossing over us and mapping their constellations. Jaye and I sat quietly, motionless.

Then she swung her feet to the floor and pulled down her sleeve and her hand stole into mine. Our fingers twined together. Her palm felt cold and small, smooth. Her pulse was a faint steady rhythm I learned to anticipate. It sped up a little when she closed her eyes. I shut mine, too. There was warmth emanating from her side of the cab. I squeezed her fingers, which made her squeeze mine, and soon it turned into a game lacking rules or points. We were just children. Keep that in mind before you judge us.

Jaye

No one called me Jaye before my mother and I fled California with our clothes crammed into Hefty bags. At school, I'd envied the girls whose names promised bubbly handwriting and canopy beds and boy after sweet boy. Mandy. Monica. Alexis. Their names seemed perennially fashionable, and their lives followed accordingly. Mine sounded old as rust. It made me feel as though I'd been cast in a play no one read anymore. While my mother spent our highway hours playing cassettes she'd recorded at the Highland house—sermons spanning multiple tapes, mumbly songs with too much distortion about the Seven Seals—I tried on new names. Jaye sounded powerful and pretty, like a bird, a winged creature that could fly and attack and look down on the world. What's in a name? The future.

We drove through darkness. The desert silvered alongside us, an endless moonscape that would have given me vertigo in daylight. We stopped for gas and hovered above foul toilet seats. At first, we resisted the temptation of honeybuns and candy, merging back onto the blacktop eating gummy peanut butter sandwiches with an air of prudence. But outside Phoenix we bought a bag of cheese tamales. In Tucson, it was Skittles and hot chocolate, and because our heater couldn't keep out the desert cold, I stole the WORLD'S GREATEST FATHER sweatshirt. Between Las Cruces and El Paso, we came upon a squat Chinese restaurant that had once been a filling station; a pair of maroon concrete Buddhas sat where the pumps had been.

We drove alongside a molten sunset pooling on the horizon. Our car never broke down and patrolmen never pulled us over and my mother's credit card always worked. In Pecos County, she used a pay phone to call my school and say she was taking me to visit a dying relative. The registrar offered sympathy, promised to gather my assignments and mail them to us once we had an address. My mother took it as an endorsement of her choices.

Our conversations were practical and fleeting. Where to stop and when. How to adjust the temperature. We played games with license plates and road signs. My mother let me drive some. She praised where I gripped the wheel and how often I checked my mirrors. I kept expecting her to bring up Perry teaching me to drive, followed by a full and multi-chambered defense of her behavior, but she never mentioned him. She never asked if I felt guilty or afraid or wanted to turn back.

And she never brought up my father. I imagined her imagining him: He returns from his route and finds her note under the television remote. He's furious and throws it a maddeningly short distance. Then he sulks to the kitchen and eats too many toaster waffles, devising ways to make her feel crappy when we return. Who could blame him? I imagined giving him the sweatshirt I'd stolen, imagined him wearing it while he rolled morning papers and bragging that his daughter had filched it. My father who would, to the world's surprise, set so much in motion. My father who must have also felt not visible.

It seemed we were on a strange vacation, a silly girls-only indulgence, a dollar-store version of a spa week. And I felt less like the daughter trailing her mother's whimsical heart and more like the camp counselor letting kids believe they were getting away with their hijinks, tempting fate and courting danger, when really there was no risk at all. We'd be gone a couple of weeks, I thought. I hoped it'd be long enough for me to return to school appearing worldlier, more jaded, more alluring. I would let the facts—or those I invented—of the trip slip to a few people and word would spread. My presence would command attention. I'd lure boys in and withdraw my affection until they were wild with desire. The girl who drove to Texas with her crazy mother. The girl who lost her virginity to the rugged son of an oil baron, the girl who lived in a commune with a man who believed the world was ending. The girl who came back changed, who would only answer to a fiercely feathered name.

ON THE LAMB

PODCAST EPISODE 11
GUEST: Tom Carroll
RECORDED: May 2024
            Phone Interview

That man you're asking about, that piece of dog shit, that pissant pedophile, cost me a family. No father's supposed to outlive his wife or daughter. That's just not the way the movie plays. You look for where you fouled up. You think: What if I'd called Johnny Law sooner? What if I'd driven out to dumbfuck Texas myself and knocked on the door of his flimsy, shithole ranch? What if I'd been more ambitious? Or what if I'd never met her in the first place? Then would she still be alive? Would Marie be married to a doctor or lawyer, taking cruise ship vacations and teaching her girl to do the ballet? In your head, you tell yourself you're not the reason why. You say you weren't the one buying all the guns. You weren't the one bedding mothers and daughters in the same house. But in your gut you know you're not innocent either. You can only go so long before you're choking on guilt like a dry bone.

Roy

That week, every afternoon quivered with the possibility of her return. Piercing hope, exquisite agony, the quicksand of fatigue from having hardly slept the previous night because tomorrow might bring another encounter. I loitered by the field where she'd found me before, hoping she'd come back. When she didn't, I convinced myself she was on her way and dallied another hour. I paced and blew into my hands and tried to think of jokes to tell her. Then I booked it home, certain she was dialing my number right then. When the phone stayed silent, I assumed her mother had grounded her for our drive to the feed mill, and I took comfort in the bond it forged between us. Like that, we shared a past. I wondered if she had sisters or brothers or belonged to any clubs or played sports. On Thursday, a seething headache. I noticed myself smiling randomly, like a saint or lunatic, then backtracked through my thoughts to find her joking about Jupiter. On Saturday, as my father said grace at supper, I started to nod off. Every topic seemed worth discussing with her; I understood truths I'd never considered. This name I couldn't help whispering. This gift I didn't deserve. Everything fated, causal. Had I spent even three hours in her presence? My heart enraptured, in ruins. At church on Sunday morning, I prayed to find Jaye in one of the pews, then I prayed my mother had forgotten to say a girl had left a message for me.

Our church was Calvary Baptist, a white clapboard building near the town center. Out front, a banner hung between two poles like a volleyball net and read, NO PERFECT PEOPLE ALLOWED. There were rarely more than thirty of us in the pews, but the tight space made the congregation seem full. It was mostly hunched liver-spotted men and blue-haired women who'd started attending as children and had never been swayed by the megachurch west of Waco. Solid Rock Worship Center ran commercials during the morning newscasts and all day on weekends. They had spiraling graphics and an 800 number. Our public access channel replayed their Sunday services throughout the week. My grandparents had been married in Calvary. My parents, too. Pastor Joe always made a point of asking the wheezing congregants to pray for Mason.

Pastor Joe was about seventy. Baggy jowls, bolo ties, a voice like soft running water. He also taught Bible classes at my school. Coop and I had him after PE. Pastor Slow, most kids called him. I'd called him that, too, trying to seem cool, but always felt slimy afterward.

This Sunday morning, he held forth on doubt. My father had gone to serve a warrant with Sammy, so my mother and I had a pew to ourselves. Everyone stood to read from Matthew 11, the chapter where the imprisoned John sends his disciples to question Jesus in Galilee. We said *amen* and sat back down, the pew's patina so smooth it might have been cut from river rock. Washed-out light filtered through Calvary's windows. A man coughed in the back of the church, then, as if in answer, another man up front coughed, too. Pastor Joe talked about doubt in the Book of Job and Ecclesiastes and Lamentations and some of the Psalms. He admitted to harboring doubts. Faith requires doubt, he said. Jesus will never turn an honest doubter away. Doubt is not sinful. Doubt is not unbelief. But doubt is poisonous, insidious. You have to act on your faith, not your doubt. It's what Noah did when he built the ark. What Joshua did when he marched around Jericho. What Daniel did in the lions' den. At the end of the service, he reminded everyone to pray for Mason.

It rained while we were inside, but now the sun was fighting through the clouds. Walking to the car, I said, "Were there any messages for me on the answering machine?"

"Still no, sweet potato," my mother said. I couldn't remember having already asked.

We pulled out of the parking lot. The wet asphalt reflected cars' turn signals. Beads of water jiggled off our windshield like insects. Soon we were eastbound on the highway.

My mother said, "Pastor Joe's always good to remember your brother."

"I liked his sermon. I like how doubt isn't a sin."

"If doubt's a sin, your mama's a goner."

"It's not," I said. "We just have to be like Moses when he crossed the Red Sea. Or like David when he fought Goliath."

"Like Abraham when he offered his son to God."

"Right," I said. "Exactly."

"Then praise be," she said. "Because I've already done that."

ON THE LAMB

PODCAST EPISODE 8
GUEST: Rhonda "Turtle" Tilly
RECORDED: February 2024
           Gatesville Correctional Facility
           Mountain View Unit
           Gatesville, Texas

Ever since I was a little one everybody calls me Turtle because of the scoliosis humping my back. Born and raised in Bay St. Louis, Mississippi. I stayed there until moving to the great mistake of Texas. I'm eighty-nine years young but don't feel a day over twenty-two. That's what the Word will do—keep you young. Each checkup, our doctor here at the prison gives me a good going-over and says, "All your parts match." But that's probably not on your docket, is it? You want to know about the girls and the Lamb and were they diddling around any. Or is it the guns this time? Reporters, social workers, badge toters—everybody claims different reasons. You know what I say? I say, if we were the ones to shoot first, then why did we stop? Weren't it their men who ran out of bullets that day? Wasn't that said at the trial? Why didn't we just mow 'em all down when they asked for the truce? If we was so bent on killing. If we was so heathen-ish. Why not shoot them through them cattle trailers they came in on? Thinking they were so sneaky, so smart. They were blind. Deaf and dumb, too, I'll tell you what. I start seeing red when you all come pestering. Burns me up. You don't even know what to ask. Wouldn't know the right questions if they danced up and kissed you. We were out there in all that dust, all that heat that spoiled food if you didn't get it to your mouth fast enough. And the cold, too, come the winter. Cold as a cast-iron commode, that's what we'd say. It got bracing when the wind cut through them walls. Just plywood, mind you, no insulation or plaster. "Prepared for war," isn't that something they said? Prepared for *war*? We weren't even prepared for a cool front! That's what beautiful Bev and I would giggle about once we started bunking together. We were all just trying for heaven. That's all we did, day and night, try for that reward, and if more folks lived that way, the world'd be better off. The girls and guns make no never mind.

If I'm asking the wrong questions, what are the right ones?
What about the sheriff's boy?

Roy

The Garden of Eatin' was beside the Gallop Inn, a cinder-block motor court outside of town. It was a haul from Calvary Baptist, but my mother had driven straight there like we had a reservation. We sat beside a window overlooking a grain field soaked to the color of deer hide. The table was waxy with coats of lacquer and years of cigarette smoke. It was also scored with names and cryptic messages: *Penny Nichols, Sweet Eugene, One More Hour*.

We shared a plate of nachos. My mother got sliced jalapenos on the side because I'd always been afraid to try them. We'd hardly come to the Garden since Mason left for Iraq, but the waitress recognized us and brought out a stack of hot flour tortillas. "De nuestra familia a la tuya," she said. I slathered mine with grape jelly and butter. My mother turned her attention out the window. There was only the field drying out in low sun and highway overpass and motel, but she seemed lost in whatever the view conjured for her. We ate without saying grace.

After lunch, we drove farther east. I worked to see the land the way someone who'd just moved here would. There was beauty in the symmetry, a surety in the understanding that crops would rise and color the world. Or so I hoped. Maybe Texas would feel too rural or plain or foreboding if you came from California; maybe the furrowed dirt would resemble rows of new graves—I didn't know. Out there, among the wide-open grasslands and endless sky, you felt pleasingly inconsequential.

My mother was driving just to drive. I remembered her saying she used to take me on late night rides when, as a baby, I wouldn't sleep; the tire sounds calmed me. I couldn't recall when or where she'd said it, but I suspected my father didn't know about those drives. And now I believed we were forging another secret. It was insignificant and random but still one that should stay between us. Even then, before the real trouble commenced, I understood the consolation of complicity.

We drove behind a pickup with a black dog in the bed. He paced from one side of the truck to the other, panting and peering over at the asphalt. My mother eased off the gas, cautious and scornful. Then we were behind another truck with the words CHEAP PROPANE spray-stenciled on the tailgate. We drove into the high marshlands on a winding two-lane road with blind corners. Ranch houses, thick live oak, automobiles in various states of disrepair. At each crossroads, my mother slowed and craned her neck to read the street sign before accelerating through.

"Are we lost?" I asked.

"Not today, sweet potato," she said. "Not us."

The road bent south, then east, then south again. We were a long time beside a pasture with a herd of black cattle wading in puddles. At a crossroads, my mother pulled onto the shoulder. I thought she was angling for enough room to turn around without sliding into the ditch. Instead she shifted into park and sat still behind the wheel. I gazed out over the rise and fall of the land, the blond grass as thick as fur. Just then the world seemed reduced to flat blocks of color—the dingy gray soil in the fields, the bone-white gravel road, the midnight blue of the car's hood. I realized I was bracing, clenching my fists. I worried my mother was going to confide something that could only be spoken in isolation. I waited, rehearsing emotions in my mind, trying to guess which mask I'd need to don.

But she just opened the door and walked up the rutted road. There were stands of sumac and Lacey oak, and a rusted wire fence around an expanse of goldenrod. My mother looked like a woman whose car had run out of gas. Without my noticing, the sun had burned off the clouds. She shelved her hands over her eyes and peered for a time in each direction, then began walking again. She cast a long thin shadow; the farther she went, the more it stretched, like it had caught a sharp corner and would pull and pull until it snapped. Another gust of wind blew, and my mother pinched her collar to her neck. I pulled the key from the ignition and started after her.

ON THE LAMB

PODCAST EPISODE 8
GUEST: Rhonda "Turtle" Tilly
RECORDED: February 2024
Gatesville Correctional Facility
Mountain View Unit
Gatesville, Texas

That business with the girls was a head-scratcher, okay? Just when I thought I'd gotten hold of it, beautiful Bev would come along saying she'd seen this or heard that. Or Olga would. Or if they had it stitched up, I'd be the one with some new nasty morsel. We looked up the ages of girls in the Scripture. For a long while we were waiting to see which way things would swing with Gina's girls, Eden and Ruthie, but that's about when they made the drive in from California. Once they got to the ranch, we tuned in to them like a movie.

Why is that?
Same reason I told you to be thinking about little Rodeo.

I don't follow.
When the Lamb came scooting back from California, he went on and on about this new queen of his heart. He'd stroll around the ranch in a dreamy daze, half rapture and half torment, then if he caught you, you knew you'd be late to wherever you'd been heading. Ten words a second with gusts of fifty, that's what I said. Beautiful Bev would say he'd gone to California and gotten vaccinated with a Victrola needle. That's extra funny because he hated vaccinations. But anyway, once they showed up, we thought things might shuffle in a hurry. He believed he'd found the one who'd bring on the last phase.

Marie Carroll, you mean.
No, the daughter. The daughter's the one that turned him inside out.

Jaye

Waco was pawn shops and potholes, taco stands and shopping strips and low-slung neighborhoods and endless, almost aggressive drab. Everywhere another car lot, another stray dog, another wavy chain-link fence, another church. The Church of the Reconciliation. Most Precious Blood. Our Lady of Perpetual Help. Shepherd's Way. Solid Rock Worship Center looked like a multiplex surrounded by acres of parking. In the bunched center of town, a small chapel sat behind a tattered banner reading, NO PERFECT PEOPLE ALLOWED.

My mother was as disappointed as I was—why drive this far only to wind up in another place as flat as a board and dull as dirt?—but feigned optimism. We passed a boarded-up mall, a puny airfield, and a painted cutout of a woman in a string bikini towering over a strip club, her breasts like planets.

Then the town was behind us. In California, every place blurred into the next, but here we were abruptly and resolutely spit out. I thought we should have stopped for directions or supplies. Plowed fields flanked the road. Every mile or so there was a one-pump filling station, a barbecue shack, a lonely house in sore need of paint.

The Gallop Inn was a long one-story building bent like a horseshoe. My mother got out but left the engine running, which made it seem like she was going to rob the joint. I watched her talk with the front desk lady and imagined her applying for a job, citing her cleaning-woman credentials, bartering services for a place to stay. But then they looked at me and smiled, and I understood she was spinning a yarn designed to elicit sympathy. I offered a tentative wave. I tried to look frail in case that helped. The lady handed my mother a key and gestured toward the rear of the property. My mother trotted out of the office, but I saw she wanted to run, to jump and click her heels together. Even when she was behind the wheel, she had to button down her excitement and fight the smile spreading across her face.

"What is it?" I asked when she parked in front of room 22.

"A sign," she said.

She'd convinced the woman to let us shower. We were only a few miles from Perry's ranch—he'd named the motel as a landmark—and now that we were close, it was time to get prettied up.

What did I expect? Acres of white fences and longhorn cattle grazing fields of clover? Mounted cowboys roping sheep? Or had I imagined the place more like a temple? A soundless expanse where gauzy-robed women balanced bowls of water atop their heads on their way to wash an elder's feet? Maybe I conceived of a swath of land unmarked by time, where believers focused their spirits by raking pebbles and chanting. A serene stretch of hills and streams. Maybe I expected all of it. Maybe the place was always meant to disappoint me.

When I finally laid eyes on the ranch, I thought: junkyard. There were rusted-out cars and lean-tos pieced together with scrap lumber. At one point, there had to have been some effort to paint the buildings a bleached gray, but the work was unfinished, giving the ranch the appearance of hasty abandonment. Skinny chickens scattered when my mother pulled through the steel cattle gates. She steered along the gravel road toward the main building and said, "I should have worn different shoes." At the motel, she'd changed into a prim floral dress and sandals. Clumps of salt grass and gray dirt and stagnant water. When we parked, curtains parted in a second-floor window. We took in the stables and water tower and grouping of off-kilter sheds atop a sad hill, and below us what looked like a gun range in a dead pasture. I expected someone to call out, to offer a folksy welcome or warn us away for trespassing. But there were only clucking chickens and the knocks and pings of our cooling engine. My mother shrugged her shoulders and led us toward the long building. The heat was gluey and disgusting. We had to avoid anthills the size of cake dishes.

The door took muscle to open—either it was poorly hung or the hinges were bent. Inside, a dim foyer opened to a long narrow corridor. The floor was untreated plywood covered here and there with dingy woven rugs; the corridor was so tight my mother and I had to walk single file. Her sandals swept and slapped the floor with each step. Sweep, slap. Sweep, slap. Eventually she took care to walk quietly. Doorways opened off either side of the hall but lacked actual doors. Sheets and beach towels had been tacked in the openings for a semblance of privacy. We were in barracks, sparse rooms with bunk beds and uneven shelves fastened to the walls. Suitcases were stacked into makeshift bureaus. I worried we were in the wrong place. I worried we weren't.

Then the mess hall. Rows of trellis tables and a cafeteria serving line, the same setup as every school I'd attended: plastic trays, towers of plates and bowls, chrome rods to slide your food along. In the back corner, a commercial-grade popcorn machine. The faint scent of dripping butter made my mouth water, though the thought of eating left me seasick. Maybe I winced. My mother twisted back at me like I'd called her name. I shook my head. She surveyed the tables, chose one in the middle of the room, and took a seat. I thought it would be funny to approach her like a waitress. *"Welcome to Wacky Waco's! What kind of crazy will you have this afternoon?"*

I studied a bulletin board papered with various pieces of handwritten Scripture. The tilting, misspelled print of children, the fanciful script of women, so perfectly spaced and slanted I could imagine waste bins over-flowing with inferior attempts. I opened one of the mess hall's rear doors, but it only revealed a clumpy dirt field. Another door led to a darkened gymnasium. Weeds pushed through the cracks in the concrete floor. There were basketball hoops and aluminum bleachers, but the space had been given over to storage. A few silk-screen setups in the middle of the room, an island of ink cans and boxes spilling white T-shirts printed with the words *God, Guts, Guns*.

I returned to the mess hall and followed my mother back through the corridor with the sheeted doorways. How easily I could anticipate the force of her devastation. How clearly I could imagine our sulking back to the car, her sobbing too hard to crank the ignition and throwing me the keys. In California, she'd clean herself up in another motel mirror and rehearse apologizing to my father. Maybe those same thoughts were dog-ging her, or maybe it wasn't contrition she felt, but anger. She'd aban-doned her efforts to walk quietly. She yanked back the sheets in a few doorways like she expected to find people snickering behind them. It was hard for me to keep up. The corridor, the air, *everything* smelled a little like shit.

Then, ahead of me, my mother froze. The corridor had delivered her to a door with a circular window, and without turning, she motioned for me to stop. I halted. I watched her hand the way I'd watch the head of a cobra. Eventually she beckoned me discreetly, with her fingers. She didn't turn from the glass. Once I was within reach, she curled her arm around my waist and guided me between her body and the door so I could behold what had already loosed the tears from her eyes: Perry in his chapel, Perry pacing on his plywood stage, Perry mouthing a question and dozens of people seated on bleachers answering in unison, Perry raising his gaze to the ceiling and thanking God, and then, at last, Perry catching sight of us and offering the tiniest nod, like he'd known we'd come, like we'd kept him waiting and he wouldn't forget it.

Roy

When I caught up to my mother, she was leaning over a cedar fence rail. At the top of a hill stood some derelict stables, then a hundred yards below was a water tower and storage buildings, a few rusted-out cars, and, farther down still, an algae-choked pond. Insects rattled invisibly around us until a wind sang across the high plain and quieted them. The tall grass undulated as if brushed by an invisible hand. Above us, two turkey vultures glided in expanding circles.

"They're looking for lunch," I said.

"Can you believe I've never been here? I stayed home when y'all delivered the horses."

The backs of my knees prickled cold. My ears heated up. Years had passed since my father and I had brought the pinto and bay to the Lamb's ranch, but I still should have had my bearings. From where we stood, the main building was obscured by the hill. It briefly occurred to me that we'd arrived here by chance, that my mother had just sought it out because she'd inadvertently driven in this direction, but I was grasping. She was a pragmatic woman and had chosen the circuitous route to avoid seeing anyone. To avoid anyone seeing us. This was the secret we'd been making. We were here because my father wasn't.

The vultures flew a higher, slower circle before banking off. Insects started rattling again. When we'd gone too long without speaking, I said, "Were you worried Dad and Sammy would be here?"

"I don't know what all I'm worried about. That's part of being a mother I didn't expect."

"I won't tell him we came," I said.

Her eyes stayed fixed on the land before us. She shifted her weight from one leg to another. I wondered what time it was, if my father had gotten home yet, if I'd be able to keep myself from telling him. The smell of cold air passing over soaked earth and dead grass. I hoped we'd leave soon.

"What if he's right?" my mother said.

"Sammy, you mean."

"Perry," she said.

"Right about what?"

"Anything, everything. What if he really does get messages from God? Would that be any crazier than the stories Pastor Joe reads every Sunday?"

"I don't know," I said, and just then, I didn't feel as though I knew anything at all, not one single thing.

"I don't either. Could be he's a lunatic pervert or he's got a hotline to heaven no one else can use. Could be both. Could be the word 'or' isn't useful anymore," she said. "But now that we're here, I don't know why federal agents are nagging your father."

"Maybe that's why Sammy is going after the Lamb," I said. "Maybe he wishes he had the hotline—"

"Do you feel endangered? Do you sense Perry has a secret arsenal pointed at us right now? Do you hear anyone screaming for help?"

"I don't even hear anyone at the shooting range. They're probably at a gun show," I said. "But the ranch is pretty far down there."

"And we're pretty far outside of town. We're on the backside of nowhere."

"You think they deserve to be left alone," I said. "You're saying they don't pose a threat."

"I'm saying they're minding their own business on land they own. I'm saying I see viable shelter and open pasture."

"I see fallow fields," I said, joining in. "I see—"

"I'm saying who cares what they believe. I'm wondering who gets to decide where we find comfort or what we worship," she said. "Isn't it their right? Isn't that what Mason is over there fighting for?"

"He's not fighting anymore. He's mostly building—"

"What I'm saying, sweet potato," she said. "What I'm saying is you can tell your father we came out here. You can say I drove us out here, and we survived just fine."

Jaye

Instead of entering the chapel, we returned to our car where my mother kneeled and checked her reflection in the side mirror. She brushed out her hair, smoothed her dress, shook dirt from one sandal then the other. Based on how Perry used to celebrate our arrival to the Highland house, my mother might have expected him to cut the sermon short to welcome us. If anything, he extended it. An hour passed before people filed from the building. I recognized a few from California. With each new cluster came a wave of lightheadedness. A bent woman, her spine like a sickle, was walking beside another woman with splotchy pigmentation. A woman in an electric wheelchair that seemed too small for her girth, and a blind man being led by an exuberant, laughing lady. Then a gaggle of children burst through the door like it was the start of recess; a young girl swinging a pink knapsack by its strap stumbled to her knees and began bawling. Two girls around my age rushed to calm her. It seemed a cast of people Perry had convened for our benefit. Behold the dreadfully optimistic. Behold the broken-bodied and soul-cured. Behold the whole ragged flock, the long procession of the emaciated and the obese, the dirty and the dazed and the lit from within.

When Perry emerged—so late that my mother had begun speculating we'd missed him—he had a child straddling his shoulders. The boy had a mess of curls and an open-mouthed smile like he'd just been tickled and hoped it might happen again. Perry held the boy's ankles like parachute straps and when he spotted us, he instructed the boy to wave. He complied, all irresistible giggles and too much energy, so we smiled and waved back and I despised how this put me at ease.

Perry ambled toward us wearing his carnival-barker grin. His shirt was open as usual, but at least he was wearing boots. Dirt caked under his nails, his stubble beard patchy and dry. Locking his eyes on my mother, he said, "'I was naked.'"

She leaned forward like she'd misheard and didn't want to do it again.

"'I was naked and you clothed Me; I was sick and . . .'"

"'And you visited Me,'" my mother took over. "'I was in prison and you came to Me.' Matthew 25:36."

Perry trapped the boy's feet in his armpits and hooked his fingers under his tongue and let fly a screechy whistle. Then he clapped. She blushed, tucked a hank of hair behind her ear, smiling up at him. I wanted to kick Perry between the legs. Instead, I kept my eyes on the child and said, "Who's this monkey?"

Perry reached for the boy's waist with both hands, then lifted and twirled him to the ground like a helicopter blade. It was clearly a maneuver they'd performed before, one the boy surely looked forward to every time. His laugh was a hiccupping rasp. Perry said, "This here monkey is Kanaan. Kanaan Cyrus Cullen."

"He's yours?" my mother said. Shock pinched her voice. The smile and blush drained from her face.

"My only begotten son," he said. "Seneca is around here somewhere, his mama. She's one of our teachers."

"Did you ever mention having a—"

"Kanaan is a unique name." My mother cut me off. She was, I knew with my full heart, willing herself to believe this didn't change anything, didn't sully him, didn't make her a fool for leveling her life to stand before him like a stooge. She said, "I'm sure he'll live up to it."

Perry kneeled and directed his son's attention up to us, like he was pointing out a distant mountain range. He said, "Can you say hidy? Can you welcome Daddy's friends? They drove a long way for us."

Kanaan buried his face in his father's neck. The boy's T-shirt swallowed him like a dress. My mother kneeled. She inched toward them.

"Now you're shy?" Perry said. "You're a chatterbox during study, but now you're Mr. Meeky Mouse?"

Kanaan nodded.

"Well," Perry said, spinning him around and sending him into another giggling fit. "No son of mine is going to keep a couple of fine-looking ladies waiting for no introduction. Kanaan, meet Marie."

And like that, Kanaan, laughing and swimming in his shirt, hugged my mother. Her eyes closed.

Then it was my turn. I kneeled.

"And this," Perry said, "this is—"

"Jaye," I said. "Call me Jaye."

"Jane?" Perry said.

"Jaye."

"Like the letter?" he said.

"Like the bird."

Perry was about to protest when Kanaan glommed on to me. He was squirmy, laughing with his eyes shut, climbing me like a tree. I stirrupped my hands into footholds. But I never took my eyes from Perry, my gaze daring him to try the girl he thought he recognized.

ON THE LAMB

PODCAST EPISODE 3
GUEST: Priscilla Martinez
RECORDED: September 2023
High's Café
Comfort, Texas

I was with Child Protective Services. Sheriff Moreland sent me out to check on those children. On their welfare.

And?
They were just happy. Children grow up believing their normal is everyone's normal. There was no sign of physical or sexual abuse or neglect. Nada. They had names I worried would hold them back—Eternity and Kanaan and such, but their names made sense where they were living their little lives. They were eager to tour you around. They had pets and chores. Mr. Cullen doted on them, and they doted on him. I put all of this in my report. I'm sure you can still find it.

I guess I'm wondering if there's anything you'd like to add. In hindsight, I mean.
One of our trips out there was a scorcher. Like a furnace in the desert. They had themselves a couple of ponds they used for swimming holes, but we had all these interviews to conduct, so the kids couldn't run down to the water to cool off. They were fussy. We were all wilting.

We were in their mess hall with all the trellis tables. As the day wore on, we start to hear kids laughing outside. That high sweet laugh kids have when they're without a care in the world. If there's a prettier sound, I haven't heard it. When we came out, we saw what Mr. Cullen had done—rigged a blue tarp into the bed of an old pickup and filled it up with water. He made those kids a swimming pool out of a rusted truck and a tarp roped to the bumper and door handles. I'd never seen such a thing. They were in it splashing and cooling off. The adults were bringing water down from the tower.

Do you think he did that to impress you? Do you think he was trying to manipulate you?
I think he was doing the best he could with what he had. I think they were hot and he found a way to cool them off and put smiles on their faces. If they were here today, I think they'd tell you he loved them to no end.

Roy

Two weeks after Jaye and I drove to the feed mill, I brought Mason's lock-picking kit to school. It wasn't something I'd ever done, for it seemed like courting trouble. In classes, I tapped my pencil against my palm, tapped my shoe on the floor, kept checking the clock. "Are you waiting for a starter pistol?" Coop asked at lunch. When the bell for the next period buzzed, I slipped out of the building and off school grounds.

The afternoon was summer bright, but the sun couldn't blunt the cold. Every few minutes wind rearranged the air. I ventured into neighborhoods I'd never visited, wondering if I was close to where Jaye lived. She hadn't called, but still I hoped she'd pull up beside me in her truck. All I saw were delivery drivers and old folks squinting at the road. A dog growled behind an age-grayed fence; the planks bowed when it lunged against them. Blocks away, the unhinged man who drove a van with speakers bolted to the roof implored sinners to repent. Coop and I had named him the Holy Roller.

The Live Oak Mall was boarded up and cordoned off by a temporary hurricane fence. I circled the entire building twice to check for an opening and security guards. When traffic passed, I turned my back to the road. Near the JCPenney's entrance, I found a curled-up section and crawled under. Pebbles dug into my palms, my knees. My heart was a jackhammer.

The lock on the Penney's entrance was a standard cylinder. For all the locks I'd picked, I'd yet to walk through an unknown door. I used a hook pick and tension wrench, half-hoping the pins wouldn't fall or the latch wouldn't click. It took six seconds.

I entered through what had been the shoe department. The space wasn't dark, despite the boarded windows. There were skylights, I recalled, but that also felt like a realization only dawning on me now. "Hello," I said, my voice carrying some. Empty racks and spindles stood throughout the store; they looked like skeletons of starving animals, which made me think of the mammoth fossils that had been found jutting out of a ravine across the freeway. A scientist had come to talk to us at school about the museum they were building around the site.

"Hello," I called again, louder. "Hello."

Odd walls had been tagged with spray paint, the letters as elaborate as calligraphy. Then I realized I'd been expecting everything to be grime-caked and busted up. The opposite was true. The storefronts were cleaner than the windows in my house, and the tile floors in the center of the mall gleamed like they'd been recently polished. Everything preserved, everything ruined. It gave me an anxious underwater feeling, uncomfortably like the dream I'd made up for my mother, as if I were swimming through the wreckage of a sunken ship. I wondered if I'd become psychic.

I picked into what had been the Record Bar first, then Cutlery World, then the place where they printed photos on mugs and aprons. All the locks were mortise cylinders, each popping more easily than the last. In a few stores, there was left-behind merchandise—a jug of protein powder at GNC, a sheer scarf on a mannequin at Joske's. I couldn't remember why I'd ever longed to pick into the mall. Coop used to love visiting the Coin Nook, the tiny storefront that sold stamps and rare currency. He'd once convinced a worker to gold-plate a silver dollar, which my father said was a federal offense.

Leave, I thought. Go home.

But I went deeper. A cardboard cutout of a marine in dress blues stood at attention in the window of the old recruiting center. It was where Mason had enlisted. In Boots and Britches, I found boxes of leather belts. They were tooled with stagecoach scenes and eagle wings and lassoes. The leather smelled new and rich. At first, I only took a stagecoach one, but then grabbed different sizes, thinking they'd make fine souvenirs for Coop and Mason and maybe even Jaye. I didn't know if anyone would wear them, but I liked the idea of presenting them with spoils of my disobedience.

Outside the store, Sammy Gregson was waiting for me. He sat on the stone ledge of a dry fountain, shaving his fingernails with his pocketknife. I was holding ten belts. He said, "I wear size 34 and prefer brown."

I should've been apologizing or pleading for him not to tell my father, but standing there, my prevailing fear was not giving a belt to Jaye. I'd already started banking on my delinquent status, the bond it might create.

"The silent alarm still works," Sammy said. "We get a call from a dispatcher in Omaha when there's a break-in."

"The door was unlocked at Penney's. I climbed under the fence, so technically I didn't break in."

He guided his knife blade around his thumbnail. He said, "Probably I forgot to lock up last time I ran out some scum. That makes both of us lucky I'm the one who caught the call."

"Are you after his job?" I said.

The question made Sammy cross himself and kiss his knuckles, then he went back to carving his nails. Behind him were the motionless escalators, the mosaic blue tile of the tiered fountain that used to trickle between them, the giant terra-cotta pots that still sprouted leafy artificial plants. It seemed we were on a stage, performing for a balcony audience.

I said, "Is that why you're pressing the Lamb about—"

"You know I can arrest you, right?" he interrupted. "Breaking and entering, trespassing, burglary, possession of stolen property, truancy—you understand you're currently up what's *technically* called shit creek, right?"

"I want to know if you're going to run for sheriff."

Sammy inspected his nails. He blew on them. He switched hands and set to work with his knife again. He said, "Perry stirred his own pot. I was leaving him be and everything was coasting along until—"

"I saw what you did to his booth and—"

"*Until* I ran into Old Bill McElby a while back," Sammy said. Old Bill was a mailman and a pool player, a gravel-throated man everyone in Waco interacted with sooner or later. "He was delivering a package out there, but the box was busted, so he got a look-see inside: grenade casings. Now we're hearing he might be converting semi-automatics to full-auto. The illegal conversion or manufacturing of Title II weapons is a serious crime, Roy."

For a while the only sound was the knife on his nails, a slow sawing. Dripping sweat in my armpits, on my neck and back. I realized I was listening for footsteps, expecting someone else to find us.

"The thing is," Sammy said, "I'm certain I locked the door when I left last time. And I'm *pretty* certain you'd need tools to pick a door like that, tools that may or may not be military in origin."

"The door was open," I said. "Someone else could've left it that way."

"Do I think he's a cult leader? A huckster who wants to liberate young girls from their panties? I do. Do I think he's a heretic? Absolutely," Sammy said. "But right now he's up to something and we need to snuff it out. Once all the evidence comes to light, your father will agree. He's big enough to admit when he's wrong."

"But what if Perry's right?" I asked. "Would it be crazier than the stories of Moses and Noah? Who decides who we get to worship?"

Sammy snapped his knife shut, pocketed it. He dusted his nails on his trousers. He said, "You're too good a kid to ask that, Roy. Too smart, too."

"I've been out there. It's peaceful. I didn't feel endangered. I didn't hear anyone yelling for help."

"If he told any of his followers to put a gun to your head, they wouldn't think twice. If he said drink Kool-Aid leftover from Jonestown, they'd pour each other's cups."

"You'll lose if you run for sheriff," I said.

"I don't care about that, son. I care about those mothers and babies out in the sticks. We've got out-of-state parents calling about missing children. The way this is going, it doesn't end well, and I don't want that on my conscience," he said. "And believe it or not, I don't want it on your daddy's neither."

He started to say something else but just shook his head and began walking back toward Penney's.

"You're not going to arrest me?" I said.

"You should keep those belts," he said without turning. "That's quality leather."

"I don't want them anymore," I said. "I'll put them back."

Sammy laughed a quick, violent laugh. His boot heels clicked on the tile.

"What's funny?" I asked.

He paused to peer into what had been the pet store, cupping his hands around his eyes to see in the glass. He stayed that way long enough I thought he might've spied a left-behind parakeet flitting in the darkness. When he moved on, he looked like a guard making rounds. I expected him to twirl his baton.

"What's so funny?" I said again, brash and surprising.

But Sammy never answered. He crossed himself, kissed his knuckles, and receded into the void.

ON THE LAMB

PODCAST EPISODE 5
GUEST: Bill McElby
RECORDED: November 2023
                        Brazos Billiards
                        Waco, Texas

You were a mail carrier in Waco. Did you alert Sammy Gregson to a shipment of hand grenades going to the ranch?
I never cared for him when he was a deputy. High and mighty don't impress me much.

But you did inform him, yes?
No.

He said—
I was knocking balls around with Shelly Pennington at Bananas Billiards. We played Nine Ball on Tuesday nights. I gave her the seven and the break. She had a good draw. On Tuesdays, ladies played for free.

Anyway, she drove for UPS, so we were always swapping stories. One night she's going on about people sending dope in diaper boxes, so I told her about how I'd seen what looked like inert grenades that Christmas. Well, little Sammy overheard. He was rattling around, crossing himself, hollering down some well. So he comes strutting over and asks me to tell him what I saw. Then he starts clucking about federal offenses. We always said he was on a first-name basis with the bottom of the deck.

Has your opinion changed over the years?
I wish my jaw had been wired shut. I wish Sonny's or Chelsea Street had better tables, but they only had bar boxes, so we went to Bananas. But if those others had better tables maybe we wouldn't have seen little Sammy. I tell myself it's on him, but I'm the one he overheard. After all this, not a day's gone by when I didn't wish I'd been born without a tongue.

Jaye

We went back into the long building, following Perry. It was just the three of us. A British woman had taken Kanaan for a bath, the smell of dried manure on her rubber boots. Perry introduced her to us, but I missed her name—Heaven or Nirvana or some nonsense. He ducked into each door like he'd misplaced a vacant room but couldn't recall where. He kept saying, "Don't you worry, girlies."

The problem was we wanted a room together, but there were only single empty beds on the women's floor. The men lived upstairs where there were plenty of vacancies, but Perry said, "If I put a couple of beauts up there, those hairy-legged boys'll break every commandment asking for a dance." Still I worried he'd split us up, worried the short duration of our stay would work against us—"Surely y'all can have a wall between you for a few nights, no?"—but then an arthritic woman came out of a room covered by a Texas flag towel and said she'd bunk with someone named Turtle. The woman held a suitcase in each hand and an old table fan under her armpit. She looked like she hadn't slept well in years.

"You're heaven-sent, Beverly," he said. He threw his head back and lidded his eyes in holy gratitude. After a few quiet seconds, he dashed ahead to help Beverly with her load. My mother ran up and relieved her of the other suitcase. I offered to help, too, but my heart wasn't in it. Beverly seemed like a sweet, docile woman. My resentment toward her was profound.

Our room was the size of a small walk-in closet. The bunk-bed frame was varnished two-by-fours, and the mattresses were covered by children's sleeping bags, one with a unicorn print and the other depicted a bunch of apples. The window was loose, smudged, cracked. Under it were nail gouges from a fallen shelf. "We'll get maintenance on that," Perry joked. He glanced around the room, clearly pleased. Probably he expected to be commended on a job well done, thanked for such luxurious accommodations. I worried my mother might.

But her eyes lit on a five-gallon paint bucket in the corner opposite our beds. It was faded orange, almost the same hue as the Bibles from the house in California. She said, "We should take that to Beverly."

Perry's mischievous grin again. He said, "She'll use Turtle's."

"Use?"

"It's thy throne," he said. "Your commode. I'll see about rustling up another one. Plenty of us share, but I'm sure there's an extra floating around."

"There aren't bathrooms?" I said and recognized, at last, the odor that had so persistently tinged the air: human waste.

"We're a work in progress. The good news is not one person in Scripture used a toilet. If chamber pots were good enough then, they're good enough now."

"So we go in the bucket and then . . . ?"

"We've got an old septic tank down the hill. I'll get Senny to show y'all."

My mother nodded, taking it in. She said, "Toilet paper? Are we allowed to use that?"

"Why wouldn't you be?" he said, insulted.

A week, I thought. Maybe less.

ON THE LAMB

PODCAST EPISODE 8
GUEST: Rhonda "Turtle" Tilly
RECORDED: February 2024
　　　　　　Gatesville Correctional Facility
　　　　　　Mountain View Unit
　　　　　　Gatesville, Texas

What did you see in him? What was the allure?
Like I said, you wouldn't recognize the right question if a neon sign was pointing at it.

Help me out.
It wasn't never about what we saw in him, but what he saw in us. With my particular situation, I think he believed I might amount to more than my misdeeds. He spotted a lacking in me, a hole filling up with ugliness like swamp water, just poison and leeches, but there was a potential for redeeming. He could roll up his sleeves and scrub me clean. Of everybody on earth, of every person in history, I was one of the few worth the hard toil of saving. He'd talk about the long odds of us meeting, how a minute earlier or later and we'd still be lost, and how it was our trespasses, not our good works, that delivered us to each other. The pain we'd perpetrated had meaning. Our crimes weren't wrong, they were the plan. He put into words what I'd always felt.

Which was?
That the healthy ones ain't in need of a doctor. That Jesus wanted to eat meals with the fallen, and sure enough I'd been setting my table all along.

Roy

Outside the mall, falling dusk. I walked with my face turned down against the chill, hands shoved in my pockets. Headlights washed over me like search lamps. I shivered and worked to stay angry with Sammy. I tried convincing myself I'd gotten away with something, but I knew I hadn't.

When I got home, my father was on the phone in the garage. The door was raised despite the cold, and I gathered he'd been watching for me. As I plodded up the driveway, he cut his conversation short. Sammy, I thought. Or Mr. Leal, the school principal. As I stepped inside, he pulled the door down behind me. It sounded like a roll of thunder.

"Your mother left supper in the microwave," he said in the kitchen. "She's at Raybourn's."

I warmed my food—two pieces of fried chicken and a few green beans—and poured a glass of milk. My father filled a coffee mug with dregs from the pot and zapped it in the microwave. At the table, we bowed our heads for a quick prayer. He blew on his coffee until it cooled enough to drink. Panda came in to rub against our boots. My father swished each sip in his mouth before swallowing.

I was about to confess everything—driving to the ranch with my mother, picking into the mall, getting busted by Sammy—when he said, "School going okay?"

"Pretty much," I said.

"Any activity on the Rosie front?"

"I don't really see her," I said. "We have different classes."

"I wonder what you'll remember when you're my age," he said. He sipped coffee. "From your studies, I'm saying. Right now the only lesson I remember was about the British using falcons to hunt down German homing pigeons when they did their secret flights. I learned that in Mrs. Guidroz's class."

"Mom would probably like to know about those birds," I said. "And Mason, too."

"You know I love you, right?"

"Yes," I said. I laid my fork on the table.

"Everyone keeps things under wraps. Sometimes the reasons are good, sometimes not."

A jolt passed through me. I looked at my plate. I hadn't eaten as much as I would've guessed. I said, "Do you?"

"Have things under wraps? Plenty. I'd be happy to tell you, but I don't need to. I've made the same mistakes Grandpa Huey did. The same'll be true of us."

"I don't understand," I said, though maybe I did.

My father drained his coffee, then stood to rinse his mug and stayed looking out through the dingy lace curtains.

"This business with Perry is getting muddy," he said.

"Some kids were saying McElby delivered grenades to him."

"Normally I'd say old McElby could talk the legs off a chair, but I might be looking the wrong way. That's something to consider."

"I don't think you are," I said and hated that I'd afforded Sammy any credence. "They were probably just trying to impress me. That happens sometimes because you're the—"

"I'm heading out there Sunday morning to try to get a bead on what Perry's doing. I could use some help if you're not tied up."

"What kind of help?"

"The kind you keep under wraps," he said.

"Okay," I said.

"We'll figure this out. We'll see if it's chicken or feathers."

"Did it work? The thing with the falcons?"

"Those pigeons never knew what hit them," he said. "They were dead before they took off."

Jaye

Breakfasts at sunup: watery oatmeal or coffee, eggs and bananas and sugarless cereal. It was the hardiest meal of the day, everyone eating hunched over the trays at the long mess hall tables. Then came Bible study and morning chores. Lunch was salad and watery soup and unleavened bread and breakfast leftovers. People chattered during lunch, usually about the previous study—what they liked, what confused them, what made them uncomfortable and how that must have been Perry's intention, how his provocations were devised to reveal higher law. Because I didn't go to the studies, the words were like pieces of a silly movie: trumpets and dragons, angels and locusts and rooms a thousand years wide. Then more chores until supper, which was usually popcorn and the last of the day's leftovers, and then evening study and lights out. Evening studies went the longest; sometimes people were only in bed for an hour before someone started clanging the breakfast bell.

Each day swallowed the next, the next, the next. Tomorrow was as dismal as yesterday, as boring and predictable as today. My mother and I kept not leaving. I lost so much weight my clothes swallowed me. Day by day, my ribs and collarbone and knuckles protruded more, as if winds were feathering sand off the sharp edges of buried shells. My cheeks hollowed. My jaw and jugular emerged. I used a shoelace for a belt. There weren't many mirrors on the ranch, but when I caught sight of my reflection, I didn't register the skinny thing I saw. With my newly thinned body and angled face, I pantomimed ballet poses and studied my figure. Even in wobbly arabesques and off-axis pirouettes my body appeared toned and elegant. The word *lithe* scrolled through my mind. *Languid.* The cult diet, I thought. Everyone should try it! I longed to saunter past the popular kids back home, prompting the girls to skip lunch and the boys to gawk at my hips. I hoped I'd look this way when I returned, hoped I'd forgive myself for taking any pleasure in the way Perry was, by proxy, sculpting me.

Everyone did chores. Most of the men worked construction, repairing what was failing or fortifying what had somehow stayed upright. Big Lyle headed up the work crews. He was an ox of a man who relayed instructions with his chin and eyes and meaty hands. I thought he might be mute, might have had his tongue cut out. One afternoon I'd watched him lug one barrel after another up the hill to the stables. His beard was a bushy bell and his hair was longer than mine, a fist-thick braid that reached his belt. Rumor had it that he'd known trouble. Depending on who told the tale, he'd been a hit man or bank robber or captain of a biker gang. They said he never left the grounds, though weeks came when he seemed to vanish. Each of his thighs was the size of my waist.

Lawrence had converted a small first-floor room into an office where he did bookkeep and legal work. He'd been a lawyer in England. "The Biblical Barrister," Perry called him. "Our Christian Counselor!" His office had shelves of legal books, a fax machine and phone, which I sometimes used to call my father. He had a thin gray mustache that I wanted to wipe off with the cuff of my sweatshirt.

Virgil oversaw the garage on the southern edge of the property; he did automotive and small engine repair. People from town hauled edgers and motorcycles and outboard motors in need of fixing. He did the labor while Perry took the credit. If Big Lyle was Perry's muscle, Virgil was his whipping boy. Half lieutenant, half lapdog. He floated above and among the others, assisting here and there, relaying Perry's instructions and gripes. People resented that he had the power to grant or deny their precious access. They subjected him to the anger and pessimism they wouldn't dare show their savior. On Wednesdays, Virgil drove into town for supplies—free food he'd scored from restaurants and grocery markets, bread and perishables that had passed their sell-by dates.

The women did everything else. Seneca and Annie had been teachers in Massachusetts, so they schooled the kids between meals and studies. Seneca—Senny—was Kanaan's waifish mother. Annie was in her thirties and did spontaneous cartwheels. Victoria was a midwife from Oregon and shaped like a bowling pin. She had a room attached to the gym that served as a clinic, a vaguely sanitary place for treating cuts and twisted ankles, for checking old folks' blood pressure and wet, rattling coughs. All the women and girls wore their hair down and ironing-board straight.

My mother was put on the cleaning crew with Sage and Charity, Virgil's wife and daughter. Sage headed up kitchen duties; Charity did laundry. Charity was fourteen, her skin so gecko pale I could see blue veins in her wrists. Gina and her daughters, Ruthie and Eden, worked the gun range because Perry's theory was shooters spent more with ladies at the till. Ruthie and Eden were fraternal twins with matching acne, a year younger than me and a foot taller. Back home, we might have sat at each other's lunch table. In Texas, I avoided them so I wouldn't have to say goodbye when we left.

A small coven of older women managed the gun show operation— Beverly, Turtle, and Olga. They tallied how much ammunition Gina and her daughters moved, kept a running inventory of the guns Perry bought and sold, unpacked cases of MREs when they arrived and added them to the thousand or so stacked in the walk-in pantry. They ordered whatever they could find cheap from military surplus catalogs: plastic canteens, web belts, ranger patches, and fatigues. I liked those ornery women. Their shuffling walks, their habit of sneaking into each other's rooms after hours to nurse hard candy. I admired the way they bitched under their breath when someone, usually Virgil or Lawrence, asked them to do anything other than what they were currently doing. I tried to sit near them at meals to listen to their sniping. "Almost three dollars for an MRE? I told him to pound sand," Beverly said one day. Another time, Turtle called Perry and Virgil "Popeye and Olive Oil." We laughed until Olga started hyperventilating. For Christmas, they gave me the gas mask.

ON THE LAMB

PODCAST EPISODE 10
GUEST: Virgil Bernthal
RECORDED: April 2024
          The Chapel of Light
          Waco, Texas

I think some listeners have trouble understanding what drew so many to him.
So many? We couldn't have filled a dollar matinee!

But what was the appeal? Why would people uproot their lives and move to Texas for him?
Honesty, openheartedness, vulnerability. He owned up to his wrongdoings and didn't hold anyone else's against them. Don't have a green card? Come on in! Stay awhile! Made some big mistakes? Well, partner, so have I. He went out of his way to welcome and protect us, so we reciprocated. We found purpose in the labor, in what he asked of us, how tomorrow was always going to be harder than yesterday.

And didn't the disciples leave their families to follow Jesus? Nowadays every churchgoer in America believes it was the right move and claims they'd've done it, too, but when the time came, y'all chose air-conditioning and espresso. You want sitcoms over salvation. You want churches the size of shopping malls and preachers with bleached teeth, but no one ever thinks to ask why so many people are buying what *they're* selling. Hypocrisy, pure and simple. Make no mistake: Your life makes a lot less sense to me than ours ever did to you.

Roy

"Just wander off," my father said driving out to the ranch on Sunday afternoon. He wore his Eisenhower jacket and I was in my canvas chore coat, but underneath we still had on church clothes. We hadn't gone home to change. In the Bronco, my father's pager vibrated. He glanced at the number, then silenced it. He said, "Once I get him talking, just wander off."

"Maybe I'll say I want to find the horses Mom gave them," I said.

"That ought to do it," he said.

We passed the Garden of Eatin' then traveled a more direct route than the one my mother had taken to the property. The sky was a dome of solid gray, and I had the idea that we were on the inside of a pearl. Every few miles, we'd crest a hill where my father had to steer into the gusts of wind to stay on the road. The heat was cranking. When the windows fogged up, he switched to defrost.

What my father needed was for me to look for milling machines at the ranch. Earlier that morning, he'd flipped an old water bill envelope and drawn boxy pictures of one. They reminded me of the band saw in the industrial arts room at school. He told me to peek through windows but not to open any closed doors or enter buildings without being invited because that would be illegal. I still couldn't tell if Sammy had said anything about the mall. Before leaving the house, I'd slipped Mason's lock-picking kit into my pocket.

"If I find anything, I'll come back without my jacket on," I said. "That'll be code for locating evidence."

"I doubt it'll come to that."

"But if I do."

"Leave your jacket on. Your mother'll skin my ass if you catch cold. She's already on me for bringing you out here."

"I don't mind going," I said. It was true. Unlike when we'd gone to serve warrants before, I wasn't apprehensive. I sensed the day would swing in my favor. It was, I imagined, how my father felt all the time.

"We'll pick up something from the Garden on the way back," he said. "She likes those nachos."

"Good idea," I said.

"My ideas don't come much better than that, detective," he said.

Jaye

Perry never assigned me chores. He told Seneca and Annie I could help teach—"She's got a bunch of learnings in her noggin"—but they said it might be confusing for the other students. Although Charity, Ruthie, and Eden were around my age, they were learning long division and similes, subjects I'd finished years before. In California, I'd been studying calculus and anatomy and Steinbeck. Eventually the twins approached me for help with homework. They came clandestinely and individually. Ruthie came under a pretense of getting to know me; Eden usually offered a Bible study. Neither sister seemed to know the other was struggling with the same lesson.

I spent the days after Christmas roaming the ranch. I expected Perry to rein me in, but he let me wander. Maybe he wanted to appear blithe and indifferent, as if his mind were so vexed with problems of holy design that a wandering girl would never register. Maybe he believed all my hours alone would awaken a yearning for rules and company. I strayed farther by the day. I followed the fence around the pastures. I snuck dry oatmeal out of the kitchen and scattered it for the chickens, saved hunks of bread for the squirrels and grackles. I could coax the pinto horse toward me with hay and a sugar beet, but the bay just pinned her ears back and stayed away. "I understand," I told her and made it my project to win her affection.

In one pasture, I found an old refrigerator that had been used for target practice; in another, the rust-brown shells of three old cars. Every other day I seemed to happen upon a new grouping of oil drums, my own private Stonehenges. The horse stables crowned the hill. From there, I could watch everyone below: Annie spinning her impromptu cartwheels until they made her woozy, Sage and Charity reading their Bibles in private

mother-daughter studies, Victoria clanging the bell for meals, Perry pea-
cocking around or skidding to a stop on the motorbike he'd been given
when he returned from Israel. More than once I saw him unzip his pants
and piss in the dirt. There were always people around, pretending not to
notice. Sometimes he waved to them.

During studies, I snuck up into Perry's room. Everyone called the space
his "quarters," but it reminded me of a boy's treehouse. The steps and rise
of the staircase were so uneven I usually stumbled. It was a crow's nest
above the gym, the highest space on the property with a window in each
of the four walls that afforded him a complete view of the prairie. On clear
days, I saw church steeples in Waco, the vague outline of Solid Rock's
giant cross far west of town. When fog rolled in, I imagined myself in a
lighthouse.

The room was bigger than everyone else's. His was a queen-sized mattress, the only one on the property, and the sheets were always balled at
the foot of the bed. A fraying Navajo rug slid around the floor. He had a
rabbit-eared television, a nightstand with a phone, and an inlaid rifle cabinet, the doors of which he left open and used to hang shirts. There was a
knee-high fridge stocked with grapes and chocolate milk and packages of
sliced cheese. Everywhere stray guitar picks, like he regularly tossed a
handful over his shoulder for luck. The viscous scent of gun oil pervaded,
but lurking under it was a musky, fermented odor I couldn't name. I
started keeping track of what he'd eaten since my last visit. I ate grapes
and slice after slice of cheese. I slipped the cellophane wrappers into my
pockets, and they crinkled loudly as I walked. The following day I dropped
them in the trash barrels to be burned.

I wanted to find something that would incriminate him, at least in my
mother's eyes, something so heinous that we'd leave him in the middle of
the night, the way we'd left my father. If one of his guitars was there, I
ratcheted the tuning pegs until the strings were taut. I watched his TV and
called my father from his phone. We talked about Texas and California
and my mother and the new president. When the conversation turned to
either of us, we told kind lies to assuage the other's guilt or worry. We
laughed more than I could ever remember. I heaped on the I-love-yous.

Maybe I wanted Perry's anger. Maybe I thought my trespassing would
get my mother shunned. Late on New Year's Eve, when I was waiting for
the ball to drop on television and everyone else should have been in their
Bible study, someone knocked on his door. I poured myself off the bed. I

flattened my body on the Navajo rug. Whoever was knocking didn't put much effort into it, or the effort was exerted toward keeping quiet. I tried to divine who was out there—my mother or someone sick or someone old or someone very young—but they left soon after. Eventually I climbed back onto the bed. On television, the ball dropped. Couples kissed and horns blew and confetti swirled like snow. Happy New Year. Welcome to 1993.

Roy

Pickup trucks and cars crowded both shoulders of the gravel road, bumper to bumper like at a livestock show. I worried we'd clip the side mirrors. "Like threading a damned needle," my father said as he steered. Eventually, we turned off the road and bumped along the rutted driveway that wound toward the main building.

The property was teeming: women bustling with laundry and boxes of potatoes; men hammering and sawing, toting lumber and ladders; children scattering feed for chickens and then chasing them away, laughing. Little knots of people stopped what they were doing to watch my father park in front of the chapel, then they returned distractedly to their chores. A man and woman were barking in a foreign tongue to each other, ushering three children into a building as if seeking shelter from a storm. I could hear the pop-pop-pop of gunfire from the shooting range. Two men burned trash in a barrel, billowing blue-gray smoke like a distress signal.

My father nodded to men as they crossed our path. Tipped his hat. He reminded me of an old-time lawman, strolling into a dusty one-horse town, saloons and blacksmith shops on either side. I had the sense that word of our arrival was spreading behind the walls. Women wore shearling jackets over long cotton dresses and rubber boots. The closer we got to the gun range, the louder the report of rifles. Each shot sounded like a hole being punched in metal. On one of his calls, Mason had told us about bullets splitting the air beside his head. He said, "You feel their heat." My father walked at a faster clip than I did, and every so often, he glanced back for me to hurry up.

I must have been hearing the motorbike's engine all along, but the noise didn't register until Perry ripped by and skidded to a stop in front of my father. His back tire churned up a fan of dust. A long pole was attached to the motorcycle seat, flying a small American flag. He wore sunglasses and calfskin gloves. His hair was blown out from the wind. He cackled about some joke in his head. I took a step back.

Perry dropped the kickstand, then climbed off and smoothed down his mane. Smiling, he said, "'So he invited them in and gave them lodging. And on the next day he got up and went away with them, and some of the brethren from Joppa accompanied him.' Acts 10:23."

"Afternoon, Perry," my father said.

"Hidy there, Sheriff," he said. I thought he might salute, but he just turned to me and said, "Deputy Rodeo."

"We came to see how y'all're getting along."

Perry puffed out his chest and stretched his arms as if just waking up. He said, "Appreciate the wellness check, Sheriff. That's a right Christian undertaking."

"The shooting range is hopping," my father said.

"Sundays are made for Scripture and target practice," he said. "We've had booths at shows the last few weekends, so all these gunslingers have been chomping at the bit."

"What would you say if the taxman paid a visit some busy Sunday?"

"I'd remind him we're tax-exempt and refer him to the IRC, section 501(c)(3). I'd assure him any money changing hands here is a donation to our church," he said. "Then I'd ask him if he'd prefer to shoot or pray."

Movement behind us, around us. I suspected men were approaching and awaiting a signal from Perry. My father swept his gaze over the grounds like he was considering buying it. Far up on the hill, a huge man was wedging a cedar post under the roof of a stable.

"And how about you, Rodeo?" Perry asked. "You causing trouble this winter?"

"I'm okay," I said, wishing I had a clever answer, wishing my voice was deeper.

He grinned in a way that made me glance at my father. When I turned back, Perry was still looking at me. He said, "What makes me think you'd sing a different tune if your daddy weren't here? What makes me think a sheriff's son commits crime the way a preacher's daughter commits sin? What makes—"

"Or," my father interrupted him, "say it's not the taxman calling, but the FBI? What would the answer be then?"

"I'd ask how I can be of service," the Lamb said. "They wouldn't be the first ones coming out for the guns and staying for the fellowship."

"I'm serious now," my father said. "I'm not here to lollygag. If you've got something out here you shouldn't, this is when I can help. Right here, right now."

"We've got nothing to hide. We know what's coming."

My father scanned the customers down at the shooting range, then the men and women moving around like carpenter ants, the children chasing chickens. Everyone's breath issued in clouds.

"Do you still have those horses?" I asked.

"If I didn't, your mama would cook my goose," Perry said. "I ain't fearful of no government lackeys, but I know better than to cross Mrs. Lynnette Moreland."

"I'd like to see them," I said.

"Up in them stables I reckon," he said, jutting his chin at the hill. "Feel free to muck out their stalls."

I looked at my father, wondering if he'd let me go after all. He nodded. "And, Rodeo?"

"Yeah?" I said.

"If you cross paths with any of my girls, mind your manners, okay?"

"Of course," I said.

"Much obliged. A little devil like you can tear this whole place down faster than double-struck lightning."

Jaye

The night after New Year's, my mother woke me up in the dark. She said, "I think he's onto something. I'm starting to see it."

"I think you're in love," I said from the top bunk. "That'll cloud anyone's judgment."

"Have you ever been in love?"

She wasn't trying to corner me, I knew that from her tone, but I felt trapped by my own inexperience. Despite the cold seeping in, I pushed down my unicorn sleeping bag. I'd never kissed a boy for fear of being rejected or ridiculed for my technique. I was afraid of what seemed imminent gossip—not stories that I put out easily. I would have welcomed slutty rumors and occasionally considered starting them myself. What I feared were accounts of my innocence.

"A few times," I said, trying to sound both impatient and sage. "They didn't end well. I don't think this will either."

"I probably shouldn't be having this talk with my daughter," she said. "I haven't really made any friends here yet. The other women seem suspicious. They can be a little standoffish."

True. The other women kept her on the periphery. Even when she interacted with them—on the cleaning crew, at meals, walking around the grounds—she seemed adjacent to the others. Always I played a consoling role, the responsible party, offering a pitying voice of feigned reason. But I liked them isolating her. It was easy to imagine them freezing her out so completely that they'd present Perry with an ultimatum: her or us. It was easy to imagine they'd be the reason we'd leave.

"I'm sure things will thaw soon," she said. "They're just protective. He

means so much to everyone, and here I come strutting in from California
and—"

"Have you fucked him?" I interrupted. I wanted to sting her with the
question, but mostly I wanted her to know I wouldn't allow myself to be
shocked by her behavior. If anyone was going to be caught off guard or
offended, it would be her. The edge in my voice was new and invigorating.

She stayed quiet in the dark. I imagined her eyes wide and fixed on the
bottom of my bunk. No doubt she was debating how forthright to be, debating whether to punish me for my insolence or share tawdry details.
Outside, the night wind rattled unseen things.

"No," she said calmly. "I haven't laid with him, but I wouldn't rule it
out."

"Then I'm sure his harem will welcome you into the fold in no time," I
said. The room was spinning a little. Boundaries were blurring, dimming.

"I think your father and I were meant to be together long enough to
make each other happy and to have you, and we did both of those things."

Now I kept quiet. I sensed the impression my body made in the mattress, the irrefutable proof of my sad existence.

"I know you've called him," she said. "Maybe you didn't tell me because you thought I'd be angry or hurt, but I'm glad about it. Your father
loves you, and our problems will never affect that. He's always glad to hear
from you."

"I wanted him to know we were safe," I said. "I wanted to talk with him
on Christmas. He thought we'd be back by now. I did, too."

"You're our sweet girl," she said. "We did a good job with you."

"So you've called, too."

"I have," she said, a little brighter. "We've had productive talks. Hard,
but productive. I told him I sold my car."

I'd allowed myself to believe the car was in Virgil's shop, but now I understood why I'd never asked her about it: I'd known the truth all along
and it terrified me. I said, "So we're never leaving."

"Perry needed a loan. He'll buy us a nicer car after the next gun show,"
she said. "I know it sounds crazy. Your father thinks I've gone off the deep
end. It doesn't feel that way to me. If you'd like to leave, we can make
those arrangements."

"I don't think people who've gone off the deep end can tell when
they've done it," I said.

"I've always felt like I was figuring life out a day too late, and now I feel like Perry's given me a map, like he's given all of us one."

"And where does this magic map say we're going without a car?" I said.

She shifted on the bed below, tugged on the sheet. The longer she went without speaking, the worse I felt. I derided my lack of compassion, my entitled indignation. Let her enjoy herself, I thought. Let her feel loved and tend her faith. I was trying to remember if I'd left anything in the car. Tears in my eyes.

I was about to apologize when she said, "It's late, Jayebird. Let's rest. Thank you for talking to me."

"I'm sorry," I said.

"You have nothing to be sorry for," she said. "Try to sleep a little. There'll be plenty of time for bad news tomorrow."

Before that night and without realizing it, I'd been avoiding Perry. I scarfed my meals quickly and far away from wherever he sat. When morning studies let out and he mixed with the others, I stayed in our room or explored the pastures. When we did run into each other, he held my gaze too long. His voice dripped like honey. As I walked away, his eyes bored into me.

But after my mother and I talked, I started actively hiding. In the water tower. At the shooting range. In the mess hall, and once in one of the two rooms where they kept their guns and ammo. I watched him through curtains and around corners and from high above. I didn't venture out until I knew he wouldn't intercept me. A few times he spotted me in the field and hollered my name, but I ignored him. When I snuck into his room, I poured his milk out the window and put the empty carton back in the fridge. I pushed my nose into his sheets and pillows for any scent of my mother.

She'd started returning to our room later and later. Through our window, I watched the others spill out of the chapel, felt them clomping through the corridor to their rooms, heard them bid each other good night and then collapse into bed. Each night, the same sudden swell of activity followed by the same hushed stillness. From our room, I could see a sliver of Perry's window. The light would come on shortly after the study concluded. If my mother returned to our room late, she carried her shoes. If she cried, she did it into her pillow. The sounds of trying not to make a sound.

Roy

When my mother and I had peered down from the road, the structures seemed small and cloistered, but on the land itself, everything seemed too far apart and all the walk-worn paths uphill. Every few minutes, I turned to locate my father. He stood with his arms crossed, listening to the Lamb run his mouth. The Lamb was brandishing a Bible now, a copy so thoroughly handled it hung as limp as cloth in his hand. There was less gunfire than I would have expected with the range so packed. People were waiting for my father to leave.

Every structure appeared unsound. Angles were off, no surface exactly plumb. None of the windows I looked through were hung correctly. Sections of the main building were washed in a coat of gray paint, but the job was seemingly abandoned as each bucket emptied. When more paint was procured, it looked to have been used to start another section rather than finish the previous one.

I kept expecting to be grabbed by my neck and dragged into a lightless room. I braced every time I approached a corner then forced myself forward. When I encountered anyone, I acted like I was running an urgent errand. The men and women I passed paid strict attention to the boards they were sawing, the children they were wrangling. We gave each other wide, wary berths then moved in opposite directions.

On the trail leading up the hill into a pasture, I saw two girls striding by a willowy woman on a Navajo blanket. The woman was watching over three boys who seemed to be collecting twigs and depositing them in a pink knapsack the smallest boy had on his back, a quiver of bent arrows. One of the girls said, "Eternity wet herself. We're on the hunt for a clean smock."

"Again?" the woman said.

The girls nodded in unison. Their faces were pink with acne.

"Smock," a boy said, probably for the first time. "Smock. Smock."

Then the other boys erupted into the alphabet song, high pitched and starting at the end: "Now I know my ABCs! Next time won't you sing with me!"

"We'll add Eternity to the prayer list," the woman said.

The girls didn't answer. The boys started at the beginning of the song. Below us, a rifle shot cracked open the air.

When I reached the stables, the horses were nibbling clover through the corral fence. The man I'd spotted installing the post earlier was gone. So was the post. Still, the stables seemed sturdier than anywhere else on the property, like whoever had built them had learned from mistakes down the hill. A new plywood deck skirted the tack rooms, firm and square and level. The corral's cedar gate had been reinforced with planks of knotty pine. Oil drums filled with sweet oats and grain, stacked bales of hay, leather bridles hanging on nails. Another barrel with shovels and pitchforks and a post-hole digger. Everything smelled pleasantly of sawdust and horsehair, and there was nothing that resembled a milling machine.

After the stables, I got turned around. I thought I was walking back toward my father but wound up deeper in the pasture. A few old cars were rusting under a stand of persimmon, like stray livestock slumbering in shade. I remembered that one of Coop's many theories was that cars marked the tunnel entrances, so I went farther out of my way to investigate. The cars were gutted, nothing more than flaking shells bound by thick tangles of weeds. I crouched to check under the chassis for secret panels or passages, but the ground was untouched. *Toilets or tunnels? What would you install first, detective?*

When I stood, a couple was passing on the path below. The man had a long four-by-four post across his shoulders, each arm extended and snaked around it. Either he was being punished or enacting some passion play. It seemed a brand of medieval torture. I thought the woman might start whipping him.

Then I recognized him: Virgil. He was just carrying lumber. In his Cajun accent, he said, "Well then light my head on fire and put it out with a hammer."

The woman laughed like she'd been hoping he'd say exactly that.

Once they were far enough down the trail, I started toward where they'd been. I hadn't realized I was so close to the water tower and its cluster of sheds, but they soon emerged on the other side of a small rise. I touched the lock-picking tools in my pocket.

A wooden ladder leaned against the water tower. Virgil and the woman must have been working inside it. The hatch on the underside dangled open, so they'd probably been going for supplies and would return soon.

Because the doors to the sheds had no locks, I didn't need my tools. Rusted nails protruded like so many thorns. The exposed studs were termite-grooved. Inside one shed was a faded canvas cot and a chalkboard. White cobwebs hung tattered in corners, clumped with dust. Another shed reeked of stale cigarette smoke. I thought it was a place for secret meetings.

The last shed was sturdier with a poured cement foundation and packed with supplies—hoses and metal toolboxes and buckets full of pipes and fittings. A stepladder hung from hooks on a wall. A metal shopping cart was loaded with tarps and water jugs, a box of bright orange Bibles. There were bicycles and a child's red wagon full of maracas and tambourines. One wall held shelves of books: manuals on small engine repair, carpentry, and water filtration, books about the Chesapeake Bay and the Blue Ridge Mountains, a tall and thick volume on sailboats, a stack of Bullet Bibles, and a set of structural engineering texts in Portuguese. No milling machines.

Instead of moving everything to use the ladder, I took the tambourines out of the wagon and dragged it across the floor. The wheels were rusted in place and screeched on the cement. I stopped to listen for Virgil. Intermittent gunfire from the range. When it seemed safe, I stepped inside the wagon and tiptoed to reach the fake Bibles. Their lack of heft shamed me. Relieved me.

I was about to step down from the wagon when the question formed in my mind: Sailboats?

The book was right in front of my face, taller than the others. In my hands, it was unevenly weighted, awkward and heavy in places, insubstantial in others. When I opened the cover, I saw why. It was a box, not a book.

Inside, swaddled in burlap, four hand grenades.

Everything silenced. I had the headlong sensation of being on the edge of a cliff, that one misstep would be deadly. I inspected each grenade, praying—silently, earnestly, urgently—that I'd recognize a way to disprove Sammy. Their knobbed bodies in my palm were icy and horrid; the pins securing the hammers seemed too loose. My hands started to sweat. To shake. I knew I was clutching a live explosive, knew I would drop it. I situated the grenade back into the burlap. Although both my feet were planted, I was wobbling. The wagon slid an inch. In my mind it did. I wondered if I should take one of the grenades to my father or if I should walk down with the box in front of me like a tray, a brazen offering, or—

The bottom of the wagon gave. All at once, I was falling. For so long. For too long. My legs out from under me, my hands clutching the box of grenades to my chest. Air. Gravity. A tinny, high-pitched noise that rang and lingered. Things kept coming down even after I was on my back—Bullet Bibles and the water manuals and a toolbox. The bicycles, too. The tambourines.

Jaye

I was eating breakfast with Turtle and Bev when I felt Perry's bony fingers clamp down onto my shoulder like he'd pinned a snake. He said, "Morning, my dears. Mind if I borrow the little one for a spell?"

We exited the mess hall with everyone pretending not to watch. My mother sat with Sage and Charity, and though our eyes met, I couldn't tell if she'd orchestrated this. Perry held the door open and smiled back at his flock; he intended for them to see us leaving together.

"Let's hoof it down to the garage," he said. He paused to light a cigarette and the wind carried the odor of butane past me.

The garage was near the cattle gates at the entrance, a quarter mile away.

"You'll be late for study," I said.

"I'd like to see them start without me," he said.

Gravel crunched beneath our heels. Perry blew smoke from one corner of his mouth. A couple of rabbits nibbled alongside the driveway, then bounded into the brush. The garage didn't seem to be getting any closer.

"She cries when she comes back to the room," I said. "She thinks I'm asleep, but I'm not."

"That grieves me to hear," he said, sounding genuine. "Some women don't mind the sharing, but it wears on others. I wish I knew the remedy."

"Maybe fucking just one would help," I said. I wanted to shock him the way I'd shocked my mother. If anything, it made him feel more at ease. He sucked on his cigarette then flicked it away.

"Everybody thinks I'm living the dream, scoring with a bunch of ladies. Well, it's no party, I'll say that."

"Should I feel sorry for you? Applaud you for breaking up—"

"You're young yet and you're a female," he said, "but think on it like this: How many problems does every married couple have? How many did your folks have? How many times does Virgil squabble with Sage? That new president and first lady? And that's just one man and one woman. If everybody struggles like that with just two people, why would I take on a bunch of women if I didn't have to? And why do these ladies come my way? Because of my good looks? My bank account? Get real."

"You're tearing up families," I said.

"You have to crack some eggs to fry an omelet," he joked. When I didn't laugh, he turned serious, almost petulant. "The families don't matter. We're all vessels, and by the end, we'll get cracked, too. That's when the glory comes. When meaning comes. You have to get to a point where you want to be broken. Where it's an honor. Where the breaking is all that matters."

I felt a little entranced, and I resented it. Just then it was easy to envision us as the last two people on earth, like his rapture had already come and we were left behind in the dingy fields with ants and vultures. The garage loomed now. I thought I'd go in and never come out.

"Why the garage? Why can't we just walk and talk?"

"Because I can't show it to you out here," he said.

"I don't want to see your crotch," I said.

"If I had a nickel for every time I've heard that . . ."

Scraps of sheet metal were propped against the building. Old rotting lumber had been stacked around the east-facing side.

"She's here because she thinks you're special," I said.

"She's dead wrong on that count. If that's too big a disappointment, she should leave. Anybody can waltz right out those gates. Plenty have. It breaks my heart, but I'm not blocking any exits."

"Don't ruin her," I said.

He was trying different keys on the garage door. Once the lock snapped open, he turned to me. He gazed at me in a way that no one ever had, maybe no one has since.

"Ruin her?" he said.

"Yes. That's in your control."

"Jaye, darling. I'm trying to save her," he said. "I'm trying to save all of them. And do you want to know why?"

"Not really," I said.

"Because *they're* special. Not me. Everyone who comes here is special. They're here at a critical time in history, at the *end* of history, and they're here for a reason."

"Whatever," I said.

"Everyone," he said. "Including you."

"Me?"

"*Especially* you," he said. Then he sent the garage door clattering up into the ceiling. At first, I didn't apprehend what I was seeing. I hadn't forgotten about it, but I hadn't ever expected to see it again. My hand was on my mouth and my eyes were infuriatingly wet, and I thought, Do. Not. Cry. But it was too late. Maybe because I was so tired or worried about my mother, maybe because Perry had sold her car, maybe because I hated how I'd followed him to the garage and how I wasn't immune to his aberrant thoughtfulness. I didn't know. Nor did I know how Perry understood this was his best play.

That red Chevy truck had crapped out fifty miles shy of Waco on his drive back from California last year. It was towed to a mechanic in town where it had been ever since. Every week the mechanic claimed it was close, then something else went kaput. Perry explained how he'd sold my mother's car to pay for a new transmission and engine block. The truck needed work, but it was running again. With gun show season coming, they'd need it to haul inventory.

"And I'll come clean with you," he said in the garage. "I was thinking since you're such an expert driver, you might start helping Virgil on his supply runs. Maybe that'll be your contribution, shopping and whatnot. Maybe accompany us to the shows and help us sell these hillbillies their weaponry."

"Virgil already asked me to prime the water tower," I said. It was mostly true. Virgil'd caught me climbing the ladder once. He said the plan was to redo the tower in the next year and collect rainwater for vegetable gardens. He said I could come keep him company if I got bored.

"Well," Perry said, "then you can do that, too. 'It is the hardworking farmer who ought to have the first share of the crops.' 2 Timothy 2:6."

"I don't have my license yet," I said. "I'm not sixteen."

"Mary was about your age when she birthed the Christ. If she can handle that, you can keep from steering into a ditch."

"That's what you want me to say when the cops stop me?"

"Don't give them a reason to pull you over," he said like it wasn't something I'd think of on my own. "But if that happens, just say you're running errands for me. I'm in good stead with Sheriff Moreland."

"Sure," I said, already imagining driving the truck alone. I saw myself parked on a dirt road, sitting on the tailgate with a Coke and some perfect song on the radio. And I saw my mother and me leaving. I said, "I just don't want to get you in trouble."

"Little girl, if you get me in trouble, it ain't going to be over no speeding ticket."

ON THE LAMB

PODCAST EPISODE 1
GUEST: Professor Eliza Ashcraft
RECORDED: July 2023
            Phone Interview

Dr. Richard Hannah and I served as consultants in 1993. We also testified during the trials.

Consultants for?
The FBI asked for our input based on research we'd published concerning sects, marginalized systems of belief, and new religious movements.

Cults.
Not a term I'd use here.

Why not?
For one, epistemological transparency. Mr. Cullen was open about his beliefs, methods, and doctrines. Typically, a "cult" will obfuscate how it diverges from organized religion. Cullen was also forthright about the group's finances. His records were accessible. Any moneys coming in were used legally and for the benefit of the group and its assets.

He had multiple wives. He slept with teenage girls.
My understanding is that the charges of plural marriage have never been substantiated. His relationships with minors are another matter entirely, and certainly disturbing if true, but I'm a scholar not a litigator or member of law enforcement. I'm only able to speak to the substance of his doctrines, the viability of the church. All of this happened some thirty years ago, which, in western culture, is ancient history, but in my area, it's no time at all. It's like that joke: What's the difference between a cult and a religion in America?

I don't know.
A hundred years.

Jaye

So I bought groceries and collected day-old freebies. I emptied the tank so I'd have to go out again for gas. Everywhere I went I used the toilet and all but bathed in hot water from sinks. I parked outside the little airfield and ate a hamburger without wiping the juice off my chin. I trailed a man with loudspeakers sprouting like cactuses from his Econoline roof and listened to his proselytizing. In some neighborhoods he spoke Spanish. He drove as slow as an ice-cream man. I wondered if Perry viewed him as a rival.

Here's some of my shame: Once I had a way off the property, I felt free. I felt chosen. Like rules were being broken on my behalf. I felt more forgiving toward my mother, even toward Perry. If my mother was in our room at night, I told her where I'd gone during the day. She asked about the truck, if I liked driving, if I ever got lost or scared. She said Perry had a lot of faith in me, wanted to make sure I felt at home here, part of his family. She never asked to go on my drives, and I never invited her. Nor did I ever propose we break away in the middle of the night and hightail it home. The truth is that when I was on my constitutionals I never thought of not coming back. In short order, now that we had the option to leave, the prospect stopped crossing my mind. Just as Perry had planned.

Every weekend a gun show in a different city. Our caravan left before dawn on Friday mornings. Perry and Virgil always went, and usually Sage and Charity. Sometimes Lawrence or Gina. We spent that afternoon erecting our booth for early bird nights. The dealers were the same sad-eyed men, their same chain-smoking wives. Perry led me around and introduced me. He called me "the lovely Jaye," "the California cherub," "the prettiest little getaway driver" he'd ever known. The men shook my hand. The women hugged me so tight I came away smelling of their jasmine perfume and Parliament cigarettes. They started whispering as soon as Perry and I turned around. "They're a bunch of inbred hicks," he'd say. "Jealous philistines."

On Friday and Saturday nights, we lingered in the auditoriums and hid in bathrooms hoping the staff would lock us in and we could sleep under the tables. It worked about half the time. Perry hated paying for motels, no matter how cheap. If the weather wasn't too bad, we'd sleep in our vehicles. Virgil laid the seat back in his Volvo. I slept in the cab of the truck in my clothes and shoes. I put the folding sunshade in the windshield and hung a plastic poncho in the rear window and trapped towels in the door windows. Perry put sleeping bags in the bed of the truck and stretched out with Sage or Gina, and some nights they wouldn't shut up until three or four. They talked about inventory and Scripture and Perry's life, about Song of Solomon and the Seven Seals. He strummed his guitar and improvised songs about outlaws and God.

I'm sure there were other times it happened, but I only heard him having sex once. This was in Corpus Christi where we were camped in the parking lot of a beach church called Island in the Son. At first I thought the wind was rocking the truck, but then I heard a voice whisper, "We need to go to the dunes. She'll hear." I told myself it was Sage but worried it was Charity. They stayed in the bed of the truck, and soon the rocking motion was like bouncing down a potholed hill faster and faster. I was queasy, tingling. I was afraid my mother would ask if anything had happened between Perry and someone, afraid I'd throw it at her in some random argument, afraid Charity would confide in me. I imagined her wrists flexing, the blue veins under her translucent skin coursing and swelling with fast blood. Just before the truck stilled and everything got quiet, Perry panted, "There's my precious angel. There she is."

After that, I wore my gas mask the way girls with regular lives wore sunglasses. I didn't want Perry to see how closely I watched him.

ON THE LAMB

PODCAST EPISODE 1
GUEST: Professor Eliza Ashcraft
RECORDED: July 2023
                    Phone Interview

What attracted people to the Lamb?
Belief.

Can you elaborate?
Christianity bases its claims on belief in Christ. Practice flows from belief. Mr. Cullen's beliefs were also millenarian, which dictated how he and his flock practiced. Millenarian groups believe that time is imminently coming to an end, and salvation is reserved for the faithful.

The allure won't make sense to most of us, but that's what attracts and binds the flock. These groups tend to emerge in times of national or global stress. In this case, the first Gulf War. Millenarian leaders claim divine wisdom, so global events are interpreted through symbolic readings of Scripture. The followers feel like they're receiving an exclusive invitation, and they feel less alone. There's a sense of promise. They believe the best is yet to come, their sacrifices will be justified, and the person they're following is the only one who can lead them to paradise.

You sound like you're describing someone falling in love.
Because I am.

Roy

Everything hurt. I'd landed on my back and elbows because I refused to let go of the grenades; the impact of the fall had knocked the wind out of me, but the most acute pain was on my shin. I raised my pant leg to find a slanted red scrape and then I could feel nothing but warm blood pulsing along its edges. Tetanus, I thought, and began inventing explanations I could offer my mother. I was still clutching the fake sailboats book when I poked my head out of the shed. From that bluff I could see the whole property below—the car shells and buildings and believers milling around. My father was still with the Lamb. Nodding. Other men flanked the Lamb now; they didn't look especially intimidating but were, I sensed, reinforcements. I didn't like my father being outnumbered.

It still seemed inconceivable that I'd been the one to find the grenades. The odds. The percentages. I was trying to figure the best route back—straight down the hill betraying where I'd been or the long way through the pasture—and I still couldn't decide whether to bring all four grenades, or one, or none. Was it more dangerous to bring all of them swaddled in the sailboats book or to stash a single grenade in my pocket? What was the right thing to do? The bravest? The—

Then, from above: "Rodeo?"

I scrambled back into the shed like a cockroach skittering from light. Without thinking it through, I slipped a burlap-wrapped grenade into my coat pocket and returned the book housing the others to its shelf.

"Rodeo?" the voice said again. "Rodeo? Where'd you go, Rodeo?"

The shed had no windows, so I craned my neck around the doorframe. I could see the legs of the water tower, weeds, and bare dirt. You're concussed, I thought. The possibility came as comfort. Everything existed at a remove, like I'd fallen, not through the rusted bottom of a wagon, but into an inconsequential dream. The grenade in my pocket, that voice calling out to me, its absurd familiarity. I stepped out cautiously. I stopped just beyond the door and waited, primed to slip back in.

Then she said, "I have to stop sneaking up on you like this."

Jaye. In the water tower. Peering down from the hatch at the bottom, smiling, her gas mask crowning her head and her braid hanging down like a rope.

My vision seemed clear, but I felt adrift from my body. Surely I was hallucinating. I was unconscious, on the floor of the shed. Or the grenades *had* exploded and these were the last fantasies of a dying boy. I was about to wake up in the hospital or not wake up at all.

"I fell," I said.

"Sounded like a doozy."

"I think I have a concussion. I think I'm maybe hallucinating you."

"Oh, I'm a real dream come true," she said.

"I don't understand," I said.

"And I don't know how I'm going to finish sealing this tank before dark," she said. "Get up here and let's sort out these pressing issues."

She held the top of the ladder while I climbed. I had to twist sideways to squeeze through the hatch, and yet the tank was bigger than I'd expected, rounder. Wavy light leaked through the corrugated tarpaulin overhead. Even the smallest noises—my boots on the floor, Jaye moving the paint pan—amplified and echoed. Like we were inside a bell, every sound chasing itself around the dome until it rang away or escaped through the hatch. The air inside was thick, nauseating. Jaye wore a long-sleeve thermal and faded overalls.

Nothing seemed real. I tried to center myself and fit the impossible facts together by cataloging what I knew: My father was down the hill, talking to the Lamb. I'd fallen. Jaye was here, at the ranch, inside a water tower, and now I was with her. There was a grenade in my pocket and she didn't know and I didn't know how to tell her. Jaye was here, and I was here, and I was here and Jaye was here, and it made no sense but she seemed unjarred. She'd returned to working the roller over the walls. It was like a sponge being squeezed. The fumes made me dizzy. I said, "You never called."

"False. I called every chance I got and the line just kept ringing."

The relief. The formidable calm that follows a truth revealed. I said, "My father's been getting a lot of—"

"And I called about an hour ago and talked with your mother. I assured her my intentions were no good."

For weeks I hadn't allowed myself to confront the idea that Jaye was gone, either because she'd lost interest or her mother had taken her back to California or the older suitor had—and like that, I remembered where I'd first seen her old red truck: in the parking lot of the gun show when my father had his talk with the Lamb, the night we met.

"It's the Lamb," I said. "*He's* your boyfriend."

"Strike two. He's my mother's boyfriend. I'm not washed in the blood."

"I don't understand," I said.

"You say that a lot. But here's the thing: I may have exaggerated that boyfriend stuff. I may have been trying to appear *desirable*. Girls do this."

"So he's not—"

"Unlike my mother, I despise him. She puts him on a pedestal then complains about her sore neck."

I touched the grenade in my pocket while Jaye explained how she got from California to Texas. She said the Lamb aimed to start a program called New Light that would precede an event called the Wave Sheaf.

"What's the Wave Sheaf? What's New Light?" I asked.

"Kids," she said.

"I don't under—" I caught myself. I said, "What do you mean?"

"Kids are the New Light. He needs to bring a couple dozen of those little saviors into the world lickety-split. They're going to mind the store after Jesus flies back home. Or something along those lines."

She poured more primer into the pan, then started rolling another section.

"Do you believe in what he says?" I asked. "Are you going to marry him if your mother says you should?"

"I've got my eye on someone else, but he's playing hard to get," she said, glancing over her shoulder to see my reaction. Her eyes dilated as did each chamber of my heart.

"What's he like?"

"I'll tell you, but after that, it's my turn to ask a question. Deal?"

"Deal."

"Okay, so, he's real mysterious," she said. "And holy shit, would Perry hate it if he knew about him. He'd be furious, enraged. And scared."

"Because of the mystery man's father?"

"My turn," she said.

"Okay," I said, thrilled, terrified, hopeful.

"Why are you here?"

"Why are *you* here!"

"Pilgrim," she said, "we made a deal."

"I'm helping my father. We're trying to find—"

She made a loud harsh noise like a buzzer. She said, "Sorry, we were looking for: 'To see a girl I can't stop thinking about.'"

"To see a girl I can't stop thinking about," I said.

"I knew it," she said. "My next question has to be whispered. You'll have to come closer."

I rose and kept my hand on the wall as I made my way to her.

When I was two feet behind her, she said, "Closer."

I stepped forward, and she said, "Closer."

Then I was against her back. I could smell the heat of her body, the rubber of the gas mask, her unwashed hair, dried sweat behind her ear. The earthy odor of days in frostbitten pastures and nights without bathing.

"Here?" I said.

"Closer."

I laid my hands on her hips. Her back against my chest but she turned her face toward mine. Our cheeks touched. I heard her lips part. Her breathing was shallow, jagged, like she was shivering. She leaned into me gently. So gently. She was still holding the paint roller. After a long while, she swallowed and said, "Ready?"

"For what?" I said.

"My question, Rodeo, my burning question."

"Yes," I said. "Ready."

"Why haven't you kissed me yet?"

"I think I'm scared," I said.

"Of what?" Her eyelashes brushed my cheek.

"That you don't want me to," I said. "That you won't like it. That you'll think it's a sin or—"

Her mouth on mine, smaller than I'd imagined and just then I could have counted the thousands of times I'd imagined it. She gave me more of her weight. She moaned a little and the sound, that small hum and vibration, moved through my body like blood.

When she pulled back, I opened my eyes to see what was wrong, but hers were still closed. She wore a goofy smile, like she was drunk. She said something about sin.

"Do what?" I said, quiet, trying not to break the spell. "Did you say 'Sin'?"

"I said, 'Again,'" she said. "Again."

"You mean kiss you again?"

"Kiss. Sin. Whichever, pilgrim. Just give it to me again."

This time she spun to face me and let the roller drop onto the floor. I wondered if any primer had splashed onto my boots or church pants, but then we were each other's breath. Her hands on my face. Her finger in my mouth, then another, her fingerprints delicately on my tongue, dissolving like snowflakes. I was aware that we were high above the ground. The sensation of being borne aloft. We were suspended, hovering between the past and future, between earth and heaven.

Then we heard a noise and froze; people passing beneath the tower. I flattened my back against the tank.

Virgil called up, "Jayebird?"

"It's me," Jaye said. Her wide eyes fixed on me. Her finger on my lips, shushing me. I wanted to softly bite it. Her wicked smile. She said, "I'm finishing up."

"Soup's on."

"I'll be right down," she said.

"I'll help," he said, stepping onto the ladder. "Looks like a raccoon or opossum got into one of the sheds. It's a mess."

Jaye grabbed the bucket of primer and lunged into the hatch, blocking his view. "Just take this," she said. "I'll be down soon. Tell my mom, okay?"

"Oh, okay. Sure thing," he said. "I'll grab you some popcorn before it's all gone."

The ladder creaked. Eventually his footfalls grew faint. Jaye gazed at me, smug and curious.

After a time, I said, "I want to see you again."

"I know," she said. She was standing now, her arms around me, her hands clasped behind the small of my back.

"Tomorrow," I said boldly. "At the field."

She touched my cheek with her palm. Everything felt real again—the scrape on my shin, the ringing in my head, the grenade in my coat pocket, the knowledge of where we stood.

"Promise me," I said.

"Promise," she said. "I'll say I need tampons. He hates that word."

Then, despite the keen awareness of pushing my luck, I said, "You didn't say what the Wave Sheaf is."

"I didn't?"

"No," I said. We kissed again.

"My apologies, pilgrim," she said. "But it's really nothing important. Just the end of the world."

Part Two

The Red Horse

February 1993

Jaye

After my pilgrim and his father drove off, Perry called an emergency study. Virgil, Sage, and Lawrence fanned out, wrangling people into the chapel. Bev clanged the dinner bell for five minutes straight. Big Lyle posted himself outside the barracks, a rifle slung over his shoulder. He was a redwood that people had to sidestep to enter the building. Seneca and Annie had been down by the oblong pond, brushing out each other's hair or writing lesson plans, and when they hustled up the hill, they had to keep doubling back to stomp on stray papers Annie dropped. She spun no cartwheels, a bad omen to be sure. My mother plucked clothes off the line and wadded them in her wicker basket; she was harried and, I knew, worried she'd be last inside. When the basket was full, she abandoned the rest of the clothes and tried to catch Seneca. Parents chased children. Bev never stopped sounding her alarm, so it seemed a tribulation was about to befall us—an avalanche or flash flood or some other indifferent act of nature, of a cold and riled god.

Their study ran all night. I listened outside the chapel door with my legs cramping in the cold. Perry said, "They've sent out scouts, okay? It's what I've been barking about. It's real bad news. Probably the best news: '. . . and on her forehead a name was written, a mystery, "Babylon the great, the mother of harlots and abominations of the earth." '"

His voice cracked as though he'd suffered an onset of puberty. He shouted. He sobbed. Then a kid, likely Eternity or Kanaan, began screaming. The child quieted long before Perry did. He led everyone in a fifteen-minute prayer. When a coughing fit seized his chest and throat, I bolted down the corridor, worried someone might run for water and find me lurking.

The night was a gauze of glistening stars. Like a swath of quartz in black granite. I considered going to our room and wrapping myself in my sleeping bag, but instead I went to the gym. I ran wind sprints to pump feeling back into my body. Everywhere—in the cobwebbed corners near the ceiling, in the sound my soles made hitting the ground, in the hollows of my collarbone—our kiss.

I took a bowl of stale popcorn to our room. I climbed onto my bunk and balanced the bowl on my stomach. I flicked pieces into the air and made a game of catching them in my mouth. For every piece I caught, the chances of Roy running away with me increased. The lights were off, which made it harder, but the moon was emitting a cold, smooth-edged light, so I could see well enough to catch almost as many as I missed. Between each toss, I listened for people in the hall. It was daybreak before my mother crept into our room. Outside, birds were calling to each other, lonely and curious as to who had survived the night.

I thought I'd sleep through the day, but as soon as I started drowsing, I remembered the clothes left on the line. Below me, my mother's breathing had evened. She snored softly, and I was awash in a sad protectiveness, wondering if she felt visible yet, if being seen might eventually open her own eyes. I worried Perry would humiliate her for abandoning her chores, worried Seneca or Annie would turn her in or retrieve the orphaned garments and take credit for correcting her error. I climbed down, grabbed my gas mask. When I leaned down to tie my boots, bits of popcorn fell to the floor. I found two other pieces in my hair. I ate them, and the chewing only made me hungrier.

The empty wicker basket was beside our door. Outside, the ground was bejeweled with frost that cracked beneath my boots. The clothes on the line were also crystal-crusted, so I snapped each garment like a bullwhip before laying it across the basket; when the frost exploded, it put me in the mind of glass shattering. I could think of nothing more satisfying.

I pulled my gas mask over my face when the wind picked up. After I'd finished with the clothes, I walked down to the pond to see if it had frozen. It hadn't. The sharp noses of a few turtles breached the surface. I ran my fingers through my hair, hoping for more popcorn I could throw to them. Off and on, the lenses of my gas mask fogged with my breath, warming my cheeks. A blue iridescent dragonfly skidded over the water.

When I turned around, Perry was standing up where the land began its downward slope. I didn't know how long he'd been there.

"That mask ain't got no filter. It's as worthless as an ice tray in hell,"

Perry said. His voice was raw from talking all night. "I'll have somebody scrounge one up for you."

My breath was coming fast. My head swam. I said, "It's a fashion statement. Form over function."

"'Let your light so shine before men that they may see your good works and glorify your Father which is in heaven,'" he said. "If I looked like you, the last thing I'd do is wear a mask. You're hiding your light under a bushel, darlin'."

"I need to get back to our room," I said. "I'm cold."

"But I come bearing a gift," he said, sidestepping down. When he was a few feet away, he stopped. A wide smile overtook his face. He said, "Close your eyes."

"No chance."

"You don't like surprises?"

"I love surprises," I said. "I don't like you."

Perry smiled again, wider still, like he was in on a secret. He extended his right arm like a plank. His fist was closed. He rotated his wrist, tauntingly slow, and then one by one peeled open his fingers. In his palm, a chrome-plated derringer with a mother-of-pearl handle. When I didn't reach for it, he slapped his forearm with his other hand and the pistol catapulted in my direction. I caught it with both hands for fear of it hitting the ground and going off. I'd never held a gun before.

"Hot damn!" he said. "Most girls'll run if you throw a gun at them. Most men, too."

"Why are you throwing guns at people? Are you arming everyone in case the sheriff comes back?"

"Oh, he's coming back all right," he said. "He may not even know it yet, but I do."

I hoped he was right. I hoped Roy would come back, too. I hoped it'd be later this morning, and I hoped he'd kiss me without my asking. I said, "Maybe if you weren't boning Charity, Johnny Law wouldn't be so interested."

"That's what's called a pocket pistol, a whore's gun. See how there's no hammer? That's so it won't get stuck on your garter belt."

"I'm no whore," I said.

"No, but you're always roaming these here pastures. What happens if you meet Mr. Copperhead or Mrs. Coyote? I'm giving it to you as a token of trust. See, the more I watch you, the more alike I think we are."

"I'm not like you," I said.

"You understand me, and like it or not, I understand you. You can apprehend the significance of all this. Not many can. You're the exception."

"We're nothing alike."

"Didn't we both change our names? Didn't we both wind up here, on this scrappy parcel of land, at this very moment? Think of them odds! I mean, why weren't you born a man in the Dark Ages? Why ain't I on a fishing boat in Japan? What's going to transpire could only transpire on this hard Texas soil."

"Is that what you told Charity? Was she an exception, too?"

"Charity's part of the plan," he said. He fished in his baggy shirt pocket for a half-smoked cigarette, then patted his jeans for a lighter. It took him a few tries to fire up.

"Virgil must be so proud," I said.

"He is! Sage, too," he said, expelling smoke over his shoulder. Far up the hill behind him stood the water tower. Farther up still, the stables and horses. "Their girl is part of something real rare, something that dwarfs this dime-store world."

"I think this is all going to crash down. I think my father would break your neck if you told him I was part of your nasty-ass plan."

"See? We agree again. I'm under no delusions about this ending well for me. No, ma'am. I'm just trying to fulfill my duties before the sand runs out of the hourglass."

Perry dragged on his cigarette. He flicked the butt and it arced over me before landing in the water. A couple turtles swam toward it, thinking it was bread. I wished I had a way to warn them.

"I'm going to the store later," I said. "I need tampons."

Perry winced.

"Tampons! Tampons, tampons, tamp—"

"Message received," he said, walking away. "And I appreciate the tip about your father. I won't tell him anything if you won't."

"I'm not an exception!" I yelled into the gas mask. "I'm not part of your shit."

"No, ma'am, not you," he said in a singsong tone. His back stayed to me as he ascended the hill. "You traveled all this way for the scenery and snapping turtles."

ON THE LAMB

PODCAST EPISODE 10
GUEST: Virgil Bernthal
RECORDED: April 2024
                The Chapel of Light
                Waco, Texas

I admit I had doubts about his relations with Charity. Sage and I prayed on that for days. We cried and raged in every direction—at each other, at him, at God.

What was the Lamb's response?
He asked for our blessing. He was as conflicted as us. I believe that. He knew how the request could be misinterpreted. We shed tears together. We carried each other's pain. Growing pains. God was stretching us in new ways, testing us. The Lamb said we'd ultimately view this as a kind of choosing, a privilege. He said Charity would, too.

And did you?
Sage did. Absolutely she did, and I feel grateful for that. Charity, I don't know. I hope so. Personally, I'm still trying.

Were you relieved when he turned his attention to Jaye?
A part of me was. Not a small part. Not a proud part.

Roy

After supper on Sunday, my father oiled his belt and boots; he did mine, too, and my mother's and her purse. She took a shower so long it emptied our hot water tank. I went to my room and promised myself I wouldn't touch the grenade; I'd stashed it in my suitcase in my closet as soon as we'd gotten back from the ranch. I worked locks to occupy myself. I pulled on the gas mask I'd bought for Mason. I debated taking down my posters in case Jaye ever visited. Within fifteen minutes, I'd done everything I could think to do and was unwrapping the grenade. It looked like a hideous pineapple. The cold heft in my hands. How thin its pin, how insubstantial the barrier between safety and destruction. There had to be more stashed around the property, and yet I hadn't been able to bring myself to tell my father what I'd found. My thoughts rioted, stuttered, guilty and afraid and riven with the demented hope that I'd overlooked an obvious clue that would deem the grenades harmless. Were there blank explosives like there were blank bullets? Did they expire? I wanted to talk to Mason without our parents on the line, to confide in him, to hear his counsel. When my hands started to quake, I returned the suitcase to my closet. I buried it under a stack of board games I couldn't remember ever playing.

Eventually my parents slipped into the backyard and the filmy odor of cigarette smoke wafted. I opened my Bible to Revelations and read like I was cramming for a test. No matter how I positioned myself, I couldn't get comfortable. I kept throwing off my grandmother's quilt and then pulling it back on. I wanted to know how the stories of the Wormwood star and the abyss and the trumpeting angels could seem imminent. Any word I didn't know—*Nicolaitans, censer*—I tried looking up in the dictionary I'd won in the spelling bee. I considered calling Coop, which he would've relished, but didn't want to explain my sudden interest, didn't want to betray Jaye and her mother.

I remembered how she kept saying "Closer," how she kept her finger on my lips when she called down to Virgil. Closer. Closer. But then I'd think how she was at the ranch and Sammy had said the Lamb was bent on separating girls from their panties, how he could approach her whenever he wanted, might be making his way to her right now. Someone might as well have been holding a pillow over my face.

"Chop chop, lamb chop," my mother said on Monday morning.

She was in my room, tugging open window blinds. Light crashed in. She tossed a shirt and my brown corduroys onto my bed. Grit in my eyes, in the folds of my brain. A few locks and Mason's tool kit lay beside me on the blanket; my Bible was on the floor, face down and open like a shot bird. Then my mother was back in the hallway, saying, "We're late."

The morning was crisp, as though a film had been stripped from the provincial sky. I ate a piece of toast in the car. There were pockets of runny melted butter in every bite. I was still waking up.

"Where's that sweet grin coming from?" my mother asked.

"I dreamed Mason came home," I lied.

"My money would've been on that call I took from Lady Jaye yesterday."

She glanced at me, then reached over and parted my hair with her fingers like she sometimes did before we stepped into church.

"I might go to Coop's this afternoon," I said.

"You have crumbs all over your chest. Don't dust them off in here. Do it when you get out."

"We're working on a project for class," I said.

With everyone already at work and school, the streets had emptied out like on holidays. I tried to remember if I'd closed my closet door.

"She was nice on the phone," my mother said. "She sounded pretty."

"Thanks," I said because it felt like a compliment. We passed a vacant lot being graded for construction. A clutch of workers smoked in hard hats.

"Maybe you'll tell me about her someday," my mother said. "And if you'd ever want to invite her for dinner or—"

"We're taking it slow," I said. "We don't want to rush things."

"She was very polite," she said. "And she's crazy about you, sweet potato. She's no better at hiding that than you are."

In the gym locker room—wooden benches painted dark evergreen, equipment cage that reminded me of jail cells downtown—I listened to Coop talk while he changed out of his school clothes. He was summarizing a bus stop brawl between Shane Buford and Tommy Fuentes: Shane had pulled Tommy's shirt over his head and kicked his legs out from under him. But then Tommy had dragged Shane to the ground and started raining down blows. "He was tagging the shit out of him," Coop said, shadowboxing in front of the lockers. Ultimately the bus driver shouldered through the fight circle and broke it up. I thought Coop might be inventing everything. I'd taken shop class with Shane and Tommy last year.

"Why would they fight?" I said. My mood had darkened. I wanted to catch Coop lying to make myself feel better. "They're friends."

"That ended with Sabrina," he said. Sabrina Grant wore big bows in her ponytail, ran with an elite crowd, and smoked brown cigarettes behind the tropical fish store. Her parents owned the gun shop that had been in the mall before it shuttered. Coop said, "Why aren't you changing? Today's dodgeball."

"My stomach hurts," I said. "I might go to the nurse."

"You should've gone earlier. You could've seen Shane. Tommy tagged him and busted his lip," Coop said. He must have heard someone say *tag* recently. At that point in our lives, a lot of kids staked their identities with particular words and phrases. Barry O'Dell described every noise as *elephants trying to fuck*. Judy Mahurin was constantly talking about *partying*—*I want to party with him* or *we partied at the feed mill* or *oh sure, Roy, like you even party*. I didn't know if I said anything too often, but I usually felt sorry for kids when I knew what words they'd use before they did.

"I might skip the rest of the day," I said. "But I told my mom I was going to your house after school. I said we had a project."

"You're acting weird. Are you on the rag?"

"My mother's upset about Mason. He called yesterday but we couldn't hear," I lied. Normally, I refused to invoke my brother. Mentioning him felt chancy, like tempting misfortune, but sometimes I needed the leverage of pity.

Coop nodded, all conciliatory. He kneeled to tie his laces. His gym shoes were his school shoes, dingy and blown out, a size too big from Goodwill; I had to look away. Someone turned off the industrial fan in the back of the locker room. Coop said, "What kind of project? I don't want to say the wrong thing."

"She won't call. I just didn't want her to worry," I said. The locker room had cleared out.

"She's always going to worry, sweet potato," Coop said. "You're the one she's got left."

Jaye

O ur room was an empty icebox. My mother would have started on her morning chores right after breakfast. I slid into my sleeping bag with the outside cold still knitted into my clothes. I couldn't get warm no matter how tight I balled into myself.

I'd started drifting off right when someone knocked on our doorframe. When I peeked into the hall, Big Lyle was lumbering away. He'd left a tray outside my door: a bowl of oatmeal, a bruised banana, three slices of white bread, and a cup of coffee. The bowl and mug were covered in cellophane.

"Thank you," I called out. No response. I felt like a prisoner in solitary confinement who'd been granted her single meal of the day. Big Lyle's shoulders were as wide as the corridor. His braid bounced against his massive back. When his boots hit the floor, thunder.

I inhaled the oatmeal and gulped down the coffee, both lukewarm. The banana disappeared in three bites. I wiped the bowl clean with the first piece of bread, then I sopped up what was left of my coffee with the second. I meant to save the third piece, but without realizing it, I'd torn it in half and consumed it in two bites. I climbed back into bed, nursed a sated sleep.

When I opened my eyes hours later, the twins were standing one behind the other in front of me. Eden was in back with her head tilted so it appeared to be attached to Ruthie's shoulder—two acne-pocked faces, one body, inches from my nose. I recoiled and slammed against the wall behind me, the ceiling above. The twins started cackling. They doubled over. They were so loud they covered each other's mouths.

"What the flying fuck?" I said.

Their eyes saucered. They turned to each other, then, scandalized, erupted in laughter again. I wanted to scream in their faces and shoo them from my room, but soon, despite my ragged, angry fatigue, I was giggling. Then I was gut-laughing on my bunk, tears glazing my cheeks, my face pushed into the mattress in hopes of no one else hearing. If I stole glances at them, it only made us laugh harder.

When the fit turned us loose, the twins sat beside each other on the floor, their backs against the wall and their hips touching. Ruthie looped her arms around her shins, rested her chin on her knees. Eden's legs were extended and straight like she was in a kayak. The twins took turns describing last night's study, passing the story to each other as if sharing a bowl of chips. I had the feeling they'd been waiting to unload everything on me. Like they'd spent the morning divvying up who would say what and in what order. While Eden spoke, Ruthie straightened her spine and neck, maybe trying to correct her posture. At one point, Eden placed my gas mask on her head like a tiara.

They said Perry had worked himself into a lather at the study. "If we would've been in the front row, we'd be covered in his spit," Eden said.

"Poor Senny," Ruthie said. "Poor Victoria."

"Poor Mom," they said in unison, but it didn't faze them.

I was going to make a joke about how those women were probably well acquainted with his spit, but I couldn't nail down the phrasing. The twins riffed off each other as they recounted what they'd heard. Perry was convinced Assyrian authorities would assail the ranch. He spoke of marauders blasting up through the floor and hog-tying children. Or they'd soar in on silent black-winged gliders. Or parachute in from undetectable planes. He kept stopping to peer gravely through the chapel's small window behind the stage. He went on about Babylon and the fall of Jericho and the wars of Saul and the Four Horsemen. Ovals of dark sweat soaked his shirt. He untucked it, unbuttoned it, removed it, and mopped his flesh. When he tossed it toward the bleachers, Charity caught it and clutched it to her chest. Perry said the sheriff and his son might have been decoys, a distraction so Special Forces battalions could start slithering from underground like the snakes they are.

"He called Rodeo a *snake*?" I said, offended.

"Who?" they said in unison.

"The sheriff's boy," I said. "He called him that at the gun show."

"We never get to go to the gun shows," Eden said.

"We ask every time, but Mom says we're not ready," Ruthie said. She took the mask from Eden's head, as if deeming her unworthy of the crown. "But we're allowed to work the range here. Stupid. Charity always gets to go."

"They're boring," I said. "You're not missing shit."

"I keep hoping someone'll teach me to drive. Maybe then I'll get invited," Ruthie said.

"Same here," Eden said. "It bites."

Had I thought teaching them to drive would result in their fleeing, I would've offered right then. But I knew they wouldn't. After all, I had the keys to the truck and no matter how many times I left the ranch, I kept coming back.

"I'm pretty sure Charity hates going," I said.

"I'd trade places with her in a heartbeat. We both would," Ruthie said and looked at Eden for confirmation. Eden nodded. "It's because she's part of New Light."

"You know about that?"

"Duh," Ruthie said.

"She's lucky," Eden said. "She's chosen."

"We thought you were, too," Ruthie said. "We thought that's why y'all moved here, but every time we think you're with him, we'll find him doing something else or you'll be out with your horses."

Each word blotted the one before. I couldn't parse what I was hearing, what it beckoned or negated, like my understanding was a ball bouncing in and out of a roulette wheel. Out of nowhere, I felt a dismal sluggishness. I wanted to fall asleep and wake up in my bed in California.

"New Light's disgusting," I said. "Everything about this place gives me diarrhea. That there are no working toilets is a perfect metaphor."

"For what?" Eden said. The question seemed earnest. Her eyes were on mine like when I helped her with math.

"Everything is shit," I said, realizing I didn't have the metaphor fully worked out either. "Everything is rank and vile and—"

"Don't worry," Ruthie said. "You'll get picked eventually. Probably before us. Probably that's why Mom won't take us to gun shows. You're next. For sure you are."

"No chance," I said.

"No, it's true," Eden said. If her sister's tone had been consoling, Eden's was congratulatory. "He watches you. We've seen him."

"You're going to make me vomit up the oatmeal Big Lyle brought me," I said.

"Big Lie," Eden said.

"Big Shy," Ruthie said.

"But wait, go back: What did Perry say about the sheriff and his boy?"

"I said . . ." Perry called from the hallway, drawing the word out like part of a song. The twins snapped their faces toward each other. Their hands fell primly to their laps. I tried to remember anything we'd said that might turn into a problem, tried to guess how long he'd been listening on the other side of the flimsy wall. When he pivoted into the doorway, he leaned against the frame, tired and aslant. "I said I'd always liked the sheriff and little Rodeo, and I surely wanted to help, but until they got right with God, they were bailing out their boat with a spoon."

He'd bathed since I last saw him. His hair hung damp and stringy. The twins scooted closer together. When Perry looked down at them, a slow, squinting smile. He said, "I reckoned you three would hit it off. I had visions. Three angels."

"We're doing school," I said. "They came for math help."

"I never cottoned to math," he said. "I think something in me resisted the notion. It just seemed like somebody trying to make sense of the world with a bunch of numbers and angles. But Scripture'd already done that, you know? The problem's already been solved."

"I don't get it either," Eden said. "I think something in me resists, too."

"Yeah, it feels real fake," Ruthie said.

"I'm comforted not to be alone. If Professor Jaye didn't have her errands, maybe I'd sit in on class. Maybe now that I'm older and wiser, these fanciful concepts would take root for me."

"Errands?" Eden said. She looked at me like I'd broken their trust.

"Yes, ma'am," Perry said. He rolled himself off the doorframe and started patting his pockets with both hands. I thought he was looking for another half-smoked cigarette. "This teacher of yours has places to go and people to see."

"I need tampons," I said. I was looking at the twins but saw Perry grimace.

"'Son of man, when the house of Israel lived in their own land, they defiled it by their ways and their deeds. Their ways before me were like the uncleanness of a woman in her time of menstrual impurity,'" he said.

He pulled his white pockets out of his jeans, not finding what he needed. Then, remembering, he stood on one leg like a flamingo and worked a folded piece of paper from deep within his boot. He crumpled it into a ball and tossed it onto my bed like he was shooting a basket. It landed near my chest. He said, "Two points."

"Stop throwing things at me," I said. I intended to project confidence, but it came out whiny. I wanted my gas mask. Without it, I felt naked.

"Well, you haven't invited me into your room and a gentleman don't cross a threshold unless he's been called," he said. "I needed to get that information to you before you hit the open road."

"Just tell me," I said. The twins observed our conversation like a tennis match.

"Let's just say it's life or death," Perry said. "Let's say it's heaven and hell. Let's say if you're using my truck and my gas, then I'll be damned if I ain't getting something out of that fucking excursion."

Roy

After Coop jogged into the gym, I picked a few lockers: Barry O'Dell had a rolled-up *Playboy* I'd already seen; T. J. Palvino had the school's best soccer ball; Rob Torres had his skateboard with the graphic of a robot dog. I debated taking a shower, but worried Coach Delgado would hear, so I just dampened my hair and tried to style it in the mirror. After ten minutes, it only looked drenched. I wished I'd worn the hat Virgil had given me, wished there was one thing I could do to raise my stock.

Because Pastor Joe sometimes subbed for Coach Delgado, I knew it was his off period. I wanted to hear him talk. In his classroom, he was decorating the bulletin board, tacking up richly colored illustrations: Moses parting the Red Sea, Jesus walking on water, David slaying Goliath. His small radio was tuned to the Christian station, a program about Samson bringing down the temple. I recognized the host's voice from the radio my parents had on our kitchen counter. Pastor Joe's back was to me, and when I cleared my throat, he jumped.

"Sorry," I said.

"Roy?" he said, glancing at the clock.

"I'm going to the library. I just saw you in here."

He relaxed. In the past, he'd been summoned when Delgado was sleeping one off in the locker room or teachers needed help breaking up a fight. Now he crossed the room and turned a wooden chair in my direction. He said, "Come in, come in. Sit, sit."

He wedged himself into the neighboring desk, which made him look giant. I thanked him for always remembering Mason in prayers at Calvary.

"You must be counting the days to September," he said. "Your parents, too."

"Yes, sir. We're excited."

"No doubt Mason is as well," he said.

"He called last night," I said, wanting to speed the conversation along. "We talked about all the weird stuff the Lamb believes from the Book of Revelations."

"Revelation," he said. He folded his hands on his small desk. "There's only one, and one's enough."

"I just think he's twisting up Scripture to get with a bunch of girls. I think he's a heathen and huckster and all this stuff about the Wave Sheaf is pure BS. New Light, too. I think if he told his cult to drink the Kool-Aid, they—"

"Where is this coming from, Roy?" he said. "Where are you hearing things about the Wave Sheaf and . . ."

"New Light. He needs virgins to have kids who'll inherit the earth. They're the light. They're what's going to be new."

"Is this something your father is investigating?"

"I was just talking to Mason. I was going to look stuff up in the library."

"In the strictest terms," he said, "the Wave Sheaf would have been the barley, the first fruit to be harvested."

"How does it relate to the Book of Revelations?"

"Revelation," he corrected again. "And who says that it does?"

"Some kids were saying the Lamb did," I said. "We talk about him sometimes. Especially on Mondays, after we've gone to real church."

"Monday morning quarterbacking," he said.

Pastor Joe met my eyes, then shifted to gaze out the window. The light had turned dolorous. I'd pushed my luck too far. Mentioning the Wave Sheaf and everything else had turned the tide of our conversation, and it had dragged him into the undertow of his thinking. I wanted the bell to ring.

"It's probably just more BS," I said. "I'm sure he's just twisting things again."

"An offering," he said, still staring into the middle distance.

"Do what?"

"He might see the Wave Sheaf as a kind of offering. The best of the best being cut down first."

"Like he would sacrifice people?" I asked, my veins full and surging, like I'd almost been hit by a car.

"No," he said. "No, he wouldn't have to."

. . .

After the day's last bell, I hid in a bathroom stall until the school emptied. I wet my hair down again and crossed the field where the marching band was honking through practice. The sun dappled the tops of leaves in gold. In the chill, my wet hair seemed as solid as a helmet. When the buses pulled out, I caught sight of Rosie on Isaac's lap. She was in his denim jacket and looked warm, content. Barry O'Dell leaned out the bus window and yelled at the band: "Y'all sound like elephants trying to fuck!" And then someone—maybe Fat Clay who played tuba—yelled, "Tell us something we don't know, jackwater!" Then Mrs. Berryman blew her whistle and ordered the band to start over. My father had once arrested her husband for driving drunk.

In the neighborhood behind school, I could hear trampoline springs stretching and contracting in Jacob Ternasky's backyard. Jacob could do backflips off picnic tables, and Coop and I envied him more with each one. I wondered if Mason could do flips, if that was a skill you learned in the marines. It was after midnight in Iraq. For a block, I tried to picture my own face and couldn't.

When I came out of the neighborhood abutting the stubble field, the red truck idled on the far side. My instinct was to run, to make excuses for being late, to do everything I could to catch her before she sped off, but I talked myself down. I crossed the field with a forced and flagrant nonchalance. That Jaye had driven so far to meet me when it hadn't even been a day since we'd kissed in a water tower seemed its own miracle.

"I'm sorry I'm late," I said, climbing into the truck.

"You're not," she said and handed me what looked like a chicken-scratch grocery list. "But you are our navigator."

"Where are we going?"

Instead of answering, Jaye just dropped the truck into gear and twisted to check her blind spot. Then she stretched across the bench seat and gave me a kiss like a headbutt.

ON THE LAMB

PODCAST EPISODE 1
GUEST: Professor Eliza Ashcraft
RECORDED: July 2023
Phone Interview

Doesn't polygamy and sex with underage girls sound more like a cult leader than a man of God?
What I can tell you is what I told the FBI and members of Congress during the hearings: From a scholarly perspective, he was not unimpressive. His command of Scripture was sophisticated, original, and substantive. Were his beliefs unusual? Absolutely. As were his practices. But nothing about them can be wholly dismissed as manipulative or deceptive. They fell outside the norms of current Christianity, but in the larger context they were hardly exceptional.

Do you believe he was the son of God?
Certainly not, though he never claimed to be.

But you *were* sympathetic toward him?
Had Dr. Hannah and I been allowed to speak with him, I believe we might have negotiated a different outcome. We could have engaged him in a conversation about Scripture, about his doctrines and goals, that would have confirmed his beliefs were being taken seriously. If that equates to sympathy, then yes, I suppose so.

But you weren't allowed to speak with him?
No. Mr. Cullen requested to meet with us. He wanted to discuss the situation with someone who was conversant in holy texts. But the FBI forbade it.

Why?
They believed we'd be taken hostage.

Roy

We headed south on the interstate. Tractor-trailers and farm equipment crowded the road. Exhausted laborers in the beds of pickups returning from farmland. Jaye kept both hands on the wheel, vigilantly checking all three mirrors. She drove leaning forward, space opening between her back and the seat. She bit her bottom lip. The truck's floorboards vibrated. I'd never been this far from home with anyone except family. I had the intoxicating sense that we were on the lam.

I tried to discern where we were heading based on the chicken-scratch directions, but I could only tell we'd be southbound for miles. I hoped we'd stop to eat, hoped I had enough money to buy her meal. I tried to inventory what I'd bought recently and calculate what was left in my bill-fold. I wondered about her favorite food, if she drank with a straw, if we'd say grace. Jaye scratched her calf with her boot heel. She was wearing a flannel shirt and her hair hung in two thick columns that I wanted to weigh in my hands. I checked my hair in the side mirror and found a bushy half-wet snarl. I tried fixing it without her noticing. I wondered when we'd kiss again. Birds wheeled against the sky.

There came miles of loamy fields, telephone poles and power lines sagging like hammocks. Billboards for rent, a tractor supply yard, a whitewashed church with a jungle gym and marquee listing the Ten Commandments. I'd seen it all before, but beside Jaye nothing looked familiar. Next time I see this, I'll think of her. Wrong. *Every time* I see this, I'll think of her. I sneaked glances at her pale neck, her thighs in her jeans. I reminded myself to stand up straight when we parked.

The truck's antenna bowed in the wind. I studied the directions, afraid I'd be responsible for missing an exit and getting us lost. I still couldn't tell where we were going, but at once I understood it was the Lamb's hand-writing. Words were misspelled. The letters, all capitalized, slanted harshly to the right. The penmanship of a child. I wanted to wad up the paper and chuck it out the window.

"He didn't know you were picking me up," I said.

"Why were you guys even out there?" she said.

"I was there to see a girl I can't stop thinking about. My father was there because he's worried about the Lamb," I said. Then, because I hated sounding sympathetic and because I recognized a chance to impress her, I said, "We had a tip he was making assault weapons. We were looking for evidence."

"So you've been deputized?"

"Sometimes I help with warrants," I said. "It's not a big deal. My father just distracted him while I looked around for milling machines."

"What if you're setting me up? How do I know you're not deep under-cover?" she said, concentrating on the road.

"I wouldn't do that," I said.

"I know, Rodeo," she said. A mass of motorcycles passed and reminded me of a school of fish. "And believe me, if I knew where he hid his diabolic machines, I'd 'fess up."

And, like that, a chaotic swirl of sharp-edged thoughts: If my father arrested the Lamb, the risk of Jaye becoming part of New Light vanished. She'd be spared, and if I was the one who provided the evidence, I would have played a part in her rescue. But to contemplate saving her was to contemplate losing her. If the Lamb was arrested, her mother and the others would either leave of their own accord or be evicted, which would surely send her back to California. It was too easy to imagine being left behind.

"The illegal conversion of Title II weapons is a felony," I said. "If he's guilty, he'd go to prison."

"He's definitely guilty," she said. "And he's definitely got a lot of guns."

"Are they full-auto?"

"English, pilgrim."

"Machine guns," I said. "If he's got machine guns, there might be cause to arrest him. The ranch could be seized and everyone living there would have to vacate the premises. You'd be sent home."

"You'd miss the shit out of me," she said.

"Maybe for a minute," I said.

The Chevy gathered speed. I wanted her to say she'd miss me, too, or that she'd convince her mother to stay in Texas if Perry got arrested. I wanted to tell her about the grenades so she could tell me not to tell anyone else, but we stayed quiet. I was there and not there. I was beside her, and I was years ahead, regretting my decision to burden her with what I should've kept to myself. So I clammed up. She checked her blind spot and merged into the passing lane. Light was thinning, the sky frosting over.

ON THE LAMB

PODCAST EPISODE 6
GUEST: Jim Grant
RECORDED: December 2023
        Grant Firearms
        Waco, Texas

Did he have assault weapons?
See, the thing is, that's a nothing term. It's made up by people who've never bought or fired—maybe never even *held*—a firearm. It's just not in the vocabulary. That's why the first assault-weapon ban failed as policy. That was 1994, the year after everything at the ranch.

Okay, did he have machine guns before then?
Not to my knowledge, but let's be clear: It's not illegal to own machine guns. Not illegal to sell them either. There's not even a state or federal statute against stockpiling weapons or converting them. The rub is you have to register them. That dates to 1934. Congress was trying to get a handle on mobsters who liked tommy guns and sawed-off shotguns. They didn't legislate against the guns; they taxed the owners.

But Perry was buying guns to sell. New, in the box, nothing dinged up or without packaging. For him, it was about money for his church. His theory was that if the gun-control proposals became law, then the price for specific firearms would skyrocket—and he was right! He wanted as many as possible on hand. More inventory, more profit. He bought in bulk.

From you?
From anyone.

Roy

In elementary school, we took field trips to Fort Hood. It was an hour's drive, down by Killeen. One year, Coop made a shoebox diorama with plastic soldiers; his mother still had it displayed on her chipped mantel. The base had been established when the army needed open land to test tank destroyers in World War II; Elvis Presley and Jackie Robinson had lived there. It housed armored and infantry divisions and had deployed more troops than anywhere else for the Gulf War. Mason's war. Sometimes Brent Douglass, the face of Waco news, began his evening broadcasts listing the Fort Hood soldiers who'd been injured or killed. He'd show their DA photos, where they usually looked like they were playing tough and trying not to laugh. If the soldier had died, the dates that marked the short span of his life would emerge as the screen faded to black. Then Douglass would ask viewers to pray for the families and for God to keep watch over the rest of our troops.

Jaye pulled onto the shoulder near the base. A chain-link fence was topped with rolls of barbwire, which made it seem like soldiers regularly tried to escape. A drainage ditch ran between the road and steep berm rising to the fence. I expected the military police to descend at any moment. I was calculating whether it was an asset or liability to be the sheriff's son, trying to figure how my father would react when he got the call saying we'd been detained. Jaye was out of the truck before I could ask what we were doing.

She got a running start and jumped the ditch, but when she landed, she slipped in the mud and caught herself with her hands. I opened my door but didn't close it in case we needed to flee fast. I made the jump so clean I hoped Jaye might compliment me. She didn't.

The setting sun coppered the buildings and cast the foothills in a jagged relief. It was early yet, but the moon was already ascending, a faint finger-print in the east. I couldn't grasp that I'd been in school earlier that after-noon. Jaye wiped her hands on the fence and left the wires edged with mud. The main cantonment was a mile away; the tanks scattered on the property looked like drowsy elephants.

"I thought we were going to see the mammoths," I said. That had been true an hour ago, but I only recognized it now. I also didn't know what else to say and just then I wanted to say anything.

"Mammoths?" she asked.

"They found fossils. It's a prehistoric graveyard. It's supposed to be really rad," I said. *Rad* was a word I imagined people using in California. The letters tasted false.

"Or really sad."

"Elvis was stationed here. And Jackie Robinson," I said. "It's the largest base in—"

"Is this where Mason was?"

I liked her using his name, liked her asking a question that had always hovered in my family. If my brother had enlisted in the army, there was no guarantee he would have been sent to Fort Hood despite its proximity. It might have ensured he'd do his basic training at Fort Sill or Benning. But my mother was hurt he'd chosen the marines and hadn't even given the army a chance to keep him close. I said, "Fort Hood is an army base. Ma-son's a marine. They're better than the army, tougher."

Jaye took in this information. I could feel her committing it to memory.

"Perry thinks they're going to attack him. He thought they'd be out here, like, practicing," she said. "Surprise: wrong again."

"It would just be the state police," I said.

"After you guys left yesterday, he crammed everyone into the chapel and held court about Babylon. You're proof that what he's been squawking about is coming true."

"I am?"

"You, your father, the government, anyone not of the chosen," she said. "He gave me a cute little pistol."

"What kind of pistol?"

"Probably the kind that shoots out a little flag with 'sucker' printed on it."

"You believe in the Seven Seals stuff?"

"I don't know what I believe," she said, like a confession, like an apology, like she'd been hoping I'd never ask.

"Me either," I said, like an invitation, like a pledge, like I'd been waiting to tell her all along.

"You're good at jumping ditches," she said.

"You're not," I said.

"Jerk," she said. It seemed we'd kiss soon. I wanted to put my arm around her or take her muddy hand. I tried to sense if she was waiting for me to make a move. Then, unbidden, this thought: *Everyone thinks I'm somewhere else.* I couldn't tell if I felt emancipated or untethered.

"I envy people who believe in the big things," she said. "I think life would feel like a puzzle, an easy one without too many pieces. I guarantee you they're happier than you or I have ever been. I want to believe that I believe in something."

"I'm happy now. I'm happy with you."

"What if I'm just seducing you to get information about your dad? What if Perry's pulling the strings, and once I get what he wants, you never see me again?"

"I don't think you are," I said.

"What if that's what you're supposed to think?"

"I think you're happy when we're together," I said because I wanted it to be true.

"Well shit, pilgrim," she said. "Shit."

Jaye

The night coned our headlights as we left Fort Hood. At some point, the truck started dragging to the left, so I had to keep yanking the wheel to avoid running off the highway. On either side of us the darkness extended almost without interruption. Here and there a dimly lit house, the lamps on a truck's roll bar. I wanted to scream.

And I wanted to say things: That Roy didn't need to keep fussing with his hair because it looked cuter when he left it bushy. That he should've kissed me when we were beside the fence. That he should tell me to pull over and kiss me now. That I was terrified—of getting lost or breaking down or running out of gas or being clipped from behind—but feeling his weight on the bench seat calmed me, emboldened me. I wanted to say I'd look for the milling machines. Mile after mile, I kept hoping to hear my voice. He did, too, I knew that much. Sitting there like a wounded little soldier. Like a precious martyr.

Amidst the road noise, the rattling windows and floorboards, he was forming an opinion of me. My sulky mood, the glowering silence I couldn't shatter, even the way I kept mopping the defrost from the windshield with my sleeve—none of it cast me in the light I wanted. Maybe he saw me as a tease, a coquettish shill. Maybe he thought the drive was a pathetic waste of time or, worse, evidence of my devotion to Perry. Or he wished he was beside that Rosie instead, a girl I'd never seen but who linked up in my head with the perky cheerleaders back home, a girl who could probably jump a ditch and land on her ballerina toes. Probably he was thinking this was a lousy first date, crafting how to say it'd be best if we didn't see each other again.

Drive, I thought. Just drive. Blow past the exit. Keep heading north.

When he twists toward you all confused, wink. Take his hand to your lips and kiss his knuckles in the dark, a mystery and promise. When the gas needle edges toward *E*, stop to fill up and then merge back onto the highway until it's time to break west. Drive through the night like before. Stop for hot chocolate and candy. Watch sunup in the desert. Wrap him in your arms. Shiver together. Say we're going to the Salton Sea or the Colorado plains. Hold him close while morning colors the earth. Say you'll never betray him. Believe him when he says the same. Say it was a bad takeoff back at the ditch, your foot slipped, and you're really good at jumping things. Say you'll show him. Wink again, all seductive. Touch your face to his. When he asks if that's the pistol in your pocket, say, That? No, I'm just happy to see you.

But no words came. The whole scenario stayed unspoken, undone, useless as lint. Behind the wheel, I trembled and tried to believe I was just cold. When his exit came up, I took it like a plain fool, like a devout pawn, steering us toward lives that were only meant for smoke.

Roy

Jaye dropped me off at my corner, acres away from my house. She never shifted into park but offered me her hand anyway. I knew I shouldn't try to kiss her. Her mind was elsewhere, and I could feel her wishing me away so she could catch up to wherever her thoughts had gone. I stood in the road until her taillights faded. I waved the whole time.

The flood lamp over our porch doused my mother in brassy light. She sat on our top step wearing my father's Eisenhower jacket like a shawl. She was absently petting Panda, the cat eddying around her hand.

"Hi, Mom," I said when I was close enough.

"Hi, sweet potato. Did you make headway on your project?"

"A little," I said. Then, hoping I'd have another chance to see Jaye, I added, "It's hard, though. We'll probably have to do more this week."

"Y'all can work here, too," she said. Panda lay on her side, licking her paw. My mother moved her fingers as if swishing water, trying to get the cat's attention. She said, "I haven't seen Coop since the gun show. I can fix y'all snacks."

"I'll ask him."

Panda lolled onto her back. My mother looked at the cat for a long while, then said, "You might be getting a brother soon. You're not going to like that, are you?"

"What kind of brother?" I asked.

"The wiener dog variety. Raybourn might be fading. He has a daughter up in Michigan but seeing him before he finds his reward doesn't seem a priority."

Somewhere in the dark a dog was yipping. It would bark, then await a response. When none came, the dog started over. Panda twisted so my mother could scratch the places she wanted.

"I saw Pastor Joe today," I said. "He asked about Mason coming home."

"And you had your little dream about him," she said. I didn't know what was weighing most heavily on her—things with Mason or my father or Mr. Raybourn and his daughter and dog. I could tell she wanted to talk about something. Or not talk about it. Maybe she knew I was lying about the project with Coop or she'd found the grenade in my closet. I was aware of a tingling in my ears, a fuzzy ringing.

"What was it like at the ranch?" my mother asked. "Up close, I mean. What trouble did y'all find out on the range?"

"I scraped my leg on a wagon. I rinsed it with peroxide when we got home."

"No one can say you're not a nurse's son," she said. The dog barked, waited, barked again. "Did you get a feel for their lives? Did it seem better or worse than you expected?"

"Better. Everything is dingy and slapped together, but no one was ugly to us. Everyone had a job to do. They were building things and painting a water tower. The horse stables looked good. Boards had been replaced and reinforced. You can tell they care about them."

"A regular utopia," she said. "A little slice of heaven."

"I don't know," I said.

"I know you don't, sweet potato."

A cold wind shook through the bare branches down the street, then made its way to us. Panda stood and cameled her back and slunk into the dark yard like someone had summoned her. Eventually my mother set her tired eyes on me.

"I'm sorry about Mr. Raybourn," I said.

"Were you able to use your little tools out there?"

There it was, sudden and solid: the thing she'd been hoping to say or hoping to avoid. My heart went stone still. I said, "Do what?"

"They were on your bed this morning. I didn't recognize them at first, but I figured it out when I found all the locks in your pillowcase. I'm guilty of nosiness."

"Oh," I said. I couldn't tell if I was in trouble, what she knew or didn't, if she'd looked in my suitcase. "Mason sent them to me."

She looked serene, like it confirmed she'd raised us right. "I figured."

"I open stuff, but I don't steal anything. I just look around."

"I figured that, too," she said. "You've always been good. And curious."

"Dad doesn't know about them," I said.

"No reason that should change," she said.

"I took them to the ranch, but most of the doors don't have locks. Some doors didn't even have doors."

The night hollowed. Everyone I could think of—my father, Mason, Coop, Jaye, even the Lamb—would have handled this moment better. My mother said, "Are they hard to use, your special tools?"

"It depends on the lock," I said. "Some pop right open and others take forever. It's like—"

"Teach me," she said.

"You want to learn how to pick locks?"

"Not really," she said. "But I'd still like for you to teach me."

The smell of chimney smoke being hauled off by night wind. The feel of the driveway cold under my feet. The dog somewhere in the dark, silent.

"Am I missing something?" I said.

"We're all missing something, sweet potato. All of us."

Jaye

The milling machines nettled me all night. The possibility of evidence so damning, so incontrovertible, and so close squashed any chance of sleep. Just find one, I thought. Then I'd alert my pilgrim and he'd alert his hard-eyed father and when Perry, handcuffed and crestfallen, asked who had ratted him out, I'd raise my gas mask and take a bow. I imagined how Roy would visit me in California, how we'd mope when each trip started winding down, how on one of those trips, we'd drive to Vegas and exchange vows in front of Elvis. Nothing seemed impossible then, nothing too romantic or dangerous.

That I didn't know what a milling machine was meant nothing. That I didn't know if I should look for something the size of a toaster or phone booth mattered not. As my mother slept, I strategized where to search. While they sat through their Tuesday studies, I rooted through the gym's closets, the plywood lockers at the gun range, the cupboards in the kitchen. I roamed pastures, checking the rusted-out cars and the old fridge they used for target practice. I went to the garage and looked for tools I couldn't name. I peered under Perry's bed, behind his TV, in his hideous drawers. There were stray sticks of gum, guitar picks and strings, loose bullets, a dog-eared photo of a lady that might have been his mother. I planned to crumple it on another visit.

The following morning, while Big Lyle logged inventory in the small gun room adjacent to the mess hall, I sauntered in with an air of annoyance. My gas mask was on my head, the empty filter compartment extending forward like a miner's light. I took my time poking around, as if I were in the market for a few new weapons. All I saw were racks of rifles, rolls of targets, boxes of ammunition. There were a few Bullet Bibles, but the room was cramped and narrow, lacking anywhere to conceal secret machines. Big Lyle made the space feel even smaller, like we were shoulder-ing beside each other in a pantry. He stunk like a homeless man, which stirred in me a peculiar protectiveness. I considered casually saying, *Hey, you haven't seen our milling machine, have you?* but didn't want to impli-cate him. Giant as he was, he reminded me of a child who'd been unfairly scolded, a foreigner stranded where no one spoke his native tongue. He skulked from the room with his head down, like he'd found me indis-posed. I wondered if he was on his way to sell me out. When no one showed, I understood there was nothing worth finding in that room.

Because you had to cross through Lawrence's office to reach it, I'd as-sumed the large gun room was a no-go, but that afternoon his desk was empty. Standing outside the door, I could hear Turtle and Olga fussing over prices. They were leafing through military surplus catalogs at the util-ity table. If not for the walls of shotguns and their army jackets, they would've looked like a pair of grandmothers clipping coupons. They had a napkin piled with vanilla wafers between them. Olga plucked one from the stack. She wasn't wearing her dentures so I could see her pale tongue when she opened her mouth. She gummed the cookie slowly, relishing the sweetness. Turtle flipped the page in her catalog, chewing. Crumbs fell into her lap. She didn't notice.

With her eyes still fixed on the catalog, Olga said, "Take a picture, it'll last longer."

My impulse was to hasten back to our room, but Turtle said, "Or scoot in here and help us polish these off before the counselor catches us."

I crossed through Lawrence's office, passing his orderly desk, his tufted swivel chair, his shelf of drab law books. I'd snooped in there plenty. I'd called my father collect from his rotary phone, heavy and black as a car battery, and I knew all the gun show cash was in a lockbox in the desk's bottom drawer. The twins believed Big Lyle carried the key on a chain around his neck. I'd daydreamed about bringing the lockbox to Roy and letting him go to town with his tools. Maybe instead of money, the box held a milling machine.

In the gun room, Olga dropped a cookie into my palm. Neither she nor Turtle looked at me. The cookie tasted stale, brittle, delicious. Turtle gave me another.

"Where *is* Lawrence?" I said.

"He's jawing with the boss in his quarters," Turtle said.

"More like his nickels." Olga snickered, taking another cookie.

"Because of the sheriff's visit?" I said. I wanted another cookie, another twenty cookies.

"Because he fancies himself special," Turtle said and licked her thumb. "Because he gets bored sitting at his big boy desk, chirping with bill collectors. And, yes, I reckon because of that handsome sheriff. I'd like to sop him up with a biscuit."

"How much did we pay for ball caps last year?" Olga said.

"Too much," Turtle said.

"I think the price dropped some. There's some camouflage ones."

"No more hats. If it don't say Stetson, ain't nobody in Texas putting it on his head."

"We could start selling milling machines," I blurted. "I heard people asking about them at the last show."

Now Turtle set her eyes on me, arched her eyebrows. A beat later, she turned back to the catalog. She read a few descriptions in silence and flipped the page. She brought the catalog near her face to examine small print. She reached blindly for another cookie. She hummed while she chewed. Olga sniffled.

"There's two of y'all and two of them wafers left," Turtle said.

Olga nudged the napkin toward me. I took both and ate them together. I said, "Or if we already have a milling machine, we could offer to—"

"I was instructed to get you a filter for that mask," Turtle said like she'd just remembered. She tossed the catalog onto the table and levered herself up and crossed the room. It took energy, time. She withdrew a box from a cabinet and pulled out a plastic spool. Given how directly she waddled over, I understood to surrender my mask. She unscrewed the filter's compartment and inserted the spool with surprising dexterity.

"Thank you," I said.

"You best run along. These old birds got chores to do, and no telling when Lawrence'll shuffle back."

"Milling machines . . ." Olga's tone was sour, dejected.

"I was just—"

"Repeating what you heard," Turtle said. "That's no sin. But usually that's the sort of question asked by somebody with his mind already made up. Ain't no grace there. Ain't no mercy. Whoever's doing the asking usually deserves to be knocked into next month."

ON THE LAMB

PODCAST EPISODE 8
GUEST: Rhonda "Turtle" Tilly
RECORDED: February 2024
          Gatesville Correctional Facility
          Mountain View Unit
          Gatesville, Texas

So *did* y'all have milling machines?
No offense, hon, but I'm going to skip that answer. On the advice of counsel and such. I'm getting up before the parole board next year. If that pans out, then you come take old Turtle out for a nice supper, Chili's or Sirloin Stockade. I'll talk your ear off.

How many times have you been up for parole?
Ten so far.

Why do they keep denying you? Virgil was released shortly after the hearings.
Before the ranch, I put a woman down. Her man, too. I'm not proud of it, but I know it was part of God's design. Shortly after I did my deed, I used my last pennies on a bus ticket to Waco. Farthest place I could afford. Went straight from the station to Loan Star Pawn. Which is where I met the Lamb. We were both milling around the parking lot before they opened. He wanted to see if they'd bought any new guitars, and I was hungry and broke, aiming to sell my pistol. A pretty little derringer, chrome and mother-of-pearl. We got to talking, and he took me to the Garden of Eatin' for breakfast. I told him my truth over flapjacks.

What was his response?
He said, "Welcome home, girl." Then he asked for my pistol.

Jaye

Charity lay on my top bunk when I returned to our room. She was on her stomach, her cheek mashed over her knuckles and a Bible open in front of her. With her knees bent, her toes grazed the ceiling. She appeared bored, absently flipping pages, and aggrieved, like she'd been up worrying about me.

"The Lamb's a prophet," she said, her eyes still on the Bible. I'd rarely heard her speak, but her voice was always lower and fuller than I expected. "He believes in redemption and community."

"He also believes rivers used to turn to blood and donkeys could talk," I said, repeating what I'd overheard at meals. "And he believes it's cool to break up marriages."

"So did Jesus," she said. She twined and untwined her ankles. "Every disciple chose to leave his family behind. You have to love Jesus more than anyone else. That includes your husband and offspring and parents."

"Perry isn't Jesus," I said. "I'm not even sure Jesus was Jesus."

"Belief's hard. You have to trust God's truth will cure your pain. We live by faith not sight."

"You sound like a zombie," I said.

"What's a zombie?"

Oh, shut up, I thought. I resented having to peer up at her and how naturally she'd taken over our room. Now that she was here, as shameless as a teacher's pet, I realized I'd been expecting her for months. That she'd sought me out not to beg for help but to flaunt and campaign for Perry was hardening me. I peeked into the hall and under my mother's bed. I said, "There's no one else here. You don't have to talk like this."

"Talk like what?" She flipped pages in reverse.

"Charity," I said, a plea. "I know why you're here. It's okay."

"He told you?"

"He didn't have to."

"Well," she said, squinting at her Bible. "I still should've come earlier. I should've welcomed you. I think I was jealous, and jealousy is one of the sins that killed Christ. Please accept my apology."

"What are you talking about?"

"The Lamb thinks you need friends."

"Friends," I said.

"You're lonely. You need a community. You need girlfriends."

"I don't need shit," I said.

"Everyone needs things. Even God."

"I thought God was all powerful. What could He possibly need?"

She closed the Bible, raised her eyes to me for the first time. When she smiled, a petite blue vein crimped under the flesh near her temple.

"Us," she said. "He needs us."

Roy

Any lock can be picked. Warded, pin tumbler, wafers, combination—it doesn't matter. Pin tumblers are the most common, so learn those first. You need two tools, a pick and a tension wrench. In movies, crooks can pop locks with a single instrument but that's fantasy. Even if you use a bounce key tool, you'll need a mallet to knock the pins into place. It's noisy, cumbersome, unnecessary. Just get a pick and a wrench. The pick lifts the pins to the shear line and the wrench turns the plug. Different locks require different picks— hooks, rakes, half-diamonds, balls, double-sided. Hooks work well with pin tumblers. Most locks have five pin columns. Each consists of a spring, a driver, and a key pin. Insert the pick on top of the keyway and make sure there's enough room for the tension wrench underneath. The more tension you apply, the harder it is to feel the pick. You need way less than you'd assume. The weight of three butterflies.

That's what I would have told my mother if I'd gotten the chance. I'd spent most of Wednesday distilling what I knew into clear lessons. While I wanted to impress her with my knowledge, I also thought she might find some solace in the tedium of picking. And I thought it might make her feel closer to Mason, that the three of us were forging a bond even when he was still away. I also worried that once she saw how accessible the world was, how porous its boundaries could prove, she'd force me to toss my tools in the garbage.

But Wednesday was also the day Mr. Raybourn wouldn't eat. My mother called my father at his office to say she'd stay until another nurse could relieve her late in the evening. The afternoon was raw-winded. My father fetched me after school, then drove to Church's for fried chicken and yeasty rolls and then out to Raybourn's small cabin to drop off supper for my mother. I offered to run the bag inside—I was still hopeful I'd get to talk with her about locks, and I was trying to think of a quick lesson I could impart—but my father said this one was above my pay grade.

He stayed in the house so long I wondered if Raybourn had died. An old swing set in the backyard had gone to rust. There were plastic bowls for his dog's food and water, a few toys; everything paled by years of murderous sun.

When my father lowered himself back into the Bronco, he reversed from the driveway and started up the road in silence. I could see the ghosts of our faces reflected in the blackened window. We passed the sprawling low-slung oak that I remembered wanting to climb as a child.

"Raybourn's kin are driving down," my father said. "They know what this is."

"He has a daughter in Minnesota I think," I said.

"He's unrecognizable to me. He's being withered from inside out, but he used to be a bastard. He put a rattlesnake in the cab of Lalo Garcia's truck. There was a stretch where he was friendly with the backseat of this truck. He's taken a swing or two at me over the years."

I twisted to look in the backseat as if I might find something belonging to Raybourn, a handkerchief or billfold. My father said, "Your mother just sees him as a patient."

"It's like the World War II birds," I said.

"Do what?"

"Those birds that flew secret missions. We all have secrets," I said. "I won't tell Mom."

"It's not a secret, detective. She's just choosing where not to look."

For the next couple of days, my mother came by the house if another nurse could spell her at Raybourn's. When I got home on Friday, she was in our kitchen listening to her radio and drinking coffee. The scent of buttermilk soap sweetened the air. Mr. Raybourn had started eating again, a surprise for everyone. His daughter had gotten stranded in a storm up north; she'd try again when her father began his next fade. My mother said, "I watch television with the volume down or pet his little dog. I ought to write Mason a letter, but I'm trying to keep my spirits up. Mr. Raybourn deserves that."

I wanted her to ask for a lock-picking lesson, wanted her to know how the hours just fell away when you were working a difficult lock, but I also didn't want to be the one to bring it up. I said I hoped she wasn't too sad at Raybourn's.

"You've got a soft heart, Roy," she said. "You've got a nice outlook."

Then she gathered her things and told me to give Panda some tuna and was gone. She didn't know we'd run out of tuna the week before.

Everything felt adrift for me, and probably my father, too. I washed dishes and took out the trash and made my bed and Jaye never called. Without knowing when I'd hear from her, I was reduced to myself again, the version I'd been before the gun show—closed off, small-feeling, easily crushed. My father read his *Farmer's Almanac* or case files he brought from the office. He paid bills and tapped figures into his adding machine, stopping occasionally to review the long paper ribbon unspooling onto the floor.

We ate frozen dinners or canned soup. We sat at the table and listened to radio weather reports or sermons. Maybe we were thinking the same thing: that with Mason gone and my mother at Raybourn's, we'd been halved. Even our phone, which had rung so often in the weeks prior, had gone largely dormant. The heater droned. We rolled bath towels and wedged them at the bottom of our front and back doors, but still had to wear flannel shirts over our thermals. I couldn't imagine how cold Jaye was with the wind cutting through those shoddy walls.

I watched for signs my mother had told him about my locks or that he'd discovered the grenade in my suitcase. Each night I went to bed shocked I'd held my tongue. The longer I stayed quiet, the more imminent my confession seemed.

Then, at our small table on Sunday evening, shortly after we'd sat down with bowls of tomato soup and said grace, I blurted, "What's going to happen with the Lamb?"

My father's spoon was halfway to his mouth. He put it back in his bowl. He wiped his mouth with a paper towel and wadded it up. Each of us had taken two, maybe three bites. Our bowls were still full, but he gathered them and emptied them into the sink. It wasn't like him to waste food; he regularly finished what my mother and I didn't eat. I thought I'd be sent to bed without supper.

He opened the fridge and light puddled around his boots. He looked like a mechanic inspecting an engine, listening for misfire. He brought out a carton of eggs and a package of bologna. He lit the stove and rummaged in a cabinet to find his skillet, not the stainless steel one my mother preferred, but the heavy cast-iron one that I had, for no reason, always associated with his time in the service. I had the sense I was watching him behave the way he did when none of us were around.

Scrambled eggs, fried bologna. The kitchen filled with the smell of heat and melting butter, the snap of popping grease. Panda trotted into the kitchen and wove through my father's legs. He flipped slices of bologna with a spatula. The meat glistened and darkened and curled up on the edges like pie crusts. My mouth watered.

"Scare us up a couple of plates," he said.

I did, then I dropped four pieces of bread in the toaster. My father nodded once, pleased. I poured myself a glass of milk, then without asking, I poured him one, too. It felt significant and mature, maybe the most adult thing I'd ever done. I tore off two paper towels, folded them into triangles, and pinned them down with flatware.

The food was hot, over-peppered, greasy. I loved it. We ate without a word, but my father never resorted to turning on the radio. He cut a small square of bologna and fed it to Panda from his fork. Then I did.

"Your grandfather used to sprinkle gunpowder on his eggs on hunting trips," he said. "He claimed it gave him energy. I prefer pepper."

"I do, too," I said. "We should have it more often. I bet Mom and Mason—"

"To answer your question, detective," he said, "Perry's going to get himself killed. Him and all of those knuckleheads, none of them are long for this world."

ON THE LAMB

PODCAST EPISODE 1
GUEST: Professor Eliza Ashcraft
RECORDED: July 2023
            Phone Interview

If the FBI worried about the Lamb taking y'all hostage, weren't they just looking out for you?
Dr. Hannah and I remained confident he would've welcomed us. The mind that saw Scripture in the way Mr. Cullen's did would never think to hurt someone approaching him as a peer. Approaching him as an adversary is a different story. He'd see any defense as justifiable based on his beliefs.

He still could've taken you hostage.
Hostage is an interesting word, and of course it came from the FBI. They referred, almost exclusively, to the people in the compound as hostages, but nothing indicates he was holding them against their will.

Meaning you believe members of the group were free to leave.
I do.

I know Dr. Hannah shot—died by suicide. Do you think it was because of what happened in Waco?
This interview isn't about Dr. Hannah.

Of course. So if the believers were free to leave, why didn't they?
Because they were being held hostage—

You just said they weren't—
—*by* the FBI. Mr. Cullen wasn't blocking the door, the government was.

If members in the group were entertaining doubts, then they'd need only look outside to confirm his prophecy. If the FBI wanted to unmask him as a false prophet, then simply stand down. Expose his views as baseless. If he's telling everyone there's going to be an assault, then call off the assault.

What did they say?
They said our consulting services were no longer needed.

PODCAST EPISODE 4
GUEST: Special Agent Kent Unrue (retired)
RECORDED: October 2023
              Phone Interview

Kent Unrue here. I was an FBI negotiator for twenty-four years. I ran lead in Waco. I had direct and daily communication with Mr. Cullen, Mr. Bernthal, and others at the ranch.

Your goal was to negotiate a peaceful end to the standoff?
Hundred percent. The objective was to extract the hostages.

I've spoken with Dr. Ashcraft. She doesn't think the term *hostage* applies here.
Dr. Ashcraft is a college teacher. With all due respect, her opinions on law enforcement terminology are as uninformed and unhelpful as mine would be on hemming a skirt. She was called in to help decipher Mr. Cullen's ramblings about Armageddon.

But they weren't allowed to meet with Cullen?
We were working to get people out of the compound, not put more inside.

Were they allowed to speak with him?
As I said, we brought in the academics to interpret what we didn't understand. We needed to determine if there was anything to be read into his babbling, anything that might offer insight into his plan. That analysis didn't require conversation.

Do you think granting them access would have changed anything?
Negative. They would have fallen under his spell, or he'd have used something about their communication to leverage another delay. He was a manipulative sociopath with delusions of grandeur and a messianic complex. He liked to pretend he was a soldier, a rock star, a big deal with the ladies, but he was just a kook.

So why not pull back to disprove his prophecies?
The United States government does not retreat.

Jaye

I was in the stables cleaning the horses' hooves when I spotted Kanaan climbing the hill. On his hands and knees, he wore a no-longer-puffy jacket with a fur-lined hood. He'd reach ahead of himself and grab a clump of grass, then leap forward as if scaling the face of a cliff. I'd never seen him alone before. I worried he was covered in sticker burrs. I cross-stepped down the hill, my eyes darting between my feet and the child below, convinced I was going to turn my ankle and tumble onto that poor boy.

Then I saw Senny giving chase. At least it wasn't Charity. A week had passed since she'd appeared in our room. I'd been avoiding her to spare both of us the indignity of pretense or another goading conversation. Senny was halfway up the hill with her long cotton skirt gathered in one hand. She waved with her other arm. Big, slow arching gestures—all in vain because her son's back was to her. When she saw me, she shook her head and laughed, a failed attempt to disguise her mortification, and I saw how desperately she wished I hadn't been the one to witness this. I regretted my gas mask being on my head and not my face. Kanaan continued climbing. He grunted as he got higher. The sounds were exaggerated; he might have been parroting noises he'd heard adults make when they exerted effort. With his hood over his head, he appeared bigger than he was, more substantial, but the broad hill confirmed his smallness. A beetle on a ten-story building.

"Ahoy there," Senny said, embarrassed. Now she had the hem of her dress in both hands so she could watch her steps. "Ahoy, ahoy!"

A wind knifed up from the flatland, hard and splitting cold. We both turned our backs to it. After it passed, Senny put more space between her steps, like she was bounding over puddles. She wasn't wearing a jacket.

My hands had gone into my pockets, but when I touched the derringer, I yanked them out. With Kanaan nearby, I wished I'd left it in my room.

"We were settling into a children's study," she said, "then next thing I know Junior's scampering up the hill! I guess he hadn't seen enough of you lately."

Seneca was the only person who called him Junior, and I'd started thinking of it as her own glum badge of honor. The boy was taking a break on the hill, sitting on his haunches, inspecting a rock or leaf. He knew we were after him. He was taunting us.

"He probably just wanted a field trip," I said.

"No, he's partial to you. Sometimes he'll ask, 'Where's Aunt Jaye-Jaye?' If we're on a walk, he picks things up and says they're presents for you. I hope you like twigs and clumps of moss."

She wasn't lying, I could feel that. Sometimes Kanaan and I played peekaboo in the mess hall or hide-and-seek in the barracks. If I spied him away from Perry, I stalked from behind and scooped him up and said, "Up, up, and away!" His loud, feral laugh that always turned to tiny hiccups. The smell of his skin like confectioners' sugar.

On the hill, he was turning over whatever he'd found with his fingers. After a moment of consideration, he raised it to his nose. Immediately he scrunched his face and hurled the object so hard, so far, he toppled forward. Dung, I thought. He sputtered his lips and shook his head and resumed his ascent.

"I could drive for the field trip," I said. "We could go see the mammoth fossils. When I was little, we went to the La Brea Tar Pits."

"His father'd skin us," she said. She'd gained enough ground to let down her skirt. Kanaan continued upward, ignoring her. I was yards away, parallel to them. We inched toward the top at Kanaan's pace. Below, Virgil was heading toward the garage. Senny said, "The Lamb thinks fossils are a test."

"A test?"

Kanaan laughed as he crawled, a form of invitation into his private game. I wanted to run over and swing him around until he got the hiccups. His mother kicked him in the butt. He giggled each time.

"A test of faith," she said. "Tempting people to choose science over Scripture."

"He doesn't believe in dinosaurs?"

"He believes in God."

"Do *you* believe in dinosaurs? I mean, you're a teacher," I said. We'd almost reached the top of the hill. The horses were chewing hay I'd strewn for them. Kanaan stood upright and trudged to the crest. I wondered what he'd do if I showed him a picture of a T-Rex. I wondered if Senny knew where the milling machines were.

"I try to focus on what the Bible says," she said, though it sounded like she was repeating something she'd memorized. "I don't know Scripture the way I should, but I don't remember any mention of mammoths."

Up near the stables, Kanaan dusted off his pants and clapped his hands together like he'd completed an arduous job. This composed little man! He romped onto the new deck Big Lyle had built around the tack rooms, then leapt into the dirt. I made eye contact with him and suddenly we were locked in a smirking stare down. When I finally spread my arms wide and arranged my mouth in an O, he barreled over to hit me with a clumsy sideways tackle. We wrestled. After we rolled around a couple of times, I situated him in front of me. I sat on the deck with him on my lap. His back against my chest. He'd gotten hold of my gas mask and started inspecting it.

Senny had her arms crossed and her chin tucked against the wind. Her long hair lashed her neck and face; she had to pull strands out of her mouth like she'd walked into a spiderweb. She longed to be anywhere but here. Not because of the cold, but because of me. She would hurry back to the children's study and tell Gina and Sage how, on top of everything else, I was now trying to take her son.

"So who's running the test?" I asked. My arms encircled Kanaan's waist. His belly rose and fell with his breath. "Scientists? The devil?"

Senny's demeanor brightened. Her eyes lit with mocking pity. She said, "God."

"God," I said.

"Exactly," she said. Kanaan was trying to figure out how to put on the mask.

"God planted a bunch of fake pachyderm skeletons in Texas just to mess with you," I said. "That's what you're saying?"

"He put them there to teach us. So we'd learn to tell truth from falsehood."

Down by the mess hall, Olga intercepted Virgil; they were disagreeing about something as usual. I buried my nose and mouth into Kanaan's jacket. I couldn't smell his skin through the fabric, so I pushed his hood down with my chin, pressed my cheek to his thin, cool neck. After turning the gas mask every which way, he figured out where to put his face. I leaned back and helped him adjust it. I baby-talked to him. Senny watched and seethed. Even though I liked her, I didn't mind her seeing me as the sordid ingénue, the would-be slutty stepmother. I cinched the straps as tight as possible, all cooing encouragement. No matter how I worked them, there was still enough give that the mask would drop forward, the filter Turtle had given me hanging to his chest like a trunk. The mask was made for adults, not a little boy, and try as we did, we weren't going to be able to make it work. The form was never going to fit. You should remember that.

Roy

Because my father's words kept looping in my head, Monday was nothing but panic, a plague of serpentine and hideous fears: Jaye calling and choking out that she'd been shot; the believers drowning themselves in the ponds at the ranch; my mother finding the grenade in my suitcase and showing it to my father and it exploding between them. At school, I endured the drone of students and teachers, the hallway claustrophobia between bells. I asked for hall passes and wandered aimlessly. On classroom doors were posters for Young Life and pep squad fundraisers, art class drawings and paintings rendered in mockingly bright colors. The case of sports trophies seemed frivolous indulgence, so I picked the lock and laid each one face down.

Every time I passed the pay phone at the front of the school, I tried to gather the nerve to call my father. I paid strict, nuanced attention to the way the adults carried themselves, searching for any hint they'd caught wind of a tragedy. It was only after gym class—which I spent on the wooden bleachers, faking another stomachache—when I realized I'd assumed my father's prediction was happening today. There's still time, I thought, and it allowed me to breathe some. I dillydallied on the walk home, doubling back once, then twice, hoping Jaye might pull beside me in her truck. The Holy Roller crept by in his van. "Repent now," he crowed through his staticky sound system. "Repent, my brothers and sisters. Repent, my children, and free yourself eternal!" It seemed a sign. I decided to hand over the grenade when my father got home from work.

But when I reached our street, he was already at the house. My grandfather's truck was in our driveway, too. *Motherfucker,* I thought, and ran. I threw open the door and found the men at the kitchen table with papers spread in front of them. My father's eyes raised toward the bird clock. Grandpa Huey said, "Sheriff on your tail?"

"I think I thought something happened," I said. My voice wobbled.

"Granny needed her sewing machine tuned up, so I hauled it to the Singer shop," Huey said, coming to greet me. He pulled me to his chest. "Then I swung by the office and convinced this youngster to play hooky."

His answer came so easily, and seemed so plausible, that I knew he was lying. It dropped a scrim between us. On his shirt, the smell of hay dust, of my grandparents' shadowy house, of Mason somehow.

Behind him, my father gathered the papers they'd been reviewing; he was hustling as if someone else needed the room and he'd kept them waiting. The files were wavy from years of inattention and humidity. I couldn't read anything on the folders but understood they belonged to Huey and were the actual reason he'd made the drive in from San Saba.

My father moved to the stove. He clicked on a burner and set the cast-iron skillet on it and took out the carton of eggs and package of bologna again. Huey pulled a grip of flatware from the drawer and passed it to me. I started setting the table. If our house had felt lopsided in my mother's absence before, now it tilted in the opposite direction. I thought Huey and my father had probably been at the table all day and had lost track of time and my arrival had been a disappointment. The bird clock read a little after four o'clock, two hours earlier than we usually ate.

"Is Mom coming?" I asked.

My father dropped a piece of bologna into the skillet. He said, "She's staying put for now. She'll holler when her stomach starts growling."

"Raybourn's always been stubborn," my grandfather said. "No reason to die differently than you lived."

"You knew him, too?" I said.

"Sheriff knows everybody. Or at least everybody that needs knowing. Everybody you don't want to know."

My father cracked eggs into the skillet. He poked at them with the spatula and dusted them with pepper. The sizzle got louder then quieted like distant dwindling applause. Huey was taking mason jar glasses down from the cupboard. He wore a sheathed hunting knife on his belt. He talked about life in San Saba—the pecan harvest, the petty politics of a small town, a friend whose memory was failing, how he'd lifted a rock and found a tangle of scorpions.

When he was done, I said, "Did Dad tell you we drove out to the ranch?"

A look passed between the men, furtive as a snake, before they returned to what they were doing. Huey said, "He was catching me up when you rolled in. Little Perry's given folks something to chew on, hasn't he?"

"Chow time," my father said.

The three of us sidled past each other in the tightened kitchen. Huey handed me a plate. My father lifted the skillet from the stove and dished out steaming eggs and meat. I imagined this was how my father and grandfather had eaten when they were in the service, how Mason did, but it had never happened in our house. The day's rules were being rewritten.

Huey said grace, then we dug in. The eggs had a crust of black pepper and just then I *did* remember him making them that way when Mason and I used to stay overnight, telling us we weren't old enough to eat them with gunpowder. The memory hadn't surfaced when my father mentioned him before, though I couldn't say why. At that time in our lives, cause and effect seemed out of order, subject to whim and coincidence.

"Eggs aren't part of supper often enough," my grandfather said. "If it were up—"

"When do you think everyone's going to get killed out there?" I interrupted.

Another look snaked between the men. There was nothing furtive in their eyes now, nothing quick. The bird clock ticked, and the dingy lace curtains hung on either side of our window. Huey took another bite and chewed for a long time, then wiped his mouth with a napkin the way my father did. My father laid his knife and fork on his plate. I thought he might throw out our food again.

Huey said, "Perry's a loose—" just as my father said, "I shouldn't—"

Huey raised his palms: *I surrender.*

"I shouldn't have said that, detective," my father continued, taking up his fork and knife again. He cut a bite of bologna, lifted it to his mouth. He nodded at the taste; had anyone else cooked it, he would have paid them a fine compliment. I knew all of us wished I hadn't mentioned the ranch. He said, "Perry's bullheaded. He's riling up some men he shouldn't, but we've yet to find any laws being broken. That all of this could simmer down is still in play."

"But you don't think it will," I said.

"What I think doesn't matter. All that matters is what I can prove."

"What if we'd found milling machines? Or if he had, like, grenades?"

"He's a loose cannon," Huey said. "He thinks he's smarter than he is and thinks God's on his side. Those aren't winning hands."

A rush of lightheadedness, an assault of memory: the ballast of the grenade, the impact of my fall, the smell of her unwashed hair. I was burning up in my clothes, embarrassed and fearful, feeling besieged by the tyranny of choice, the double-edged blade of confession. I said, "But if you could charge him with something, if you could prove he had grenades, would it make—"

"Hey," my father said. It was the voice he used when some drunkard was swinging at him, when my mother fell to pieces over Mason being gone. He said, "Hey, it's okay now."

Grandpa Huey regarded me aslant. I couldn't tell if he wanted to squeeze my shoulder or flip the table.

"Hey," my father said again, warmer. There was misplaced relief in his voice, and coward that I was, I hid behind it. He said, "Perry's out there and I'm right here. We're all safe now. Nothing's going to happen to anybody who matters."

After supper, Huey helped with the dishes and told a story I'd heard before, the one about arresting a man who smuggled parrots and boa constrictors up from Mexico. The kitchen light was on, but no others; night had claimed our other rooms. Panda strutted in and started wetting her paw with her sandpaper tongue to clean her face. When Huey shut off the tap, we could hear the scratchy sound of her licking. I felt like the men were prolonging the chores on my account. I said I had homework and excused myself.

Through the wall, I could hear their voices. It was easy to envision them drinking beer and returning to Huey's files. I tried fitting myself into that scene, figuring how it'd be for me to take my seat among the men. I could see their eyes dilating as I stripped the burlap from the grenade. I could imagine my father strapping on his gun belt, Huey lifting his .30-06 from the rack in his truck, the lightbar spinning red atop the Bronco as they sped off.

And maybe that would have happened, maybe I would have kept my promise to myself and handed over the grenade if the phone hadn't rung.

My mother, I thought, calling for supper. I was anxious to talk. But it wasn't her, and the voice in the receiver wiped away my best chance to make some difference.

"Tell me," Jaye said, "what's a girl got to do to see some dinosaur bones around these parts?"

ON THE LAMB

PODCAST EPISODE 6
GUEST: Jim Grant
RECORDED: December 2023
            Grant Firearms
            Waco, Texas

Did you sell him grenades? Milling machines?
I'm not aware of him having either, but all I can say for certain is we had nothing to do with any such transactions.

So was the raid warranted?
I don't think so.

You sound unsure.
Look, do I think he was up to no good with girls? Probably. Hassie and I talked about it, made sure he was never alone with Sabrina. But maybe I convinced myself I was just an overprotective father. He was a paying cus-tomer, a good-ole-boy nice guy, and you want to extend folks the benefit of the doubt. That's part of being Christian. And Texan. He was buying more every month. That's my cross to bear. In hindsight, I think he was probably guilty of statutory rape. That's how they should've gotten him.

Then why don't you think the raid was warranted?
Because the Bureau of Alcohol, Tobacco, and Firearms has no jurisdiction over statutory rape.

Roy

We talked every night that week. During evening Bible studies Jaye would sneak into the Lamb's bedroom—his *quarters*, she'd say with an eye roll I could hear—and dial my number. My phone usually rang around ten, but I was stationed on my bed by nine, at once bracing for her not to call and cataloging what I wanted to say when she did. All day, every day, I strategized how to come across as funny and brave. Then, inevitably, every word and joke I'd planned evaporated when I picked up the receiver. My voice was girlishly high—with excitement, nervousness, relief that she'd called, that something awful hadn't occurred since the night before—and the syllables tumbled out too fast. I mispronounced words. And yet each call was a balm, her voice allaying numberless terrors, like that moment when Panda appeared on our porch after days away. Oh good, you're back, I was so worried.

Or maybe we talked for two weeks. In my memory, the days refuse to sort themselves out. We described our rooms to each other. We listed what had happened since we'd last hung up, then she'd usually offer something about her childhood (she had once won a ukulele on a cakewalk) or her father (she'd loved occasionally getting up early and throwing his paper route with him) or California (she'd always wanted to visit the Salton Sea). She'd say how happy she was when the horses recognized her trudging up the hill toward their stables, how they ambled over, shy and majestic, nickering in a way that sounded like laughter. I told her about picking into Live Oak Mall and how, when I was younger and felt insecure about being the sheriff's son, I'd lie to my classmates, claiming I'd gotten licks in the principal's office or was grounded at home. "My angel who invents trouble," she said.

The longer I went without mentioning the grenades, the harder it was to imagine bringing it up. When Jaye said she'd searched for milling machines but couldn't find any, I thought it might suggest that Perry toed the line more than we believed—maybe he also invented trouble! When she told about what she feared was happening with Charity and how Virgil condoned it, I almost retched. Every night, we talked until she heard people leaving the chapel. I paced to stay awake or opened my window to fill the room with frigid air. I started sleeping through algebra.

On Thursday night, she said Perry had found her in the mess hall at supper, complimented her hair, and suggested she start combing it out straight and wearing it down. He'd said Valentine's Day was coming up on Sunday and seeing her hair like that would be his gift. She told me she might hack it all off. I didn't think I should admit how much I loved her hair, so I just suggested she pile it under a hat. I spent the rest of the week imagining her hair cut in a high-and-tight like Mason's.

I went to Coop's on Sunday. His house was a cottage with a cramped pink-tiled bathroom and three dim bedrooms and too much furniture; his grandmother had brought all of hers when she moved in. I never remembered how small it was until I was in the hallway stepping aside or backing up to let his mother or grandmother pass. The floors sagged. One leg of the kitchen table was shimmed with an old *TV Guide*. The air-conditioner grills were furred with dust. I found myself trying not to see things as I made my way to Coop's room.

He had a twin bed and a boxy television and a chest of drawers that he was incrementally covering with radio station bumper stickers. One wall had the triangular YIELD sign we found after a storm and another had taped-up pages from magazines—*Soldier of Fortune, Circus*, the *Sports Illustrated* swimsuit issue.

We watched a kung fu movie he'd recorded. We rewound the tape to replay fight scenes. We imitated how the hero bowed before and after every battle, a slow forward bend at the waist, palm over fist in front of his chest. When the movie lulled, it occurred to me I should've gotten a card and present to give Jaye next time I saw her. I wondered how to make tonight's call more romantic. Coop was standing up now, swinging his nunchucks. He'd gotten a lot better with them. His routines were so much faster and more fluid that soon I understood he'd invited me over because he wanted to show off. It was a little after eight o'clock. On television, a villain was training for a fight by kicking a piece of bamboo with his shin. The wood was sheened in blood.

"How much longer is this?" I asked.

"Two more fights."

"I need to get home. My stomach's thrashed," I said.

"Just watch the next one. He tags this dude with a wheel kick you almost have to slow-mo to see."

"Next time," I said. "Don't record over it."

"Are you having diarrhea?"

"Do what?"

"You're always sick to your stomach. I figure you're either pregnant or suffering the squirts."

"Oh," I said. "There's just a lot going on."

The phone rang and Coop made a show of answering fast, swiping the receiver mid-ring like it amounted to a martial arts feat. I started for the door. I knew he'd be petulant and I'd feel guilty later, so before stepping into the hall I turned and did the kung fu bow toward him. When I righted myself, he extended the phone.

"For you," he said.

ON THE LAMB

PODCAST EPISODE 11
GUEST: Tom Carroll
RECORDED: May 2024
        Phone Interview

What do you mean, if you'd "called Johnny Law sooner"?
The police, the feds, the cavalry. Who the shit knows if it would've made a difference, but these are games your head plays. You wonder if the dominos would fall a different way if you'd pushed the first one with another finger. You wonder what small thing would've worked. All that butterfly flapping its wings and changing history horseshit. It tears you up.

But you did call the police? The sheriff?
He had my wife and daughter. I called anybody I could think of.

What did he say?
The sheriff? He said I had to file a missing person report. I said they ain't missing, dude. I know exactly where they are and who they're with and I've got a hell of a good idea of what's going down and it ain't legal. I said my daughter's calling me from the shithead's phones. I said, this is an easy win for you, an open-and-shut case, so get your happy ass out there and restore my family.

ON THE LAMB

PODCAST EPISODE 12
GUEST: Sheriff Elias "Eli" Moreland (retired)
RECORDED: July 2024
                Waco–McLennan County Central Library
                Waco, Texas

Tom Carroll called more than once. I understood his position, but no crime had been committed in the state of Texas. His daughter was in her mother's custody. A parent has the right to take a minor on an extended vacation. I told him to call the truant officer in their school district.

What if he believed she was in danger? Or being groomed to marry the Lamb?
CPS filed report after report saying the children were safe. The marriage angle is no better. At that time in Texas, if you had parental consent, you could be married at the age of fourteen. For all I knew, Mrs. Carroll drove her daughter to Texas to be Perry's bride.

I can empty that ashtray, Sheriff Moreland.
Call me Eli. I'll use the cup.

Roy

Jaye had called my house earlier than usual and my mother gave her Coop's number. She was at a pay phone downtown. Perry was sitting in with a band at the Chelsea Street Pub, and she wanted me to meet her for Valentine's Day. Coop watched me on the phone; he was skeptical and envious, as shocked as I was, so I tried dragging out the conversation. I asked if she'd cut her hair, and she said, "Come find out if you're so curious." I felt kinged.

Chelsea Street was downtown, five miles away, maybe more. Even in Coop's narrow room, I could feel the temperature dropping. I imagined huddling with Jaye for warmth. I tried to think of the fastest route, shortcuts, obstacles to anticipate. When I asked Coop to borrow his bike, he said, "You can ride on the handlebars."

"You don't have to come," I said.

"Either I go, or my bike stays here," he said. "Ladies' choice."

Air so cold it shocked my lungs. Wind that smelled not just fresh, but wholly new.

I rode on Coop's handlebars with my legs dangling on either side of the front tire. When we coasted into downtown, the streets were barren. The mechanical tick of the chain cranking over the sprocket sounded like something being hoisted up from a great depth. Traffic lights flashed yellow. The reflection of us on the bike floated across the night-mirrored storefronts, and my head swam a little in the empty intersections. It was the same disorienting sensation as walking on a stalled escalator. We passed the shoe repair place and St. Vincent de Paul and the tobacco shop whose sweet moist odor had always saddened me. The buildings looked so desolate in their darkness that the desire to pick into them never formed. Everything too still, too quiet.

Then, a whistle. A single long note with two loops in the middle, issuing from an alley behind an antiques mall.

"That's her," I said.

"If not, I have my nunchucks."

Coop carved a wide U-turn with the bike. I spread my legs like wings for balance. I felt giddy as a child.

Jaye appeared in the street, sauntering toward us. I wanted to spring to the ground but didn't trust myself not to face-plant on the asphalt. Coop pedaled and the bike gathered speed and I worried he'd force a skid or pop a wheelie to impress her.

But he slowed to a smooth stop. On the ground, my feet were blocks of ice.

"Boys," she said, a greeting. She hadn't cut her hair after all; it was in a long single braid. She wore her WORLD'S GREATEST FATHER sweatshirt and white jeans and her hiking boots with red laces. I wondered what Coop thought of her, what she thought of him. The idea of them meeting made me feel like I could lose both with a single wrong word from any of our mouths.

"Sorry we're late," I said. "We—"

"I'm Coop," he said, thrusting his hand forward. "I thought he'd made you up."

"Why?" she asked.

"It's a common tactic. Invent a girlfriend who goes to a different school or lives in another county."

She squinted at Coop, then turned to me with her head cocked. She said, "Are you spreading rumors, tarnishing my reputation, calling me your girlfriend?"

My ears, and then my whole face, went hot. Coop watched me, mischievous and interested and a little apologetic. I said, "I want to."

"Want to what?"

"Say you're my girlfriend. Call you that, I mean," I said.

Jaye raised her eyebrows: *Well?*

"I'm sorry I haven't had time to get you a Valentine's present," I said.

"I don't care about that," she said.

"I don't either," I said, not sure if it was true.

Jaye was still looking at me, waiting. I didn't know what I was missing. I turned to Coop.

"Ask her to be your girlfriend, sweet potato," he said.

"You never told me you were friends with a genius," she said.

"I'm in advanced algebra," Coop said. "Did he tell you I'm starting a band?"

I found Jaye's eyes and said, "Will you be my girlfriend?"

"But of course," she said and spun on her heel. She started walking away, while Coop and I stood frozen. Over her shoulder, she said, "Now let's go find those old bones."

Her truck was parked in the lot between Chelsea Street Pub and a derelict red-brick hotel. The once-grand building had been boarded up my entire life. I vibrated as we walked the empty street. Coop rode ahead on his bike, showing off, doing bunny hops and donkey kicks. I could hear the band playing and a man crooning, though I couldn't make out the lyrics or tell if it was the Lamb. I didn't care. Let him sing, I thought. Let him wail. Jaye took my hand. Our arms made a pendulum between us. I forgot the cold.

Coop lifted his bike into the truck and then, to my surprise, jumped onto the tailgate to ride in the bed. Jaye drove through the abandoned streets, heading west. When I offered directions, she said, "Your job is to sit there and look handsome." Our windows were up, but I hoped Coop had somehow heard. I watched him in my mirror, his squinting eyes and whipping hair. We went under the highway overpass, and he absently reached up trying to touch it. He had no shot, but I thought the attempt defined him in an essential way. I felt guilty for wishing he'd stayed home.

When we arrived, the mammoth site was locked. Coop swung himself out of the truck bed and made a big show of scaling the wrought iron fence. The building was still under construction. A crane and pallets of lumber and concrete pipes so tall we could have walked through without crouching. Everything was gray in moonshadow. Above us, the stars burned clear and bright and close. Like bullet holes, I thought. Jaye leaned against the truck, regarding the gauzy smear overhead. I stood beside her, awed not by the stars but that we were together. I hoped Coop saw that we were holding hands again.

From the top of the fence, he said, "Aren't y'all coming?"

"I didn't know it wasn't finished," Jaye said. "I thought we could look through windows and see giant tusks and rib cages."

"That's what's inside!" Coop said. "I bet we can see if we climb—"

Because I sensed that Jaye didn't want to risk it, I said, "There's an alarm. Sammy gets a call from a dispatcher in Omaha. He arrests two or three people a month."

"Why are people in Omaha concerned about a worksite in Texas? Maybe the fossils are from aliens! Or Bigfoot or—"

"Or maybe I wanted to get my pilgrim into a secluded area and commit unspeakable acts," she said. Her tone was distracted, noncommittal. My blood flared electric. "Maybe I wanted to relieve him of his virginity on Valentine's Day."

"Gross," Coop said and jumped down. He landed in a ninja crouch and immediately started swinging his nunchucks. The night seemed to pant.

The mossy smell of mesquite trees wrapped in cold air, the whirring of insects unseen. I tried to think of something to tell Jaye, something flirty or edgy to urge the conversation forward. In the moonlight, her neck looked fluted. Her skin so pale it seemed forever untouched by the sun.

And then, for the first time in my life, I realized the mammoths had likely drawn some of their last breaths right where we stood. Before I'd regarded the massive bones with the same fleeting interest I had in arrowheads. Now, I remembered the scientist doing her presentation at our school and saying the animals had been caught in a flood. Most of the skeletons were juvenile, which meant it had been a nursery herd. Based on how the skeletons were positioned, the scientist believed the few adults, all but one of them female, had encircled the young in a failed effort to shield them. I imagined the lives of those ancient creatures, how they'd roamed the prairies and grown taller than houses before lumbering into the ravine. Then I saw the water roaring from the Bosque River and overtaking them, drowning them like flies as they fought to save their bloodline.

Coop finished his nunchuck routine and did his kung fu bow. He hung the weapon around his neck and said he liked Jaye's sweatshirt.

"I stole it," she said.

"My dad's gone," he said. He lowered himself to sit cross-legged in the parking lot, then, unprompted, he described how his family had gone to sleep on a Friday night, but on Saturday morning, his father had vanished. No note, no nothing. His mother had only ever said his father needed to clear his head and he'd come back to his senses—and his family—soon. For years, Coop had asked about him—why he'd left, if she'd heard from him, when she thought he might return, *if* she thought he might return—but the story never changed. His grandmother moved in with all of her furniture. He avoided any movies with upstanding or missing fathers. His mother plucked all the man's photos from the albums and tossed them in the trash. She pawned her wedding ring. Coop didn't know if the man was still alive, let alone in Texas, but he'd hallucinated him a few times over the years, conjured him behind the wheel of a car on the freeway, in line at a feed store, climbing into a city bus. When Father's Day came around, he'd go to the drugstore and rip the cards in half.

Jaye and I listened without speaking. Coop took his nunchucks from his neck and absently rubbed them together as if starting a fire. The night's chill was settling between the trees. I'd never heard Coop talk in this subdued tone, and I was assailed by a violent tenderness. That there would be aspects of his life I didn't know. That he'd had experiences without me. That his view of the world might be broader or darker than mine—all of it felt like judgment, like failure. Just then I could imagine nothing worse than my having taken his pain for granted. I arranged what I hoped was a stoic expression on my face. I didn't want him to see my feelings welling up.

The bullet-riddled sky seemed lower now, each pinpoint blazing. I had the hope, then the conviction, that we'd see a shooting star. Coop was saying he believed his mother and grandmother knew more than they let on. Maybe his father had left for another woman. Maybe he was in prison or dead. I'd heard him spin those theories, but when we were alone, his voice was bold, and his father's fate was a mystery he'd relish solving. The father-shaped hole in his life distinguished him, strengthened him, made him interesting. Tonight, with Jaye, I understood I'd failed to fathom how deep the hole was and how he'd been working to climb out for years.

"They think they're sparing me," he said. "But it feels like I'm being punished."

"What if they don't know where he is?" Jaye said. "What if they're being punished, too?"

Coop picked up a pebble and skipped it across the parking lot.

"The stars look like bullet holes," I said.

Jaye raised her eyes to the sky, then Coop did. We stared in silence, all three of us. I thought I heard an airplane but couldn't find it.

"Has your mom gone out with other men?" Jaye asked.

"She mostly just watches TV with my grandmother. Sometimes the three of us play cards. My grandma cheats," he said. He skipped another pebble. "Sometimes I worry his leaving has cracked me in ways I can't see. I worry I won't notice what's wrong with me until too late."

"You're taller than I'd pictured," Jaye said. "You're going to grow into a strapping, handsome man. You'll have this mystery in your past. Women'll line up to try to fix you. Take it from my mother."

"I'll keep you posted," he said, chagrined. A swirl of pity and envy in my chest, the ironic but not unfamiliar desire of wanting to trade places with him.

"And, pilgrim, you're wrong," she said. "The stars look like lace, something gorgeous a bride would wear to a midnight wedding."

ON THE LAMB

PODCAST EPISODE 9
GUEST: Anonymous ATF Agent (retired)
RECORDED: March 2024
                  Phone Interview

Why start a podcast thirty years later? Just for the anniversary? Because podcasts are all the rage? Need to blow some money as a sponsor?

I lost folks in the fire. If I talk to enough people, I'm hoping I'll understand.
Hope in one hand, shit in the other. Tell me which one fills up first.

What about ATF having no jurisdiction over child abuse, or the idea that the warrant was invalid?
It's not so uncommon, is it? Bring someone in on one charge to pave the way for another.

But it's not illegal to own machine guns if they're registered. That goes all the way back to the 1930s.
Exactly. Al Capone went down on tax evasion.

So the weapons charges were the way in because that's where you had jurisdiction? But how can you charge him for owning weapons that are legal?
Owning automatic weapons is different from manufacturing them, which is what we had reason to believe he was doing. Hand grenades are illegal.

Did he have grenades?
According to the mailman he did.

Did you find any at the scene after everything ended?
Who'd you lose in the fire?

You didn't answer about finding grenades.
Ask the FBI. Once those swinging dicks took over, we were denied access. Who'd you lose?

Friends.

Roy

We drove back downtown and parked in the same spot from before. In front of the pub stood a loose scatter of men and women smoking. A few glanced our way, vaguely intrigued, then lost interest. After Coop lifted his bike out of the bed, he went to shake Jaye's hand again, but she batted it aside and brought him in for a hard squeeze of a hug. I stepped away to afford them privacy; I wanted to appear princely.

My lips tingled. My nose dripped. The ripe stench of the dumpster, of motor oil on asphalt. I ambled in the parking lot, listing toward the music. It got louder when someone opened the door, then softened by degrees as it closed.

"You can't know that for certain," said a woman in front of the pub. Her tone was ominous, forceful. "There are contingencies, Virgil."

I ducked behind the dumpster. If I crouched, the space underneath afforded me a clear view of the group. I recognized the woman as the one who'd been walking beside Virgil in the pasture. One man had been behind the Lamb when he spoke with my father at the ranch. Two others were familiar from gun show booths. They seemed agitated. They had, I thought, stepped outside to discuss a subject that required more privacy than the bar provided, but whatever Virgil'd said had derailed them. I wondered if any of the women were Jaye's mother. I stood up, afraid they'd catch me on the ground.

Jaye came up behind me and slid her hands into my coat pockets, rested her cheek on my shoulder. Coop was biking home. My hands found hers in my pockets. Our fingers braided into the same fists. In my memory, everything is obvious, laid out like tobacco curing in the sun. I remember cigarette smoke on a whistling night wind, the new odor laying over the already familiar rankness of beer-soaked garbage. I remember the tickle of her hair on my neck, errant strands that had slipped from her braid. I wasn't worried about when Jaye and I would kiss again or what Coop would say next time I saw him or if I should say anything about the grenades. We were in the dark, and I closed my eyes. For a few minutes that Valentine's Day, we stood together as defiant as stars on a cold night, and it was almost possible to believe the trouble was behind us.

But, of course, I also remember the Lamb's voice, how his was the face I saw when I opened my eyes.

"'Woe to those who deeply hide their plans from the Lord, and whose deeds are done in a dark place,'" he said. He was leaning against the dumpster in a casual slump. The lenses of his amber-tinted glasses reflected a streetlamp. "Isaiah 29:15."

"Hi, Perry," Jaye said. "I want you to meet Royal Moreland."

He turned his gaze to me, slow and tilted like a praying mantis. He wore a western shirt with silver piping and tight jeans, a hole fashioned over one knee. Jaye squeezed my fingers. He said, "I know little Rodeo. Know his daddy, too."

"Oh, right," Jaye said, her cheek still on my shoulder. I could feel her jaw moving. "They came to visit."

"The sheriff and I chewed the fat while little Rodeo scampered off and didn't give me a chance to say a proper goodbye."

"I was looking for the horses," I said.

"No excuse for poor manners," he said, shaking his head. "No excuse for disrespecting your host. If you were mine, you'd feel the rod."

"He's not yours. He's mine, and if anyone's going to spank him, it'll be me. We're lovers."

The Lamb laughed, a laugh that started thin and bitter but swelled into a hammy cackle that demanded everyone's attention. I could feel Virgil recognizing me.

When Perry quieted, he pushed himself off the dumpster with his shoulder. He shook his head, dubious. He slipped off his glasses. Part of me expected him to hand them to Virgil before he bum-rushed me. He fogged the lenses with his breath, wiped them clean with the hem of his western shirt. He took his time. The group by the curb watched his every move. I'd never seen him speechless, unable to even trot out a verse from Scripture.

Finally he said, "Then I'm rightly sorry to bust up your date on such a special night, but we need to load out and let these heathens run off. Their precious TVs ain't gonna watch themselves."

"I'm giving Roy a ride," Jaye said.

"Not tonight you aren't."

"It's too cold for him to walk," she said.

"He can call 911. He can put that thumb in the wind and take his chances on a good Samaritan, but there ain't no more room in my truck."

"Perry, come on, it won't take—"

"Enough," he snapped.

"I can walk," I said. "It's not too far."

"See? Listen to little Rodeo," he said. I was happy Coop wasn't there; I wished he'd never left.

"Fifteen minutes," Jaye said. "I'll be back in fifteen—"

"Tomorrow," Perry said. "Give him all the rides you want tomorrow. Right now it's time to say your farewells. Right now I need to get home and put that lonely mother of yours to bed."

ON THE LAMB

PODCAST EPISODE 11
GUEST: Tom Carroll
RECORDED: May 2024
        Phone Interview

How often did she call you?
A couple times a month? I do remember she called two nights before the raid. He'd embarked on one of his all-night Bible-thons. She was too smart to buy that shit, so while they were getting worked up, she snuck up to his room and called. Valentine's 1993.

How did she sound?
Like herself. Maybe more talkative? She told me about her beau. I guess a father's supposed to be bent out of shape about that, but I liked that smile in her voice. I told her I looked forward to meeting the young man. She thought I'd like him. She said she loved me, and she'd call me when she got another window.

And?
And what? And nothing. That's it. That's all she wrote.

ON THE LAMB

PODCAST EPISODE 10
GUEST: Virgil Bernthal
RECORDED: April 2024
           The Chapel of Light
           Waco, Texas

What was the Lamb's reaction after leaving Chelsea Street that Valentine's Day?
Furious at first, but that gave way to a resignation. I told him there'd been agents in the pub, and I'd heard them talking about a big operation. They didn't mention the Lamb or the ranch, but it perked up my ears. His, too. He'd weep for a couple of miles, then laugh for a couple of miles, back and forth the whole drive.

Because?
I think it brought everything home, confirmed what he'd been preaching. Probably a part of him had hoped his visions would prove wrong. Another part had to feel vindicated, though. Happy, too, maybe. He knew there'd be blood and suffering and loss of earthly life, but glory would follow. Ignoring the signs would do no good. He knew he didn't have long.

Until?
The end. Or the beginning. The beginning of the end. I don't know how to say it, really. I'm not a smart man. That night, there was a sense that things had commenced. A clock was ticking backward, and its hands were moving with an awful quickness.

Part Three

The Black Horse

February 17, 1993

Jaye

L ater we would learn the government didn't notify the hospital. No rescue vehicles awaited, no fire trucks. Over a hundred agents were dispatched for the warrant service. They came in three gooseneck cattle trailers with tarps strapped over the tops to keep drivers from seeing the armed and helmeted battalions inside. Later it would come out that the tarps had, in fact, attracted attention, and some drivers—and their children, heading to school—had even waved. The agents stuck their tongues out, silly and smiling. Later, we'd learn that, unlike the hospital, the local press had been alerted. A few agents carried small video cameras along with flash-bang grenades and AR-15s. Internally, the raid was called Operation Primetime because they hoped footage would be picked up by national media. A thrilling display of heroism, a spectacle of moral and tactical might, a do-over for fiascos in Montana, Idaho, Jonestown. At least one agent, shot through both knees, was driven out on the hood of a Dodge like a dead buck. Later, the camera footage would be lost before anyone could review it. Later, a lawyer for one of the slain agents would testify his client had retained his services the day before the raid to draft his will, just in case. Later, *much* later, another agent would adopt a pseudonym and self-publish a paperback book submitting that members of the tactical team had been drinking at Chelsea Street on Valentine's Day night, and Virgil had overheard them discussing their strategic plan and fed that information to Perry who then began preparing for war.

Roy

That morning, the muffled sounds of my father's stirring elbowed into my sleep: water pushing through the pipes in the walls, the first heave of the heater, the punch of his croupy coughs from the previous night's cigarettes. Eventually I heard his voice, forgoing any effort to stay quiet, and understood I wasn't dreaming. He was on a call in our kitchen. I ferreted through my sleep memory for any racket of a ringing phone but found nothing, which meant someone had paged him and he'd dialed out, which meant there was an emergency.

I clicked on my lamp and dressed in clothes from the day before. I parted the curtains to see how the world looked when I was usually sleeping. Our house was wrapped in silver fog, dense as cotton.

In the kitchen, my father was buckling his gun belt. He unholstered his Colt Python and checked the rounds in the cylinder and, with the barrel angled toward the floor, squinted at the adjustable front sight and the bead of lime-green phosphorescent paint he'd dabbed there to help aim in the dark. On the table were boxes of ammunition. His shotgun leaned against his chair.

"Back to bed, detective," he said, still eyeing the sight.

"Why aren't you eating? Why aren't you making coffee?"

He took up his shotgun, the 12-gauge I'd always been afraid to shoot because Mason had said its recoil would put me on my ass. My father began pushing shells into the chamber with his thumb.

"School's canceled," he said. "Snow day."

"It's not snowing."

"Lunch meat's in the fridge," he said. "Cans of chili in the cabinet. I'll be back by suppertime. Or your mother will. She did the overnight at Raybourn's."

"Back from where? Where are you going?"

"No TV," he said. He patted his pockets to make sure he had everything. "No radio. If anyone calls, let the machine get it."

"Why won't you tell—"

"Enough, Roy," he said. "That's just enough now."

As soon as he left, I went for the television. The multicolored test pattern was still on. I expected the phone to ring. I moved from one room to the next, peering through the windows, expecting to see I didn't know what. I checked to make sure the grenade was still in my suitcase. A swath of sputtering rain passed through before the fog turned opaque with the sunrise. When the early news aired, the stories focused on the weather.

When the doorbell rang, I yelled.

"Turn to Channel 3," Coop said. He pushed past me like he needed to use the toilet. His nunchucks were in his back pocket. His bike lay in the yard, the tires still spinning.

"They're just crowing about the fog," I said.

"Not for long," he said. "Guarantee you that."

Jaye

ut in the chapel that morning, instead of "crediting Virgil for the information," Perry said he'd been visited by a vision of tribulation, of an imminent battle, of grave and virtuous sacrifice. "'Do not fear what you are about to suffer,'" he said. "'Be faithful unto death and I will give you the crown of life.' Revelation 2:10." He instructed the women and children to gather weapons and bring them to the men. They carried as much as they could—the women handled the guns; the children toted cartons of ammunition like boxes of crayons—but had to make multiple trips. The men stayed behind, discussing strategy and imploring God for strength and loading rifles with shaky hands. Once they were sufficiently armed, Perry led the group in a rambling prayer. His arms were raised, palms toward the ceiling. He swayed. He grinned. He shed tears. He ordered the women and children to get to their rooms and take cover.

I was eating waxy slices of cheese in his room, his *quarters,* debating if I could call my pilgrim before he went to school. A messy fog had settled over the lowlands, which made me feel once more like a lighthouse keeper. When I saw trailers clattering toward the property, I assumed it was another one of Perry's money-grabbing schemes. Cows? I thought. Really? The trucks idled outside the locked gate, all rumbling engines and purling exhaust. I imagined them as cargo boats, navigating curtains of tufted mist to deliver livestock. No one on the ranch ate beef—it was banned like jewelry and textbooks mentioning Darwin. Maybe he planned to start a dairy or trade the herd for more guns.

"Mooooo," I said. "Mooooo."

A man swung down from the passenger seat of the first rig. He wore a bulky padded vest. He was dressed in all black, ironically obvious against the fog. With a pair of bolt cutters, he clipped the gate's chain as effort-lessly as snipping a rose. It flopped open like someone shrugging their arms in defeat. Then, one after another, the rumbling engines dropped into gear and the trailers advanced while the man swung open one of the gates. He didn't have a chance to get to the other one before the second truck plowed through and crumpled it. As the trailers roared up the long driveway, dozens more black-clad men spilled out. Like someone had kicked an anthill. Goggles and helmets and pants tucked into combat boots. They carried rifles with scopes thick as baseball bats. They posted themselves behind trees and fanned out in an elaborate, almost elegant choreography. Every barrel aimed our way. Oh, I thought. Right. This.

ON THE LAMB

PODCAST EPISODE 9
GUEST: Anonymous ATF Agent (retired)
RECORDED: March 2024
                Phone Interview

I was in the rear of the second trailer. Before we breached the gate, our CO was talking to the agents. After each exchange, he'd do something to their necks. It took him a while to get to me. When he did, he asked for my blood type. I told him and he dabbed his finger in an inkpad and wrote it on my neck. That had never happened before, and I promise you it hasn't happened since.

Roy

Coop had been in first period when Coach Delgado waved Mr. Wilson out to the hall. "Wilson just kept shaking his head," Coop said. After class, he'd staked himself outside Pastor Joe's room and heard the first reports coming through the AM radio on his desk. Coop lit out while the other kids shuffled ignorantly to second period.

The Price is Right had been interrupted by Brent Douglass at the newsdesk. Douglass never did early broadcasts unless events were dire or celebrity-related, tornados or Nolan Ryan visits. Over Douglass's left shoulder hung a BREAKING NEWS graphic. He said, "We'll get a live feed up soon, friends. We're on top of this."

"What's happening?" I said.

"Gunfight at the Kinky Corral," Coop said. He was crouched a few feet from the TV. "Showdown at the Raunchy Ranch."

My legs hollowed. I leaned against my father's recliner. I said, "The Lamb?"

"Being led to slaughter as we speak," he said.

The live feed kept crapping out. We glimpsed Lova Flores—all makeup and hairspray and shoulder pads—in front of a hazy field but her mic failed. Then the signal dropped. The haze could've been fog or gunsmoke.

Douglass received information in his earpiece: The Bureau of Alcohol, Tobacco, and Firearms was in the process of serving federal warrants, one for the arrest of Perry Cullen and one to search the grounds for illegal firearms. There were unconfirmed reports of gunfire.

I thought I might pass out. All I could think of were the grenades. In the shed, my closet. Now my silence, my cowardly and self-serving indulgence, had led here. The vicious consequence of—what? Love? Indecision? Nothing seemed pure or clean. Was it too late? Couldn't be. Had to be. I went to the bathroom. I bit the inside of my lip as hard as I could to focus myself. I opened the tap and prayed aloud.

When I returned, the BREAKING NEWS graphic had been replaced with a photo of Perry: tweed blazer, wide-knotted tie, tinted aviators. His hair parted in the middle, shoulder-length, feathered. He looked at something out of frame, smirking. The photo had been taken at the courthouse when he'd filed a request to change his name. Now the photo was stamped with harsh red letters: UNDER FIRE.

"Is he dead?" I asked.

"Not yet, but I wouldn't get too attached to him."

"Have they said anything about the casualties? Or anything about—"

"Easy, hoss," he said. "You were gone two minutes. You missed Douglass saying the live feed sucks and then the pest control commercial where the lady sings, 'Buenos noches, cock-a-roaches.'"

"I just think it's sad," I said, then wished I hadn't.

"Sad that some wingnut is getting his due?"

"No, everyone else," I said.

Coop twisted to regard me. He peered in my direction like I'd gone blurry and when I came back into focus, he didn't appreciate what he saw. He said, "If they're dumb enough to fall for his act, we're better off without them. Sometimes you have to thin the herd."

Jaye

I bolted from Perry's room. I worried I'd trip down the stair-
well, so after the first couple of steps, I hurled myself over
the rest of the flight. Landed with a thud. A pile on the floor.
Heaved up. My elbows and knees pumped like pistons. The whole time a
voice bellowed outside through a speaker. Measured and monotone, the
voice of God. *This is a raid. This is the Bureau of Alcohol, Tobacco, and
Firearms. We have a warrant for the arrest of Perry Norman Cullen. Surrender immediately. This is a raid. This is the Bureau of . . .* Norman? I
hadn't known he had a middle name but knew he'd be embarrassed by
that information getting out. Knew he'd be furious they used his real
name, no doubt to belittle him. Good, I thought. Even as I scrambled
toward the chapel, even as the cattle trailers rumbled close, I took pleasure in more of Perry's ordinariness being exposed. Norman. I wondered
if my mother knew, if Charity did, Roy. Norman was the name of a kid
from my elementary school who ate his own dandruff. When I rounded
the corner that would deliver me to the chapel, I kicked my own foot and
slammed my shoulder into the wall and bounced off.

But then, a wave of people barreling toward me—dark open mouths
and screaming eyes and twisted arms clawing and clawing like a mass of
bodies sliding down a cliff. Sage and Senny and Victoria with little Kanaan
scooped up and crying in her arms. No, not crying. Wailing. His feet swam.
I longed to cradle him, to fold myself around him, to position my body
between his and everything else. The wave overtook me, pushing and
shoving and spinning me and sending me back the way I'd come. Ruthie
and Turtle and my mother. Screaming and screeching, louder than the
blaring voice of God, and someone praying behind me. *Please Jesus, protect us, the children, come help if you can.* The funk of fear-sweat, of egg

breath, coffee breath, of oatmeal and unemptied buckets of fresh excrement. An elbow in my sternum. A shoulder to my cheek. *We have a warrant. . . .* The hallway hot and too narrow and Turtle slumping and my mother hoisting her up and someone saying, "Where is he?"

"He *told* us," Turtle said. "He said this day would come! And mercy me, here it is!"

"He answered the door," Sage said. "Virgil's there, too. It's some mistake."

"It's beginning," my mother said. Drippy, soiled wonder in her voice.

We were running, lunging forward until we bunched together, temporarily halted every time someone stumbled. We all almost fell but there was no room to fall; bodies held us up. We panted. We couldn't catch our breath. Then we'd start running again. Cattle in a chute. I was in the middle with no idea where we were going. I lost sight of Kanaan, couldn't hear him anymore, couldn't process if that was good or bad. I was disgusted by my mother and trying not to trip again and thinking how all the doors out of the building were behind us.

Women ducked into their rooms. Senny propped her mattress upright against her window. She upended it so deftly, with such fluid confidence, it seemed a skill she'd practiced. Had there been drills before we arrived? Beverly thudded to the ground behind me and started wheezing; I hadn't even known she was there. Every window rattled. Ruthie's face was bleeding, some pimples had popped. She draped Bev's arm around her neck and strained to hoist her up. Someone's wiry hair stuffed into my mouth. A hand flailed, bony knuckles in my throat that made me cough. All around, chaos and lurching commotion. Sage swung into her room and pulled a knapsack from under her bed and grabbed her pillow. Charity screamed so long a vein emerged in her neck, thick as a garter snake. My mother clamped a hand over Charity's mouth. . . . *Alcohol, Tobacco, and Firearms. We have a warrant for the arrest of Perry Norman Cullen. Surrender immediately. . . .* Then, at my knees, Kanaan! He'd wrangled his way out of Victoria's arms and slipped under all of us, on all fours like a dog, and scurried back the way we'd come. "No, no, no, no," Victoria said, "Kanaan, doll, come here, baby." "He wants his daddy," someone said, as if charmed, and I fought against the bodies to try reaching him. He rose to his feet and took the corner. Victoria shoved back through us and went after him. I wanted to follow them, thinking that made more sense than anything, but my mother hooked my elbow and dragged me into our room.

We dropped to the floor, flattened ourselves. We crawled toward the interior wall, the one separating our room from Gina's. The hall quieted. The herd had dispersed, everyone sheltering in their rooms, huddling in corners and under mattresses, catching their breath. The loudspeaker outside muted. Over, I thought. Safe.

That was when the bullets started opening the walls.

Roy

My mind in revolt. It cornered and bludgeoned me, just as it had when Mason deployed, when he'd been downrange in Iraq, when he failed to call. I imagined Jaye being tackled by federal agents. Or in handcuffs being shoved headfirst into a paddy wagon. Or my father had sighted down the barrel of his Colt Python, put the phosphorescent bead on Virgil or the Lamb, but right as he fired, the man moved and the bullet struck Jaye. Or she was scrambling to find a phone to call me when the Lamb intercepted her. He took her hostage, clutching one of the grenades I'd left behind, the pin already pulled.

When the news paused for another raft of commercials, Coop said, "Is your dad out there?"

"Do what?" I said.

"Your father? The sheriff of McLennan County?"

"He left early. He knew it was going to be bad."

"I bet he'll tell us what Douglass won't. Can I stay for supper?"

"Let's go," I said, already standing.

"Go where?" he said.

"We need to be out there."

"At the ranch?"

"If we leave now—"

"On my bike? That would take us all day even if we don't get T-boned by a car or catch hypothermia, which we definitely would."

"We can just ride to your house, or to where my mom is, then we can take one of the cars," I said. The plan came to me one word at a time. I tried to make it sound plausible.

"So we'll boost a car and gun it to where all the cops are. What could go wrong?"

Douglass returned to the screen and blathered: warrants, assault weapons, standoff. I heard words instead of sentences. Hail of gunfire. Cult leader. Contraband. Combat gear. I sat back down, felled by the crude knowledge there was nothing to do but wait. Coop rolled onto his stomach, his legs stretched out and his elbows propped up, his chin cupped in his palms. He looked like a kid watching cartoons. The soles of his dingy sneakers were bone smooth, no sign of any original tread. Of everything from that morning, this is my clearest memory: sitting in my father's chair, looking at the worn-down soles of my friend's thrift store shoes, understanding we weren't going to survive.

Jaye

What I kept thinking was how pissed my father will be when I die. At Perry, obviously, but also at my mother. Maybe at me, too. He'll be furious and my mother will feel guilty and I'll never drive the red Chevy again and Roy's ears turn red when he gets shy and I was going to lose them, too. Those red ears. I'd been eating sliced cheese, so that will have been my last supper. I changed my name and I was going to die on an unsanded floor where I can smell grainy fog through hole-ridden grainy wood, and each shot like something being torn, the stars like lace, like bullet holes, and poor Roy will hear about this, sweetest Roy with his ears turning red in his baseball cap and—

"Where are you—stay down!" my mother screamed. She swiped for my ankle with both hands, but I kicked free. I stood and reached under my mattress for the derringer. Then I dropped to the floor again and rushed back into the hall, crouched, hopeless, going back toward the chapel. Maybe I wanted to get to Kanaan. Maybe I wasn't thinking. My body led; my mind followed.

Seneca's mattress still leaned in front of her window, but bullets had chewed it up. Fluff fell like snowflakes. Shattered glass on the floor like broken ice. The outside noises—the rumbling diesel engines and men yelling and the pop-pop-pop-pop of rifles—were louder in her room. She lay on her stomach, taking cover, facing the wall. There was glass on her back and in her hair and she didn't know about it; child that I was, I didn't want her to cut herself.

"Senny," I called. On my elbows and knees, whisper-yelling: "Senny! There's glass! In your hair!"

She couldn't hear. Another round of shots. Like the anguished whine of a circular saw. Her mattress wavered but didn't topple. More foamy fluff, floating and eventually falling. The floor pinched and bit into my elbows as I crawled toward her. I wanted to put the pistol in my pants but couldn't make myself. I worried the mattress would fall on me. I blew the smallest shards of glass out of my path. A girl making a wish on dandelions. Bullets were spraying another part of the building like oscillating yard sprinklers. Everything smelled thick, pulpy.

"Senny," I whispered when I got close.

She stayed facing the wall. In shock, I thought. Terrified. So terrified she didn't realize her hair was in a puddle of dark syrup, congealed cola. How had I never found such contraband when I snooped in her room? What else had I missed? Were the milling machines *here*? A memory flash: Perry's love of Dr Pepper. Where did she get a can or bottle of maple— No. Not syrup. Not soda.

"Senny?" I said. I rose. I kneeled over her. Glass dug into my jeans, my knees. "Seneca?"

The puddle was spreading. Seneca's eyes were half closed. Only now did I see that her right arm was twisted under her body and her feet were pointed toward the door, her upper and lower halves lay wrenched in opposite directions. A perfect circle, a dark hole, just below her shoulder blade, blood leaking under her and forming the hideous puddle. Her hair in it, leaching it up.

ON THE LAMB

PODCAST EPISODE 9
GUEST: Anonymous ATF Agent (retired)
RECORDED: March 2024
                    Phone Interview

We were outgunned, plain and simple. I remember hearing we shot some eleven hundred rounds of ammunition, and they shot over ten thousand. That first cease-fire occurred because we ran out of ammunition. Hell of a thing. We were walking backward toward the trailers with our hands above our heads, and our blood types smudged on our necks.

What was happening during the first cease-fire?
We called for backup. Someone went to Walmart and bought more ammo.

Roy

I fixed us lunch—fried eggs and bologna and glasses of milk. I brought out TV trays my mother had gotten with her grocery store points the year after earning the bird clock. Chewing, we stared at the news. I covered my eggs in pepper the way my father and grandfather did, hoping Coop would notice and ask about it. He didn't. During a commercial, he went to the cupboard for the bag of white bread. He moved fast and kept looking back at the TV to make sure he wasn't missing anything. He slapped two slices onto my tray and used his bread to mop up grease on his plate. He said, "You're a good cook. If you had bigger boobs, I'd marry you."

An hour crawled by without change. We kept expecting something to give—for the live feed to connect or for Douglass to sign off and in-progress soap operas to resume. I washed dishes while Coop worked out a nunchuck routine in slow motion in the living room. Without my asking, he turned up the TV so I could hear. The station was dispatching additional reporters and camera crews. Eventually news came of a cease-fire.

Coop was lying on the floor again, on his back, his ankles crossed and a couch cushion under his head. For hours, I'd been bracing for him to leave. Only now, watching him try to find a comfortable position, did I understand how badly I needed him to stay.

By midafternoon, the graphic of the Lamb was replaced with a photo of Lova Flores. She'd called in to the station, her voice static-barbed like Mason's always was.

"What can you tell our friends at home about this dangerous standoff, Lova?" Douglass asked.

She said there were six dead law enforcement agents and four dead cult members. Twelve wounded agents had been evacuated to the hospital.

The media had been pushed back, forced to set up miles away in the parking lots of the Gallop Inn and the Garden of Eatin' where a law enforcement spokesman gave them intermittent updates. Despite a lull in the shooting, authorities had worried the cult would take potshots at reporters. The FBI would be on the ground within the hour. So would the National Guard. While she spoke, the station rolled footage of the ranch's mangled front gate.

I'd stopped listening. My brain was trying to assess the likelihood that my father and Jaye were among the casualties when I heard Lova Flores say she'd caught up with Sheriff Moreland just before her crew was escorted from the scene. Coop sat up and glanced back at me, his eyes as round as doorknobs. I moved down beside him on the floor. Then my father was on the screen, walking toward the camera; Lova and her cameraman had intercepted him. The footage bounced as they jogged. Beads of water on the lens blurred the image. My father's Stetson was soaked and pulled low. The collar of his Eisenhower jacket was raised. Everything looked saturated, wind-sheared. He squinted—either from the wind or impatience.

Off camera, Lova said, "Do you think the cease-fire will hold, Sheriff?"

"That'd be best for everybody," he said.

"Have you had contact with Mr. Cullen today?"

"No, ma'am."

"Is there anything you'd like to say to him if he's watching?"

"I'd tell him we've all had about enough. I'd say, 'Perry, it's time to quit this.' I'd say, 'Let's lay these guns down because it only gets worse from here.'"

ON THE LAMB

PODCAST EPISODE 10
GUEST: Virgil Bernthal
RECORDED: April 2024
        The Chapel of Light
        Waco, Texas

Outgunned? That's rich, real rich.

There were, what, a hundred of them? Two hundred? How many in each cattle trailer? Government agents with military technology. How many snipers—ten? Not to mention everything they'd use later, or the reinforcements from the FBI, the Texas Rangers, SWAT.

Weren't there about a hundred of you as well?
Thirty women, give or take. Another twenty or so people that were elderly or infirm. Then the kids and adolescents. We're down to maybe twenty of us who were even physically capable of taking up arms, let alone how many of that number knew how to shoot. *Outgunned.* What does that say about the prowess of the agency—of the United States government—if a handful of Jesus freaks can *outgun* them?

But didn't they run out of ammo? Isn't that what being outgunned means?
I think it means we had some help.

God, you're saying.
What's the alternative? Some Bible thumpers defeated Uncle Sam? That so much planning and training and equipment was no match for little old us? Sounds fishy, but what do I know? Either way, it sounds like something I can shake hands with.

Jaye

rom behind Seneca's mattress, I could see the helmeted men in their stations. They advanced and stopped as deliberately as chess pieces. They had the same yellow letters on their backs, bold and capitalized: ATF. Two men charged toward the building with a long steel ladder, which I thought they'd use as a battering ram, but just before reaching the wall, they jammed its feet into the mud and angled it to lead up to the roof. All in a fluid pole-vault motion. Then, from nowhere, a third man appeared and ascended. The other two followed, scrambling onto the roof of the chapel, heading toward Perry's quarters, exactly where I'd been moments ago, a lifetime ago. A window shattered. Then another.

When I turned to bolt back into the hallway, I almost kicked Seneca's legs. I'd already forgotten about her. "Sorry," I said, not thinking.

In the distance, sirens. I crawled out of the room. Beverly was praying loudly in her bunk. Behind me, Sage found Seneca and shrieked, "Oh my God! Senny!" Children cried wetly from invisible spaces. Then came the sudden stench of piss and shit, ripe and cold; someone's bucket had fallen over or it had been shot and the waste had splattered. The ruckus of men running on the second floor, the muddled cacophony of frantic voices. An arc of gunfire cut up the hallway wall just before I stood to run. The bullet holes left a candy cane shape. A sickle.

Then the floorboards and walls started trembling. The air pulsed around me. A heavy rumble, the noise spinning louder and broader, building to an encircling roar as it wheeled closer. I dropped to the floor again and scrambled into Turtle's room, curled into a ball in the corner. Windows rattled in their casings. Now the roar thundered overhead, bearing down, deafening. Like we were inside a massive engine. Like we were the wheat in the thresher. Of all days, I thought, a tornado? Now? I expected the roof to peel off. Expected windows to implode and walls to cave. Yes, I thought. Please.

Through Turtle's window, I saw helicopters banking to the east. Three black shapes like sharks in cloudy water. The rumble receded.

More ladders had been wedged against the building. Men scaled the roof while others flanked the front door below. The fog had thickened. The scale of the enterprise was disorienting, overwhelming. All these people, all this artillery, because Perry maybe did it with Charity? Because he had some guns he wasn't supposed to? Everything seemed such a gross miscalculation that I felt sorry for him. I considered throwing the derringer out the window so I wouldn't have it on me when I was arrested.

On the roof, a helmeted man used the butt of his rifle to break a window. I watched the shards cascade into the fog. The man was wedging himself inside when a light flashed and a rifle's report broke through every other sound. The man whipped back and opened his pink mouth and flipped onto his stomach, writhing. Then another flash and report and his body spasmed and stilled. The man slid off the roof, an egg out of a skillet.

The window started vibrating again. The helicopters were coming back.

Roy

"I saw Lova Flores at H-E-B last year," Coop said. This was an hour after she'd interviewed my father. The station hadn't resumed regular programming—which I'd convinced myself would signal the worst was over—but at least they'd started breaking for more commercials. Panda had climbed into Coop's lap. He said, "She was hosting a blood drive. She was shorter than you'd think. Prettier, too."

"You tried donating blood to flirt with her but weren't old enough," I said because I knew he was about to tell that part of the story. Even on regular days, he liked describing the encounter.

"Yeah, but she definitely smiled at me," he said. "She'd probably remember me if I saw her again. For sure she would."

After a commercial for the junkyard by the airport, Douglass said the FBI had begun a dialogue with the Lamb over the phone. They were negotiating the release of some eighty hostages, mostly women and children. Ten of the twelve wounded agents were in critical condition at the hospital. SWAT teams had arrived on scene; law enforcement had the fortified compound surrounded.

"Fortified?" I said without meaning to.

"Do what?" Coop said absently as he scratched Panda.

"I didn't say anything," I said.

An hour later, it had started raining again and Lova Flores wore a plastic poncho. She interviewed a newspaper reporter whose Datsun had been hit by bullets at the ranch. The interview took place in front of the Garden of Eatin'. The camera circled his car, zooming in on the perforated quarter panel.

"You should invite Jaye over," Coop said. He was on his back again. His arms extended toward the ceiling, holding the nunchucks like a wide bar-bell. Panda had disappeared.

I made a show of twisting to see the bird clock in the kitchen. I said, "She's still in school."

"I liked her. She's easy to talk to. Did you ever find out how she got into the gun show on early bird night?"

"How long do you think before the Lamb surrenders?" I asked.

"Why would he surrender?"

I didn't know how to respond. Now that negotiations had begun, his surrender seemed a given. I wanted the phone to ring. I said, "Because he's surrounded? Because there's no other way out?"

"If he comes out, he goes to prison and the losers worshipping him have to find another leader. Turn to Channel 5."

I flipped the channel; I couldn't remember how I'd wound up with the remote. The reporter Joseph Pena was talking to a National Guardsman.

"Channel 10," Coop said.

Bernard Vessey was behind the newsdesk. The same photo of the Lamb hung over his shoulder, but the caption read MESSIAH MAYHEM.

"Try CNN," he said.

"I don't think we have it," I said. I scrolled back to Channel 3. Lova Flores was on the screen, but the newspaper guy was gone. The wind tugged at the hood of her poncho.

"Well," Coop said. "I promise he's on CNN, too."

"So?"

"So, the longer he refuses to come out, the more attention he gets. There's no reason to give up and every reason not to. I bet he drags his feet until he's had his way with each chick at least one more time. Probably twice."

Jaye

An avalanche of noise, of blinding strobing light, everywhere and from every angle. Like someone had thrown a match into a fireworks stand—a chain of explosions chasing itself through the corridors. Bullets strafed the walls around me; I watched hunks of wood fly like tossed hay. I couldn't catch my breath. The space convulsed, then the convulsing was inside me. My body shook against the floor, but I couldn't discern if the movement was my own or the building's. An earthquake from when I was a kid, my mother on her back in our tub, then me on top of her, then my father on top of me, trying to keep us from being afraid—"We're a Carroll sandwich!" Now, overhead, Perry's men were running, then stopping, then reversing their course. The reek of spent gunpowder, of diesel fumes. The floor rough against my cheek and something wet and cold, too—my snot or spit or, if I was crying, tears. I couldn't tell. I willed myself to rise and run but stayed on the floor. The periphery of my thoughts—my memory, my understanding—was dulling, retreating until there was only the physical now. A now that I couldn't remember having begun, a now that had always been. My body prone, my unresponding heart. A crash behind me, something clattering down and taking smaller things with it, things that broke and scattered when they hit. Behind my eyelids, streaks and flares of violet, starbursts and pinwheels bursting against blackness, appearing with one blast then obscuring the next.

And still more noise—the walls absorbing what they could, the helicopters and yelling and sobbing and coughing, my breathing coming too fast and the awful high-pitched gurgling of our chickens as they were being shot and people pleading with God and barking orders and information: *Get down! Over here now! They're still coming! I can see them and they're still coming!* Then a single shot and the sickening muffled thunk of its impact, a sledgehammer into a sandbag. Then an enormous gasp—like someone breaching the surface of water after too long below. The gasping continued and turned wet, and a man cried out, "No! No no no no!" Then, as if all the agents were ordered to aim at the same thing and hold down their triggers at the same time: The dinner bell tolled tolled tolled tolled until it dropped to the frozen earth and silenced.

Roy

"**F**riends," Douglass said into the camera. His voice was dyed in seriousness. "We're getting information. News is coming in."

He pressed his fingers to his earpiece, nodding. I raised the volume even though we could hear fine. He squared the edges of the papers on his desk—bottom, side, top, side.

"Spill it, Douglass!" Coop said.

"I told you he'd surrender. I told you—"

"Friends," Douglass said, "this just in."

The Lamb had been shot. Twice. Once in the side and once in the hand. Neither wound was mortal, but the bleeding had been hard to stop. According to Lova Flores's sources, he'd faded in and out of consciousness.

There was more. The Lamb had also accused the ATF of killing two toddlers. "I've got baby blood all over the walls," he'd reportedly told the negotiator. "You think someone ain't going to hell for that one?" In a subsequent call, he denied having ever claimed such a thing. As part of the negotiations, the FBI was coordinating with a Christian radio station in Dallas to broadcast a sermon from the Lamb later that evening. The Lamb demanded that he deliver the sermon live, but the feds would only agree to a taped message, fearing he'd use the platform to incite violence. In exchange for the tape being broadcast in its entirety, the Lamb promised to turn himself in tomorrow.

When Douglass broke for the pest control commercial again, I said, "Do you think he's denying that two kids died or denying that the people shot were kids?"

"Do what?" Coop said.

"Do you think the Lamb's lying about how old the two kids were or about them being shot at all?"

"He lies about everything. For example, being God."

"But about this specifically, which do you think sounds more likely: that they were toddlers or that two people were killed?"

"Who cares?" he said. "Once you say you're Jesus, you've lost all credibility."

"Listen," I said. A commercial for a kolache shop came on the screen; the kid in it had been in our class for a week before his parents transferred him to private school. My neck was sweating. The inside of my mouth was pasty. Coop was waiting for me to speak. I said, "Listen. I need to tell you something."

ON THE LAMB

PODCAST EPISODE 4
GUEST: Special Agent Kent Unrue (retired)
RECORDED: October 2023
            Phone Interview

His claim about baby blood on the walls? No dice. Cullen *was* shot, flesh wounds on his hip and wrist, but those could've been self-inflicted for all we know. Everything that man said was falsehood. I was trying to persuade him to release his hostages, and he's tittering about the Fifth Seal. I said just give me one kid as a show of good faith, and he said he'd surrender if we played his radio sermon. Took me about half a minute to peg what a slippery son of a bitch he was going to be. But as a negotiator, even in such an atypical scenario, you play along. You work with what you've got. In this case, I'd inherited a squad of hick cops and a deranged evangelical who's armed to the teeth.

What was atypical about the scenario?
He had all the leverage.

Why?
Because there was nothing he wanted.

Nothing?
Nada, zip. He just wanted to be left alone, and there's no way I was going to give him that.

Jaye

The chapel was deserted. I'd expected to find Victoria and Kanaan hiding there. I eased the door closed as quietly as I could, convinced one squeak of the hinges would cost me my life. The shock of having not yet been shot. The incontrovertible understanding that the next sound would be the last I'd hear. That I was racing across a rickety bridge, the planks collapsing under my heels.

The shooting turned intermittent. A single shot there, a terse rattle of automatic fire there. Either the helicopters had landed or flown too high to hear. God took a breather from his homily. I squatted on my haunches with my hands steepled in front of me, the derringer between my palms. I was breathing in through my nose, out through my lips, trying to puzzle out where Kanaan might be, what I should do, what I shouldn't. If you'd seen me, you would have thought I was praying. You would have thought what a devout girl, what a dispossessed angel.

I couldn't guess the safest way to move: I scooted on the floor, I crawled, I pressed my back against the wall and cross-stepped. Through the glass, the cold mist gauzed my view but did nothing to hide the men in helmets and goggles. Their numbers had multiplied. Men everywhere—in clusters and alone, sprawled on the ground behind rifles on tripods, taking cover behind rocks and automobiles, on the roof of the mechanic shop.

A pulse of shots issued from our second floor, lewd cracks in the quiet. The men under the fog made themselves small. Two of them—one behind a cattle trailer, the other atop the shop—returned fire, bursts of hideous illumination.

Time dilated, lapsed, divorced itself from the clock. The chapel existed in a gray ghostlight. I expected the door to open. Either it would fly off its hinges as ranks of men stormed through or someone, Virgil or Lawrence, would twist the knob. In my ears, the softest pleas of my heart.

On the stage were guitars on stands and a small drum kit. Opposite it was the tiered pine seating that reminded me of gym bleachers and commanded most of the room; the scalp of any adult on the top row would rub the ceiling. The back of the bleachers abutted the north wall, and because neither side was flush with the eastern or western walls, they had been sealed off with scrap particleboard. I positioned myself on the eastern side. I tried prying off the particleboard, but it wouldn't budge. Another solitary rifle shot, another strained and precarious silence in its wake.

When the voice of God returned, its tone was more plaintive: "Perry, come on out now. No one else needs to get hurt. Let's end this thing on a good foot."

Hurt? The word seemed encouraging—like Seneca would survive, like I'd misjudged her condition and should've stayed beside her. Maybe the falling man had jumped to safety. But such possibilities never gained full purchase in my mind. Senny was dead, and she wasn't alone. Dank cold seeped into the chapel. Between the bleachers and the wall, my breath squeezed.

"Come on out, Perry," the voice said. "Let's call it a day. Everybody wants to go home in one piece."

On the floor above, the resolute snap of magazines being loaded into weapons. I'd moved to the other side of the bleachers, nestled between the western wall and the seats. This space wasn't nearly as tight as the other one, further proof of the slapdash asymmetry that defined the ranch. Why I'd moved—or when—was again lost on me. Earlier I'd been over there; now I was here. The derringer was still in my hand. I never considered putting the barrel to my temple and pulling the trigger. Not once.

Roy

Once I started talking, I could hardly stop. I told Coop how Jaye had surprised me in the truck and how the FBI had been calling my father and how I'd picked into the mall and Sammy had busted me. How I went to the ranch with my mother and then with my father and how Jaye and I had kissed in the water tower and how she'd been calling me from the Lamb's room. As I spoke, I lived each moment all over again. When the impulse to embellish and exaggerate arose, I resisted—not for Coop's sake, but mine. I was at once speaker and audience, experiencing the story both halved and doubled. That I'd held it in so long was a shock; that I'd caved was a thrilling, comforting shame. Part of me heard it as a rehearsal for how I'd eventually relay everything to Mason. Every time I came close to mentioning the grenades, I circled back and added a detail to what I'd already said. I couldn't bear to hear him suggest the raid was my fault, couldn't risk him being so disgusted that he'd leave me alone with the news and my guilt.

Coop was sitting on the floor and by the time I'd finished, his back was to the television. He'd pivoted in my direction like a sundial.

"Holy shit," he said, stunned and staring.

"I know," I said.

"You can pick locks? Like any lock?"

"Yeah, but that's not really important right now."

"No, I know," he said. "But we could get into the AV room at school and take the video camera. We could get into the equipment cage and get the good football before anyone else."

"Definitely," I said. "But we need to find a way to get out to the ranch and—"

"Did you check the Coin Nook when you went into the mall? Did they leave anything behind? I still have my gold-plated Susan B.—"

The sound of tires in our driveway. Coop and I scrambled to look through the slatted blinds on opposite sides of the television.

My mother climbed out of her Oldsmobile. She wore her denim shirt and jeans and looked haggard, a little angry. I wondered if this was how she always appeared when she came home to wash up. She shut the car door with her hip. On our porch, she surveyed the neighborhood again, gazing up at the telephone lines where two grackles were swaying. When she turned to unlock the door, Coop and I jumped back to where we'd been.

Before she'd gotten inside the house, I said, "Dad told me to stay home."

"They're butchering the Lamb," Coop said. "There's a truce now, but there was a lot of shooting earlier."

"Good afternoon to y'all, too," she said. She brought in the smell of the velour upholstery in her car, and in her hair or breath, a hint of a recent cigarette.

"Dad said he might be home for supper," I said.

She hung her purse over the back of a kitchen chair on her way to the fridge. She took out a can of beer. She said, "It might just be us tonight, fellas. I can make us some spaghetti or tacos, or y'all can—"

"You talked to Dad? Did he say what's happening?"

"He described it as a clusterfuck. I believe it's a technical term," she said, taking a drink, then lifting her eyebrows as she swallowed.

"Did he say anything about the casualties?" Coop said.

"I don't think he knows," she said. She was leaning against the fridge. I half-expected her to slide to the floor. "I don't think there are clear lines of communication. I told him to come home, but he thinks he'll be marooned out there all night."

"We could go see him," I said. "We could take him something to eat."

"I also said if anybody shoots up my horses, they'd do themselves a favor by killing me, too."

Coop stayed a couple hours after supper, but when it became clear my father wouldn't be home tonight, he headed out. He lifted his bike by the handlebar grip and walked it down our driveway. The chain and sprocket clicked. I stood on the porch. My breath dispersed in the beam of our floodlight. Strange that everything seemed so at peace—the lighted windows in small houses, woodsmoke in the breeze. Behind me, my mother was standing in the living room, a few feet from the TV, flipping channels.

At the bottom of the driveway, Coop swung his leg over the seat. He pulled his nunchucks out of his back pocket and slid them down inside the front of his zipped jacket. He had both hands on the grips, one foot on the pedal and the other on the ground.

I said, "I'll call if I hear something."

"No news is good news," he said.

"Maybe," I said.

"He's just busy and she's holed up with her mom," he said. His voice sounded the same as when he'd been talking with Jaye about his father, soft and even, grief-touched. Earlier, we'd both fallen into a routine of good humor for my mother's benefit, and it was a relief to dismiss such pretense. He said, "They'll get in touch soon. Your dad will come home, and she'll call on the phone."

"Sure. Okay," I said. I wanted to sound unswayed, but I relished his confidence, as if he knew something I didn't. I envied it. Resented it. I worried I'd say something sentimental.

"Or maybe everyone used the tunnels and the whole ranch is empty."

"They don't even have toilets," I said.

"Maybe they're in Mexico, scarfing enchiladas. Maybe they're across the border, sitting on toilets in a fancy resort, laughing at the FBI watching an abandoned building."

"Thanks for coming over," I said, maybe for the first time in my life.

Inside, my mother was in my father's spot at the kitchen table, the chair where his shotgun had been propped that morning. She scrolled through channels, jabbing at the buttons on the remote two or three times for every station that went by.

"I can change the batteries," I said. Her eyes stayed on the TV. The channels were either commercials or repeat stories about the raid. She paused on each one. With Coop gone, I felt feeble and anxious.

"I wonder if this has gotten to Mason," she said.

"I doubt it," I said. I needed to believe the story was insignificant, an event that only seemed consequential because of our proximity to it, no different than an outbreak of oak wilt. "We'll have to tell him when he gets home."

"It feels like two of my three boys are at war right now," she said. "I don't have enough worrying left."

On TV, a reporter I didn't recognize was talking into a microphone under an umbrella. I listened for rain outside.

"Do we have CNN?" I said.

"The Ted Turner channel? We'd have to check the *TV Guide*. He's married to Jane Fonda. She protested Vietnam and sunk her career."

"We used our TV trays today," I said.

"If this keeps going, maybe all those extra cans of soup I bought will be worth it."

We were almost out of soup, but I didn't want to say that. I said, "I think it'll end soon. Perry said he'd surrender after they play his sermon."

"What world is this?" she said.

"I don't know."

"Good," she said. "I hope you never do."

Jaye

I n the chapel, my fear of an army storming in morphed into a sense that everyone else had already quit this miserable place. My mother had left me behind; Kanaan had already forgotten me. I wanted to stomp my feet on the floor like a furious child. I'd been sheared from my own existence. I'd been orphaned by blood, by hope.

Occasionally a lone gunshot punctured the silence, as if the men pulling the triggers were falling asleep and their fingers were twitching. The inside of my ears ached. I started cataloging everything I'd never do, the particulars of which were now feverishly jockeying in the queue of my thinking: Learn to sew or bake biscuits from scratch. Take a bad driver's license photo or earn a diploma or board a plane. Catch snowflakes on my tongue. Swim with dolphins or pay rent or break a bone. Spy a double rainbow. See the mammoth bones. Or Barbados. Attend a concert or bury my parents or hold a monkey or land a job. Get a speeding ticket, a tattoo or yeast infection. I wouldn't live to see my face folded with wrinkles, a female president, or what would become of this desolate stretch of land. I would never return to California. I would never flaunt my new thin self in front of the girls I'd envied, never capitalize on the mystery of my disappearance. I would never have sex or marry Roy. Never see my parents again, my own face, his.

Silence sprawled. I stayed between the wall and bleachers. My arms hugging my shins, my forehead on my knees, teeth chattering. It had to be warmer outside than in the chapel. Something about the greenhouse effect, which I'd been studying in earth sciences before we set out for Texas. Mr. Kilgore, my teacher, a perpetual sheen of sweat on his face. He would've appreciated a postcard from the mammoth grave. My knees shook. I set the derringer beside me on the floor so I could cover my fingers with the cuffs of my shirt. I pulled tighter into myself.

Who was still alive, cowering in a corner like me? My first thought was of my mother; I trusted something would have shuddered inside me had she died. She was alive because I was alive. And, because I was supposed to outlive her, I knew I would not. The invalid reasoning of a shivering child, the misbegotten audacity of faith.

Kanaan. Virgil. Victoria. Beverly. Gina. Lawrence. Big Lyle. Ruthie, Eden. Charity. A precarious roll call in my mind. I tried cataloging everyone at the ranch I'd avoided meeting, the ones from whom I had averted my gaze for months; foolishly I'd thought not learning their names had some bearing on the hold this place would have on me. The wheelchair woman. The Portuguese family who spoke no English but communicated in smiles and deferential gestures, and yet who hung on Perry's every utterance. The blind man and his bubbly guide. The woman with the skunk-white streak in her hair, whom Turtle suspected had been a pimp. The man with jaundice that almost seemed to glow. The kids who were forever singing their ABCs.

I tried convincing myself that Seneca alone was gone. When that center wouldn't hold, when everyone else seemed simultaneously alive and dead in my ignorance, I started bargaining. I was content to stop myriad hearts to save Beverly, Turtle, Olga, or even Charity. It was easy to imagine sacrificing the blind or jaundiced man, the lady in the wheelchair: Their lives, I reasoned, had to be defined by miserable voids. After that, I traded Perry's life for the lives of my horses, then people I knew. When that wasn't enough, I came up with a hierarchy. Take Victoria and Gina, I thought, take Lawrence, the twins, Sage and Virgil in exchange for Lyle. Take Lyle, take my mother, take me, take every last one of us, including the pinto and bay, including the whole lot of ragamuffin kids, but leave Kanaan.

Then, at once and everywhere, another landslide of unbearable noise. It was bottomless and booming, utterly solid. Like two locomotives barreling toward each other. It surrounded me, a vast and thundering cavern that immediately collapsed and grew louder still. I fumbled for the derringer. I fell onto my side. My fingers laced behind my head and my biceps squeezed down on my ears. My body, a knot. Time concussed. Matter overwhelmed, matter made small. The sense that something this loud could not exist. That it was the only thing that had ever existed.

Then what had been so massive and loud and solid broke apart. As if the sky had shattered and pieces of it rained down. Even with my eyes pinched shut, I could see—I could feel—the succession of the rounds. Their light. Their heat. Perry's men firing from above and the helmeted soldiers shooting from underneath, from all sides. I couldn't figure who had the advantage. The guns sounded bigger, angrier, worse. I was shrieking. Maybe the huge noise had penetrated me, maybe that's where it had gone, and I was fighting to expel it. My throat was shredding. No help coming, no savior, no hero. A long spray of bullets ripped through the chapel, first through the western wall over my head, then into the wood enclosing the bleachers. The shooting corroded the air, scalded it, contaminated it. If I'd been standing, the shots would have sawed me off at the waist. If I'd been sitting, I would have been scalped.

Another spray, higher this time, chewing up particleboard like a chain saw, buckling the seam on the side of the bleachers, blowing off the top of a middle panel, and—

Part Four

The Pale Horse

February–March 1993

Roy

My mother was asleep on the couch the next morning. On TV, there was footage of agents in tactical gear conferring in low fog. I stood watching from the hall then went back into my room. I felt dislocated and divided, living one life where there wasn't a grenade in my closet and one where there was. Boredom and panic and a suffocating kind of lonesomeness took turns on me.

When I emerged again, my mother was gone. Her coffee mug was washed and drying with other dishes atop our checkered dish towel. She'd dashed a note on the back of an old envelope: *Another snow day. Huey coming to get you. Love, Mom. P.S. Still no sermon.*

Lova Flores reported that Black Hawk helicopters had been used in yesterday's raid, and as of this morning, officials were requesting ten Bradley Fighting Vehicles from the Texas Army National Guard.

"Friends," Brent Douglass said, "this is a dark day."

"Some kind of jackpot, ain't it?" my grandfather said after he picked me up. We were in his F-150, towing an empty horse trailer. When a rig passed on the highway, the trailer fishtailed. Silver stubble grizzled Huey's jaw. Every few miles he'd stroke it with his free hand, scraping his knuckles over one cheek and then the other. It seemed new to him, something he was assessing, an animal he might keep or set free. He wore a canvas jacket that almost concealed the .357 on his belt. It was a Colt Python like my father's, the gun he usually kept in his Bullet Bible.

"I bet it ends today," I said. "He's claiming he'll come out after the radio plays his sermon."

We were driving to retrieve the horses my mother had given the Lamb years before. A woman named Robichaud had found them nibbling grass on her property last night. She lived a few miles from the ranch but recognized the bay and pinto from the Lamb's pasture. Normally, Robichaud would have driven to the ranch herself—she'd had neighborly exchanges with members in the past—but she'd heard the gunfire and watched the news. So she called the sheriff's office, speculating the horses had gotten spooked and jumped a fence. Sammy talked to her then radioed my father who'd called my grandfather. He knew the Robichauds from the days when the game warden caught them spotlighting deer.

The sky hung low, a translucent mother-of-pearl, as if its richest colors had drained out. A farmer drove an old tractor in a field. He was twisted in his seat, observing what was happening behind him instead of watching where he was going. It was the kind of thing I'd tell Jaye about on the phone, then she'd tell a story it reminded her of from her own life. The farmer shifted a lever that made his old machine buck. He swayed in his seat, oblivious to everything except his own aftermath.

We exited the highway and hit a line of stalled traffic on the feeder. Ahead, the parking lot for the Garden of Eatin' and the Gallop Inn was thick with news vans. Reporters with microphones stood in front of men shouldering video cameras like rocket launchers.

Maybe the idea had been coalescing since I'd climbed into the truck, I couldn't tell, but before I had the chance to reconsider, I said, "The news said they were bringing in tanks. Can we go see them?"

"Tanks," he said in disbelief. "On American soil. We're at war with ourselves."

"It's just what the news said."

"They should've let your daddy handle all this."

"Maybe we can see him, too," I said.

"There'll be checkpoints set up to turn away lookie-loos."

I remembered Mason saying car bombers targeted checkpoints in Iraq. Brent Douglass had reported it, too. Outside my window was a stand of stunted trees, a rotted-out skeleton of a half-collapsed shed.

"It's okay," I said, pouring on the disappointment. "I just wanted to tell Mason I'd seen them."

We were still behind traffic. I longed to be the kind of boy who'd throw the door open and run the corded fields until I found her or someone cut me down with a rifle. A brace of cowbirds exploded from a tree and pinwheeled against the pale sky. My grandfather checked his side mirror, then mine.

"You know," he said, cranking the wheel to the right, "I bet your daddy wouldn't mind laying eyes on you."

"I'd like to see him, too."

"And I bet Mrs. Robichaud wouldn't mind spending the afternoon with them horses," he said. He nosed the truck onto the road's caliche shoulder. "Hell, she might even thank us. More time with a horse is about the most anyone can ask."

"Definitely."

We bounced past the line of cars. I looked back at the drivers watching us leave them behind. Pebbles rang against our undercarriage, rattled into the fenders.

"He'll like seeing you, too," I said.

"It'll be a fine reunion," he said. "We'll make something of this sideshow yet."

The rutted road leading to the ranch was even tighter than when I'd come with my father. Vehicles crowded both shoulders, tilting away from the road like they had been pried apart. The trailer jostled. Huey had to park half a mile away.

We walked the road single file, Huey in front. When vehicles barreled through, we squeezed between bumpers of parked cars or made ourselves flat against truck beds. People nodded at Huey as they passed. A burly man carried a video camera like a toolbox while a woman beside him flipped through a notepad. She said, "Are we doing VO or sound bite?" Ahead, a man jogged across the road and disappeared into a small RV. When we reached it, he was squatting behind an editing console and fiddling with dials like he was playing a video game. The odor of kerosene. Thick cables snaked through weeds.

Uniformed lawmen paced while others stood sentinel—Texas Rangers, Highway Patrol, and State Police. When Huey caught one glaring in my direction, he waited for me to catch up to him and then laid his large hand on my neck, staking his claim. The lawman looked away. There was the increasing rumble of so many generators. RVs and vans and people leaning into doors for clipped conversations. The feeling of wandering through

a morbid festival. A military jeep was heading in our direction, a mounted
M60 bouncing as if on choppy water. Huey guided me across the road
where we sidled between two vans. Someone had laid a plank over a ditch
full of dingy water.

We came into a clearing, a red clay lot that had been commandeered as
a staging area. A line of media workers stretched beside a Salvation Army
truck where a woman distributed coffee and sandwiches wrapped in wax
paper. I scanned the crowd for Lova Flores, hoping to have something to
offer—or lord over—Coop. A cluster of men in front of a long trailer
laughed about something. From the pitch of their voices, I suspected the
subject was indecent and worried my grandfather would confront them.
They wore dark glasses and windbreakers. FBI, I thought, and I was awash
in oily resentment. When I turned to my grandfather, he was talking to the
lawman who'd clocked us on the road. I joined the sandwich line as cover.

I could barely make out the ranch in the misty distance. A mile away,
maybe two, beyond sloped pastures and curving roads, the structures were
hemmed in by an armada of tanks. The cannons pointed at the barracks.
Snipers were sprawled atop three cattle trailers. Behind the tanks and up
the hill stood the storage sheds and the water tower, and still farther up
were the horse stables. I wondered if anyone had yet found the grenades,
if another sniper was hidden in the water tower. It wobbled me. If I'd been
living two lives this morning, now they had crashed into each other and
become a single wretched existence that was the consequence of my
spinelessness. The Salvation Army van and red clay earth started swirling,
each spinning on a different axis. I kept closing and opening my eyes, hoping to steady myself, hoping the world would come into better, more forgiving focus.

"Detective?" my father said.

He was in front of me, though I had no clue how long he'd been there.
Once I registered him, I threw my arms around him. My cold cheek
against the collar of his jacket. Even with my eyes shut I knew people were
watching. My father hugged me but soon put space between us. He had
his hands on my shoulders.

"What's got hold of you right now, detective?"

He pulled me out of line and nodded for the woman behind me to take
my place. He looked me over like I'd fallen from a tree. His eyes were pink
with exhaustion, his face darkly lined. I said, "I'm okay."

"You look chewed up and spit out, son."

"We're picking up those horses," I said. "I wanted to see the tanks. I wanted to see you."

"Some old boy radioed the command post when he put eyes on—"

"Has there been more shooting?"

"Nothing's happened for hours. We're all fighting to stay awake."

"Have you talked to him?" I'd lowered my voice, aiming to elicit confidential information. "Do you know who got killed inside?"

"They cut the phones. They've got a line set up for the negotiator, but it's just a pissing contest. This whole thing's—"

"There's no phone?" I said. "What if they need help?"

"These boys might not be in a hurry to offer assistance, detective. Perry's posse took out four agents and put a dozen more in the hospital."

Somewhere a two-stroke engine coughed to life. The axis wobbled again. Behind me, the line advanced. A woman with crimped hair and acid-washed jeans opened her compact to assess her makeup. A load of Skid-O-Kans was being delivered. I could smell gunmetal.

"What about the kids?" I asked.

"I'm hoping they'll come out soon enough. They don't deserve this. Perry's got to know he's whupped. They'll kill the power if it stretches out much longer."

"When?"

My father shook his head. Behind him, lazy shafts of sunlight were hitting the tops of the trailers, pooling gold in the satellite dishes. He said, "I'm kindly impressed they haven't done it already."

Huey and I drove back with the radio playing too low to hear. The trailer rode smoother with the horses inside. Dusk fell fast over the scrubland. Neither of us spoke. Words were too feeble.

When he pulled in front of our house, the porch light was off. My mother must've gotten stuck at Raybourn's. I knew Huey expected me to open the door and step down. I took hold of the handle but couldn't make myself pull. At best, Jaye was alive, and when she looked outside, she found tanks aimed at her from every direction. A war zone, I thought. Without meaning to, I shook my head.

Huey said, "It'll be—"

"What if Perry has grenades?"

"Then I reckon he would've used them."

"What if they're elsewhere on the property? Somewhere he can't reach?"

Huey stroked his stubble. He was trying to unknot what I was asking, and why, and why now. I could feel him discarding possibilities as his thinking proceeded toward truth. The neighborhood was black, pressing in. The truck idled. Huey turned to me, then forward.

"It's been a long day," he said. "We could both do with some rest."

"I don't know," I said. On the radio, the deejay blathered about music being a form of prayer. I thought he'd play the sermon next, but he put on an old song my mother and I sometimes heard driving to school. The windshield was fogging. I said, "Would proof of grenades make any difference now?"

"Sammy tossed his booth and came up short."

"But—"

"And you and your daddy drove out there and didn't fare no better."

"I know, but if—"

"Perry's been on this path his whole life. Nothing was ever going to change that."

"There's a girl," I said. "She's inside. Her mother—"

"Don't!" he said, his voice filling the cab. He shut his eyes tight, suddenly sore at himself. He clicked off the radio. He regarded me again, longer this time, and even in the dark, I saw he understood.

"I'm sorry," I said.

"We saw your daddy and collected these horses. That amounts to a good day," he said, recalibrating. "The innocent folks out there, those women and children, they ain't done nothing but get snowed. If that's a crime, we'd all be in jail—you, me, your daddy, the whole country. Soon enough Perry'll wind up in Gatesville, and the rest of us will have to work to remember him."

"Pretty soon this will all be a long time ago."

"You sound like your daddy."

"So do you," I said.

"It's better than him sounding like me."

"I just keep worrying—"

"You're fourteen years old," Huey said. "All you ought to be worrying on is studies and chores. And you damn sure don't need some skirt setting you up for a fall."

"She's not. She hates—"

"Things can seem awful real when you're a boy. They can look a lot like what you want them to be."

"Okay," I said.

"But once you're grown, you look back and just see fantasies and boogeyman dreams," he said. "Whatever you're worrying on right now, whatever you think you saw, or felt, it's just a boyhood make-believe. It's something you could spend your whole life too embarrassed to ever mention again."

ON THE LAMB

PODCAST EPISODE 8
GUEST: Rhonda "Turtle" Tilly
RECORDED: February 2024
Gatesville Correctional Facility
Mountain View Unit
Gatesville, Texas

What was happening inside the ranch while the sermon aired?
We listened, but afterward we ate sheet cake Ruthie and Eden had baked. We sang songs. We eulogized those we'd lost—I'm the one who celebrated beautiful Bev's life; to this day I still think of things to add—and we prayed for them that were shot up and looking none too good. Victoria was Florence-Nightingaling around. Annie, too. We cried rivers. We turned giddy. Delirious, maybe. We took to calling it a barn dance. I think a few people got up to some diddling. Bullet holes in the walls. You could smell winter.

And the Lamb?
Weak, hurting. No one ever speaks to how his side was pierced and there was a hole through one of his palms. No one connects them dots. He was on a cot in the mess hall; he didn't feel good enough to get upstairs. Virgil pulled the plug on our singing because the Lamb needed sleep. Most folks started packing. We'd been told Uncle Sam had chartered buses for us, and they were waiting there in the night. Sage and me went to the kitchen and made sandwiches for everybody to take out.

Roy

The sermon aired close to midnight. The Lamb spoke of sacrificial turtle doves and red heifers and the pharisees who refused to believe Christ was virgin-born. Then came repentless foes and grace pouring from Jesus's lips to the children of men. Then Job's bed of ash. Once he started reading from Revelation, I snatched up my Bible. My finger traced the verses. He touched on the Seven Seals—the four horsemen and the martyrs crying out, the moon turning red and the sky receding like a scroll.

"Well, okay now, that's pretty interesting," the Lamb said, like a lesson was emerging. "Don't add or subtract anything from this book. Don't prank. Don't trifle. Why? Well, because there's a sword in the king's right hand and the arrows are sharp in the hearts of the king's enemies. Isn't that fascinating? I think so."

I could hear voices in the background—men and women bickering, children crying. I strained to believe I heard Jaye. Except for a sharp wince followed by a lapse in the sermon he didn't sound like a man who'd been shot twice. Or a man who'd shot anyone. For a while he seemed determined to speak clearly and avail himself as a responsible servant trying to finish the mystery of God. But as the sermon continued, his words started tumbling over themselves. He cracked jokes, giggled. He asked someone for a sandwich, then continued speaking with food in his mouth.

"Well old Solomon doesn't seem like too nice a guy, does he? Not if you're his enemy. I wonder why that is? Well, let's see," he said. He'd trail off and pick up again in a different place, doubling his speed or mumbling like a drunk. On television, the buses idled in the dark. Their hazards pulsed red through a haze of exhaust. The Lamb held forth about a great dragon and flashes of light and peals of thunder. I couldn't tell if he was citing Scripture or staring out his window.

Coop called when the sermon ended, but right as he started talking, my call-waiting clicked and I hung up on him. Before I had time to hope it was Jaye, my mother said, "I don't know, sweet potato, there might be a few lights burnt out on his string."

The television camera kept blurring, and every time the picture cleared, I expected to see a parade of people exiting. My mother said she hoped my father was staying warm, remembering to eat. The news coverage reminded her of when Mason's war started and when the *Challenger* exploded. I didn't like hearing her this way, so when call-waiting clicked again, I said I had to go.

"New theory," Coop said. "The sermon was pre-recorded, right? So what we just heard wasn't happening when we heard it, right?"

"That's what pre-recorded means. The FBI worried he'd incite violence on a live feed. They wanted to make sure there wasn't any kind of threat."

"You don't think talking about arrows in your enemy's back sounds threatening? You don't think reading all that scary shit from the Book of Revelations is—"

"Revelation," I corrected.

"Do what?"

"There's just *one* revelation," I said. "I thought you had a theory."

"What if he wanted everybody focused on their radios, so nobody noticed groups of people crawling across the pasture. Dead of night, tons of fog—textbook getaway weather."

"He wanted to deliver the sermon live," I said. "Recording it wasn't his idea."

"Maybe that's what we're supposed to think."

I changed the channels and landed on an infomercial for a magic sealant. The host cut a hole in the bottom of a skiff, sealed it with red goop, then motored around a swamp.

"So," Coop said, "what do you think?"

"I think they'd put in toilets before they put in tunnels."

"Because a shitter matters more than an escape route?" he said. "Remind me never to join your cult."

Jaye

hen I returned to our room—in frantic disbelief, terrified and almost giddy, my nerves vibrating like plucked wires—I halted in our doorway and gagged. Annie was on her knees, soaping our floor, and Victoria was wiping my mother's face with a wet cloth. She was on her bottom bunk with her eyes lidded, pale as alabaster. She'd been shot. Twice.

I felt top-heavy, like a tree being felled, and knew I was fainting but couldn't stop it. Victoria lunged from the bedside and braced me. I stayed standing, stayed awake, but the world—the room, the women, my mother, my own body—was at a remove. I took my mother's freezing hand and tried to follow what Victoria and Annie were relaying: Turtle had heard my mother scream then ran for Victoria. She'd lost a lot of blood, which was what Annie was trying to scrub off the floor. The shots had come through the walls, but Big Lyle had already puttied the holes. While I was gone. While I abandoned my mother. Left her for dead. Victoria had bandaged her leg—the bullets had blown completely through her thigh and calf—and she was in and out of shock. Victoria said if we kept the wounds clean and infection free, and if we prayed enough, my mother should pull through.

"I was looking for Kanaan," I said. "I found Seneca and I just—"

"God wanted you safe," Annie said, wringing her rag into a bucket. The water was a putrid pinkish gray. "He spared you to take care of your mama."

"I should've stayed here," I said, then stopped. I felt faint again, hollowed, not like I was going to puke but like I already had.

"If you'd stayed, then we would've found you the way you found Senny,"

Victoria said. "Your mama and the Lamb both took two bullets. It's divine symmetry, I think. There's meaning in suffering."

My mother squeezed my hand. With her eyes closed, she said, "You smell like clay."

The two women looked at me. Victoria rose and wiped my face with her cloth. She dusted off my shoulders and plucked flecks of wood from my hair. She said, "And you look like you've been digging ditches."

"I'll wash up soon," I said.

"You came back," my mother said. "You came home."

Then I did puke. In Annie's bucket. Chunks of the cheese I'd been eating when the trailers crushed the gate. Bloody water splashed back on my face.

Roy

The morning after the sermon, the newspaper headline was: HOLY WAR. The next day it read: PROPHET OR PROFIT?

My mother ferried me to school. I told her how good the horses looked when we loaded them into Huey's trailer, then I invented a sappy dream I hoped she'd like, then I said the believers would probably come out before supper. Nothing took. In the parking lot, she didn't fix my hair or adjust my collar. She kissed her fingertips and touched my forehead before I opened the door. A beleaguered blessing.

In morning classes, teachers tried adhering to lesson plans, but students just asked about the raid. After lunch it was all group work, which amounted to kids pushing their desks together to discuss the Lamb. Judy Mahurin wanted to party at the ranch after everyone committed suicide. Shawn and Shane Buford said their troop leader was going to take them out there to watch "history unfold." Stevie Dylan said Barry O'Dell said Pastor Slow said the Lamb had the number of the beast carved into his chest. Students clocked my movements then averted their eyes. Quick, surreptitious glances like swarms of gnats. By fourth period, custodians were wheeling in TV carts.

In World Geography, my desk was near the front of the room, which put me right beside the cart when it arrived. The live feed showed Brent Douglass interviewing a DPS officer about checkpoints and rerouted traffic. He droned on about public safety. I couldn't tell if the clock over our map of Texas had stopped, but at best there was still half an hour before the bell, then all of fifth and sixth periods. I closed my notebook and sidestepped between desks. Mr. Wilson ordered me to get back to my seat. I left without closing the door.

. . .

The exodus kept not starting.

I turned on the television in my room, then in the living room, and paced between them. Brent Douglass began referring to the ranch as the bunker. Lova Flores described it as a compound. The FBI took over. Every channel aired a press conference where Special Agent Kent Unrue, a pasty man in a starched white shirt said Perry Cullen had reneged on promises to surrender. Unrue claimed Cullen had threatened to kill himself on camera and had over a hundred hostages, predominately women and children. Some were wounded, but Cullen was denying EMTs access. He'd been shot twice. Authorities were still working to confirm identities of the deceased cult members, but Cullen wasn't cooperating.

After the press conference, Brent Douglass said that despite the bloodshed, there was some positive news. I was in the hallway but rushed into the front room and raised the volume. Reporting live outside the Gallop Inn, Lova Flores said there were no vacancies in any Waco hotels, and since the raid two days prior, the city's economy had gotten a million-dollar boost.

My mother brought tacos the following night. We prayed and ate at the kitchen table. I figured we'd keep the TV on, but after a few bites, she got up and turned it off.

"I don't want to talk about what's transpiring out there, okay?" she said.

"Me either," I lied.

After supper, she took a long shower. I turned the TV back on. They were speculating about how much money the Lamb raked in at gun shows. When I heard my mother coming from their room, I clicked it off. She wore dark jeans and a teal sweater I liked. She had an overnight shift and didn't know if my father would be home tonight, so she invited me to sleep in Raybourn's guest room. I said I'd be fine at home, which got us trying to name another time when I'd slept alone in the house. We couldn't.

"Everyone's growing up," she said.

I brought my locks into the front room and worked them while I watched TV. I picked up the receiver every half hour, checking for a dial tone; I kept convincing myself it had gone dead to explain its silence. One time I put it to my ear and only heard hollowness, like the throbbing air inside a shell. Immediately I thought my suspicions had come true and started imagining how many calls I could have missed.

"Hello?" I said just to hear my own voice.

"Shit!" Coop said. "It didn't even ring!"

"Did you call me?"

"Does a coyote shit in the woods?" he said. "Did it ring on your end?"

"No," I said. My locks were on the couch, a scattering of chrome and brass that resembled holiday ornaments. How had Christmas happened just two months ago? Just then I couldn't remember our tree or meal or gifts or trip to church. On TV, a reporter interviewed another reporter.

"How'd you know to pick it up then?" he said.

"Did you want something?"

"I wanted to see if you'd heard anything," he said.

"Just what's on the news. My father hasn't been home."

"After you bailed from school, everyone started guessing how long it would last," he said. "O'Dell bet Fat Clay his stereo that it'd be over by Monday. They shook on it."

"What was your guess?"

"That they'd already escaped," he said.

"The FBI talked to him. He refused medical supplies. They know he's inside."

"Since when do we trust the FBI," he said.

"They're in there. Nothing else adds up."

"Or maybe *he's* in there, but everyone else slipped out."

I flipped through the channels, found nothing new, started over.

"Are you still there?" Coop said.

"If everyone slipped out, why hasn't she called?"

ON THE LAMB

PODCAST EPISODE 8
GUEST: Rhonda "Turtle" Tilly
RECORDED: February 2024
                          Gatesville Correctional Facility
                          Mountain View Unit
                          Gatesville, Texas

Why didn't you leave after your barn dance?
God told us to wait.

Meaning, the Lamb.
All of us were free to go, and some eventually did, including my own sorry self. But the Lamb was just following orders. Think of them times the FBI claimed one thing and did the opposite. Said they wanted to keep their promise, but somebody higher up said no dice. Same thing. Our head honcho—and here I'm speaking about the Lord our God, not the Lamb, don't get that twisted—issued an order.

When did the order come down?
The next morning. Our plan was to tote the Lamb out on his cot like a stretcher. We had our sandwiches.

But then he's strutting in like a peacock. He sits himself up on a stool and it turned into a regular study. Soon enough he's covering his favorite topics—the Seals and the constitution and how Nebuchadnezzar, destroyer of nations, laid siege to Jerusalem and threw Daniel's men into the fire, but God saved them. Then he starts weeping, letting out what he'd been holding in for so long.

One by one, folks got up and passed before him, like at a funeral. We gave him soft hugs so as not to further injure. We said we loved him. The procession took a while. Then he said, "I've come to tell y'all we've got to pump the brakes on this hot rod."

What was your reaction?
I gathered up them sandwiches. I didn't want what food we had left to spoil.

Jaye

week of my mother trembling in pain and from the cold except when she was trembling and soaking through her clothes in fevered sweat. I spent the hours wiping her down with a wet rag and apologizing. People delivered food to our room; by the beginning of the second week, there was only the stock of MREs to eat. Lyle emptied our bucket each day. The twins said they'd heard the bodies of the dead—Senny, Tiago, and Beverly—had been stacked in the freezer. Later Ruthie said they'd been misinformed: Lyle had spent the night burying corpses behind the gym. Or burning them.

When she had enough energy to speak, my mother begged me to leave. She implored me. She asked me to forgive her for dragging us to Texas. She screamed at me, demanded I save myself, said she'd die happy knowing I'd gotten out. I believed every word and knew she desperately wanted me gone and never once considered leaving without her.

"I chose to come," I said, pouring water into a paper cup and keeping my voice upbeat. "I invited myself, which was really quite rude. You should ground me."

"I'm getting what I deserve, paying for sins. You're suffering for my selfishness. If you left, you'd be giving me the best gift."

"When you can put weight on your leg, we'll leave together. Here, sip."

She leaned forward, closed her eyes, drank. When she sat back, she said, "Don't you love me?"

"You know I do."

"Prove it," she said.

"We'll leave together. We'll call Dad from that skanky motel. He'll come get us."

"Everyone's going to be arrested. The kids'll become wards of the state," she said, eyes watering. "If you go now, they'll send you home."

"Leave before Perry repays you for our car? Not on my watch, sister."

"Baby," she said. "I'm not going to make it."

"Don't say that."

"I've ruined your life," she said.

"Mom."

"We shouldn't have come. I've gotten us both—"

"Mom!"

"You need to—"

"I met a boy," I blurted.

Roy

Another day plodded by, a week, more. Every evening, my hope had been ground down by half. My memory dimmed, numbed. I had to concentrate to remember if I'd eaten lunch or how I'd landed back in front of the television or what had transpired in the interim. Each morning I'd recovered just enough to be crushed when the day ended uneventfully. Raybourn lingered, and my mother started sleeping at his cabin because the overnight nurse had quit. Mason didn't call, but worse than that, I'd forgotten it was the time of month when he might've. When I finished off the last of the cereal, I broke up stale Oreos, dumped them into a bowl, and poured milk over them for breakfasts. The kitchen counter accumulated unwashed dishes and bread crusts and half-empty Coke cans. The garbage filled with the molded trays of TV dinners. I realized I'd missed trash day only after an animal tumped over our can and scattered the week's garbage across our yard. When monotony metastasized into a helplessness, I tore the posters off my walls, so only the huge Semper Fi banner remained. When Panda killed a sparrow and left it on our front steps, I used my *God, Guts, Guns* baseball cap to scoop up the feathered corpse. It was both lighter and heavier than I'd anticipated. That was the night before garbage day the following week, so I tossed the bird and then the hat into the trash can with my wadded-up posters and dragged it to the curb. Then I went inside and let televised reports from the ranch lull me into a dismal approximation of sleep.

The news changed depending on the day and channel. Four dead agents and fifteen wounded. Three dead agents and six wounded. Six dead agents, untold wounded. The National Guard had brought in twelve armored fighting vehicles. Six armored fighting vehicles. The tanks had been retired after the Gulf War, although it would be illegal for the military to be used against civilians. A hundred hostages. Three hundred. They were chained in the fortress. The Lamb kept negotiators on the phone for hours, spouting apocalyptic prophecy. Negotiations were stalled. No comment on negotiations. Law enforcement was furious, frustrated, pleased with the progress so far. Because there were so many officers from different agencies, they were having trouble getting on the same radio frequency. Communication between the agents and leadership was stilted, compromised, open, and clear. A unit of grief counselors, all veterans, had been flown in to work with agents involved in the raid. The Lamb had a harem of ten wives. Twenty. There were machine guns inside. Homemade improvised explosives. Military-grade firepower. The cult members had shot first. Fired blindly through the walls. Ambushed the ATF as soon as the cattle trailers had arrived. The water tower was outfitted with a .50-caliber machine gun and needed to be razed. The Lamb's wounds were infected. They were miraculously healed. He was deranged. A biblical savant. His mother was being brought in to assist with negotiations.

With each newscast, the pool of reporters sprawled, thickened. Lova Flores said over two hundred journalists were on-site, representing nearly twenty countries. At press briefings, the media looked like worshippers themselves, kneeling before the podium, their microphones extended like holy offerings. When it came time to pose questions, their voices rose and fell like a choir. As side-blown rain moved in, their hooded ponchos made them look like monks.

Federal authorities had commandeered a wing of the hospital. Agents with automatic rifles guarded the entrance while plainclothes officers were positioned elsewhere. Lova Flores was organizing a blood drive. On the midday news, a doctor said they'd been treating the kinds of wounds he'd only seen in Kirkuk. Seven agents remained in critical condition. When a reporter asked the doctor to identify the caliber of shells used, the FBI's communication liaison—a prim woman with a flat gold necklace over her maroon turtleneck—butted in and said such information couldn't be shared about an active investigation. She also said the discharge of wounded officers would not be publicized for fear that supporters of the cult would stage an ambush.

And supporters there were. They posted up in a gravel lot near the southern checkpoint. Protestors, fundamentalists, survivalists, and all manner of conspiracy theorists descended with misspelled placards and bullhorns. Like the press, their numbers kept rising. They screen-printed shirts. They made button pins. They published their own newspaper focusing on government cover-ups and how the coded symbols on U.S. currency had foretold the siege. Some believed the government might wall off the ranch to turn it into a prison. They sold their wares along with patchouli, hot chocolate, and BBQ. Lova Flores interviewed my father who said the citizens had the right to free assembly and he didn't expect them to break any laws. His beard was growing out, and because it made him look different than I remembered, I wished he'd shave it. Another reporter profiled a family of four donning combat gear. They'd driven from New Hampshire in their Suburban. The driver's side was emblazoned with a hand-painted Gadsden flag; the Second Amendment was scripted in its entirety on the passenger side. The Holy Roller parked his own van out there. Anarchists and evangelicals passed around a motorcycle helmet for donations.

Nothing made sense, least of all why the news wouldn't confirm who'd died inside the ranch. My ache—for clarity, for headway, for her—had become my bedrock, each day accruing an additional layer of estrangement and each evening another stratum of despondency. Then I realized that if Douglass didn't run a photo of Jaye, I couldn't identify her. It was a gut punch. How gullible I'd been, how arrogant, trusting I'd have time to learn her life. I knew the staccato rhythm of her laugh and the shallow contours of her knuckles and how she flapped her hands before every sneeze, but not her parents' names. Not even hers.

The coldest spring in a decade, and the weather was turning again. A norther was coming down, bringing rain. One meteorologist predicted sleet. Another forecasted hail. They begged people to keep plants and pets inside. I slept in my jeans.

ON THE LAMB

PODCAST EPISODE 2
GUEST: Constance Cullen
RECORDED: August 2023
Phone Interview

So the FBI had you talk with him?

They wanted me to tell him to come out, which I did, but I knew it wouldn't do no good coming from me. He'd been shot and said he was dying. Said he didn't mind. Said he was sorry he couldn't save me, but I'd chosen the left-handed path. He said he loved me and apologized for missing my birthdays. Said he hoped I'd gotten good presents. He said I had a grandson, but I'd never meet him. He was trying to hurt my feelings. I deserved it. You have children?

Yes.

One wrong word from them can be venom. That don't change. Your boy's surrounded by tanks and on every channel in the TV, and all they want is to crucify him in front of their cameras, but he's still your boy and you just want him to say he's missed you. I got what I earned, and probably so did he. Difference is that if it weren't for me, all those people, all them children, would've been just fine. They'd have had lives and families and children of their own that would twist their hearts in their hands like dirty rags.

Roy

The ringing phone must have woken me, though I couldn't remember falling asleep. Now I was in the dark kitchen, holding the receiver with both hands. Maybe I'd already said hello. I figured Coop was messing with me again. The TV was still on.

I was about to hang up when I heard, "Champion?"

"Mason?"

"Champion? You there?"

"Mason! Yes! Hi!"

"What in green hell's happening? We're watching television in the canteen, and I see Dad talking in front of tanks!"

"Is it Sunday?" I asked. A sting in the lining of my arteries, stark pain behind my eyes. I pinched the bridge of my nose. I couldn't square Mason, half a world away, watching the same station that was on my screen, seeing an interview with our father that I'd missed. I could hear people in the background.

"It's Saturday morning here," Mason said. "Friday at home."

"You're just calling because you saw Dad on TV? You're not shot or captured or anything?"

"You're seeing more combat than we are, I'll tell you what," he said. I pictured him in our school cafeteria but surrounded by rowdy men in desert camo with high-and-tight haircuts. He said, "All I do is frame walls and play Nintendo. How long has Dad worn a beard?"

"Just since he's been at the ranch. He can't really come home," I said. Then I told him about Huey coming for dinner and our rescuing the horses. I said I was shocked the feds hadn't cut the power yet, passing the idea off as my own. I told about the rain and freezing temperatures and how I'd been sleeping alone in our house. Behind him, other contractors whooped like someone had won a big pot in a poker game. The connection was clearer than usual. I felt guilty my parents weren't there to hear it. I said, "I'm pretty good with the kit you sent. I picked into the Live Oak Mall. I've got a new girlfriend."

"Right on," Mason said, but there was nothing behind it. "What's the old man say about this ruckus?"

"He thinks it'll end soon," I said. I was cherry-picking our father's language, I knew that, but wanted to guide us toward optimism. I needed Mason to agree and ask about Jaye and offer advice.

"Why not just arrest him? Why call in the heavy artillery?"

"I don't know," I said. A schematic rendering of the ranch appeared on television. The caption read: SINFUL STRONGHOLD. "There's a decent chance he has grenades."

"And, what, he bagged federal agents? That's confirmed?"

"Some were definitely shot," I said, remembering a term Mason had used when he was in-country, "but it could've been blue-on-blue."

"Then it's over. They'll light him up."

"When are you coming home? Mom thinks Sammy's going to run against Dad. With everything going on, we could use your help."

"September," he said. Maybe because of the clearer connection or because I was listening in a way I couldn't with my parents on the line, I understood he was lying, papering over a decision he'd already made. He would stick to his story then claim the trip had fallen apart at the eleventh hour. That would keep happening. He'd stay over there for years—who knew how many? He was curating his experiences the way my parents did, the way I did, showing only what he wanted us to see. I needed him to be different, better. I was indignant toward all of us.

"Will you still call on Sunday?"

"Not unless I see something on the news. It feels like I'm at home seeing all this on TV," he said. "Tell Mom and Dad I've got a leave-weekend in April. I'll call then."

"That's a month away," I said. "Can you at least call Mom at Raybourn's? She's depressed without you here. She's always worrying. She cries a lot— *a lot*. It's fucked. If you—"

"Champion, I'll—"

"If you came back, she'd be happier. You could help with the Lamb, too. You could offer tactics you learned in-country and—"

"Champion," he said again. "I'll call in April and be home in September. That's no time at all. But I can't help with this. The book's already been written and put on a shelf."

"Then how does it end?"

"The way they all do," he said, laughing darkly. "With everyone in the ground."

Jaye

I told her about my pilgrim's bushy hair and ears that turned red as onions when I teased him. I said I could hear how deeply, how particularly, his mother loved him just in the few words we'd exchanged on the phone, how she seemed proud I was calling for him. I said my horses had originally come from her and that cleaning their hooves and combing out their tails had made me feel closer to him. I said he listened to me in ways no one ever had, like his whole life had been spent anxiously awaiting my opinion on Thousand Island dressing and time travel. I told her about our late-night calls, how his voice turned faint and lilting when he refused to admit he was sleepy. Because I couldn't gauge if it would hurt or help, I resisted saying he made me feel "not invisible." But he did! I told her he made me feel less alone, but the deeper comfort was thinking I might be doing the same for him. I told her about big brother soldier and father sheriff and his heartbroken buddy. I told her about Perry's pouting when he found us in the parking lot.

"You haven't been able to call him?" she asked.

"The phones are dead."

"He's probably worried sick. He probably hates me."

"He loves you. Without you, we would have never met," I said, jokey. Then, serious: "He's excited to meet you."

"Jaye."

"You'll be walking in a week. Maybe sooner."

"Honey," she said.

Roy

On a Wednesday morning in early March, in exchange for milk and antibiotics, a blind man and his guide came out. That evening, three children and a lady in a wheelchair exited in a swap for boxes of medical supplies: gauze and bandages, peroxide and more antibiotics. Then on Thursday, a woman with a wide ivory stripe in her raven hair left and more supplies went in. Soon, I thought. Every night, tomorrow.

But after Thursday, no one else left. At daily press conferences, a spokeswoman vowed the Bureau was committed to a peaceful resolution, but Cullen had stopped accepting their calls. She said Cullen's behavior evidenced his callous disregard for human life, his sociopathic disposition.

"He's claiming to be an angel," she said, "but if that's true, there's horns holding up his halo."

When there was no news, broadcasts were pieced together with whatever producers could drum up. One segment attempted to explain the Lamb's belief system: The Second Coming was near and would be preceded by jihad. After the vanquishing of unbelievers, the Lamb's offspring would inherit the earth and Jesus would return. In another piece, the pastor from Solid Rock said his congregation was praying for the hostages. The manager of Chelsea Street claimed the Lamb never talked religion at the pub. He could pick a decent tune and always tipped the staff before loading out. Coop told me about an hour-long program about Jonestown that aired on CNN. A doctor explained how superficial Perry's wounds probably were. At one point, a channel ran a tight shot of tanks rumbling along a dusty road so I thought they were vacating the ranch, but it was stock footage from Kuwait. After sportscasters rattled off local baseball scores, they showed footage of media members tossing footballs or prac-

ticing golf swings around the staging area. They drove balls into the Lamb's
pastures.

Whatever was on, I watched. I couldn't look away. No one could. We
were all hostages.

Because another hospice nurse had quit and it was getting harder to ferry
me to school, my mother arranged for me to stay at Coop's. I packed a
couple changes of clothes and my locks. I folded a T-shirt around the
burlap-wrapped grenade and used another one to keep it snug. On the
drive, I rode with the suitcase on my lap to keep it from jostling.

"You're sweating," my mother said and touched my forehead. "You're
burning up. Do you feel sick?"

"I'm okay," I said.

At Coop's, I slid the suitcase under his bed and rolled out a sleeping bag
on the floor. I never slept long. When my eyes wouldn't stay closed, I
stared at the suitcase or gazed through Coop's smudged window. I picked
the closest star and tried to believe Jaye was doing the same. The notion
never quite took, so then I imagined a universe where a person could rearrange the stars to relay a message to someone else, a night sky inscribed
in cryptic code, an illuminated language of loss.

Coop's grandmother tended to get up for a couple hours every night.
She watched reruns, opened squeaky cupboards, hacked her croupy
coughs. Once she was seized by such a violent choking fit that I woke up
Coop, but after raising his head to listen, he said she was fine. Raccoons
rooted through garbage cans. Night winds coiled in and out of tallow
branches, raked them against the house.

Walking to school each morning, we split a package of Pop-Tarts.
Teachers assigned busywork and postponed tests, biding time until students could focus on something other than the ranch. Each day the home
ec classes baked brownies or magic bars for a teacher to deliver to law
enforcement at the ranch. After homeroom on Thursday, Rosie pulled me
aside to say she and Isaac were praying for my father, and Solid Rock was
devoting a prayer group to ending the siege. I couldn't think of how to
respond, so I just said you could never have too many prayers. In every
class, people studied me and whispered. Teachers gave me all the hall
passes I requested, either because they pitied me or getting rid of me

made their jobs easier. On Friday, I saw Shawn and Shane Buford being escorted to the principal's office.

"They got busted for cheating," Coop said walking home. Backlit clouds ridged the sky. "They're in in-school suspension all next week."

We passed the tropical fish store, the barber, the two-story apartment building. A woman sat on her balcony chewing a cigar. Coop was saying Lova Flores's blood drive would be at the Ford dealership. There would be tacos and T-shirts; he wondered if they'd relax the age requirements given the circumstances. I tuned out and, a block later, tried to catch up.

"Like maybe we could swap skills," he said.

"Skills?"

"You can teach me how to pick locks, then I could teach you nun-chucks."

I couldn't tell whether he really wanted to learn to pick or was just de-vising distractions. On my second night at his house, he'd suggested we build a house of cards. The next night it was trying backflips like Jacob Ternasky. We failed at both.

"I can show you how to pick a padlock tonight," I said. "We can work in front of CNN in case something happens."

"It's Friday," he said.

"So?"

"So we have to play penny-ante poker with my mom and Nana," he said.

We'd cut across the Masonic lodge parking lot. I had no idea what the Masons were or did, but I knew they'd given my father a plaque that hung in his office.

"Can we watch TV while we play?" I asked.

"You'll lose more if you don't pay attention," he said. "Also, she cheats. If she cleans her glasses before she bets, fold. That's her tell."

"Maybe I'll just stay in your room. I can say I have homework."

"I want to learn to open whichever locks are at the mall," he said. "You should've checked Coin Nook. They might've left behind pieces of gold. Actual treasure. Literal booty."

"That wouldn't make any sense."

"Says the burglar who didn't think to check," he said.

. . .

All weekend, the world was paled by cold and draped in the thinnest rain. Lova Flores postponed her blood drive. A gust of wind plucked an umbrella from a reporter's hand. More than once, Coop stood by the window and said, "It's fixin' to come one." Brent Douglass kept describing the weather as "biblical." Then he'd replay the footage of the reporter losing her umbrella.

Every time the phone rang, I had to stop myself from diving for the receiver. The calls were always from Coop's mom's clients. She worked at a beauty shop in a strip mall out by Solid Rock, but on weekends women paid her cash to perm their hair in the kitchen. She did two on Saturday and one on Sunday. The ripe chemical smell seeped under Coop's door as I tried to teach him how to pick locks.

He sucked. He rushed or applied too much pressure with the wrench. I told him to imagine the weight of three butterflies, but he just got frustrated. A rotten part of me liked seeing him fail, liked that I could do what he couldn't, but I also felt like a cruddy friend and failed teacher and was relieved not to have tried teaching my mother. When he showed me how to swing nunchucks, I suspected he made the routines harder than necessary to even the score. I gave up after I missed a grab and sailed the sticks into the YIELD sign on his wall, the impact so loud his mother abandoned her client in the kitchen and rushed to check on us. Wearing latex gloves, she pointed at us and said, "No more, Cooper."

On the one-month anniversary, every channel recapped the raid and standoff. We'd gotten used to the reports the way we had war coverage. They led every broadcast, and each night, Douglass signed off with the same live shot from the ranch: the barracks' windows illuminated against the dark. The yellow squares made it look like a passenger train about to depart on an overnight journey.

A blue norther dropped temperatures the next week. Brent Douglass talked about ruined crops, icy overpasses, a burst water main in front of the tobacco store downtown. Another station ran video of telephone lines heavy with icicles and showed reporters at the ranch fashioning a sickly knee-high snowman from the slush.

On Thursday night, Coop's mom and Nana bickered about opening the oven to take the chill out of the house. Nana flipped channels until she landed on the public access channel rerunning a Solid Rock sermon.

The pastor said the word *rapture* was nowhere in the Bible. Nana took up the remote again and switched to a sappy movie. I was on the sagging couch and about to excuse myself to Coop's room when Brent Douglass interrupted the movie with breaking news.

The government had, exactly as my father had predicted, cut the ranch's electricity. An Australian film crew had captured the moment on camera. In the footage, the lights went out so suddenly, so completely, that for an extended moment the only image on the blackened screen was our own reflection, entranced and aghast and under a scrim of dust.

When the feed cut back to Douglass, he said windchills were expected to drop into single digits.

"Those poor babies. They deserve better," Coop's mom said.

"She must be so cold," I said without thinking.

Everyone turned to me. Coop's mom said, "Who's cold, sugar?"

"The lady with the stripe in her hair," Coop said, covering. "We were just talking about her."

"She got out, remember?" Coop's mom said. "She's probably in jail, but warm at least."

"What world are we living in?" Nana said. "Freeze to death or come out with your hands up. Welcome to Texas. Welcome to the United States of America."

ON THE LAMB

PODCAST EPISODE 10
GUEST: Virgil Bernthal
RECORDED: April 2024
                    The Chapel of Light
                    Waco, Texas

When they cut the electric, those tank drivers probably heard us hootin'
and hollerin'! We were bitter cold but smiling.

Why?

"And great drops of ice, every one about the weight of a talent, came down
out of heaven on men; and men said evil things about God because of the
plague of hail, for the plague thereof is exceeding great." Revelation 16:21.
If anyone doubted before, the message was right clear now. Cold focuses
the mind. The so-called authorities thought they were putting us in a vise,
but God was using them. They were delivering His message, assuring us
we were on His path.

The building wasn't insulated.

We huddled together and held studies. We wrapped ourselves in wool
blankets. We broke up Senny's bed frame, and then Tiago's, and made a
fire with the wood in the mess hall. We were at war. Ask any veteran and
he'll likely have a similar experience of being pinned down. The difference
is we were at home, on domestic soil, and the enemy was our government.

Jaye

A month, entire and interminable, and my mother still couldn't put weight on her leg. Victoria thought the bullet had split her femur, but there was no way to be sure without X-rays. On the night they cut the power, I hooked my elbows under my mother's armpits and eased her from bed. I slid our sour mattresses onto the floor and pushed them together so we could snuggle. I dismantled the bunk-bed frame and fashioned the boards into a makeshift doorway barrier to blunt the drafts.

"You're resourceful," my mother said. Her breath plumed in the cold. "It's admirable."

"Frostbite is the mother of invention," I said, but I was proud.

The next morning Perry paraded through the barracks with Bev's army coat draped over his shoulders like a king's robe. He lingered in each room to inquire who needed an extra blanket or another MRE. He claimed to be doing wellness checks but just seemed to be fishing for sympathy, veneration. It was a desperate and mystifying victory lap, as if the government had played right into his hands by cutting the electricity. He described an ice storm befalling all of Egypt in the book of Exodus, then led everyone in a long-winded prayer. He said Lyle was in the mess hall building a fire to warm their bodies and spirits. I heard Ruthie and Eden shriek, swoon. Turtle sobbed. Victoria announced that Perry's recovery was a miracle that defied science, and everybody in the hallway cheered. When he appeared in our door, I pointed the derringer at his heart and threatened to pull the trigger if he came back. We were both waiting for someone—anyone, everyone—to scream or scold me, to bust through the barricade I'd built and slap the pistol from my hands. When no one did, Perry nodded and sulked off toward the mess hall with his flock filling in behind him. I thought my mother would rail at me in private, but she just said, "We raised you to be a fighter. That's something to celebrate."

After I drew the derringer on Perry, he only braved our end of the hall to fetch Kanaan. The boy would slip through my barricade, then crawl between me and my mother on our mattresses. He learned to avoid her leg. The three of us huddled together under blankets, but no matter how close we were, the cold found its way in and laid claim. Sometimes Kanaan asked about Seneca and cried, but there were also stretches when he seemed untroubled, content to chatter on about what he hated (the stench of everyone's buckets, the weight of wet clothes, having his fingernails trimmed) and what he found "tasty" (popcorn, grapes, clouds). He started sleeping between us at night, and soon Big Lyle brought the boy's clothes and few belongings into our room. With his crayons, I sketched pictures of pterodactyls and told him everything I could remember about dinosaurs. I promised to take him to see the mammoth bones. When Perry came by, he behaved like a father who'd lost a custody battle. Polite or crabby depending on the day. My hand trembled over the pistol grip in my pocket, ready to draw. My mother never spoke to him again.

Three nights later, the government pointed massive spotlights through the building's windows. It was a brightness I'd never known; it seemed they'd fitted a blinding halogen dome over the ranch, and the intensity of the glare bleached every color, bleached the darkness itself. I considered tacking one of our sleeping bags over the window but knew we'd freeze without it, so we turned to face the wall. I expected my mother to cry and demand I surrender to the authorities, but instead she started making shadow puppets for Kanaan—rabbits and ostriches and rhinos! That I had no clue she possessed such a skill charmed and bewildered me, made me wonder what percentage of her life I knew. *Let's trade secrets*, I thought. *Tell me every last thing.* The next night the cruel relentless glare was replaced by strobes. The three of us pretended to be robots. In the morning Victoria told us Turtle'd had a seizure violent enough that Olga shoved a spoon in her mouth to keep her from swallowing her tongue. The next night they doused the lights and blared horrific noises—hours of dental drills and lambs being slaughtered, the screaming so loud it tore at my gums—so we sang made-up songs about dinosaurs. We tied shirts around our ears—"Sound helmets," Kanaan called them.

When Victoria came to change my mother's bandages and said Turtle had left, I was hurt the old biddy hadn't come to say goodbye. I thought

Olga must be so lonely, but maybe she'd left with the others and I hadn't heard. Maybe she'd died. Maybe she'd never actually cared for Bev or Turtle. Most likely none of them trusted me after I asked about milling machines. Victoria didn't like the bedsores or color around my mother's thigh wound, so she spent longer than usual on the cleaning. My mother bit down on the blanket when Victoria got in there deep. When the pain was so bad she needed a break, she couldn't stop shuddering. She was in agony, and so very cold. I slid under the blankets, pulled her close, tried to absorb her shaking. It did no good.

As Victoria started wrapping up, I asked if anyone used the chapel anymore.

"The Lamb's deemed it unsafe," she said. "He's conducting studies in the mess hall. It took the least damage. You should come."

"We do our studies here," my mother said, shivering. "With each other."

"And Junior," I said for the first time and loved how normal it sounded, the name of a boy living a fine, predictable life far away from this freezing filth.

"I know he's taken a shine to you since we lost Senny," Victoria said, leaning close to my mother's leg, blotting the wound with peroxide.

Unplanned, I said, "My boyfriend and I are going to adopt him. Then we're going to get married."

The women turned to me, then each other. My mother shrugged. Victoria said, "Have you run this by the Lamb?"

"Not yet. But he's going to prison, so there's time."

Roy

On the thirty-sixth morning, an anemic Thursday, a stooped woman exited the building with her hands up. Brent Douglass reported that she'd suffered a grand mal seizure and needed medical attention, but the FBI denied any link between her condition and their tactics of directing strobe lights and loud noise into the ranch. An hour later, a mother and her children came out. I remembered her from when my father and I visited the ranch; she and her husband had been arguing in a foreign tongue. Coop and I thought everyone else would leave soon, but the evening news only brought footage of a tank crushing Jaye's red Chevy truck.

The next day I got a hall pass in language arts. The door to the narrow in-school suspension room was slightly ajar; Shawn and Shane were randomly filling in circles on a Scantron, not even pretending to look at the test questions. They wore their uniforms, which meant there'd be a scout meeting in the cafeteria after school. Outside the teachers' lounge—that wing of the building always smelled of ink-dampened paper—Mr. Leal was talking to Mr. Wilson. Both men had their arms crossed and resting on their bellies. The trophies had been righted in their case. My boots scuffed the gleaming floors.

I picked into the school's storage room. I left the light off but could see card catalogs and folding metal chairs. There was a filing cabinet packed with answer keys for tests given years before, maybe when Mason was a student.

I didn't hear the door open, just close. I slammed the file drawer shut and whipped around.

"Your girlfriend stole our pecans at the gun show," Shawn Buford said. Shane was beside him. They stood shoulder to shoulder with their backs to the door. They were thick-necked and a head taller than me, but with their matching uniforms and merit badges, they looked like costumed children. I was trying to connect Jaye being at early bird night to the Boy Scout pecans. Shane said, "We count how many bags we start with and how many sales we make. Plus we basically saw him swipe them."

"Oh," I said. "You mean Coop."

"Yeah, your girlfriend."

"We see y'all walking to school together," Shane said. "Holding hands."

"We don't hold hands," I said.

"Didn't you used to ride the bus? Did you quit because Rosie started jerking off Isaac in their seat?"

"I have to go back to class," I said.

"You mean you have to go find your girlfriend," Shawn said. He puffed out his chest. Shane copied him. They were blocking the door like bouncers. "Because she's afraid to walk home by herself."

"Exactly," I said. "Would you please let me through so I can find her?"

"Or else what?" Shawn said.

"The bell's about to ring. You'll get busted if you're not in ISS."

"We'll say we caught you going through private files," Shane said. His breath smelled like Skoal.

"The sooner you let me go, the sooner I can get Coop to pay for your nuts."

"You mean your girlfriend," Shawn said.

"Right. My girlfriend."

"Or maybe we should just collect the money from you," Shane said. "With interest."

"Or maybe we ought to call the sheriff and say his fruity son was skipping class?" Shawn said. "I guess he might be hard to get hold of while he's screwing the pooch at the ranch."

"What?" I said.

"You heard me," Shawn said. "Everything that's happening is his fault."

"If he would've arrested that sicko before, that old lady wouldn't have choked on her tongue, and the brave men who died would still be alive," Shane said. "If he was any good at his job, those kids would still have fathers. They're dead because he's too much of a—"

My fist caught him on his neck. I'd been aiming for his mouth. It was the only punch I threw. They left me on the storage room floor.

ON THE LAMB

PODCAST EPISODE 4
GUEST: Special Agent Kent Unrue (retired)
RECORDED: October 2023
                 Phone Interview

What did you think about the power being cut and the use of psychological warfare?
I wasn't consulted. Those were tactical decisions. It's uncommon, but there are occasional discrepancies between the approaches of negotiators and tactical teams.

Are you saying you disagreed with—
We'd been there over a month. People's patience was toilet-paper thin, and forgive me, you couldn't take a dump without it making the news. The stakes kept going up. But we *had* successfully negotiated the release of some hostages. More trickle than flood, but people *had* come out. And Mr. Cullen was increasingly unstable. On that topic, there's zero debate. He was erratic and irrational, and he'd been under enormous stress for, what, more than five weeks? So I advocated staying the course. Not because I harbored any sympathy for Cullen, not at all, but because we had a plan in place that was working. And, yes, absolutely, because I had real reservations about deploying tactics meant to drive a crazy man crazier.

Roy

"I grabbed your books when you didn't come back," Coop said, handing them to me after school.

We were by the flagpole debating which way to walk home. I'd voted for the field, but Coop wanted the sidewalks because a hole in his shoe was about to open. I couldn't tell if he knew I'd gotten my ass kicked. Shawn had stomped my ribs like he was trying to kill fire ants, and Shane had spit in my hair. Now the ROTC cadets stood at attention on the breezeway. I was bracing for Shawn or Shane to tackle me from behind until I remembered their scout meeting.

"I picked into the storage room," I said. I watched for any reaction, but Coop just kept looking around, maybe mapping different routes home. "I lost track of time flipping through old answer keys."

Then his eyes sparked. He said, "Shit me."

"They were old tests. I looked—"

"No . . ." he said, his gaze trained on a point behind my back, "your dad."

At the intersection, my father's Bronco. The windows were up, but I could see him talking into his CB. All at once I was shouldering through the hordes of kids, running with my books clutched to my aching ribs and waving my other arm as though trying to flag a plane.

"Wait up!" Coop called. "It's hard to run with my shoe!"

I passed in front of the Bronco. My father stretched to unlock the passenger door. I was huffing, trying not to show how much my side hurt. Coop caught up just as the car ahead turned left. I climbed in first; he followed. With the three of us, the cab was tight, and the pressure pinched my rib cage. Coop didn't shut the door the first time, had to slam it again.

"Is it over?" I said.

"You boys can sure book it," my father said. "When are track tryouts?"

"I'll go out for football this fall," Coop said.

"Were you coming to get me?" I said.

"Is it illegal for dear old dad to give his boy a ride home on a cold afternoon?" my father said. He was trying to jest but sounded shaky. He wedged his hat between the dash and the windscreen. The bones in my knees rubbed against each other through my pants. I could feel where my hip was touching my father's pistol.

His beard was bushy and dry; it made my own neck itch. He was in a fresh uniform, though, and if I inhaled, I could smell his Brylcreem and cakey deodorant. I didn't know what to read into these things. I wished he would've shaved. I hoped he never found out about Shawn and Shane; I worried he'd blame himself for my weakness. I ran my fingers through my hair to make sure I'd gotten all the spit out. The motion killed my ribs.

"Actually," he said, "I'd like to ask you boys a favor."

"Absolutely," Coop said, leaning forward, ready to enlist.

"With a warrant?" I said. "Is it something at the ranch or—"

"What if you lay off the TV for a few days?"

Coop eyed me, confused, then we both turned to my father. His gaze stayed on the tar pavement. It seemed like we were being grounded. The Bronco's hood rattled as we drove over a patch of road being repaired.

"Just the news, mind you," my father said. "If you want to watch a game, no problem. I'm only saying leave off Brent Douglass and his compadres."

"Why?"

"The feds have their marching orders," he said. "This'll be wrapped up soon. After that, we can all ruin our eyes watching the news."

My father parked behind Coop's mom's Nova, and Nana stepped outside. As we climbed the porch, he joked about apprehending a couple of roustabouts. She laughed and invited him for a supper of breaded cutlets and okra. He asked for a raincheck and thanked her for looking after me. I was sweating under my clothes, remembering how Shawn or Shane had kneeled to punch my kidneys, how I kept thinking they'd bust up my face but they never did. Coop's mom joined Nana on the porch and also asked my father to stay. "His dance card's full," Nana said. Shortly before he left, my father told me and Coop to run along so the adults could have a word.

Once inside we peeked through the front-facing bathroom window. My father did all the talking. Nana's hand flew to her mouth.

The TV stayed off during supper. After the meal, we cleaned the kitchen and played cards, then found an episode of *The Carol Burnett Show* we could pretend to enjoy. Each time I excused myself to the bathroom, I expected to piss blood.

I assumed we'd watch the news once Coop and I shut ourselves in his room, but he worried his mother would check, so he just played a tape of martial arts movies he'd recorded over Christmas break. We turned the volume up higher than normal and speculated about how and when the standoff would end. I said three days; Coop said four. At some point, he fell asleep—a relief. I resisted the urge to check the news, hoping such restraint might make some difference. My ribs hurt least when I lay on my back. On the screen, a ninja traversed rafters inside a carriage barn while his pursuers bungled the search below. Clueless, they argued and scattered. The ninja did a front flip from the rafters and landed silently on the hay-strewn floor. He mounted a horse and escaped into the night.

My mind was skittering, hectic. I couldn't find a path back to the calm life before I'd climbed into the water tower. Every thought arced toward Jaye, toward her horses that somehow, unlike any of the believers, had managed to flee.

When the movie's credits rolled, I crept into the darkened house. I'd been counting on finding Nana awake. I wanted to know what my father had said that made her hand fly to her mouth. I doubted she'd allow me to watch the news, but she might summarize anything she'd learned after we'd said good night. The kitchen was dark, vacant. The television was just a darker patch of dark in the living room. Back in my sleeping bag, I told myself that had something happened, the women wouldn't be sleeping. I told myself the quiet was a promise.

And yet it echoed like a threat. Because I felt guilty. Complicit. Because I couldn't remember a time when my father had exerted such effort to shield me from seeing something. If anything, he'd sought to teach me the countless ways people could be cruel, dangerous, unpredictable. He didn't want the world to ambush me with its violence or despair; rather, he wanted my guard up. I was timid, but I was his son. Or maybe because I was timid, because the gene that infused him and Mason and Grandpa Huey with courage had skipped me, he'd gone out of his way to show me

who and what to avoid. But now my father was forbidding me to look, or-
dering me to turn away. It didn't make any sense.

Until it did. And once I understood what he didn't want me to see, I
understood what my father himself wasn't seeing, and then I understood
everything else, too. It had all been so simple, and right under my feet.
"Oh fuck," I said aloud and covered my mouth. "Fuck, fuck, fuck." I lay on
the floor cataloging evidence and searching for holes or flaws, but I
couldn't ignore the answer to the question I should've been asking all
along: How *did* Jaye's horses slip from their stalls? Through Coop's window, the night was starlit cobalt. Would I have put everything together or
felt the riotous electricity in my chest if I hadn't found the grenades, if
Shawn and Shane hadn't beaten me? If my father hadn't asked his favor?
It didn't matter, for suddenly it seemed my life, my future and my soul,
was in peril the longer I stayed on the floor. I pulled on my pants and
jacket; I slid my lock-picking kit into one of my coat's pockets and the grenade into the other.

When I shook Coop awake, he said, "Five more minutes."

"It's still night. It's one in the morning."

"Did something happen?"

"Not yet," I said. "But soon."

"I'm going back to sleep."

"I got in a fight with Shawn and Shane today," I said. "I lost."

"I know. They told Barry O'Dell."

"Great," I said.

"They suck for double-teaming you. You would've won a fair fight. We'll
tag those Cub Scouts when they least expect it."

"You can't go back to sleep," I said.

"Watch me, sweet potato."

"I need your help," I said.

"With what?"

"We need a flashlight," I said. "And your bike."

Jaye

I woke between my mother and Junior. He was asleep, breathing evenly, his tender chest rising and falling against mine. The world was hushed, sheathed in ice and darkness. My heart, though, in chaos. Even before I rolled toward her, I knew my mother had died.

I rose. I shifted the barricade away from the door, careful to keep quiet. I roused Junior—shhhhh—and swaddled him in a blanket and carried him into the corridor. I tried thinking of anywhere except Perry's room to deposit him, but my mind was clogging and I was about to cry and it suddenly seemed unforgivable to saddle Junior with my grief. Perry had started sleeping in Seneca's room, so I tiptoed in and laid his son beside him. Perry stirred without waking, and within a minute they had both drifted into decent sleep. "I'm sorry," I mouthed to the boy.

When I crept into Big Lyle's room, he was sitting on his bed, fully dressed, with his boots planted on the floor and a rifle planked across his lap. I couldn't tell if he'd been stationed there all night or if he'd heard my footfalls and was waiting to neutralize the intruder. His long whiskers pricked my lips when I leaned close to his ear.

"I think my . . ." I whispered, then had to pause. "My mother died."

He received the information. His eyes roved from wall to ceiling to floor to wall. Then, as if released, he leaned his rifle against his bed frame, stood, and opened his arms. I shook my head even as I stepped forward. With my face in his jacket, I could hardly hear myself bawl.

Roy

When we arrived at the mall, my eyes and lips were dried out, stinging with cold. It was all I could feel other than the weight of the grenade in my coat pocket. I scaled the fence, climbed down the other side. Coop was wearing his favorite camo cargos. He tried passing his bike to me over the top, but the handlebars swiveled and he couldn't lift it high enough above his shoulders for me to grab. We tried prying up the fence's bottom but couldn't. When I suggested just laying the bike flat against the pavement, he said, "What should I do after that? Put a sign on it that says 'Free Bike'?" He peddled behind the mall and hoisted it into a dumpster. The noise carried around the building to where I was trembling. It took him forever to walk back.

In that freezing air, my fingers were stiff as kindling. Working the lock, I couldn't feel the tool touching the pins. We were at the JCPenney's entrance, Coop observing over my shoulder and shining the light on the keyhole to no avail.

"Maybe they changed the lock," he said. When I'd offered to get him into the Coin Nook, he'd burst out of bed and started pulling on his clothes. I'd thought he expected me to chicken out, but now I understood he'd come as much for the prospect of gold coins as for the chance to watch me succeed. Such camaraderie made it hard to concentrate. I cracked my knuckles, blew into my hands. I made a show of it in case I'd need an excuse later. I tried again, nothing. Slid in the wrench, the pick. Closed my eyes to envision the tumblers, the pins. The combination of pressure and position eluded me. My ribs burned.

Coop said, "What if we tried the Mervyn's entrance or— Shit! Was that it? Was that the click?"

The door opened. Coop swatted my backside like I'd scored a touch-down. I could feel him wanting to holler or whistle but restraining himself. We passed the hulls of the Record Bar, Pampered Pets, the cardboard marine in the recruiting center. Coop said he remembered getting free samples of sausage from Hickory Farms before Orange Julius replaced it. The flashlight beam played over the glass storefronts and tile. Walking ahead, Coop reminded me of a child at an amusement park. He smiled and swung the light toward the ceiling and into the dry fountains. I liked seeing him happy, the purity of his astonishment. I hated myself for drag-ging him into this.

"After we open the AV closet and get the video camera from school, we should come back and film a horror movie," he said. "*Mayhem at the Mall!*"

"Absolutely," I said. "It's an egress lock. I've opened it plenty."

Coin Nook was empty, but Coop's disappointment only lasted about five seconds and then we were back in the mall and he continued casting his movie. I wasn't really paying attention but gathered he would play the villain and needed Jacob Ternasky to do stuntwork. Backflips seemed cru-cial to the plot. I picked into Boots and Britches again and directed him toward the boxes of left-behind belts. I wandered by the fountains, listen-ing for the clack of Sammy's boot heels. I was surprised he hadn't arrived yet and worried what would happen when he did. For as long as I could remember, I'd been afraid of getting hurt or in trouble. I'd long expected—or at least hoped—to outgrow such anxiety, but now that mind-set seemed just as childish. Life, it occurred to me, might just be a series of decisions shaped by the fears you could tolerate, the pain you could disguise enough to survive.

"How long do you think we've been here?" I called to Coop.

"Ten minutes, fifteen at most," he said. "Can you get into Cutlery World? They might have left some knives behind. We could use them for close-ups in the movie."

"Last time he was already here," I said.

"So let's go to Cutlery World," Coop said, leading the way. "If he shows up, we can be on my bike in three minutes through the Sears exit."

I was trying to think if I'd done anything differently before. I was jumpy, thinking about not being able to get Coop's bike over the fence. I won-dered what else I might not have anticipated. I considered pulling the grenade's pin and chucking it back toward the recruitment center.

The only things in Cutlery World were flattened cardboard boxes and stacks of outdated knife catalogs. Coop sat down to flip through them. When he found pages he liked, he tore them out, and I knew he planned to hang them in his room. I was wondering what would happen if I pulled the fire alarm when I heard boots hitting tile.

"Shit," Coop said. "Let's get out—"

Then a flashlight beam a thousand times brighter than ours was in my eyes, blinding me. Sammy said, "Again, son? Really?"

"Take us to the ranch," I said, trying to block the light with my hand.

"Do what?" Coop said, shocked.

"Take you where now?" Sammy said.

"To the ranch," I said. "The standoff."

"Roy, what in Sam Hill is wrong with you? Why would I—"

"Come on," I said, racing past him. "We're short on time."

ON THE LAMB

PODCAST EPISODE 3
GUEST: Priscilla Martinez
RECORDED: September 2023
High's Café
Comfort, Texas

Sheriff Moreland called me at about two A.M. He'd heard the FBI was going to end the ordeal. He wanted me on-site for when the kids came out. He expected everything to start right around dawn, so I threw on some clothes and did my hair and makeup as best I could. It's silly, but I wanted to look presentable for the children. I wanted them to know I'd gotten ready for them to come on out.

ON THE LAMB

PODCAST EPISODE 12
GUEST: Sheriff Elias "Eli" Moreland (retired)
RECORDED: July 2024
                    Waco–McLennan County Central Library
                    Waco, Texas

I met Priscilla at the eastern checkpoint. I didn't trust them to let her through without someone vouching. They planned to breach before sunup.

You knew it was going to be bad.
I had that hunch when I saw them prepping tear gas.

But law enforcement uses tear gas often enough.
This all came out in the hearings.

I know, but you weren't called to testify.
Neither side would have appreciated my opinions.

So why the hunch?
CS gas isn't meant for confined spaces. It's combustible. Best-case scenario after prolonged exposure is brain damage. It's banned in prisons.

Were they using it to guarantee the Lamb would come out?
Hell if I know. It's a weapon of war, not a tool for law enforcement. Maybe a case could be made were the building in Iraq or Afghanistan, but not central Texas. A third of them inside were children. I thought he'd at least send them out. Weren't they the ones that were supposed to inherit the world? Weren't they the new beginning? Well, weren't they?

Roy

O ut on the blacktop highway, the night was glutted with stars. The cruiser was baking, its heater in a higher class than my father's Bronco's. Neither the hood nor windows rattled. There was the steady hum of the four tires on the asphalt, the engine doing its efficient work. I imagined the din of the tires rippling under the soil like concentric circles in a pond. A rosary hung from Sammy's mirror. It swayed when the road dipped, vibrated when we hit a flat stretch and he opened up the engine.

"I call shotgun on the way back," Coop said from the backseat. He was holding his bicycle's front tire on his lap. We'd had to detach it to fit the frame into the trunk. "I feel like a criminal back here."

"You are a criminal," Sammy said. "You were apprehended for B&E. You're an accessory to the destruction of private property. Smart money says y'all are both cuffed before dawn. Smart money says this scheme of yours won't work."

"It'll work," I said. In the mall, I'd explained that I'd broken into the mall as a way of summoning Sammy without using the phone because I knew calls to the sheriff's office were taped. I promised to lead him to where the grenades were hidden, so he could take credit for finding them. There were glaring holes in everything I said, but Sammy and Coop seemed too surprised to notice. It was exactly what I'd been counting on, exactly what was required if the next steps in my plan stood a chance.

Now, in the cruiser, Sammy said, "Hell, Roy, why not call your old man?"

"Because you're going to run for sheriff. If you take down the Lamb, it'll be a landslide. I want you to win."

"Bullshit," he said. "Bull-ass-shit."

"My father's give out," I said. The headlights parted the dark ahead. "My mother, too. You win and I get my family back. I'm being selfish."

For a couple of miles, we rode in silence as Sammy and Coop pondered what I'd said. I was pondering it as well, thinking how the words were all true and a lie at the same time. My feet were thawing. I couldn't tell how fast we were going.

"You're leading me on a snipe hunt. How about we add filing a false police report to the list of charges," he said. "I mean, come on—if they've got grenades, why haven't they lobbed one or two at the big bad government?"

"They can't get to them," I said. "They're in an outbuilding, but everybody's stuck inside. The shed's about halfway up the hill, between the ranch and horse stables."

"And you didn't think to mention this before? It wasn't worth your breath when you and your old man were on the actual premises?"

"I was afraid."

"But now you're not," he said.

"Now I'm too afraid not to tell," I said.

"Plus we realized we'd never seen them at the gun shows," Coop said from the backseat. He was animated now, pleased to assist. Maybe he was also signaling he'd forgiven me for misleading and using him. I hoped so, and I hoped he'd eventually forgive everything to come. He said, "If they were something he could legally sell, he'd display them on his table. I would've bought one."

Sammy eyed Coop in the rearview mirror. Static crackled through the CB radio. When it quieted, he said, "I tossed his booth back in January, but there was no contraband. I *knew* he had something, though."

"I know exactly where they are," I said. "Just get us through the checkpoint."

"All those women and children with him," Sammy mused. "A man claiming to be Christian, hoarding weapons to wage war against his own nation. How does any of it make any sense?"

"It doesn't," Coop said.

"We're close," I said, touching the grenade in the dark. "Really close."

Jaye

ig Lyle led me back to my room then stopped just before the door. Upstairs, I'd told him I didn't want anyone to know she'd died, and he'd nodded exactly once. I had no idea why I'd asked that of him, except I didn't think they deserved to know, to grieve, to claim they'd miss her when they'd never actually welcomed her. Or maybe telling anyone else would make her death more real. Everything was already too real. Nothing seemed real at all. I was afraid to go in the room, afraid I'd made a mistake and would find her awake and angry, heartsick that I'd returned when she believed I'd finally left; I was afraid I hadn't made a mistake at all and wouldn't be able to withstand seeing her body. I wanted Roy beside me. I stayed in the hallway.

Lyle palmed the small of my back, eased me forward. He was, I somehow knew, worried about the coming dawn. I went inside. Our room still smelled of her life, and though her skin was cold, it seemed no different from mine. I knelt beside her on the mattress, listened to her chest but heard nothing and felt no breath. I took care not to jostle her hurt leg. Gradually, vigilantly, I rolled her onto her back. I laid her hands on her heart. I brushed hair from her face. I wept and begged her forgiveness.

Roy

The checkpoint was a slant-leg canopy tent on the shoulder and three highway cones blocking the road. As we approached, I kept expecting critical news to crackle through the CB, but the radio stayed quiet. It could have been the silence was coordinated, a concerted effort to maintain the element of surprise. Or it was proof of how disastrously communication had wilted between the feds and local authorities. Or—and this has always seemed the most likely explanation to me—it was just the luck of our timing. Had we set out five minutes later, the radio might have conveyed warning after warning. Or the checkpoint might have been impassable. Or Sammy might have already been speeding toward the ranch when he'd gotten the call about the mall's alarm. He might have left us there with our petty crimes and futile plans.

But when the checkpoint guard saw Sammy's cruiser approaching, he removed the middle cone and waved us on. The cruiser jounced along the rutted road. I wanted to feel relieved, like another part of the plan falling into place amounted to permission, but I knew I'd crossed a bleak threshold. Had I banked on the night ending in Coop's room or at the mall? Had I undertaken the excursion with a coward's confidence, curious only to discover which impossible circumstance would spare me from following through and send me safely home? I just knew I'd never expected to make it this far. We were east of the ranch, near the dark top of the hill, because I'd told Sammy to follow the meandering route I'd traveled with my mother. The night's pins and tumblers continued to fall into place, opening door after door. Locking me in. Locking me out.

WE BURN DAYLIGHT | 287

My memory had the land sloping away from the road; we were on a berm, traveling between split-rail fences. Gravel crunched beneath the tires. From farther away came the rumble of heavy machinery.

"Who's doing construction this early?" Coop asked.

Sammy pressed a lever on his door to lower his window. A sudden dump of loud and freezing air. The cruiser was going fast enough that its antenna bowed.

"It's the generators for all the cameras and satellites," Sammy said.

"My window won't roll down," Coop said. Then, understanding, he said, "Oh, right."

Night poured itself over the folds of the earth, coating the hills and filling the valley below. For a mile, there was nothing to see beyond the window; the land blackened against the glass. Then, in the middle distance below, emerged the ethereal bone-white outline of the corral fence, the corrugated metal roof of the tack rooms. We were so close. I worried I was wrong about everything. I worried I was right. At once there was a sheen of sweat between my skin and my clothes; I had to open my mouth to breathe.

"Can you pull over," I said.

"Here?" Sammy said. "Why?"

"Can you just stop the car? I think I might throw up."

"Hell's bells, Roy," he said. He left off the gas.

"His stomach's been thrashed," Coop said. "He's gone to the nurse a bunch."

"Don't hurl in here. I just had this interior detailed and if—"

I swung open the door as the cruiser slowed. Had I waited any longer, I knew I would falter. I stumbled, tripped, skidded onto my side, and rolled. Sharp, piercing pain flared in my ribs. I put all my effort into shielding the grenade in my pocket from any impact. Then I was on my feet, running through the dark pasture, pebbles flinging from my coat, my hair. The arrhythmic punch of my boots upon the earth, the crust of frost giving way to soft grass underfoot. In my coat pocket, the grenade knocked and bounced against my thigh, but I clutched it mid-stride and tucked it to my chest. The steep contour of the slope revealed itself in increments under starlight. Sammy was out of his cruiser now, calling my name. Then Coop was, too. Maybe they were already growing wise to how I'd duped them, where I'd been heading all along. I kept running, putting distance between us, and soon their voices were scattering on bitter wind. Without looking back—had I turned around, I would have given up on everything—I knew they were standing on the road, bewildered and betrayed, watching me disappear forever.

ON THE LAMB

PODCAST EPISODE 7
GUEST: Sammy Gregson
RECORDED: January 2024
Keller-Williams Specialty Realtor
San Antonio, Texas

Where did you think he was going when he bolted from the cruiser?
Nowhere. I thought he'd lost his mind and was trying to outrun himself. I thought we'd find him in a heap in the field, blubbering and apologizing for concocting the whole sorry story. He was a kid who'd never known real trouble and his family was getting ripped apart. I thought he was playing a prank that outlived its shelf life. I didn't know about the girl then.

What about you? Did you know where he was heading?

No. He just told me we were going to the mall.
Forgive me if I call bullshit. Bull-ass-shit.

It's true. I thought maybe he saw someone, his father or Jaye. Or he was going through the pasture for a shortcut. I didn't know he had everything already worked out.
Mighty convenient.

I think he was trying to protect us. If we'd known his plan, we'd be complicit.
In my view, what happened that night is no different from these sickos who point toy guns at law enforcement so the boys'll light 'em up. Suicide by cop. If he wanted to protect us, I'm sorry to say he failed.

You didn't start the fires.
I should've radioed ahead from the mall. It wouldn't have mattered in the grand scheme, we know that now, but my conscience might be clear. I was prideful, selfish, already imagining myself with my feet propped up on the high sheriff's desk. No, I didn't start the fires, but I drove the car that delivered him to those who did.

Roy

The stables smelled of alfalfa and manure and the sweet oats in the tack room barrels. I had Coop's flashlight but couldn't risk giving myself away by turning it on. I imagined I was already in the crosshairs of snipers' night-vision scopes.

It was an hour before sunup, but the sky was already brighter than the earth. With every step, I felt increasingly certain this whole exploit was a foolish indulgence that would only bring more trouble to people I loved. That what I'd convinced myself was here, what I believed everyone else had missed but I alone could locate, was nothing but lovesick fever. I crawled around the stables, discovering nothing except brick-hard dirt. In the tack rooms, I pressed against the lower sections of the walls. I tipped feed barrels. I stomped the floor.

Outside, the lowland lay steeped in shoaled fog. Soon the horizon would emerge in the soft pink hues of ocean shells. No sign of Sammy's cruiser on the ridge above. Likely he and Coop had sped to the command post. My father would already be zipping his jacket and checking his flashlight, his sidearm and walkie-talkie, and heading to where I'd bailed from the car. It was another consequence I'd failed to anticipate. He would be livid, wounded by everything I'd withheld. All for a girl I hardly knew who was probably already dead. I turned to look in every defeated direction.

I paced the deck skirting the tack rooms. The leftmost panel of plywood was loosely anchored; the board shifted on its joists each time it bore my weight, so I started avoiding it. *Think*, I thought. *Think*. Every idea reeled out of reach—save the knowledge that I'd acted in perilous haste on nothing beyond a half-assed plan. From now on, my parents would regard me with skepticism and disdain. So would Coop. Even if they forgave my lies, they would never trust me again. Nor should they.

Then, I halted. Like I'd stepped on a land mine. The stars in their time-less stations, emitting their last light before dawn. The smell of dust and my own breath. The insects and faraway generators and the wind spread-ing the limbs of mesquite. Everything was as it should be except for that loose panel, a quarter sheet of plywood that had been securely fastened when I was last here.

Jaye

When Lyle at last stepped somberly into our room, I rose from the mattress. I tottered. I couldn't quite keep my balance, had to grab the doorframe. I offered to help lift her, but he motioned me into the hall. I tried to think how to tell my father and Roy, what words would serve best. I tried to imagine telling Junior. I searched my memory for today's date, but I couldn't even determine the day of the week, the month, the year. Or the color of my mother's eyes, what we'd talked about before bed. When Lyle came out, my mother was rolled into my blanket. Mine, not hers. I found her face in the fabric and touched my lips to her forehead. I covered her again. Then Lyle was out of the corridor—I would never learn where he carried her or laid her down—and I returned to our room. I dropped to our mattresses and curled into her blanket, pressed my nose into her pillow. "Your mother is dead," I said. "You're alone here." When the tears came again, I wiped them on my sleeve to preserve her scent on her pillow. Soon night would be gone. I needed it over already. I needed it to never end.

I was still on our mattresses when the tank cannons punched through the walls. I watched the gas distort everything. I watched the air catch fire. It didn't occur to me to move.

ON THE LAMB

PODCAST EPISODE 4
GUEST: Special Agent Kent Unrue (retired)
RECORDED: October 2023
           Phone Interview

So why did the FBI decide to end the standoff that morning?
Again, tactical decision. My team wasn't consulted.

Did the tanks breach the building because not enough people were coming out?
It's common for negotiations to ebb and flow.

Does that mean—
The decision of when and how to end the standoff was made by the attorney general of the United States. It was based on information provided by the agents and directors on the perimeter. What happened was tragic, no question, but there's also no doubt about who bears responsibility: Cullen. We can debate tactics and strategies, tanks and tear gas, but if Cullen hadn't abused those kids, we wouldn't have been there.

But even the attorney general testified there was no evidence of child abuse.
The responsibility is Cullen's. He did this. The tanks went in because he wouldn't come out.

Roy

In the end, a wooden hatch. A hole with the circumference of a barrel. The understanding that I was kneeling over the mouth of a tunnel emerged in stages and only as I eliminated every other possibility. There was an absence where there should have been solid, hard-packed clay. The hatch had been forced open from below: Someone had come out. Maybe the person had gone back into the tunnel and couldn't properly refasten the lid from below, or maybe they'd fled so hastily that they'd forgotten to cover their tracks. Maybe *everyone* had fled, exactly as Coop'd posited. I wanted to find and congratulate him, to apologize, to applaud his sage foresight. I lay on my stomach. The scent of buried earth, of air trapped in emptiness. The suggestion of a whistle as a breeze hit the tunnel's mouth like someone blowing into a bottle, the promise of an echo so complete that despite my desire to stay quiet I had a nearly overwhelming impulse to scream into the void. The swooning sensation of peering over a canyon. Blindly, I groped for a handful of dirt and flicked it into the hole. A cascade, earth on steel, sluicing out of earshot. When I could think of no other gauge, I plunged my arm inside as far as I could and clicked on my flashlight. The tunnel was a succession of oil drums that extended far beyond the reach of my beam. None of it made sense—that Coop had been right about the tunnels, that my instinct about where they'd lead had panned out, that Jaye, who must have used the tunnels to free the horses, might still be alive. I held the grenade in front of me, bit down on the handle of the flashlight, and crawled in headfirst.

I followed the shallow luminescence of the beam. The barrels were too narrow for my shoulders to stay square, so I twisted and trench-crawled at an angle. Every few feet my elbows got trapped against my chest. Or my aching ribs. I rolled to move on my back, angling forward one shoulder blade at a time. That the roof would collapse seemed certain. That the tunnel would be cut off ahead of me. Then behind. That I'd suffocate. That rats would scurry into the tunnel from below. Their bodies wedging between my neck and chin, their bony feet on my pinched eyelids, their hairless tails dragging between my nose and lips. Or my presence would awaken a den of snakes. I wouldn't know they were slithering down until one was in my shirt; I could already feel its cold belly on my spine. The only hope of anyone ever finding my body was the stench of my decomposing organs. Once the odor dissipated, I'd be lost to the living. My breathing gone again; I couldn't catch it. I wanted out. Needed out. I was sweating under my clothes; I needed to peel off my jacket but couldn't budge. I tried to push back, to backtrack, but the pitch of the tunnel had become too steep and I lacked the strength or leverage to move. I could smell my panic. I couldn't tell how far I'd gone. Twenty feet? Fifty? Or how deep I'd crawled underground, how much earth was suspended over my back, how much weight the rusted metal carapace could withstand. Or how long I'd been inside. The steel tore my pants. A sleeve. My knuckles. There came a dented barrel, tighter by almost half. I got caught with one arm stretched ahead and the other locked under me. I'd been trying to roll onto my side. My shoulders jammed painfully toward my gut. Like I was wrapped in duct tape. Like someone had put a plastic bag over my head and cinched it around my windpipe. I couldn't cough. I choked. Another thought of snakes: I was a field mouse, already dead and swallowed, the reptile's ancient muscles crushing my irrelevant bones. I screamed—mealy bile in my throat, a thick rope of spit from my chin to the barrel. The noise died out. I kicked and writhed and fought and at last my arm found enough give to break free. When it did, I lost hold of the flashlight and it clattered ahead, spinning like a top until there was only the smothering dark.

ON THE LAMB

PODCAST EPISODE 9
GUEST: Anonymous ATF Agent (retired)
RECORDED: March 2024
　　　　　Phone Interview

I was leaving for physical therapy when the phone rang. Another former agent was calling to tell me to turn on CNN. The screen was just fire and black smoke. Black smoke is never good.

The agent calling had been with you during the raid? He also quit?
I didn't say the agent was male. But yes. Last count I think about sixty of us walked after the raid. I was in the hospital, but I heard a lot went to church directly from the ranch. If you weren't bleeding, you went to repent.

How did it feel watching CNN that morning?
There were people inside that building who'd killed my friends, men with families who were just following orders. Someone in that building put a bullet in my own leg. But we should never have been there that first morning, so who can I really blame? When I saw all that black smoke on my screen, I couldn't help but admire them.

Admire?
They stuck to their beliefs. They said if you hate us so much, burn us alive. If you can't stand the sight of our kind, then turn our home into a gas chamber and point your precious cameras at us, zoom in as close as you can and watch us inhale.

Roy

B
arrel after barrel after barrel. The pitch steepened. My heels higher than my head like a shot buck, hung to drain. The tunnel stayed black and constricted, and each time some piece of my clothing ripped, the noise swirled at me from every direction. Then a segment too tight for crawling, so I flattened out and dragged myself forward by my elbows and whichever hand wasn't holding the grenade. Six inches each time, maybe less. Progress became more difficult, like I was submerged in quickly drying concrete. Entombed. Then, ahead, a sliver of a pale glow, no bigger than a tiny candle viewed across a field: the flashlight! I tried to move faster only to crack my head on the metal, only to wedge my shoulders again and lose more time prying myself free. Sweat and blood sopped my hair, stung my eyes. Each part of my body turned foreign.

The opening. About a hundred feet away. I learned to exhale before every movement. If my lungs were full, the space was too tight. I strained against the last barrels—toward the hazed radiance of the flashlight, toward a pocket promising easily drawn breaths. Every foot a mile, ten miles. The tunnel ended in a precipice, but the drop to the landing was farther than I'd anticipated and I hit hard. My muscles had knotted up. I fumbled for the flashlight and whipped it around the space: clay walls and the crude timber framing of a mining shaft, a sloped cavern. The ceiling was too low for me to stand, but even that much room offered enough space to shake feeling back into my limbs. Tools leaned in the corners— a pickax, shovels, buckets, a wheelbarrow. A breach in the opposite wall. I shed my coat, threw it to the dirt. My shirt was soaked. My dry mouth tasted of vinegar. I desperately needed water. I sucked salty sweat from my shirt. I crouched beside the breach, listening for noise or voice. I aimed

the flashlight into the passageway—more rough framing and a blind corner. I couldn't figure whether to follow that path or climb back through
the tunnel in hopes of telling Sammy what I'd found. The flashlight beam
in mottled dark. I was almost to the blind corner when I thought to turn
back for the pickax.

Stillness. Silence. Through most of the corridor, there was enough
room for me to walk with my spine hunched. The constant threat of phan-
tom attackers, the terror of knocking loose the framing, the tunnel collapsing. The knowledge that the pin would slip from the grenade in my hand,
that explosion was imminent. Every few steps, I snuffed the light. I held
my breath to listen. Then I clicked it on and forced myself forward.

The tunnel kept jagging directions. One stretch was taller and braced
with plywood walls. When I entered a long straightaway, I tucked my head
into my shoulder and plowed through at a full run. With each step, I was
more convinced I'd emerge not in the ranch, but in a random field or beside the highway. I had seen no option to take a different path, but I knew
I'd made a wrong turn. From behind, the imaginary men gained ground.
Ahead, I could almost hear Perry and his people stalking toward me.
Ghosts everywhere, furious and disturbed spirits, the dead, holy and un-
holy alike, debating how much longer to tolerate my smug imposition.

Then, on the surface above and ahead, an annihilating detonation. A
noise like a crane dropping a ton of debris to the ground, and the impact
shook the earthen corridor and knocked loose a cascade of rocks and dirt
behind me. I was fear-stricken, but then the fear vanished; there was no
longer room for it.

ON THE LAMB

PODCAST EPISODE 4
GUEST: Special Agent Kent Unrue (retired)
RECORDED: October 2023
            Phone Interview

Was the FBI aware of the tunnels?
Mr. Cullen denied us access to the building.

What about the stables or other exit points?
Our primary focus was the health and safety of the hostages inside.

So you learned of the tunnels after the building burned?
The FBI's position is that Mr. Cullen set fire to the building to destroy evidence. In the case of the tunnels, he didn't succeed.

Was the CS gas a mistake?
Our mistake was taking Mr. Cullen at his word.

Did you find evidence of milling machines or live grenades?
That information has been sealed.

Roy

An extension ladder, twenty feet tall. Beside it, a bucket of flashlights and kerosene lanterns. For the climb, I hooked the safety lever of the grenade in my back pocket and bit down on the flashlight. I extended my arm as high as I could, hooked the ax blade on a rung, then scaled. Each time I reached the ax, I stretched up and hooked it again. Pain lanced the space between my ribs. Eventually I climbed high enough to see a shredded piece of particleboard hanging askew. It swung inward, so I had to descend a few rungs and use the ax handle to pull it open.

I emerged between a bullet-riven wall and a set of steep bleachers. Gray light came through the perforated wall, a broken window. I stayed low, crouching against the busted-up bleachers. I peeked around and found I was in a chapel—ruined and deserted and surely a preview of what awaited throughout the building: nothing and no one. They had escaped through the tunnels after all, or they had been arrested and hauled off. A few punctured drums were strewn about. A splintered acoustic guitar lay on the stage and another on the floor like fallen soldiers. The rumble of heavy machinery, of boards cracking. From the schematic I'd seen so often on the news, I knew I was on the westernmost part of the building and the barracks were to my right. A gluey smoke burned my throat and lungs. I tied my shirt like a bandana around my nose and mouth. I chambered the ax. I stood up straight for what seemed the first time in my life.

ON THE LAMB

PODCAST EPISODE 10
GUEST: Virgil Bernthal
RECORDED: April 2024
                The Chapel of Light
                Waco, Texas

Who else knew about the tunnels?
Not many: Big Lyle; Tiago and his wife, Leticia; the Lamb.

Why weren't others informed?
Tiago wanted a way to get his family out if INS came knocking. He paid
for the materials, designed it. He wanted tunnels leading to multiple exits
and safe houses. Our joke was that's why that first tunnel was so tight; it
was designed for a very short, very skinny Portuguese family! The Lamb
worried everything would cave in.

You don't think the Lamb ever envisioned using them?
The tunnels were Tiago's. Unfortunately, he was the second person to die
in the raid.

But, if they were already built, why not use them when things got bad?
When people ask this, I always feel sorry for them. It shows you've never
felt part of what we did. Where would we go? Why would we leave?

**Because tanks are knocking down the building? Because you might be
able to save your wife and daughter, yourself?**
Salvation was inside.

Jaye

Alifetime before, on the fog-strewn morning when the men had stormed from cattle trailers, when their bullets tore through Senny and Tiago and Beverly and my mother, when I'd fled to the chapel, I'd curled fetal while a torrent of gunfire blew apart the bleachers' particleboard façade. When the shooting stopped, the opening was right there. A hiding place, I thought. I kicked through what remained of the particleboard panel, but instead of a solid floor on the other side, I found a void and the ladder that stretched twenty feet down to the dirt. There was no thunderbolt of epiphany. No exhilaration of future escape. I stepped onto the top rung and descended because I was terrified and had no other choice. With luck, I thought I'd wait out the shooting under the chapel. Probably I'd get stuck, trapped. The goggled men would find me, shrug their shoulders, and squeeze their triggers for sport. Or they'd pull up the ladder and leave me to starve.

So I just kept trying to find different places to hide. Beside the ladder was a bucket full of flashlights. I took the only one that still emitted a weak glow. I moved with my arms outstretched or my back pressed against the earthen walls, groping through the lightless passage. I knocked my head against unseen beams. I fell against plywood framing. As soon as I squeezed into the barrels, I wished I hadn't. I assumed I was in what would become a sewer system; I expected filthy water to rush in and fill the barrels and my mouth and throat, to drown me. When I finally peeked through the hatch and saw the horses, my solitary hope was to live long enough to set them free.

The shooting had ceased. From the stables, I could see agents in flak jackets backing away from the building with arms raised. They moved cautiously, warily. Their palms were lifted in deference to some wrathful deity.

I opened the corral gate, swatted the horses' backsides, and sent them galloping into the pasture. It was as if all those months of coaxing them toward me, of earning their trust, had served only to lure them close enough to scare them away. After the horses disappeared over the hill, I crawled down into the barrels and back toward my mother. If Perry or the black-clad men wouldn't let us leave through the front door, then we'd use the tunnel and sneak out while they slept. As I inched through that claustrophobic dark, I was giddy. I thought we'd crawl out that night.

But, no. She'd been shot, hobbled, and I refused to leave without her. Whenever anyone came to our room, I scanned their eyes for my secret. Exactly what I believed would betray their knowledge of the tunnels was unclear. So was what I hoped to gain. Someone with whom to plot our escape? Someone to serve as a decoy once my mother had recovered enough to flee? Perry had to know about them. And probably Big Lyle. With a jolt, I understood where he'd been on the days when he vanished from the ranch, understood why the property was littered with barrels.

I could find no hint that the twins or Gina knew. If Virgil was aware of them, had he alerted Sage or Charity? Why hadn't they left? I wondered where the horses had gone, worried they'd trotted back to the stables or down to where the agents were gathered. I was constantly stopping myself from mentioning what I'd found. Cruel perhaps, but necessary. If no one else knew, then my reticence amounted to their prison sentence. Or their deaths. But still it wasn't worth the risk of someone ratting me out to Perry. Or someone attempting to escape and getting caught, exposing the tunnels and foreclosing my plan to abscond with my mother. Everything seemed an accident of timing, everything on the precipice of ending.

But then my mother was dead and the tanks were ramming through the building and I was on our mattresses content to watch the walls burn. And I might have stayed there had Junior not come charging through the hallway and skidding into our room. He was shrieking and clawing at his face. The gas was scalding him. I took him in my arms, then pressed the blanket to his eyes, which only worsened his pain. There was a succession of noises I'd never heard before and yet still recognized as boards exploding. The voice of God had returned, but I couldn't make out the message over Junior's screaming. He was slobbering and flapping his arms—a broken-winged bird failing to take flight. My gas mask was too big for him, but I used the roll of gauze Victoria had left behind to wrap it securely to his head. I told him to relax and breathe normal, and when he did, I knew the filter Turtle had given me in the gun room worked. We were about to set out for the tunnels when I heard Perry clamoring in the hall, screaming for his son.

"Stay here," I said to Junior.

He started trying to pry off the gas mask.

"Leave that on," I said. "You look super cool. You're a superhero mummy."

Perry was ducking in and out of rooms a few doors down. He was so frantic I almost felt sorry for him. I couldn't tell if Junior could hear him with how tightly I'd wrapped the gauze. The world was a rumble.

"Here," I said, draping my mother's blanket over his head. "Let's play hide-and-seek. Stay here and count to a hundred, then come find me. But don't open your eyes until then."

Smoke was claiming everything. Perry was in the hall, calling out, then I could hear him go into Gina's room. I pulled the blanket down over Junior, completely covering him. I said, "Start counting now."

"Now?"

"Now!" I said, all cheery.

"One . . . Two . . . Three . . ."

In the hallway, I waited for Perry to emerge. When he did, he halted, awkward and disconcerted. The air was thick with poison. Everywhere noise like countless flags whipping in gales of wind.

"Help me," he said. "I'm after my boy."

"I have him," I said, and relief passed over his face.

Then I drew the whore's pistol and shot him through the gut.

ON THE LAMB

PODCAST EPISODE 10
GUEST: Virgil Bernthal
RECORDED: April 2024
　　　　　The Chapel of Light
　　　　　Waco, Texas

Gas was filling the building. It twists your windpipe and keeps tightening. Then the fires started up, little ones at first, but they spread and merged.

The mess hall was still unscathed, though. God wanted us all in one place. It was like waiting out a tornado. Sounded like one was right on top of us. We held each other and prayed. I kept expecting agents to bust in and arrest everyone. I hoped Sage and Charity would be able to stay together at a women's jail. Then I realized people were missing—Lyle, Jaye, Kanaan, and the Lamb. I told Sage and Charity I'd be right back.

But as soon as I closed the door behind me—and I mean right when the door shut and not a millisecond later—the walls collapsed. Fire had been snaking up inside, and all at once the supports just buckled like Styrofoam and the roof was on the floor. You've never felt such heat. An avalanche of burning lumber, thousands upon thousands of pounds. A cluster bomb might as well have gone off. I heard a few screams—I can still hear them—but not many. A fire that big is as loud as an airplane engine.

I just stood there in complete shock. In an instant, everyone I loved was gone—my wife and daughter, my entire world. It was like a page had been ripped out of a book and tossed in a burn barrel. It was that final.

Then the wall beside me came down, and all I remember is the flames around me and how they mixed with the cold air. I was out in the open for the first time in more than a month. My flesh was burning. Falling off the muscle.

Roy

The innermost core of every lock is called the bible. It houses the springs, the driver, and key pins in connecting chambers. Below those are the plug cylinder and keyway. If a key doesn't match the plug, the pins won't align, and the cylinder won't have room to rotate. But when the peaks and valleys correspond, when the serrations fit together, the key twists and the pin stack passes the shear line and rises into the bible. That's when the lock opens. Really, though, the key is irrelevant. With the right tools and sufficient patience, it's not difficult to clear the shear line. This is what locksmiths and outlaws understand: The lock isn't what keeps people in or out. It's what might be on the other side of the door.

Just outside the chapel, Perry sat slumped in the narrow corridor. Legs extended in front of him, eyes lidded behind his crooked glasses, mouth agape, the hem of his cowboy shirt soaked in blood. He'd died trying to reach the tunnel—of this I was sure. What I couldn't figure was if I ought to step over his body and proceed into the barracks or go back the way I'd come. Ashen light. Smoke, and the wasted odor of sulfur. His wound so fresh it was still leaking. I'd never seen a dead man before, never considered that I might. Now that I had, I felt tainted, cracked somewhere inside. I was rooted where I stood, trying to reconcile a tight space occupied by two bodies but only one life.

Then his eyes fluttered open and found me. He said, "Hidy, Rodeo."

I recoiled. Stumbled. Hit the wall like I'd been thrown from a horse. I cocked the ax.

Perry rolled his lips, moistened them with his pasty tongue. A pox of sweat on his brow. We were in a kiln.

"Where's Jaye?" I asked.

His gaze lolled. He moved his head to the left, to the right: *No.*

"What do you mean no?" I took a step closer. My feet were sprawled wide. I knew he was dying and couldn't hurt me but still didn't trust him. I kicked his ankle, hard, like I wanted to sail a soccer ball downfield. The blow jarred his stomach, so he cried out and clutched his wound. I said, "Where is everybody?"

"I saved them."

"Then where are they?"

"They're all gone ahead."

"Stop lying," I said. The air was dense, starting to boil. My clothes were sweat-soaked, slick, getting heavier.

"You ever think Uncle Sam is making an example of me? That if you live a life he can't tax, he'll flatten you? Everyone forgets Judas was in bed with the government. It was the government that crucified—"

"I found your grenades!" I yelled and hurled the ax down the corridor and whipped the grenade from my pocket. I hooked my forefinger in the pull ring. "Now tell me where she is!"

"Jaye did what she was supposed to: delivered you to me."

"Talk straight!" I said and put the toe of my boot over his wet wound. He folded over in agony, let out a deranged guttural groan.

"Tell it true or I'll pull this fucking pin! I'm not bluffing," I said, and it was a shock to realize I wasn't. This was my warrant. A mandate like fate, holy writ. I said, "Tell me where she is, or this is the end."

"I thought she was the light, but she was temptation. That's why she's gone and you're here."

"Perry! I'm warning you!"

"The seventh trumpet has sounded, Rodeo. Show me you hear creation groaning for redemption."

"Tell me what you did with her!"

"Show me that Jaye's wet little—"

I pulled the pin and spiked the grenade into his lap. Perry winced but made no other sound or effort to put distance between himself and the explosive. In the fuming smoke, my eyes were watering and I couldn't see as I was bolting away. I kicked the ax and sent it spinning and tripped over its handle and crashed to the floor. Maybe I could've stood up, could've run and thrown myself down the ladder, but why? For just then I understood she was gone, and she was gone because I'd been too slow and selfish and small. I deserved no reprieve. I stayed down and wished hysterical apologies toward everyone I loved. I yearned to assure them that my life, however short, had been lucky and full. My heart throbbed in my teeth. Sweat leaked from every pore, a paste on my skin. I squeezed my eyes shut. I hoped my obliteration would be instant, but then it occurred to me I wasn't crying, or anywhere near crying, and I was desperate to communicate that to everyone, too. When I knew the blast was coming, I screamed not out of terror but defiance.

But there came no explosion, no eternal silence. There was just Perry's snickering, then his cackle that had him laboring for breath. Once he composed himself, he rolled the grenade toward me like an apple.

"Solid iron," he said. "I was proud of that removable pin. I thought we'd make a fortune, but Texans won't buy anything they can't wear, eat, or shoot."

A primitive bronze light washed the corridor. I raised myself to sit against the opposite wall. My finger was still hooked in the grenade's ring. I whipped it weakly toward Perry but couldn't tell how far it went. I said, "Everything about you is fake."

"Isn't this what I've always said was coming?"

"I'm tired of the lies."

"No, all you want are lies—you and all your kind. You want to hear Jaye's home. You want the TV to say justice is being meted out by patriots. Reality's a buzz saw; it'll carve up your guts. Reality is this country betrayed us, and the whole dime-store world's underestimated me the same way it's underestimated you."

"Quit it, Perry. You can't convert me."

"*Convert* you? I'd sooner congratulate you. You crawled in here while them yellowbellies outside are sitting pretty in hand-me-down war machines. We weren't alone five minutes before you tried to blow us both to smithereens. Philistines choose what's comfortable. Not me, though. Not you neither."

"It's not the same," I said, but maybe it was. I'd lost the thread of veracity. I wiped my bitter lips. I was so thirsty. My spit tasted of pesticide. In a different part of the building, another implosion—a simultaneous shatter and collapse and flexing of walls, trailed by a sheet of thick blistering air. My consciousness flickered. My eyes kept closing.

"We finished history," Perry said. "Once I'm translated—"

"You mean once you're dead," I said. It felt like a lit match was probing my eardrums. "You want me to kill you."

"Hardly."

"What then?"

"You're saved," he said. "You're saved to tell others I've had you in my sights all along but never squeezed this here trigger."

I forced my eyes open, squinted through the coarse orange haze: in Perry's lap, aimed in my direction, a 9 millimeter. He raised the gun and waggled it, displacing enough smoke to show his dejected simper. I'd underestimated him again, which confirmed that while I—while everyone—had failed to prove what he wasn't, we'd refused to consider what he might be. Merciful and ordinary. Pious and repellent. I knew this was how he lured people in, how he made them feel like they belonged with him, how it was all a crock of fantasy, but I also felt on the verge of some cosmic unmasking. It seemed the mystery of God was about to end, but then Perry jammed the barrel into the soft hollow under his jaw.

"Perry! Wait—"

The smoke convulsed. It spiraled and eventually filled back in over the body. Heat beyond heat. I felt too much, and soon I was overtaken by an otherworldly lethargy. A heavy sludge, slow and molten. My body was drying out. Whatever was inside me was moving on. And with it, my indulgent and reckless desire for courage. The corridor was being consumed by light. A hymn of burning. A canticle of walls coming down. The fires drawing ever closer.

Closer, she'd said. *Closer.*

And then, at last, a blessing: in relentless and divine relief, an undulating vision of her blooming from fumes and torrents of smoke. Everything I'd ever wanted. Her imploring voice. My given name on her tongue. She kneeled beside me, gently lifted my chin, kissed me. On her lips, absolution. My Eucharist and last rites. My Madonna and child. Time to go, she said. Up, up, and away. Okay, I thought. Okay I'm ready. Soon the ash of our bones would knit together. Let this be my quick end. Let hers be the only face I see. I closed my smoldering eyes. I spoke my final prayer.

ON THE LAMB

PODCAST EPISODE 10
GUEST: Virgil Bernthal
RECORDED: April 2024
               The Chapel of Light
               Waco, Texas

Do you think you were spared for a reason?
The others had done enough to be translated. Not me. I'm still working.

The Lamb's body was found yards from the tunnel entrance, but you don't think he was planning to escape?
He might have been looking for anyone who'd gotten trapped. He might have been looking for Kanaan or Jaye.

What do you make of Big Lyle's remains never being identified?
I think the feds did a characteristically shoddy job of cleaning up their mess. Others were never identified—Kanaan, Jaye, Roy. The lawmen wrapped my limbs in gauze and put me in the paddy wagon. We watched the building burn out. No one else walked away.

What do you mean "still working"?
I get ten or so people out to the chapel for studies each week, sometimes a couple more, but mostly I spread the message online. The website gets good traffic. I answer email and update the index. I've got a room set up for Turtle when she gets out. Folks want to meet her. We're praying for parole.

Index?
It's an online clock, counting down to the Lamb's return. I calculate dates and figures from Scripture, and track what's happening in the world that could signal the opening of the Seventh Seal. Tsunamis, famine, war. It's not an exact predictor, but the signs are there if you know how to interpret them.

How long do we have?
Not long. Not long at all.

ON THE LAMB

PODCAST EPISODE 12
GUEST: Sheriff Elias "Eli" Moreland (retired)
RECORDED: July 2024
          Waco–McLennan County Central Library
          Waco, Texas

You said the FBI's marching orders had come down the day before—what was the last straw?
My opinion? They caught wind of how flush Perry was with MREs and water, and they started doing the math on how long he could hold out. At best, they were staring down another few months of looking like Keystone Cops.

You think the government ended the standoff to avoid more bad press?
I think the shot-callers saw their jobs getting a lot easier if reporters devoted airtime to anything other than Waco. They'd been trying to choke off access for weeks. Media was two miles away by federal decree, and in most cases that would've been plenty far, but not here. With that kind of story and then a fire that big, cameras don't need to be close.

Do you think the media helped or hurt?
Even odds. On one hand, all that attention might've kept the agents in check for a spell. Who knows what might've happened with less scrutiny? On the other, the raid was just a publicity stunt, and everything that followed was propaganda. At some point, you've got to ask who came out ahead. Who had the most to gain if the cameras kept rolling?

Looking back, do you see any missed opportunities? Any ways the tragedy could've been avoided?
I see nothing but.

Who's most responsible in your eyes? Perry? The government?
In the end, there wasn't much daylight between Perry and the government. Folks counted on them, placed faith in them. They had different laws and weapons of choice, but even those aren't so far apart. They came from the same soil—the need to believe there's something bigger at work and, whether you call it God or country, it'll come save you when you're outmatched.

So they're both culpable?
We're all culpable.

What more could you have done?
. . .

Eli?
. . .

Eli, are you—
I think it was '91 when Roy and I delivered the bay and pinto to Perry's ranch. The older I get, the clearer that day gets in my mind. Mason hadn't been gone long, so we weren't used to missing him yet, still feared the worst whenever the phone rang. But that day at the ranch was a good one. I knew Lynnette was happy we'd found a nice place for her patient's horses, and it was a relief for me and Roy to take a drive together. Perry complimented the way Roy sat a horse and took to calling him Rodeo. I'll be damned if that wasn't the first time I'd seen that boy smile since his brother left. He hung back with the horses, letting the kids feed them carrots and apple slices, while I walked the pasture with Perry to check the fence.

Do you feel like you missed a clue that day?
Could be. Could also be I drank some of his Kool-Aid that afternoon and it blinded me later on.

I'm not sure I follow. Are you saying you could've brought him in on charges that would have led to a different end?
I'm saying I missed my chance. I'm saying if I'd had even the slightest inkling of what was coming, I would've come back from the pasture alone. Or, if it meant Roy would've gotten a fair shake, I would've walked Perry down to his turtle pond and drowned him with his whole flock watching.

Roy's remains have never been found. Do you have any hope that—
His coat was in the tunnels.

But—
But nothing.

You don't—
No, I don't. And none of this jaw-jacking will change it. The world keeps spinning. If we're lucky, we'll all be forgotten. What happened, happened.

I've been hurting all the years but talking about it won't help and sure won't keep anything from happening again. Hell, it's never even stopped happening in the first place. All those Sunday school empires? Every one of them fell and turned to dust, and that's our future, too.

But if their bodies weren't—
It's damned good to see you, Coop. Your mother and grandmother would be proud of how you turned out. Roy, too. All of us are, including me. But I need to get. I've got hours of highway ahead.

I think understanding what happened matters. I think their lives mattered. I know you do, too.
You were a true friend to him, and I'll always be grateful for that, but you've got to let this go. Everybody does. We aren't built to matter. That's the surprise here. That's the big finale. Tell the story a million times, a million different ways, but the ones who were punished and the ones who were pardoned ain't switching places.

Epilogue

July 31, 2024

Elisabeth

S an Saba has too many churches and too few restaurants. We live fifteen miles outside town and tend to cook at home. We went for enchiladas a month ago, pizza a little while before that. Mostly we make the drive for supplies. We turn it into an afternoon. We get coffee and split a sweet roll. Andy pokes around the hardware store. I waste all my time and most of my cash at the tack shop. Even today, when my plan was just to swoop in and grab the maple pecan pie I ordered for tonight, I found myself in front of a salt-lick display debating the merits of two different sizes. In the end, because it's my birthday, I bought both. The pie rides on top of them as I drive home. I'm late.

It is pretty here, despite the churches. We're on the northern edge of the Edwards Plateau, wedged between the San Saba and Colorado rivers in the Llano Basin. This part of Texas is rough country, rolling hills and low wooded valleys and enough blue sky to relieve any misguided sense of self-importance. Everywhere, groves and groves of pecan trees. There's also the Matrimonial Oak on China Creek Road, a sprawling live oak where the Comanches used to hold weddings. Andy and I exchanged vows there, too. Why not? We were heading back after a grocery run, and I just had this urge, a craving as deep as hunger, so I made him pull over. Later he admitted he thought I'd gotten carsick.

The tree is on the east side of the road, but its thick knotty limbs arc over and touch the scrub on the west side, forming a trellis. We heard grackles and squirrels going about their business in the branches. We said our sweet words, kissed in the shade, and were back in the truck ten minutes later. We hooked a U-turn and made for the courthouse, so Mutt Mullens, San Saba's ancient justice of the peace, could make it official. We got home before the milk spoiled. We ate sloppy joes and ordered wedding bands from the Sears catalog. We called Junior in his dorm, then each of our fathers. They were only surprised we hadn't done it sooner. Eli seemed so sure we had that we started doubting ourselves. Did we? No? Are you positive? A decade ago. Maybe two.

The ranch is just shy of a hundred acres. We have sheep and goats and chickens, too many dogs and a couple of lazy mules and our horses. We board plenty of other people's horses, offer riding lessons, and take in as many of the lost, abandoned, or abused as we can. To help cover food and vet bills, Andy built a string of little cabins for folks to rent when they want a weekend on the river. There's good money in hunting, but no amount is worth the crack of gunfire so close to home. Plus we love our deer. Most mornings, we drink our coffee watching them nibble dewy grass. When the mamas walk their fawns up from the valley for the first time, strutting around and showing off who they've brought into the world, something inside me opens. I know, I want to tell them. I get it.

We have a nice life out here, quiet. We sit on the porch and watch the weather change. We do our work and laugh at the goats and ride the pasture together most evenings. We pluck ticks from the dogs' ears and keep the fences upright. We have a TV and computer but hardly turn either on; Junior usually has to call to say he sent an email days before. We're lucky. On clear nights, the stars are so vivid, so abundant, that you forget it's nighttime. Really, you can forget just about anything you want. Out here everything feels a world apart, including Waco.

The ranch is in Eli's name. He inherited it from his parents, Andy's grandparents, but we've lived on the property over half our lives. In our first few years here, Andy never ventured beyond the front gate. The young hermit sequestered on a hundred acres. Exiled to an island without an ocean. His folks and older brother visited; they even brought Panda out to live with us on the ranch. My father came down once, then eventually bought a cottage in Marble Falls. As a housewarming gift, we bought him a wooden sign that reads: I WASN'T BORN IN TEXAS BUT GOT HERE AS FAST AS I COULD. Those were the days I'd ride into town with Huey and pick out clothes or boots for Andy and Junior. Everything seemed so precarious then, one wrong word or lingering glance away from us tumbling into the void. When anyone approached Huey—to offer condolences or swap theories or talk pecans—I'd sneak to the tack shop. If the conversation was still going when I returned, I'd be introduced as a great-niece from Meredith's side of the family.

"I'm Elisabeth," I'd say, extending my hand. "Call me Thisbe."

The syllables confounded them—"Frisbee?" they'd ask—and Huey would let it slip, as if in confidence, that I'd come from California. Then the person would offer a rueful smile. The plan wasn't to avoid attention; the plan was to keep their attention where we wanted it.

"Give folks something to chew on," Huey had said.

We were all sitting around the kitchen table, inventing histories and memorizing bogus genealogy. We'd been on the ranch for two years and had both turned sixteen. Eli had just driven in from a trip to Houston. He had an envelope stuffed with documents he'd purchased from an illegal paper mill: driver's licenses, birth certificates, Social Security numbers.

"I think I'm a troublemaker," I said. "A brawler, a kleptomaniac! I've been shipped to Texas for old-fashioned rehab. I need folksy wisdom and tough love."

"Just say you're from California," Huey said, kind, humorless. "That'll keep folks out here occupied for months."

"I need to bale hay to learn the value of hard work," I said. "I need to muck out stables and earn the trust of a skittish horse to trust myself. I need to sweat and—"

"What kind of name is Anders?"

"Anders or Guillermo," Eli said. "That's what was on the menu. I went with my gut."

"We'll call you Andy," I said. "You're a stoic cowboy, the man of Thisbe's broken-down dreams. Come hell or high water, nothing can stop y'all from riding into the sunset together."

"*Us,*" he said, leaning down to scratch Panda's neck. "Nothing can stop us."

"That's my Andy," I said. "Always looking out."

Those were also the years when Andy and I would saddle the bay and pinto, head off into the pasture, and take turns retelling what'd happened. Waco filled everyone's days. Eli attended the trials down in San Antonio and heard Virgil and Turtle be sentenced to prison. A year later, the adults gathered here at the ranch and watched the congressional hearings like they were the World Series. Andy and I endured about half an hour, but politicians arguing over constitutional language and trotting out poster-board graphs was just vanity. They assigned blame to escape their own, and they parlayed sound bites into votes. They spoke to the cameras instead of each other. They trafficked in facts and figures to avoid actual answers. They said Perry started the fires. They said Big Lyle shot him in the gut. No one could prove otherwise.

That morning, Junior and I had bolted from our room. We were breaking for the chapel and the tunnel I'd found, but as we rounded the last corner, I halted. Ahead of us in the blackening hallway, slumped against the wall, was my pilgrim. There was no rational way to account for his presence, but I knew it was him across from Perry's body. I lifted Junior, pulled his chest to mine, and whispered for him to close his eyes as hard as he could.

Then I crouched beside Roy, caressed his cheek. When his eyes found me in the haze, I kissed his faint smile.

"Time to go, pilgrim," I said. "Up, up, and away."

He rose unsteadily, a newborn colt feeling its legs for the first time. We moved through the door and the wrecked chapel. Roy descended a few rungs on the ladder then jumped the rest of the way. Junior was terrified to climb down on his own and too squirmy for me to carry. I hoisted him by the armpits, dangled him low over the opening, and said, "Look at me." Once my reflection—and the bright fire heeling and rising behind me—showed in the gas-mask lenses, I made a goofy, smiley face and let him drop. He fell right into my pilgrim's waiting arms and they both staggered to the dirt. We sprinted through the earthen passageway, passing the plywood panels and a discarded jacket, but in the last clearing we just couldn't coax Junior into the barrels. We resolved to wait for nightfall when one of us could climb out and find help. We peeled the gauze and gas mask off Junior, made shadow puppets with the flashlight, and talked about dinosaurs. When I knew my pilgrim was ramping up to ask about my mother, I shook my head.

Eventually, he said, "You said you were going to stop sneaking up on me."

"Give me one more chance," I said, but flirty.

Then heavy, labored breathing and shambling noise in the corridor. A man's deep hacking cough. We heard him stumble, then raise himself. A hundred feet away. Ninety. Eighty. We pushed Junior behind us and doused the flashlight. I drew my pistol in the granular dark. The coughing got louder as the man lumbered closer. Without a word, we scooted together to shield Junior more completely with our bodies.

Then, from the darkness: "Jaye?"

A gruff, barnacled voice I'd never heard before. I cycled through every conceivable source—FBI? The sheriff? Had Perry shot himself through the throat but survived?—then, when there was no one left to consider, I lowered my pistol. I clicked on the flashlight and kissed my pilgrim's sooty cheek, then ushered Junior in front of us.

"Lyle," I called. "We're coming."

That giant man had his flashlight propped on a child's pink knapsack, lamping the plywood panels on the southern side of the earthen corridor. He was straining to crowbar them off. I gave Junior our flashlight and had him shine it on us while we helped. The boards groaned and bent and eventually popped loose, each release like a rifle's report. The plywood concealed another tunnel. It wasn't as tight as the barrels, but the opening hardly reached my waist. Lyle never stopped moving: He tossed plywood aside. He slipped on his dainty knapsack, but backward, the pouch dangling from his chest, then he lowered himself to his hands and knees and crawled in. We were expected to follow, though he offered no direction. My pilgrim went in first, then Junior, then me.

Later—miles and hours—our hands bleeding and our knees bruised, we surfaced in the bathroom of a tiny shotgun house. A mattress on the floor, no sheets, no pillows. A small stack of thin towels. A portable TV on a card table, a single short stool. In the kitchen, cans of tomato soup, jugs of water, and the chewed-up cellophane sleeve from a loaf of bread rodents had long ago devoured. Mice droppings were everywhere, and I had to stop Junior from mashing them with his thumb, trying to taste them. Lyle kept checking the windows, peeking around curtains that had once been bedsheets. Which one of Perry's women had sewn them, I wondered. The carpet reeked of mildew, mold. After months at the ranch, it seemed a palace. A dented Chevy Caprice sat in the garage, its key on a bent nail by the door.

Suddenly, an idea: I ran to the bathroom and flushed the toilet. When it worked, I was so shocked I laughed. I couldn't wait to tell my mother. Then I remembered. I shut the door, lowered myself into the empty tub, and sobbed in a ball.

Back in the living room, Junior lay on his stomach on the mattress, holding the flashlight so my pilgrim could project animals on the wall.

Someone had plugged in a space heater and it glowed orange. Warmth smells so different from fire. Lyle stood at the counter, fighting to free a metal box from the knapsack. Once he did, he reached into the collar of his shirt and withdrew a long chain holding a key. He unlatched the box and brought out bundle after bundle of cash. Like a bricklayer, he arranged the money in symmetrical columns.

"Holy fuck," I said.

Lyle ignored me. He checked the windows again. When he came to me, he held out his huge hand and I surrendered the derringer happily and immediately. Then I pulled him in for a long, hard hug. I held on even when I knew he wanted it to end. He locked the gun in the safe and wedged it back into the knapsack.

Judging by the light framing the curtains, I guessed it was afternoon. The boys were still making shadows. In the bathroom, Lyle resealed the hatch for the tunnel and disguised it with a rug. I went into the kitchen and marveled at the money. Every bill seemed to be a twenty, then I found bundles that were nothing but hundreds. The math so bewildered me I had to move away. I found a can opener in a drawer and a single pot in a cabinet. There were only two bowls, so I warmed soup for Lyle and Junior first. After they finished, my pilgrim and I ate. I rinsed out the cans and washed the dishes afterward, then I joined my boys on the mattress.

My mother was dead. So were the twins and Annie, Victoria and Perry and everyone else. By now, the news would have reported our own deaths. We were alive and we were ghosts. We were fugitives from the law, from our families, from ourselves. We didn't know what would come next or how long we'd last, but we were warm and sated and together. My hair ached. I was filthy and stunk. I intended to rally and shower for the first time in months, but Junior had fallen asleep. My pilgrim wasn't far behind. To relax ever again seemed impossible, and yet the sound of their breathing lulled me. Lyle moved from one window to another. The last thing I remember was thinking how he resembled someone watching for the mailman. A boy awaiting a letter from his pen pal, a man hoping for a note from an old lover, a soldier receiving, at long last, news from home.

When we woke, Lyle was gone. He'd taken his knapsack and safe, a jug of water and a single strap of cash. He'd left everything else—the soup, the car, and over twenty thousand dollars. Night tinted the windows. He must be doing recon, we assumed, so we ate again and awaited his return. We turned on the television, gauged the time to be about eleven P.M., then immediately shut it off. We monitored the windows, constantly expecting to see Lyle lumbering toward us behind the clouds of his breath. When we accepted he wasn't coming back, we used the stack of towels to wipe down everything we could remember touching. We unplugged the space heater, bundled the cash in a ratty towel, and piled ourselves into the dented Caprice. A strip of masking tape was affixed to the dashboard, and on it, a warning in familiar chicken scratch: *Left blinker don't work.*

I drove. Junior slept on the backseat. I hallucinated Lyle in a cornfield, entering a truck stop, sleeping on the road's shoulder. We made a wrong turn after Gatesville. We continued south through Pearl and Brooks Crossing, west through Lampasas and Lometa. There were other travelers but not many. I never strayed from the right lane. It took us four hours to reach San Saba, twice as long as it should have. We pulled into his grandparents' ranch before dawn broke its yolk on the horizon. Lights were already on in the windows.

Junior and I waited in the car. As soon as my pilgrim stepped onto the porch, the floodlamp illuminated. When his grandparents appeared—undoubtedly braced for more terrible news—they swung the door open so hard I thought it would fly off the hinges. Then I thought it would bounce back and swat them. They were nothing but touch. After a moment, Huey kneeled before him and patted him down, making sure he was all in one piece. They exchanged a few words, then the three of them pivoted toward us. Roy waved us in, and Huey jogged down the steps.

"Rise and shine, Junior," I said in the car. "We're home."

Then came our new names, GEDs, and homeschooling. Lynnette, Andy's mother, cut my hair into a cute bob; I've worn it that way ever since. Meredith, his grandmother, taught me how to hem and let out pants. We opened bank accounts and incrementally deposited the cash. Andy grew a foot taller. He worked the pecan harvests every year; he was roped with muscle and gorgeous veins like the exposed roots of a tree. Around the time Junior started public school, we bought our first truck. (Eli had taken that old Caprice to a chop shop days after we'd first arrived. He'd also returned to the shotgun shack to properly scrub our presence.) My father sold the house in California. Everyone came to the ranch for holidays and birthdays, and there were plenty of weekends when someone made the drive just to dote on Junior or confirm we hadn't vanished again. Lynnette and I would take the bay and pinto out, and we'd pretend to argue whether they were her horses or mine. Then she'd tell me something sweet from Andy's youth. I liked hearing his people tell stories on him, liked when my father told stories on me and my mother.

Mason returned our first September on the ranch. He was quiet like all his kin, but he could also be cocksure and brash, as if being a marine sometimes elbowed its way ahead of being a Moreland. I liked him, though. He was near the end of his first term as sheriff when a drunk driver he'd pulled over shot him point-blank. Later that year, Meredith passed away, and two years after that, the doctor found tumors lighting X-rays of Lynnette's lungs like so many ominous constellations. The disease was too far along for treatment. A year after that, a heart attack felled Huey while he was helping a pal reshingle a roof. We spent every funeral at the ranch for fear of being recognized. It never got easier.

After that dismal stretch, life evened out. I gave riding lessons, and Andy built our cabins. After Lynnette passed, Eli moved to Camp Verde. We tried convincing him to move closer to us, at least to Gatesville, but he didn't want to risk it. He seems content down there. He smokes too much but claims his doctor gives him good marks at every checkup. Maybe that's true, maybe not. He could be choking to death, and he'd fight to keep quiet so as not to disturb anyone's meal. My father is probably healthier than he's ever been, and happier. He married a restaurant manager, herself a widow, and lost about a hundred pounds. He rides his exercise bike every day, watching the History Channel. When the station runs one of its programs about Waco, he scrolls through the guide for a sitcom. He wears the WORLD'S GREATEST FATHER sweatshirt every Christmas.

Junior stayed in Austin after college. He works in tech, building apps or websites or some such. Cars, I think he makes apps for cars. I don't know. His wife runs a preschool with her sister. They have two little ones of their own, Topher and Octavia. The whole family is vegetarian. When they visit, we make sure we're stocked on granola and almond milk. Topher is terrified of grasshoppers but loves to walk the pasture with Andy, catching snakes or horned toads. Every December Octavia brings holiday-themed socks to decorate the goats' horns—they're good sports—and she spends hours on our driveway riding her skateboard. On our mantel, we have a framed picture of me lying on my back while Octavia and her board leap over me. That was last Christmas. There was no takeoff ramp, and she didn't grab her board at all; we were just in awe. She did it at least four times because Andy kept botching the photo. Or he said he botched it but just wanted to see her fly again. In bed that night, he said, "It's like she's picking a lock with her feet! The dexterity! The precision and finesse!" The deer didn't come up the next morning; the skateboard snapping against the concrete must have sounded too much like rifle fire.

Like I said, a good life. For years, our biggest question was whether to tell Junior how we'd come to form this family. We'd saddle the horses and debate in the pasture. Or we'd talk facing each other in bed, grappling with the difference between kindness and cowardice. Andy believes it boils down to motivation, to self-preservation or self-sacrifice, but I'm not convinced there's much distinction. Love is equally dyed in faith and fear. One life is always another life, another thousand lives. We are the fire and the fuel, the smoke and the ash and the whirlwind that scatters everything into the night. And we're the night, too.

In the end, we told Junior our story in broad strokes and pledged to answer any question, at any point, to the best of our ability. He'd just turned eighteen. He considered including some of what we'd said in his college essay. We gave him our blessing and didn't sleep for a week. He decided against it, and after that, the subject rarely came up. Occasionally he'd read stuff online—forums lousy with religious outliers, Second Amendment knuckleheads, and conspiracy theorists—but his interest petered out after a few clicks.

Then, on one of his visits, he said, "I remember a tunnel and eating soup with a giant."

"Lyle," I said, my heart shuddering. "We wouldn't be here without him."

"Right," he said. "I get him confused with Perry."

"They were nothing alike," I said. "Nothing."

"Lyle was cool, and Perry was a dick," he said.

"That about covers it," I said.

Over thirty years. When Coop began his podcast, he posted his contact information all over those online forums. Junior alerted us, but Coop had been requesting interviews with Eli and my father forever. They only agreed for our benefit. To protect us, to circle the wagons, to run interference. And we all harbor a certain sympathy for Coop. He's done well for himself—he's a husband and father and businessman—but he can't quit

the fires. Who could blame him? He lost as much as anyone. The difference is that the people he lost are living a measly two hours away and re-
fusing to show themselves. Now that Junior's grown, there's a part of me
that hopes Coop will show up on our porch some afternoon with his recording equipment. Or that we'll drive down to surprise him. We haven't
been back to the ranch, but I wouldn't mind walking the land, paying my
respects.

Andy's conscience is like a broken ankle that healed wrong. Some days
the limp is worse than others, but even when it's unnoticeable, he's concentrating not to stumble. For me, the bouts are like migraines. I'll go
years without one, but then I'll be sacked without warning. On those days,
I can only lay in the dark and grieve. I'll remember Annie's cartwheels and
Senny's puddling blood, the twins cackling in our room and Virgil finding
me and my pilgrim in the tower, the ornery old biddies and their cookies,
and Lyle calling for me in the corridor. Then come the bladed questions.
Should we have turned ourselves in? Should we now? Should I have for-
saken my dying mother in the ranch and begged someone for help? Then
the conditionals: If Perry hadn't gathered everyone in Texas, there would
be no Junior, and I would never have met my Rodeo. If Mason had never
enlisted, he wouldn't have sent the lock-picking kit. If my pilgrim hadn't
broken into the mall and tricked Sammy into driving him past the checkpoint, there'd be no Topher, no Octavia. This is the hubris, the naivete, the
irrationality of love. I can't make sense of it any more than a soldier who,
after laying waste to village after village, marries the daughter of the last
family he killed. Were the deaths worth it? The answer depends on who
you ask, and what flag they're flying. But the truth is holy in its indiffer-
ence, as dangerous and elusive as the dead, and like the dead, always
closer than you'd imagine.

Justice and mercy. Law and grace. I can't imagine that the past is finished with us. It's as though a crucial certainty is constantly threatening an
ambush, a ruthless and inevitable revelation that will explain away all this
loss and unknowing: the ageless beliefs that sentence one man to death
and another to murder, the prophecies and lies with the same spellings,
the bastard son and our fathers and their impossible fugitive steadiness,
the fossils we'll become and the ghosts of ourselves who have already commenced their long hauntings. Did we win or lose? Are we damned or
saved? We occupy a liminal, leftover world, and we live off scraps. We
build our religion, our very existences, with salvaged and stolen parts,

waiting for the next fire. To survive is to know what no one else does: Nothing is forever. Not an alibi or shelter, not bloodline or prayer, not nation or sacrifice or any glad-hearted dream of God.

And yet. And yet our endless sky is purpling. A red-tailed hawk sits perched atop a telephone poll, scanning the bottomland for prey. When I lower my windows, the truck's cab is aswirl with the smell of soil and cooling dusk and, somehow, the rich froth of unseen rivers. I lay my hand on the pie box to keep it from falling off the salt blocks. Eli's plan was to drive up from his place in Camp Verde this morning, meet Coop at the Waco library for the interview, then come celebrate my birthday and stay with us through the weekend. If Andy slept more than two hours last night, I'd be shocked. He gets excited.

It'll be a nice visit. We'll tell our stories over supper and cut slices of maple pecan pie for dessert. I'll open my presents, then Andy and I will soap the dishes while Eli smokes under the smear of stars. Soon enough I'll feign fatigue and leave them to it. They'll oil their belts and boots and ease into their private talk about Coop and what's changed in Waco, what hasn't. They'll get to bed later each night. Eli will wake too early, like always, and fry a greasy breakfast in his own father's cast-iron skillet—eggs and bacon and biscuits and black pepper gravy. We'll eat and say we slept better than we did. We'll circle back to topics from the night before, repeating what made us laugh or adding some little detail we'd forgotten. Andy will brew another pot of coffee, refill our mugs. We'll move onto the porch and wait for the deer to make their ageless, trembling ascent from the valley.

Acknowledgments

We Burn Daylight is not about David Koresh, but I've read many books that are, and they proved essential as I worked to familiarize myself with the tragedy: *The Ashes of Waco* by Dick J. Reavis, *Inside the Cult* by Marc Breault and Martin King, *A Place Called Waco* by David Thibodeau, *Mad Man in Waco* by Brad Bailey and Bob Darden, *Stand-Off in Texas* by Mike Cox, *A Journey to Waco* by Clive Doyle, *The Branch Davidians of Waco* by Kenneth G. C. Newport, *Armageddon in Waco* edited by Stuart A. Wright, *Millennium, Messiahs, and Mayhem* edited by Thomas Robbins and Susan J. Palmer, *Beyond the Flames* by J. J. Robertson, *Waco What Comes Next!* by Livingston Fagan, *Learning Lessons from Waco* by Jayne Seminare Docherty, *Stalling for Time* by Gary Noesner, and *Waco* by Jeff Guinn. The exceptional *Virginia Quarterly Review* (Hi, Allison! Hi, Paul!) ran a piece on lock-picking that was hugely useful. I also read plenty of Shakespeare, a practice that is tremendous for the soul and brutal for the ego.

This novel owes its entire existence to family who have supported, inspired, and shown otherworldly patience while I threw out draft after draft: Jennifer. Bill. Amy. Rodney. Lori. Handsome Rob and Jen Reeves. Joseph (Manwich!), Korrine, and Ted. Brad and Brie. Nathan. Austen and Liaht, Jace and Emilia. Liebson. Ben (dude . . .). Big Ryan and Sallie (Hi, Bowen!). Yvonne, Cami (Quarter! *Now* can we get tattoos?), and Julian (your dad says, "Not even close!"). Jake the Jani—Director, Lilly, Nara, and Karlen. Peter and, of course, Jorie.

Julie Barer is a stone-cold badass, but also impossibly thoughtful and wise and just all-around peerless. I'll never come close to paying my debt of gratitude to her or The Book Group.

I'm thankful to many folks at or adjacent to Random House: Noah Eaker started this novel on its journey, and Andy Ward—whose name, no joke, makes other writers curse with envy—guided it home with grace, generosity, and clear-eyed brilliance. Azraf Khan, Madeline Hopkins, and Ted Allen showed me and these pages too much kindness. There will never be enough stuffed animals in the world to repay London King, Windy Dorresteyn, Madison Dettlinger, and Allison Rich. Mark Warren's heart and mind are Texas-sized and Caddo-deep, and these pages benefited immeasurably from both. He's always referred to this as "our book," and that's what it will always be. Always.

The Michener Center for Writers is about as close as it gets to paradise for the making of literary art, and I'm flat-out honored to work beside the staff, fellows, and faculty. I'm beyond grateful for and constantly in awe of the unit.

For myriad kinds of assistance and support, deepest thanks to: Steve (our road trip!). Frankie. Emma. Joe O'Connell (the tapes!). Conor. Cole. Michael Burnett. Whit Bodman. Brent Douglass (sorry this took so long!). Dr. Pruthi.

Thank you, as well, to skateboarding.

Which reminds me. Years ago, Bill and I went on a skate trip. I was deep into this novel and loath to take any days off, so each morning I'd work on the draft for a few hours before we went skating. On the last day of the trip, someone smashed the rental car window and stole my laptop. I was gutted and furious and afraid—afraid I'd never recover what had been lost, afraid I lacked the faith to start again, afraid I was receiving an undeniably clear sign to move on from a place and cast of characters that had come to matter so much to me. I called Apple and spoke to a kindly young man who broke my heart by confirming I hadn't saved a single word to the cloud. I called the cops, the insurance company, the rental agency. Bill and I considered scouring nearby pawn shops but knew we'd come up empty. Then, as I was waiting for a replacement car, it hit me like a mule kick: The fears dismantling me were the very fears dismantling Roy, Jaye, and maybe even Perry. Suddenly, the book was unlocking in my imagination, and once we got the new rental, I drove straight to buy another laptop. This draft began in earnest that night. So, at long last, I want to extend a huge and sincere fuc—thank you to whoever broke into our car: This book would be far worse if you weren't such an annoying and brazen punk. (Seriously, though: I appreciate you. I hope things have gotten a little better, and you're doing okay. In case it's helpful, the password for the laptop is now: Aroynt,sucka.)

About the Author

BRET ANTHONY JOHNSTON is the author of the internationally best-selling novel *Remember Me Like This* and the award-winning *Corpus Christi: Stories*, and the editor of *Naming the World: And Other Exercises for the Creative Writer*. His work has appeared in *The New Yorker, Esquire, The Paris Review, Thrasher Magazine, The Best American Short Stories*, and elsewhere. A recipient of a National Endowment for the Arts Literature Fellowship and the Sunday Times Short Story Award, he was born and raised in Texas and is the director of the Michener Center for Writers at the University of Texas at Austin.

bret-anthony-johnston.com

About the Type

This book was set in Caledonia, a typeface designed in 1939 by W. A. Dwiggins (1880–1956) for the Merganthaler Linotype Company. Its name is the ancient Roman term for Scotland, because the face was intended to have a Scottish-Roman flavor. Caledonia is considered to be a well-proportioned, businesslike face with little contrast between its thick and thin lines.